The Globe

M. KAT LINDLEY, D.V.M

pendants.pagesmkl@yahoo.com

ISBN: 099089620X
ISBN 13: 9780990896203 (LRH)

Dedicated to my three wonderful children who fill my life with love and fun. My wish is for this book to give my readers a brief escape from the trials of life. Contact me if you are kind enough to post a review and if I can I'll send you a dichroic glass pendant.

Prologue

He'd floated in the glass bubble on a vast ocean for what had seemed like a long time, and there wasn't anything he could do to change his circumstances, or even to end his life. He felt a strange, intense mixture of anxiety and boredom at the same time, which was weird because those were normally opposites on the emotional spectrum. He was a sensory-deprived, disembodied consciousness in a limbo land of hopelessness and despair. But worse than not being able to rescue himself was that he couldn't help his baby daughter, who lay unconscious on his lap, either. No one knew they were there, and if someone had, his or her life would be in danger too. But he didn't know how much longer he could exist in the torment that felt like the end of life but wasn't.

One

She'd been scared before, really scared, but nothing as intense as this moment. Everything felt like it was moving in slow motion, except for her heartbeat; its rate was accelerated, and each pump was so hard that she could feel her pulse beating in every fingertip. Her brain couldn't process any logical thoughts. She was only conscious of enhanced sensations: she was hyperaware of the wind blowing grains of sand against the outside of the cabin, the scent of the ocean nearby, and the worn wooden floor under her hands. Frozen motionless with fear, she crouched against the living room wall, as far away as possible from the object of her terror, and stared fixedly at the glass ball lying on the floor where she had thrown it in horror. A simple beachcombing treasure, it had shaken her sense of reality to the core when she had held it up to the light and a man inside had slowly turned his head and looked directly at her.

Dr. Abigail Newton, who was usually called "Newt" by her friends and family, was a scientist to the core. She moved through her days in a logical, grounded, and methodical way. Newt ordered her life with to-do lists and written goals; she had a yearly plan, a five-year plan, and even a ten-year plan for her future. She made most of her decisions using the scientific method of gathering data, formulating a testable hypothesis, and predicting potential outcomes using logic.

Some people labeled her boring, but she worked very hard, owned her own biomedical laboratory, and planned to make a difference in the world with her time on Earth. Newt was twenty-eight years old, and her current pet project was developing artificial hemoglobin, the substance that gives blood its red color. Hemoglobin fills mature red blood cells, and its job is to carry oxygen and then exchange it for carbon dioxide during respiration. Her lab's synthetic hemoglobin had huge advantages over real blood transfusions because it could be stored and transported without refrigeration and given to people without first matching blood types. She knew it would help surgical patients, save lives on the battlefield, and be quickly available at sites where multiple people were injured. Now, after a grueling two years of unrelenting work, she was on a well-deserved vacation at her family's cabin in Ocean Shores, Washington.

Staring at the glass ball in fear, her ordered and scientific mind came to her aid as she crouched against the wall. Her tight muscles were cramping from the adrenaline flood they received as her body prepared for fight or for flight in response to danger. And Newt simply couldn't maintain her frozen position any longer, so she relaxed and begin to talk to herself, as she often did when alone.

"I must have been seeing things. This reaction is ridiculous." Newt rubbed her goose-bumped arms. "It makes no sense. People aren't four inches high, and they don't live in glass globes. I'm not thinking logically here."

She stood up slowly and cautiously. "There must be a reasonable explanation. Perhaps a defect in the glass. That could happen from years in the ocean, couldn't it? Maybe a twisted piece of driftwood somehow worked its way inside the glass, and on a brief glance in the right light, it might have looked like a person staring back at me."

Those various rationalizations might have convinced someone else, but Newt was a scientifically trained observer, and she could clearly bring every detail of the man to her mind. Somehow he struck an emotional cord deep within her, and that puzzled her. He looked to be early thirties in age and was physically attractive with a square chin that gave his face a sculpted look. He was wearing worn jeans, a black T-shirt, and slightly used athletic shoes. He was sitting on a black plastic bench, his body looked well muscled and trim, and his thick, slightly wavy hair was a warm brown color. But Newt remembered his eyes as his most arresting feature: they were a dark chocolate brown, large and soft, but filled with puppy-like sadness.

The details of his appearance only registered in the periphery of Newt's consciousness, because what etched itself into her mind was the total look of despair and hopelessness on his face. At first, he sat slumped forward, and then he slowly turned his head, and for a brief moment, he looked right at her before turning back, unseeing, to his original position. But in the few seconds he looked at her, the heartbreak in his eyes hit her like a physical blow, and then she heaved the ball away in shock and scrambled away.

As Newt stood there pressed against the wall, remembering his face, her logical nature forced her to consider other explanations besides misperception. "Maybe what I saw in there was an alien from outer space or a wormhole to a parallel dimension. Or how about a time traveler or a holographic projection?" She tried to lighten her tension by teasing herself. "Maybe he will say, 'Help me, Obi-Wan Kenobi. You're my only hope!'"

Newt would have been the first to admit that she had an overactive imagination. It had helped her think up successful fresh approaches to complex medical problems in her laboratory, so it wasn't necessarily a bad thing. Also she had to factor in the fact that she was probably tired after driving from Seattle that morning, because it was now past midnight.

She reasoned with herself. "Maybe in the bright light of morning, I'll find an empty glass ball and have a good laugh at myself." She hoped it would end up that way, because a mistake was the most likely explanation for what she had seen.

Newt stretched her arm to pick up the colorful blanket her mom had knitted, which was lying over the back of the couch. Then she took cautious, slow steps forward, approaching the globe like a nervous cat sneaking up on a scary object. Very carefully, she dropped the blanket over the ball and folded it around the glass, and then she took the bundle outside into the summer air and placed it on the large front porch by the door. But just a few steps back inside, Newt didn't feel safe with it that close, so she relocated the ball well away from the house. After moving quickly back inside the cabin, she double-locked the front door and checked that all the windows were secure too.

Taking deep breaths, she looked down at her hands and saw they were trembling slightly, and then with weak knees she collapsed onto a wooden kitchen chair.

Addressing the back of the closed door, she said in a shaky voice, "I guess I really needed this break from work if I'm seeing things and freaking out over nothing." She shook her head. "I can't recall ever being this upset."

She brushed her teeth, put on a long flowered nightgown, and climbed into bed. One of the reasons Newt loved the cabin was its isolation on twenty acres of undeveloped property, because normally that was a wonderful change from her busy city life in Seattle. But tonight with the globe outside, the quiet solitude of the woods and the beach didn't seem very comforting. Instead, the long access road from the cabin to the main highway seemed to stretch twice as long in her imagination. When Newt finally fell asleep, she dreamed that the man in the moon was crying salty tears into the ocean, and it seemed critically important to understand why he was upset and to aid him. However, no matter what she tried, she was powerless to help him, and so she tossed and turned all night.

Two

The next morning as she washed her face, Newt decided to apply scientific reasoning to solve the mystery of the globe. She would let logic rule the day, proving that there was a rational explanation for what she thought she had seen the night before. But if she was honest with herself, what she really wanted to do was to kick the globe back out into the ocean as far as she could and to continue her vacation in peace without ever looking inside it again. The problem with that idea was that Newt knew her mom would be upset if she didn't at least rescue the blanket from the dew and sand it was currently lying in, so she had no choice but to walk outside and to bring the bundle back into the cabin.

She briefly considered sending the glass globe to her laboratory for analysis by her staff. Then she wouldn't have to deal with it right away, but she knew they would tease her without mercy if there wasn't anything inside it after all. And she would get gag gifts of glass balls for the next ten years at every party she held. Also pseudohilarious comments like, "Doctor Newton, an apple hit you on the head and you wigged out?" She had had her fill of Isaac Newton jokes in grade school!

Because she was a kindhearted person, she did want to help the man she thought she had seen inside the glass if he was actually there. And she wondered if he wasn't there then, why she had seen him last night? Weird situations like this just didn't happen in Newt's scientifically ordered life. It felt like she had seen a mermaid wash up on shore and then denied what she saw just because everyone knew mermaids are mythological. She understood that eyes and brains often make errors in processing visual information; that's why magic and illusions fool people.

So Newt decided to start by logging all her observations from the day before. She first noticed the glint of glass reflecting the sun as she sat on a large piece of driftwood to rest after a walk on the beach. She'd sat on that same driftwood after every walk since she was ten years old, as that was when her parents purchased the large property with its small isolated cabin. Her family vacationed there twice a year until her dad passed away, and only she and her brother, Tony ever visited anymore.

Ocean Shores was a three-hour drive from her small apartment in Seattle, and Tony's job was usually mobile, so they sometimes met at the cabin for the weekend. Newt loved the fresh air and connecting with nature in the woods and on the beach. The sound of the waves and their eternal motion soothed her somehow. She'd had some of her best ideas while relaxing there, and it was the perfect break from her usual endless, exacting, repetitive research protocols. Newt freely admitted to workaholic behavior, and she would have been in her lab every waking hour seven days a week if she hadn't had a place to get away to occasionally.

Despite all those walks over all those years, Newt never found anything like the glass ball she picked up the day before. She immediately recognized that it was a Japanese fishing float, because she had been looking for one for years. They're rare, although sometimes they wash ashore after a big storm pushes them across the ocean. They were made to hold up the edges of fishing nets to keep them from sinking deep into the ocean. Air was trapped inside the glass when it was blown into a bubble, and that made the floats buoyant. She knew that fishermen from about 1840 to 1940 used them to support large nets strung together—some of which were fifty miles long. Modern fishermen hadn't used glass floats for years; instead they replaced them with less expensive and more durable Styrofoam, aluminum, or plastic. Gift stores sold replica fishing floats for decoration, but authentic ones had been in the ocean for many years and so were an uncommon find. In addition, there hadn't been a storm the night before, and the cove was sheltered, so debris didn't often wash in directly from the ocean even when there was a storm.

She remembered picking it up and brushing the sand off and then examining it briefly, but she hadn't noticed anything inside of it. In fact, as she stared at it on the floor where she had thrown it last night, it had looked transparent and empty the whole time. She recalled seeing the worn wooden floor clearly through the sphere. The float's color was the typical green glass of recycled sake bottles exposed to the sun, and it felt neither hot nor cold when she held it. Its shiny surface was firm, smooth glass, and it was an appropriate weight for the ball's circumference of about ten inches or so. On the beach, she examined it briefly and saw no chips or cracks; at no time had it struck her as an unusual object. Newt remembered being thrilled that she found a Japanese fishing float, and she planned to show it off at work.

"OK, Newt, quit delaying. Time to take the next step," she told herself.

First, she placed a bright light on the kitchen table and gathered some basic tools like a screwdriver and a hammer; what she would use them for, she had no idea. The process was a delay tactic, she knew, but her stomach felt like it had butterflies flying around inside it. She took several deep breaths to calm herself and then walked outside and slowly picked up the bundle. After taking it gingerly inside, she placed it on the table and unwrapped the blanket to expose the globe.

The float looked like the same innocent object from the beach the day before. She couldn't see anything visible inside it from her standing position. Newt turned on the light, centered herself mentally, sat down, and peered through the glass into the ball like a gypsy about to foretell the future.

Then once again, her world tilted off its rational axis because the man she thought she had seen was still in there. This time, he slept curled on his side and wrapped in a thin, ratty army-green blanket she hadn't noticed last night. She gasped at seeing him, but she gathered her courage to look closer and was shocked to see he was not alone in there. Curled against his chest and held protectively in his arms was a baby in pink footed pajamas, so it was probably a girl. She was absolutely beautiful and had the same wavy rich brown hair as the man, and her long eyelashes brushed against her pale cheeks. She was motionless, but Newt could see her chest rise and fall as she breathed, so she was alive, like the man. But she looked more like a doll than a real child because her face didn't have the pinkish color of healthy skin, instead it was porcelain white.

Newt leaned back in her chair. She was filled with swirling emotions. Obviously, they were father and daughter. After seeing them lying close together and sleeping quietly, the connection was clear to her. It was more than their identical hair color; it was the way he held her so tenderly against him too. Watching them sleeping helplessly in their small prison touched her heart deeply, and she felt the same emotional connection to him that she noticed when he had looked at her the night before. Newt felt she must help them somehow—especially the innocent, possibly ill baby.

Three

While Newt watched the man and his baby sleeping, she ran through some possible explanations for what she was seeing. She realized that she didn't have enough data to draw the conclusion that they were people, no matter what her gut was telling her. She needed to consider other possible theories. For one thing, she could have been having a psychotic break, and it was possible that they weren't actually in there at all, even though she was looking right at them and the man's appearance was identical to what she had seen the day before. Isolation was a drawback of her situation because she needed a reality check but there was no one there to confirm what she was seeing.

To test her reality, she glanced around the cabin to see if anything looked "off" to her. It was the same familiar, boxy thousand square–foot cabin that it had always been; there was one big room with two adjoining bedrooms and a bathroom between them. The furniture was old but serviceable, designed to take the years of sand and sun. The dark wooden floor had lost its shine from abrasion by sandy feet over almost twenty years. The small kitchen along one side of the main space was partially separated from the living room by an elevated white countertop with four stools under it. The kitchen cupboards had been painted white at least ten years ago, and their surface was cracked and scuffed, but they were sturdy and made of solid wood. To Newt, the best part of the cabin was the huge front windows with a view overlooking the beach, the ocean, and the large wraparound front porch. That generous covered space had a porch swing and steps just right for sitting with a cup of tea and buttery toast. The whole space hadn't changed since her childhood, and that familiarity was a comfort at the moment.

Looking at the observation notes she had taken the day before and that morning, Newt was gratified to see they were neatly written and coherently organized as she had expected them to be. She didn't have a fever or headache indicating encephalitis, a stroke, or another disease. But to double-check, Newt ran through a standard brain function neurological test. She named the date and the current president of the United States, and she solved some simple math equations; everything checked out normally, as far as she could tell. She didn't have blurred vision, poor coordination, or dizziness, so Newt put issues with her perception low on the list of possible explanations for the man in the globe.

Next she considered that perhaps the man and baby were just a visual image. She hadn't seen any normal body-shifting sleep movements from either of them in the thirty minutes she had been watching them closely, and that was unusual for human sleep. Projecting a three-dimensional image required some kind of a screen to show the picture on, power to do the projecting, and a light source. Newt walked all around the globe that was sitting on the kitchen table, and they continued to be a convincing pair of sleeping people. She could even see the bottom of them against the glass when she gently lifted up the globe to check. She ran her hand all around the ball, looking for a light beam or a break in the image when she did so. She couldn't see anything outside or inside of the glass capable of projecting an image.

She had to conclude that at that moment, she didn't understand what she was seeing, so she needed to keep her options and her mind open. "OK, Newt, the working hypothesis is that they really are people, no matter how unlikely that seems. So until there is evidence to prove that that is not the case, I'll proceed and hope no one finds out how whacked this is," she mumbled. As the next step, Newt decided she would try to communicate with them. She tapped on the glass gently with her fingernail and then more loudly with her pen, but nothing that indicated they had heard her happened. "Maybe they're deaf or deaf aliens," she teased herself to lighten the tension she felt.

Next Newt slowly shook the ball to wake them up, but no matter how much she moved it around, they stayed upright and in exactly the same sleeping position; even rolling it around on the table had no effect on them.

"Weird," she whispered to herself.

She knew gravity should have affected anything with mass or weight, so their lack of movement might mean they didn't have any substance. Maybe they were made of gas, or other light particles. But if they had weight possibly they were independently suspended inside the globe so they stayed in place, like the globe was a gyroscope or something, she thought. Suddenly her worried tension fled, and she felt fired up with curiosity; maybe it would be a fun puzzle to solve!

Newt stabilized the globe before further testing it by wrapping a dish towel around the base it rested on. The small, flat base was where the hot bubble of blown glass had been broken off from the glassblowing pipe and sealed shut, trapping the air inside. If sound or motion didn't affect them, then perhaps they could see her through the glass. When the man had looked at her the night before, he hadn't seemed to see her, but maybe that was because of their relative size differences. If she could equalize them, perhaps he would see her.

Newt didn't have a lot of equipment in the cabin with her, but she had her laptop, a video camera, and a digital camera;

she always brought those basic electronics with her to the cabin because she loved to record images from nature. She watched what she recorded at home in Seattle when she needed to unwind, relax, and think; nature connected her to the earth and gave her a stable base in life. Her whole family felt that way about being outdoors, and she had been raised to appreciate even the smallest wonders of earth and space.

She decided that if she opened the fold-out view screen from the video camera, placed it near the glass globe, and then stood in front of the lens as if taking a video of herself, her image would shrink to his size. Then if she held a message board, she might be able to communicate with him—assuming she could catch his attention and he could see out past the glass barrier. For her to communicate with him in writing, he would need to be able to understand and to read English; if he could not, perhaps she could use symbols or sign language.

Next, she positioned her camera with its magnifying attachment pointed at him so she could see his response by sending the image to her laptop. That way, she could see the camera's view of the globe's residents enlarged on her computer screen. In the past, she had used the attachment to take close-up pictures of flowers and insects. She also wanted to record any interaction they might have as further verification that she wasn't crazy.

She paused for a moment and looked at her refection in the mirror to see what he would see when he looked at her. Newt saw practical short red hair, academic-looking glasses, a sprinkling of freckles, and a face free of makeup. She was five feet four inches tall with a slim-yet-curvy build. That was her natural shape, because she often skipped meals when she was working hard in her lab and walked to work rain or shine. She felt she did have nice bright-green eyes, but otherwise she knew her looks were unremarkable. What made her special, she thought, were her intelligence and her endless spark of curiosity.

After setting up all the equipment, she looked in the globe to see if they were awake yet. She saw he was sitting on the bench with his head in his hands again, just like he had done the day before. The baby was lying on the floor and was wrapped in the blanket. She also looked exactly the same as she had before: limp, pale, and motionless like a person in a coma.

Newt wrote her first message on the dry-erase board: **Can I help you**?

Then she turned on all the equipment, made a few adjustments, stood in position with a smile on her face, and waited for him to see her. Ten minutes later, it was clear he hadn't seen her at all, even though he had moved around the limited space, doing what looked like a stretching routine.

To draw his attention to her, she draped a dark-colored towel over most of the globe. She hoped to highlight the video screen as it lit up. Once the globe was darker inside and she couldn't see him as well, she took a flashlight and directed it on him like a small spotlight.

As soon as the beam passed through the globe's glass wall, she could tell he saw it. He had sat down after exercising, but then he leaped up with a heartbreaking expression of hope on his face, sprang to the glass, turned his head to the side, and pressed one eye as close to the globe's wall as he could. Unfortunately, that was where the flashlight beam was entering, and not where the video camera screen and the message could be seen. Newt slowly moved the flashlight around the globe's surface to direct him to the screen, and again she stood in front of the video camera with her sign and a welcoming smile on her face.

He looked at her for long seconds, and then he started to cry. No tears rolled down his face, but it was clear to her that he was weeping, because his face bunched up and his shoulders shook with emotion. He picked up his daughter and rocked her as he sobbed in the messy way of a man who was rarely out of control. The baby didn't react at all.

Newt's throat had a big lump in it as she watched him cry. How desperate he must have been for anyone to help him, she thought.

Then she wrote on the dry-erase board: **Nod yes if I can break the glass.**

She thought that would be the simplest way to release him from the globe, but after he composed himself, he signaled back "no!" with a strong shake of his head.

Newt guessed that that would have probably been too easy of a way to solve the problem anyway, because something that unusual and complex undoubtedly had a complex solution too. Next she wrote: **Do you have anyone I can contact?**

Again, he gave a negative answer, and she wondered why. It wasn't likely that he didn't have any friends or family, and the baby had to have a mother. How had he gotten into a strange life-or-death situation, and why didn't anybody care about it?

Then she wrote: **Is it possible to get you out?**

That time he nodded "yes," but she thought it was a pretty tentative gesture. It was clear he had some reservations about being rescued, and that just made her more curious about him and the situation he was in.

She felt she had to cover all bases, so next she wrote: **Do you want to get out?**

Again he nodded "yes" and pointed to his daughter, and then he cupped his hand around his ear and made a talking motion with his other hand. Newt knew he wanted to speak directly instead of using her signs to communicate. As a sound test, she put a pair of small headphones over the globe and turned on some soothing classical music at a very low volume. He made the thumbs-up sign, so she knew he could hear the music. She was excited about the development, because only asking questions that had a yes-or-no answer drastically limited their communication. Newt felt she could really get started on a solution to help him.

On the next sign she wrote: **I need to go get sound equipment.**

He nodded and made the "OK" sign with his hand.

Newt saw so much character and emotion on his face; he looked sad, yet he was staying strong, and there was something familiar about him. She searched her mind, trying to place him. He held his daughter close to his chest, rocking her gently, and she saw him bend down and give the baby a kiss on the forehead and a sweet smile. She knew he was a good man just from that small gesture of love for his child.

Newt wondered how they could be alive in there. What did they eat and drink, and why hadn't they run out of air—because she could see them breathe in and out with a normal rhythm? Obviously they couldn't have been alive as most people would have defined it. She knew that in science, the definition of "alive" wasn't always so clear-cut. Some parasites, like tapeworms, didn't eat or breathe but instead depended on their host for those functions. Viruses took what was considered to be alive to a whole new level; they were only small pieces of DNA, or genetic material, wrapped in a shell.

The man and baby appeared to her to be alive in the traditional sense, and he had responded like a normal person would have responded to her questions. She pondered the situation for a moment. Maybe what she was seeing was only part of a whole individual, like how mushrooms were a small piece of a larger fungal network hidden from sight under the soil; so one possible explanation was that only part of him was visible. Perhaps the baby was sick because the globe was hurting her somehow. If that was true, then the logical progression would be to find the missing parts, unite them together, and then set the man and baby free.

As it turned out, that sounded easy to Newt at the time, but it turned out to be the most difficult and dangerous experience of her life.

Four

Jasper Higgs had been trapped in the small round glass prison for what felt like a long time. He wasn't exactly sure how long it had been, because he had no way to track time, but it seemed like months to him.

In the computer world, he was internationally recognized as a genius-level program designer. He loved to create advanced computer games and to solve problems with custom programs. Jasper was the last child of twelve children born to a father who owned a car repair garage and a mother completely involved in homemaking. He marketed his first game at seventeen years old, and then he sold it ten days later to a major company for more money than his dad made in a year. He immediately filed for emancipation and had been living independently ever since.

Moving out of the family home wasn't such a big step for him, because his family had ignored him for years as he sat hour after hour at his computer keyboard. They rolled their eyes at him behind his back and made jokes about finding him under a cabbage leaf. It was clear to everyone that he never fit into the family and never would, so he moved to Seattle.

He knew people often ridiculed what they didn't understand, but he thought that to treat your own son like a leper was inexcusable. And his parents' blatant discrimination against him had caused him a lot of emotional pain while he was growing up. In contrast, Jasper believed in celebrating people's differences and knew that he could have made a difference in his family's lives if they had let him. Just computerizing his dad's business would have been a big benefit. His dad would have saved time spent creating laborious handwritten invoices, reduced money lost by error, and increased inventory efficiency. But even the mention of that idea sent his father into orbit.

Jasper hadn't had contact with any of his family for over ten years, and he didn't plan to see them ever again. Undoubtedly, they didn't miss him and probably even rarely thought of him, except as a joke. They didn't care that he was wealthy, because the work he did had no real value to them, so neither did the money. It was like his income was dirty, as if it came from gambling, prostitution, or drugs. Their isolation of him in his childhood had shaped who Jasper was as an adult. The nature of his work was solitary, and he seldom let people close to him physically, mentally, or emotionally. Online he was elusive and mysterious, and in person he was very introverted and withdrawn. He ran errands at night to avoid people and didn't respond to e-mails of any kind.

Jasper's isolated life started to change when he met a girl at a nightclub one night. He just sold a MMORPG—a mass multiplayer online role-playing game—for over two million dollars and wanted to celebrate. He spent a year working on its complicated design, and he was very proud of it. It was a new concept with graphics so realistic that it felt as if you were actually in the game. He knew his fans would love it. He couldn't wait to see how long it took players to get to the advanced levels, because it would take out-of-the-box thinking, and pure deviousness to get there. Most games that complex took teams to create, but he was unusual because he had skills in graphics, coding, and design, and he always worked alone.

After the game sold, he looked at his huge bank balance and realized there was no one to share his happiness with. Finally, he'd gone to a local nightclub that had been hosting a launching party for his game and sat like a quiet island in a sea of noise and color. It seemed to him that everyone else had someone to share their lives with. He felt depressed just looking around at all the people sitting in groups with friends and lovers. Then, after he had consumed a few shots, a pretty woman sat down next to him and asked if he would buy her a drink. Later that night they had gone to her apartment by taxi. He had been too drunk to use proper protection when they became intimate.

Thinking back, he couldn't remember much about that night, except for how sorry he had been feeling for himself before he started drinking. He had taken another taxi home from her apartment the next day and had forgotten all about it until she showed up at his place three months later, broke and pregnant. He wondered how she had known where he lived and suspected she had riffled through his wallet that fateful night. But Jasper wasn't sorry it had happened because baby Emma was the result of their encounter. She was the miraculous bit of sunshine that changed his life forever.

After their baby was born, Emma's mother had taken off, leaving the infant with him, and Jasper had transformed because of his new role. No longer was he the geeky guy who no one saw or talked to. Now he was the single father everyone had advice for, because no matter how hard he tried to avoid social interactions, Emma attracted people like a magnet. And he couldn't shop or run errands at night anymore as Emma slept then, so he was forced to talk to people. Women, little old ladies, dads—everyone wanted to see his cute daughter and to chat about her. To his relief, he found it much easier to talk to people when the focus was Emma than when they were looking at him for coherent conversational responses.

He came alive as a person and had a reason to live real life outside of his fantasy game worlds. He took parenting very seriously and did most of Emma's care himself. Jasper made a spreadsheet of her schedule, took her to well child checkups, and researched baby care frequently. What had started out as just a sense of responsibility for the life he had helped create quickly transformed into deep love for his daughter as a person. He spent hours playing with Emma, and she became the precious center to his life.

When Emma was seven months old, it became clear that her speech was severely delayed. It wasn't that she was a little behind based on developmental charts for normal children. It was worse, because she was almost silent when most babies babbled a variety of sounds and started to form basic words. Jasper took her to multiple specialists where she had tests and scans, but the bottom line was that she wasn't deaf, but might be mute. Speech was complex, they said, and brain development tricky, so they advised him to look into therapy and to hope for the best. She could learn sign language later anyway.

That wasn't good enough for Jasper. He tickled her and made her laugh, and she cried sometimes, so he knew she could make some sounds. He talked to her constantly, and from her reactions it was clear she understood certain words, like "bye-bye." They were both frustrated daily by the lack of communication between them, especially when she wanted something and he couldn't figure out what it was. Besides, she was obviously smart, and he was dying to know what was going on in that cute little head of hers.

One day he had a brilliant idea: why not do what he did best and solve their problem using computer technology? He knew brains emitted electrical signals that could be recorded on tracings, because they were used to determine brain activity in people with head injuries. Electrical output was easy to digitalize and to transport wirelessly, even to a remote location, with simple sending and receiving devices. The difficult part was turning those signals into useable communication, and he solved that problem with computer power. First he recorded Emma's brain activity along with video of what was happening during the same time, and then he created a program that correlated the two together. Then after millions of comparisons, if Emma was hungry or sleepy, the computer could predict what she wanted based on her brain waves. It was almost like a foreign language with a computer translator, and the result was a picture of what Emma wanted—like a teddy bear or a banana—on his smart phone or computer.

Jasper loved understanding Emma better, but he still wanted more. He wanted to ask Emma questions and to have her know what he was thinking too. That step was complex, because his brain was more mature than hers was, so he wore the device that recorded brain signals and sent them to the computer translator day and night for months. And after many refinements, the result was a complex computer chip he could hold in the palm of his hand. But in a surprising twist, instead of converting his brain's electrical activity into pictures of his thoughts like it had Emma's brain waves, it projected a three-dimensional image of him that acted out his thoughts.

He wasn't sure how his advanced computer system had been able to do that, but he'd just set the task and then let it figure out how to solve the problem. And that involved billions of calculations beyond what any person could do or understand. Over time, it had analyzed millions of possible ways to achieve the result he wanted, and then it had narrowed them down to the best solution. Apparently a total projection of him was the ideal answer to the task of turning his thoughts into a visual image.

The projection wasn't a hologram, which is a prerecorded 3-D image made by several beams of laser light on a medium and played back on a repeating loop; his computer had created an almost exact clone of him that walked, talked, and appeared to breathe. Seeing his digital image was fascinating and creepy at the same time, so it repelled and attracted him in equal measure.

He thought that his computer may have adapted a program he designed that allowed him to project game characters and images onto solid surfaces so he could turn them around and refine detail on all sides. He suspected that in all its billions of calculations, the system had rewritten that two-dimensional program code to project in 3-D. But the enhanced detail it had achieved was mind-boggling. He watched his image move around the room and speak all of his thoughts out loud, and the lag time between when he would think a thought and when his projection would react to it was so small that the projection almost became him. He had the surreal feeling that he was two people connected together by one brain.

The system had three parts: a microprocessor worn in the ear to collect brain waves, a computer to analyze them, and a chip for translation and display. Each part connected to the others wirelessly and worked together seamlessly from any location.

What the system had done did make some sense to Jasper, because the chip had taken Emma's simple thoughts and projected them as a picture of a bottle or blanket. But Jasper had asked it to translate bigger thoughts like "I love you" and "you're safe," because that's what he wanted to communicate to Emma. Thus, a total projection of him probably was the logical solution to the task, because he did love Emma with all of himself and that was a very complex task for the computer to translate.

He had been working on adjusting the chip to project only selected thoughts when their idyllic life came to a quick, horrible end. It started with a subpoena to appear in court as an expert witness in a computer hacking case. Normally he didn't leave Emma, but his housekeeper eagerly volunteered to babysit for the few hours he would be gone, and he knew if he didn't appear, the court would just send an officer to get him. He returned after four hours to find that Emma had been kidnapped and that her ransom was the surrender of his thought projection chip.

At first, his brain was scrambled by his fear for Emma and by the prospect of a confrontation with two mafia types demanding he go with them. How had they known that he wouldn't be home to protect Emma—or about the chip's existence? Then Jasper realized with horror that the system he had made to communicate with his daughter could be used to steal people's thoughts against their will. All a criminal needed to do was hook up to a victim's brain, and the chip would reveal the wearer's thoughts directly from his or her mind. Innovative ideas could be taken out of an inventor's brain and sold or developed, and finding the truth during an interrogation would become child's play. He couldn't let evil people get their hands on the chip, because it would do untold damage if they did. Formerly private brains would be free to be plundered at will! And the chip was the key piece of technology to do it, because an exceptional hacker could work backwards from it to its computer program, and brain wave collectors were a common medical device called an EEG.

With Emma missing, he had no choice except to go with the kidnapper's minions and to hope that somehow he would find an opportunity to get his daughter back—and to destroy the chip too. Fortunately, he had manufactured only a single chip that ran exclusively with his laptop's program, so he hoped that that would give him some control over the situation.

The man who wanted the chip was a recluse, so both he and Emma were transported independently to his private island for the ransom exchange. The separation effectively prevented any escape attempt, or even any thoughts other than worry about his daughter. Jasper realistically knew that once they were in the man's isolated territory, they would never be released, and Emma's life would continue to be used as a lever for his cooperation. So he would be forced to either continue to work on the chip or to sacrifice their lives, and the terror of that prospect filled his mind with desperation.

But providence favored him, because shortly after his arrival, he had a brief chance to be alone, and he concealed the chip in a Japanese fishing float. When the kidnappers couldn't find the chip, they tried to beat its location out of him, and they threatened Emma with the same treatment. But the nasty woman running the show realized she wasn't getting quick enough results that way. So she called in a computer guy who activated the chip's program on Jasper's laptop, which, in his distress, he hadn't closed out properly before he grabbed to go with the goons. After that, things got weird fast, because once the program was activated, the chip connected with it and the brain wave collector hidden deep in Jasper's ear, then he blacked out, and woke up as his digital image projected inside the fishing float--where he had hidden the chip--holding an unconscious projection of Emma.

He didn't know what was happening to their bodies back on the island, but they were probably unconscious, because he wasn't getting any sensory data from his physical self. Jasper had often observed his digital image as it moved and spoke, but he hadn't become his projection before. The feeling was awful. Like his head had been cut off, and he was only his consciousness. It reminded him of a horror film that featured a disembodied brain in a jar.

Jasper reasoned that his body must still have been alive because projecting his thoughts required the chip to gather moment-to-moment brain input from the microprocessor in his ear. He just hoped they didn't turn off the computer or look closely inside his ear. He comforted himself by knowing that at least the chip was safe, because his projection was sitting on it in the float.

Jasper's projection had all his brain's memories and knowl-edge, but his awareness was completely centered in the glass ball. He wasn't sure what was occurring in Emma's brain, and that was his greatest source of despair, because she was unre-sponsive no matter what he did to try to waken her.

Looking down at his body, Jasper could see a torso, arms, and legs, but they felt like elastic Jell-O. He moved around, but there was this weird adhesive effect, so he had to constantly fight the feeling he was still in his previous position. The glass ball was small, so the sensation wasn't a big issue, and maybe that feeling was typical for a small man in a glass bubble. Who knew? He could also look down and see an occasional brief flickering of his image that reminded him of television static when a station was off the air. He was able to move Emma's projection around and to pick up the scrap of rag he had wrapped the chip in before hiding it in the float, but he couldn't move the chip or touch the glass walls of the globe.

It was different situation for Emma, Jasper thought. Logically, she shouldn't have been a visible projection at all, because up to that point, her immature brain waves had only supported images of objects. Somehow the system had shifted to include her body's projection with his. Maybe that meant her physical body was unconscious like his was. He hadn't thought to run trials while she was asleep, so perhaps she would have appeared as an unconscious projection then, but it was a little late for that investigation now.

She lay still like a limp and broken doll. Sometimes she made sucking motions with her mouth, and he hoped someone on the island was feeding her a bottle; she also occasionally made rapid eye movements similar to the ones people make while dreaming. If Jasper physically opened her eyelids, her eyes looked like glass eyes or dead ones, and it upset him so much that he didn't do it anymore. Jasper held her, sang to her, talked to her, and apologized a lot, but mostly he cried and cursed over her. When he was despondent, he would lie next to her with his face inches away from hers and breathe with her breaths; it soothed him somehow, even though neither of them was actually moving air.

The rest of the time, he tried to keep from going crazy. He attempted to feel more normal by pretending he had a physical body in the globe. Jasper stretched and did an exercise routine, and then he ran in place for aerobics; finally, he toned with muscle resistance and tried to calm himself with yoga. He knew the exercise didn't affect his real body because it wasn't physically present, but the counting and repetition kept him from drowning in too many negative thoughts. It kept him from torturing himself by saying "we're never getting out of here!" and "what have you done to Emma, you stupid jerk? What kind of father are you anyway?"

Jasper also distracted himself by reciting poetry and any quotes from literature that he could remember. He alternated those activities with math equations, long mental letters to people he knew, and hours of meditation. Despite those activities, he had many moments when he lost his emotional grip, and he slid deeper and deeper into dark thoughts. Emma was a great reality anchor, but his intense worry about her weighted him down; he obsessed about how pale and unresponsive she was and examined her repeatedly, looking for clues about her body's health. Lately he had spent more and more time staring at nothing and feeling hope slip away.

One of the problems with being in a glass bubble floating in the ocean was sensory deprivation—he couldn't sense much outside of the glass. The wall curvature distorted anything he could see, and the many years the globe had spent in the ocean had frosted the glass in places. Though he could pick up and hold Emma, his sensation of touch was limited by his partially there body, and so it didn't feel like he was connecting with her at all.

He could hear some limited sounds—mostly his own voice, which he decided was repetitive, boring, and prone to self-pity. He sang off-key, and he was bad at remembering song lyrics, too. Overall, Jasper got so tired of hearing only his own voice that silence was usually his choice. The exception to that decision was singing and talking baby stuff to Emma even though he didn't think she could hear him.

Obviously, there wasn't anything to eat or to smell in the globe, and he didn't make spit or any other bodily secretions. He thought that was a good thing, because there were no tissues available for tears or snot when he cried and no place to discard them anyway. But that didn't mean his sensory memories didn't haunt him. Jasper's mind especially dwelt on the smell and flavor of coffee, maple syrup, apple pie, spicy salsa, fresh yeasty bread, meat grilling, and baby powder. It astounded him how clear the memory of his favorite tastes and smells were to him. They were almost better than the real thing, but they haunted and teased him often.

Jasper knew that in the 1970s, sensory deprivation by immersion in a dark enclosed tank of water had been considered a stimulus to solve problems or to come up with creative ideas. It was believed that the loss of sensation reduced left-brain cognitive function and let right-brain creativity run free. The think tanks gradually lost favor, and brainstorming became popular, but he knew the basic idea of sensory deprivation was still sometimes used in meditation and hypnosis. After being in the globe, Jasper was willing to bet that weeks of sensory deprivation would send even the strongest mind past creativity and into insanity.

No matter how Jasper tried, much of his time was spent worrying and beating himself up mentally. He logically knew that he'd made the best decisions he could at the time, but in retrospect, it felt like he had messed up every choice he made. What he had innocently created to help Emma communicate had turned into a possible weapon for their destruction because he hadn't thought ahead about all of the applications like he should have. His thoughts ran around and around the same negative tracks, causing him constant anguish.

Then suddenly into his mental mess came a bright light that sent him into immediate sensory overload. At first, he was scared as he imagined what terrible thing might be happening outside the globe. Then the light led him to the image of a beautiful woman. She seemed to be floating in space beyond the distortion of the glass wall. At first, Jasper thought she was an angel and his body was passing into the afterlife. He actually felt good about that, except it might mean the loss of Emma's life too, and he would have done anything to preserve her.

He finally noticed the angel was holding up a sign, and when he read it, all of his emotions exploded. Someone who actually cared had found them! He had reminded himself many times that they were adrift in a huge ocean and that it was unlikely they'd be found before they perished. That they had been found seemed impossible to him, and a potential rescue completely out of the question! Jasper was just happy they wouldn't die alone. He had wanted to make a will and to explain to his gaming fans what had happened; having a connection to another person, even for a little while, was everything to him—after Emma's life.

He freaked out when she asked if she could break the glass, because he had no idea what that would do to his and Emma's projections or to their physical brains with the system components so widely separated by distance. Even if he had had the time to test things completely, which he hadn't, he couldn't have imagined anything close to the situation they were in at the moment. Jasper believed it was always better to be safe than sorry, and once the glass was broken, there would be no going back if the chip couldn't handle it.

Plus Jasper needed to protect the chip from everyone until he was in a position to destroy it. The chip was the reason he and Emma were in the globe to begin with, and he didn't trust anyone with its design information. If the woman who'd found them was an innocent bystander, Jasper didn't want to put her in any danger; but if she was working for the people on the island, then he didn't want her to get her hands on the chip—no matter what he had to do to prevent it.

Five

Newt's older brother, Tony, had been born a geek. She remembered that even as a young child, he had had cardboard boxes containing wires and small unidentifiable electronic parts under his bed. Their parents had been worried throughout his childhood that he would strangle himself with electrical cords, swallow small screws, or burn down the house by overloading its electrical circuits.

In his teenage years, Tony was the neighborhood's nerdy kid and hooked up printers, troubleshot computer crashes, and educated all the baby boomers about the best antiviral software. In adulthood, all the gadget boxes under his childhood bed had morphed into an entire apartment of electronic hardware and spare parts. Tony's living space was crammed so full of computer junk that there was only a little room around the edges for him to sleep and eat. That arrangement suited him fine, but it drove Newt nuts, so she rarely visited him there. She often asked him why he didn't just rent warehouse space, but he said he wanted his inventory close at hand. She sometimes thought he was like a bird in its nest, but instead of feathers and twigs, he had wires and computer parts.

Because of Tony's geeky nature, it was natural for Newt to call him for advice about how to wire sound to the globe. She also wanted a complete list of parts to buy, as the closest electronic store was in Aberdeen, an hour away, and she didn't want to make a second trip. But Newt decided to be evasive if he asked questions, because she wanted his help without him thinking she was crazy or reporting to their mom that something strange was going on. She wanted him to tell her what to buy in plain English too, because once he had spoken to her for twenty minutes about a computer upgrade, and she hadn't understood a single word he he'd said. Then when she asked for clarification, he'd only become more technical until her eyes crossed, she'd developed a headache, and had begged him to stop. No way did she want to experience that again!

So she tried to sound casual and used her preplanned story when he answered on the first ring. "Hey, big brother, I need your help hooking up sound for a project I'm working on today."

"Happy to help, sis, you know that. What are the system requirements for it?" Tony asked.

"Well, I want to pick up and amplify a quiet sound, like a bug in the grass, and then damper my voice down so I can talk into the recording and not overwhelm the softer sound." She knew it sounded fishy, but she couldn't think of another way to explain it to him.

"OK, but that doesn't sound like a typical project for you." Tony sounded suspicious already.

"I'm trying something new on my vacation." Newt worked on keeping her voice nonchalant. "What parts do you think I'll need?"

"How about if I come over and help you set up the system? You know how I love to stay at the cabin, and I could still work from my truck." He put a little persuasion in his tone because he understood his sister better than she thought, so knew that she was up to something interesting.

Drat, he was too smart for his own good. "No, don't come. It's really not that important. Just give me some general guidelines so I can ask for the equipment I need."

There was a long pause on the other end of the phone as he processed what she'd requested. She suspected he was looking for holes in her story and deciding how to translate geek into English to explain to her what she needed for the task she outlined.

Finally, he said, "I can call the store, see what they have in stock, and design a system around that. Then it'll be ready for you to pick up when you get there, and I can e-mail you directions to put it together."

Newt thought he sounded like he couldn't wait to have a nerdy conversation with someone at the store who would appreciate the ins and outs of designing such a system.

"Man, that would be great, Tony! I'll owe you one. Just be sure the directions are simple and clear. You know how stuff like this challenges me."

"Yeah, I know who it's for. But I want to hear the finished recording someday, sis."

"I'll keep you in the loop, big brother." Newt had her fingers crossed behind her back because she wasn't going to record anything without the globe man's permission, and she hated to lie. "I love you, and thanks."

Newt loved the twisting drive to Aberdeen. It wound through salt marshes and evergreen-forested mountains. The road was a narrow two-lane highway with pullout areas for slow vehicles going uphill, which allowed faster cars to pass by them easily. But there always seemed to be a huge logging truck creeping up behind her when she was going downhill. Thankfully, there were graveled ramps pointing upward into the trees on the steeper downhill slopes, and runaway trucks could use them to get off the road and coast to a stop. Newt always wondered how often brake failure happened to justify building special ramps just for that purpose.

Newt wanted to be home before dark because another road hazard was the white-tailed deer that came out at dusk to feed on the plants growing on the edges of the highway. They favored this area because the path created by the road opened the dense forest and let sunlight in, and that encouraged the kind of new greenery deer love to browse on. Those beautiful forest creatures could cause a crash by freezing in front of an oncoming car's headlights or bounding out suddenly to cross the road. The risk of deer, the logging trucks, the squeeze of huge motor homes, and the road construction made returning home before nightfall a priority in her book. A car accident would not help her potentially rescue the man and baby in the globe.

When she arrived safely back at the cabin, she saw two blinking messages on her answering machine. One message was from Tony, who was making sure she had gotten what she needed from the store and could set it up properly; the other was from her mom, who was checking in to see how she was enjoying her vacation.

Her mother, the senior Dr. Newton, was a medical doctor who worked as a consultant for several major hospitals in Seattle and around the world. She was in great demand, commanded a huge amount of respect, and worked long hours. As a mom, she was nosy, controlling, opinionated, and overbearing, especially since their dad had died. Newt and Tony loved her beyond words, but in order to live a halfway adult life, they frequently conspired to keep things from her, because once she was involved in their business they lost any say in the outcome. Mom always knew best and frequently reminded them of that fact.

She knew that if her mother became aware of the people in the globe, she would swoop in, and Newt would never see them again. Her mom would say it was for her children's protection, of course, but Newt wanted to make her own decisions and to handle things her own way. She knew that in her mother's eyes she would always be a helpless little girl who needed her mom's sage advice in order to live her life successfully; she completely ignored the fact that Newt was also a successful doctor and a business owner too.

Newt called her mother back and left a generic message.

"Mom, everything is just great. I'm having a wonderful vacation. I love you, so don't worry about me. I'll be home in a couple of weeks. You know I love the cabin, and Tony might visit me anyway." That was Newt's usual verbal smokescreen, which was intended to throw her mom off the trail, even though she did appreciate her maternal concern sometimes.

After answering her messages, she opened the package from the electronics store and set up the equipment. The final system was simpler than she had expected it to be. It had two microphones, one to attach to the glass so she could hear the man talk and one for her to speak to him; two volume controls, one geared to tone down her voice and one to amplify his sound; a small speaker to place against the glass so he could hear her speak; and headphones for her to wear to hear him talk.

Newt knew really loud sounds could break glass, so she started with the volume at zero and very slowly increased it saying, "Testing, testing," over and over again.

The first thing she heard him say was, "Thank you so much. No matter how this turns out, I want you to know how much I appreciate what you're doing for us."

Newt replied with a smile on her face. "You're welcome, and I'm dying of curiosity. Are you real? What's your name? How did you get in there anyway? Is the baby OK, or is she sick? What can I do to help?" She knew it was a lot of questions at one time, but she couldn't help herself.

From inside the globe, Jasper puzzled over how to explain everything to her without revealing dangerous details. "I'm Jasper Higgs, and this is my daughter, Emma. I'm a computer programmer, and we're trapped in here because of a chip I invented to help me communicate with Emma."

She started to ask more questions and then stopped and gasped because the nagging thought that she had seen him before suddenly crystallized into recognition.

"Wait a minute...are you THE Jasper Higgs, computer genius, right here in my cabin?"

He grimaced. "Yeah, right here in miniature, trying to stay alive long enough to fix what happened, at least for Emma." He sounded disgusted with himself.

"I don't understand," she replied.

In an emotionless voice he said, "I don't know who you are, lady, so I won't tell you any more. I'm in here because a person I trusted sold me out, and probably for money."

Newt thought about what he said for a minute and then got angry. "You think my helping you is a setup? You just happened to wash up on my beach so I could sell you out too? That's crazy talk—think about how ridiculous that is. I would have had to have known where you entered the water and what the ocean currents were doing, and then I would have had to pinpoint exactly where you would land and when. It's a big ocean, buddy, and this is my home on a very small beach, so think again, techno-wizard."

He rubbed his hands over his face and looked distressed. "OK, even if you are trustworthy, if I tell you, it could put your life in danger."

Newt snorted. "You have to trust me because I'm the only person in a position to help you. It's a Catch-22. If you trust me, it could put me in danger. If you don't trust me, I can't help you, because I don't know what's going on."

Jasper folded his arms and glared at her. She folded her arms and glared back at him and said, "If I wanted to hurt you, all I would need is a hammer. Think about that for a minute. And what about the baby in there? I know you care about what happens to her, don't you? If I wanted to make a lot of money, I could sell you in the float 'as is' to the evening news. You couldn't do anything to stop me, and you know it."

Newt was upset because all she wanted to do was to help him, and he was throwing it back in her face. She thought that maybe she should suggest tossing him back in the ocean as a solution to his problem. But on second thought, that move would be impossible until she knew more about the baby's situation.

He paced around in the globe's small space, and then he turned his back on her awhile. Finally, he came to a decision.

"All right, I'll tell you. It started when I wanted to communicate with Emma. I made a system that collects a brain's electrical activity, or its thoughts, processes them through a computer program, and then translates them into a visual image using a chip. I made a device, kind of like an EEG, to capture brain waves. What you're seeing are my thoughts projected as a digital image of me."

Newt was stunned by the information. "Like a brain-computer interface? I know people who are working on that, but devices need to be surgically implanted, and they can't do anything like your system is doing."

"Well, mine doesn't need to go into the brain, because I designed microprocessors to fit inside the ear, and Emma and I are wearing them now. In the beginning, the system created simple images of objects on a screen, but my computer refined the results over months of constant calculations. You know how it works: give the computer a task, and it comes up with millions of possible solutions and tries them out while constantly discarding and selecting until the problem is solved in the best way. But I'm surprised, too, that it resulted in my sitting here talking to you in 3-D. Unfortunately, I got so caught up in how amazing it was that I didn't think ahead fast enough to other, less altruistic uses. Someone I knew did, though, and that resulted in Emma's kidnapping because they wanted me to trade the chip for her, the bastards."

"I'm still not sure I understand, Jasper. How is an exact copy of you aiding communication between you and your baby? And why isn't Emma awake like you?"

He almost smiled. "From the computer's perspective, it was the best way to solve the problem I gave it, which was converting complex brain activity into a visual representation of thoughts. But it's not what a human would have done with that task, that's for sure."

Jasper gently stroked Emma's hair back from her forehead. "I think she's like this because she has a baby brain, but I don't know for sure, and I'm worried about her."

"You made the chip to talk to her?" Newt didn't want to discuss the kidnapping until she had more basic facts.

"She makes almost no sounds, but I knew she wanted to communicate with me, because I could see it in her eyes. So I tried to solve that problem by designing the system that put us in here."

Newt heard the self-recrimination in his voice and tried to soothe him. "I don't see how any of this is your fault, Jasper, so put the blame on the bad guys." Then she added, "But why can't Emma make any sounds?"

"The doctor said Emma is more than just speech delayed. She might even have apraxia. Producing sound requires more than a thought—it's a complex series of fine muscle movements from the tongue, throat, and vocal cords. Somewhere along the line, she can't coordinate it all. She cries, coughs, laughs, and sneezes, but those are just reflexes, the doctor said, and not real sounds that lead to speech in time."

Newt saw he was looking sad, so she changed the subject. "I didn't know you had a daughter, Jasper."

"Her birth mother wanted to keep it quiet, and as soon as Emma was born, she signed her parental rights over to me. She never wanted a baby anyway, and I loved Emma from the first time she opened her eyes and looked at me. I just wanted to talk to her, that's all. Nothing like a frustrated father at two in the morning wondering why the baby is still crying to stimulate a leap forward for technology." He sounded tired and sat on the bench, still cuddling Emma in his arms.

Newt thought that sounded like a story to ask him about at another time. "Where's the chip now?"

"I only made one, and I'm sitting on it." He pointed to what Newt had thought was a bench.

"Do you have a plan to get out of there? Maybe destroying the chip would stop the kidnappers because then they would know a ransom was impossible."

"Yeah, but remember that our bodies are still somewhere with the bad guys. If the chip was destroyed, then our projections would stop. I want to try rescue Emma, so I need to be able to communicate. Actually, I'm afraid that at some point they'll give up on the idea of finding the chip and just dump our bodies in the ocean for the sharks to eat."

They both considered that gloom-and-doom possibility. After a moment, she replied, "So before the chip can be destroyed, your bodies must be found?"

"Yeah, but it's going to be hard to locate our bodies and virtually impossible to get to them. But I just can't let Emma die, so I've got to do something!"

She laughed. "Hey, I'm a scientist who solves hard problems. We just have to gather data, look at it logically, form a great team, and plan and execute a rescue. Believe me, Jasper, you had amazing, maybe even divine, luck to wash up on this particular beach and to be found by me."

Six

While Jasper was talking about his perilous position and she was responding, a part of Newt's brain was yelling "Jasper Higgs!" What were the chances that someone she recognized would float there in the globe—especially a person she had cared about in the past? The statistical probability of that was small enough to be immeasurable.

Newt's upbringing and education had grounded her in logic, rationally, and skepticism about conclusions drawn without testing. But like many scientists, she marveled at the complexity of the universe and the precise organization of life, so she kept an open mind about a divine influence behind it all. Serendipity was possible, but maybe something else was at work in this situation too. There was much more that was unknown than known, so Newt resolved stay unbiased as things developed.

Jasper Higgs had been her teenage crush. Other girls flitted between actors and rock stars, but he had been the only one for her. She had loved him intensely as only an adolescent can love, and even though she had had other relationships since then, Newt still had a soft spot in her heart for him. But at thirteen years old, Newt had been obsessed with him, and after prolonged Internet searching, she finally found a small photo of him and taped it to the wall by her bed. She kissed it good night every night until it turned to pulp when she was eighteen. All the while, she had dreamed she would meet him someday. Jasper's sixteen-year-old face in that photo was a three-quarter profile view; clearly, he was turning away from the camera when his image was taken, so Newt knew he didn't want anyone to know what he looked like. She had never found another photo of him since.

When he first mentioned his name, she raised her glasses and took a close look at him on the computer screen. Like many intellectuals, she had myopia and could see close up but not far away, so for fine details, she didn't need her glasses. After having felt that initial click of recognition, peering closely at him, and mentally aging him in her mind, she decided those unique, soulful eyes couldn't belong to anyone else. It really was him, and she was excited to meet him, even if he was currently tangled in a messy situation.

Although she'd seen only the one picture of him, images of Jasper's games' characters and his logo decorated her teen bedroom as posters and appeared on her T-shirts, notebooks, and inside her school locker. Most of Newt's passion wasn't based on Jasper's good looks but rather on how his games were designed. She understood him by playing the games he created; because of that, she knew he was inventive, imaginative, honest, and an original thinker.

His games had taught Newt some of the skills she used frequently in her research—things like analyzing options, predicting outcomes, problem solving, inductive and deductive reasoning, and visualization of three-dimensional structures. Unlike other popular games, his weren't mastered with violence, instead they were won with creative thinking, skill, and craftiness. Jasper always awarded honesty, kindness, helping, and teamwork, so his games enriched the character and mind of his players as they moved through the levels. Newt had loved him mostly for his games, and not just for his beautiful eyes—regardless of how much time she had spent staring at his picture.

Newt cleared her throat, which suddenly dried up with shyness as she thought about introducing herself to him, and said, "Jasper, I'm Abigail Newton, but my friends call me Newt. I have a medical research laboratory in Seattle and double PhDs in bioengineering and physiology. I've played your games since I was a teenager, and I especially love Smoke and Mirrors. I've spent countless hours battling my way through all the reflections and duplicate characters. It's so much fun, and I feel like I know you already." She tried not to gush, but she wasn't very successful at controlling it.

He turned his face away from the camera, ducked his head, and looked embarrassed. "It's always great to meet a fan."

His tone of voice said otherwise, and she was sure that was a stock answer he often used. Obviously he had issues with the notoriety of fame, so it was no wonder that she'd only been able to find the one photo of him. Newt promised herself that later on she would delve into the reasons for that, but at the moment she had other bases to cover.

"Have you heard of the hardware wizard called TNT?"

Jasper breathed a sigh of relief at her change of topic. "Sure, he's to hardware what I'm to software. He finds new things that push the envelope of technology. I've talked to him a couple of times on the phone, but I haven't met him in person."

She tried to channel her mother's steamroller attitude because she knew he would immediately object to involving another person. "His real name is Antonio Theodore Newton, and he's my brother. He's just the right person to help us out in this situation."

"Wait a darned minute, Newt. I appreciate your attempt to help, but I'm not involving you or your family in this any more than you are already."

Newt looked at him, and she could see he was angry and upset. He had raised his voice and was shaking his clenched fist at her. However, a six-inch-tall man was just funny when he was mad. She was having a hard time not laughing at him and hid it by coughing in her hand.

"Don't get upset, Jasper. Just think about it for a minute. I agree you have the right to choose how you live your own life, but what about Emma? Doesn't she deserve at least a chance to get out of there and to live normally, even if you don't believe it's possible right now?"

Jasper actually kicked at the globe's wall in frustration, but nothing happened, so it didn't disperse his anger. "That's an unfair thing to say, Newt! You don't understand the situation, and you haven't seen the people who took us. They're trained for violence and armed with guns. What do you propose as ransom for our bodies—a scientific paper?"

Newt spoke calmly in response. "Who says we're going up against armed men? Haven't you ever heard of diplomacy or bargaining?"

"You have no idea about the kind of people you'd be dealing with! But I've looked into their eyes, and they're stone cold inside! They took my innocent baby and told me they would kill her if I didn't cooperate, for God's sake!" Jasper's expression reflected his constant fear for Emma.

She felt his statement hit her heart painfully, but she stayed firm. "My mother knows many powerful heads of state, and we can apply pressure to them both through the authorities and politically too. Maybe I could even set up an Internet movement, target your fans, and collect money from them for a ransom. Most criminals shy away from the light of public exposure, so I can really blind them with it."

Jasper sat down on the chip and shook his head sadly. "No, their response to exposure or pressure would be to kill us and then to deny everything. They took Emma in broad daylight from a secure location. They knew what I was working on and when I would be gone, so they had to have established surveillance inside my very secure house. They abducted her first, knowing I would cooperate and go with them because I would be scared for her. I think they don't ever intend to release either of us. Instead, they plan to get what I can give them and then discard us. No amount of ransom would be accepted because they would have to admit they kidnapped us first, and they're not going to do that."

He sat with his head cradled in his hand and held Emma in his lap. "They're a big highly organized operation with many people involved. They took me in a limo and flew me in a private jet and then in a helicopter. Everyone I saw wore matching uniforms of black and gold, and there wasn't a shred of remorse for what they were doing to me or Emma. They just want the chip ASAP."

Newt was shocked by what he had said, but she didn't let it show in her face or voice. "Look, Jasper, don't give up. There are always several options to solve any problem. We're a long way from facing down a private army today, but let's just go step by step. There's no harm in considering all the possibilities. If it can't be done, then we'll have at least tried to figure out a solution."

He snorted. "If they even suspect the chip is here, Newt, I believe they would kill you and your entire family to get it." Jasper could tell he wasn't convincing her to give up; stubbornness was a good quality when playing his games but not in this dangerous situation. He couldn't help but like her, because it seemed she had everything he admired: goodness, ethics, generosity, intelligence, and beauty. But for Jasper, those were all good reasons to keep her out of the mess his chip had triggered.

Newt was a cautious person by nature. She didn't like heights or walking alone on dark nights; she double-checked all her doors when she left for work in the morning. Taking the kind of risk Jasper thought was involved in their rescue was foreign to her, but her mother had taught her that wrong was wrong and that you had to stand up to bullies. Besides, she rarely backed down from a worthwhile challenge. Instead she picked at it and turned it around, looking at all of its angles until the problem started to unravel.

"If it's that dangerous, Jasper, then the rescue plan must be foolproof. We'll need to account for all the variables, gather the best team, and outthink them at every turn. I know that Emma is the most at risk. Once they know she can't be used as leverage to get the chip, she'll become a liability for them, so surprise is essential no matter how we proceed."

Jasper replied in a soft voice. "If she dies, there's no point in rescuing me. I'll just jump off the first cliff I see to stop the pain of losing her."

Newt saw in his face that he was dead serious about that, so she laid her fingertip against the glass in support, and he placed his hand as close to it as he could get. They were of one mind on the importance of Emma's rescue, at least.

"OK, let me at least call Tony, and then we can put our heads together and come up with a possible plan. He suspects something is up anyway." She picked up her phone from its docking station on the kitchen counter.

Jasper shook his head. "I guess I can't stop you, but it's hopeless, Newt. I don't know who took Emma or where she is. I don't even know why you care about us anyway."

Newt smiled at him. "I care for a lot of reasons Jasper. What they did was wrong. Might is not right, and you put that moral value in your games. You're important to the world, and so is Emma. Evil needs to be stopped, and sometimes, you should know, all it takes is a few players who are willing to try."

Jasper shrugged; he was exasperated with her. "You know, life isn't one of my games, Newt. Good doesn't always win in the end, and you don't get another life or another try if you die."

"But if we outsmart them, Jasper, then no one has to risk his or her life." She wasn't waffling on that, because Newt thought she had to at least try to save them.

"I'm not sure your shiny idealism is the same as outthinking them. You're talking like a martyr. There are plenty of people who have died for their great cause throughout history to prove my point."

Newt could see his distress. She understood that he alone wanted to take full responsibility for what had happened to them. If he hadn't designed the chip, then this wouldn't have been happening, and so on. But the kidnappers really had the responsibility for their situation, so who was being the martyr? It was one of those hard choices when neither option felt good. Could she just stand by and watch him and Emma live a partial life like hamsters in a cage until they winked out of existence when their bodies died? Or should she fight back and do what was right by finding the kidnappers and taking Jasper and Emma back?

Both choices seemed risky emotionally and physically. Newt decided she needed more information to make a final decision, but her heart was telling her what she needed to do. She knew from experiences in the past that sometimes the correct route reveals itself when one has the courage to take a few steps in the right direction.

Seven

The next morning Newt stood on the cabin's front porch sipping hot coffee and watching her brother speed down the beach access road with his truck's tires throwing up gravel and sand. Tony had a theory that if you drive fast enough, the bumps and ruts in the road smooth out, making it easier to drive. That technique might work for him, but it never did for her, and it didn't look like it was working for him today either as he bounced down the road toward the cabin.

She looked up and noticed that there was a storm brewing out on the ocean. Newt heard distant thunderclaps and could see the flash of occasional bursts of lightning; there was the feel of moisture in the air as the wind picked up. The ocean's color was a dark and opaque gray, and the whitecaps on the waves extended almost to the horizon. She could see white spray as water crashed against the rocky outcrops on either side of the inlet where the cabin was sheltered. Newt loved storms; they were full of possibility for washed-ashore beach treasures the next day, and she loved the snap of electric energy in the air. Streaks of rain falling on the water were visible over the distant ocean, and she knew the wind would blow it to the cabin soon. The air smelled fresh and clean, and she breathed it in deeply as she waited for her brother to park.

Tony pulled into the turnaround circle at the end of the road and stopped. He was driving his customized brown delivery truck. He always said its plain brown wrapper fooled people and hid the totally tricked-out interior from potential thieves. Like a snail with its house on its back, Tony's truck carried everything he needed for his computer work, and much more, too. He often drove around for weeks at a time, setting up data systems for schools, businesses, libraries, and nonprofit organizations. He specialized in troubleshooting, upgrades, and repairs for older computers people just needed to last a little bit longer. Tony's overhead was low without a store or an office to maintain, so he often gave steep discounts for good causes and to people on limited incomes. His genius with data-processing hardware was in great demand by corporations, but he never let it overshadow helping people out individually.

Newt loved her brother with all her heart. He was her only sibling, and because they were separated in age by just eighteen months, many people assumed they were twins. His hair was a darker auburn red than her light red-gold hair, and his eyes were a soft grayish green unlike her bright bottle-green eyes, but their facial structure was identical. Newt thought his best feature—the one that drew in the girls—was his large open grin. But beneath Tony's handsome, amiable, and kind surface ran the constant passion to build computer systems that held more data, processed faster, were smaller in size, and could do more things. He had an amazing mind that continually worked on the next frontier for computers and associated technologies.

Tony always moved fast and efficiently. He jumped the few steps up to the porch and gave her a fierce one-armed hug; in his other arm he carried a hot spicy pizza and a small sack of ripe peaches. Her mouth watered at the smells. He knew just how Newt liked her pizza, and that was valuable knowledge in a brother. She also suspected he had stopped to visit with the daughter of the pizza shop owner. She and Tony had had an on-and-off relationship for years, but it had never matured in a serious direction; that was a disappointment for their mother, who craved grandchildren and mentioned that fact frequently.

Tony brushed Newt's cheek in a light kiss. "Hi, sis, I'm glad you called. I was just in the process of coming to see you anyway. My spider senses told me something strange was going on."

Newt kissed his cheek in return. "No amount of psychic connection would make this situation believable unless you saw it with your own eyes. So sit on the swing with me, and I'll try to prepare you if I can."

Tony gave her a quizzical look. "What? Mystery isn't like you at all. You're the most straightforward person I know."

"Yeah, but even I can't believe what's happening. It's like my life has shifted into the twilight zone."

He shook his head. "OK, time to clue me in, because this is getting weird."

Newt knew she was stalling because there was still a part of her that thought the people in the globe might be a hallucination. "I guess it's time to go in and see if you see what I see. It's starting to rain anyway."

They walked inside to the living room, and Tony's eyes immediately went to the kitchen table where the globe was hooked up to the sound and video apparatus.

"What's this, sis? Are you working on an electronic version of a crystal ball?" Tony said in a joking voice.

Newt gave him a serious look and calmly said, "I found it on the beach two days ago." She paused for a moment. "Have you heard anything about Jasper Higgs lately?"

"The super-duper computer worker, master of outrageous gaming software, and the guy you crushed on? No, not for a while, why are you asking? Want me to try and get his number for you?" He was still trying to find a joke somewhere in the situation, but Newt's serious face was throwing him off.

Newt tried to use a soothing voice. "Prepare for a shock, big brother, because he and his daughter are inside that glass ball."

"No way. You must have hit that thick skull of yours." He laughed at her, but then shot her a concerned glance.

"Look for yourself, but sit down first as it could be a shock." Newt knew the moment he saw Jasper. She felt relief because it confirmed she was not having some kind of mental breakdown. His loud gasp, which was followed by a quick shake of his head and a closer look, told her all she needed to know about her sanity. She turned on all the equipment and introduced them to each other.

"Jasper, meet my brother Tony, also known as TNT. Tony, meet Jasper Higgs and his baby daughter, Emma. They need our help to get out of there." Newt listened while they spoke to each other.

"Jazz-man, what the heck is going on?" Tony asked using Jasper's online name.

"TNT, I really pushed the envelope of what should be done, and now I'm in deep trouble—probably too deep to be saved. Your sister thinks we can fix the situation, but I hope you talk her out of that. No one should risk their life for what I did. Just destroy the chip and end this the only way possible!"

"What chip, Jazz?" Tony was confused and struggling to understand the situation.

"I'm not going to give you the chip's technical details! I don't trust anyone. The chip needs to be destroyed, and that's all you need to know!" Jasper walked around in a small circle, clearly agitated.

Newt intervened. "The chip he means is the one in the globe, and if it's destroyed, they'll die!" She pointed to the small square of black plastic inside the glass.

Tony was trying to catch up, and he couldn't listen to both of them at the same time. "OK, sis, be quiet for a minute. Relax, Jazz-man! Just clue me in about the chip as much as you can before I destroy it and kill you and the baby." He exchanged a quick look with Newt, and she knew what he was thinking: no way were they going to destroy Jasper and Emma before eliminating all other options. Tony knew what Jasper meant to Newt, and Jazz was a computer god to him; and the sweet sleeping baby had a stake in the outcome too, no matter what Jasper wanted.

Jasper took a few deep breaths to calm himself before he spoke because sharing their ordeal again was painful. "I wanted to communicate with Emma because she can't talk, so I made a system that collects thoughts and translates them into visible images. It bypasses sound production. I fed the project requirements into my computer, created an ear microprocessor for collecting brain waves, and made a chip to project the resulting images. What the system produced was a full digital copy of me created directly from my brain, and that's what you're talking to now."

He paused for a minute to let Tony think about it. "I don't know about you, but I haven't learned to control my thoughts very well, and I got so involved in the process that I failed to consider other possible uses quickly enough. Picture this: someone abducts an inventor, a rich person, or a rival leader, and then against his or her will, the abductor projects his or her thoughts. How long could anyone keep secrets without a lip to zip? The chip is better than truth serum, TNT. You know the saying 'Thoughts speak louder than words'? Well it's true."

Jasper rubbed a hand over his face. "When my body was awake, I heard my image verbally pour out my stream of consciousness, and it was scary. I never realized how strange thoughts can be, but mixed in there was enough technical stuff that my thoughts could have been a blueprint for all my designs. I was working on a thought-selecting mechanism when someone kidnapped Emma and demanded the chip as ransom. My system has the potential to make privacy a thing of the past, so no one would be safe, even in their own mind. They can't get their hands on it no matter what!" Jasper fisted both of his hands.

Tony tried to settle him down. "I get that it has a bad application, Jazz, but you built it for good reason, right? I can see how it could help people communicate, too, and that's very important. Maybe it just needs a little modification, and the bad will go away and the good will come out." He scratched his chin. "How many projection chips did you make, man?"

"Only one, and it's in here with me, TNT." Jasper sat down on it and rocked Emma. He was finally relaxing.

"That's great! At least the chip's where we can keep an eye on it. And I have to give it to you 'cause I haven't seen any 3-D images that move around and talk back. It's wicked cool, man. But where's your body, and how are the bad guys running the chip?"

"I hid the chip in the float and refused to cooperate, so they tried to locate the chip by activating it from the program on my computer. Stupidly, I forgot to shut it down completely and made that easy for them. After that I blacked out and woke up in here with Emma, so they must have thrown the float in the ocean."

"But even if the system was suddenly activated why did you black out? That didn't happen at home did it?"

"No. But wait a minute! I was holding Emma with one hand and I grabbed for my computer with the other one. I vaguely remember pain in the back of my head and falling with her in my arms, so somebody must have bashed me in the head."

"A head injury would scramble things Jazz."

"Maybe I do have some brain damage, and now the chip is collecting sound waves and light energy from in here like my eyes and ears would normally do. Then it's sending that data back to my brain, which is processing it, and returning thoughts back to the chip, which projects a digital image of me in here."

Jasper sighed. "The good news is that I don't think the bad guys can get very far without the actual chip to analyze. The bad news is that with motivation and time, a good hacker might be able to work backward from my program and eventually make their own chip. It all depends on how smart they are and how much time they have. I have layers of protection spread throughout the program's code. So even though I made activating my computer easy, figuring out what I did to make the components translate thoughts is going to be really difficult."

Tony marveled at what Jasper's amazing system was doing, but he could see the down side to it too. "See, it isn't all about destroying the chip, Jazz. Sounds like we need to get your computer and the program back too."

"You know anything can be unraveled eventually, TNT. They're going to do it, and I'm going to be remembered as the one who released human psychic destruction—just like the guys who invented the atomic bomb are for massive physical annihilation."

"That sounds pretty pessimistic, dude, but your scrambled brain and program buys us some working time." Tony picked up a pad of paper from the kitchen counter and began making cryptic notes on it.

Jasper rubbed his cheek on Emma's downy hair. "I assume my brain and body are working because they're processing the chip's information, but I must still be unconscious. And I don't know what's happening with Emma. I'm scared they will discard her as not useful anymore."

Tony thought for a minute. "Hang in there. I think they're going to hedge their bets and not do anything drastic to either of you yet. They went through a lot of trouble to get this far, so I suspect they'll try a lot harder before they give up on getting the chip."

"I'm really mostly worried about Emma being OK."

"Of course you are, because you're her dad, man! Here's a scary thought, though: can they track things back to where you are and show up here suddenly?"

"I don't think so, or they'd have found me floating in the ocean, but I don't know for sure." Jasper shook his head.

"Then could we backtrack to your computer and find your and Emma's bodies that way?" Tony asked.

"I'm sure if we tried that, the bad guys running the program would know it, and that wouldn't be a good thing."

"OK, don't worry, Jazz, we're the best in the biz. Let's scam the scammers and get you and the baby back home safe. I know between the three of us we can come up with a solid plan." Tony scribbled some more on the pad. "In the meantime, I think I can get you out of that glass bubble and back up to normal size. You'd still be a projection, but you could walk around and maybe use a keyboard. It would be lots better than being stuck in the globe. Just give me a day, and we'll be sitting on the couch watching a movie, bro."

"Thanks, that would be a great relief. But you and Newt need to think hard about the risk involved in a rescue or even in just contacting them. Two geeks and a scientist won't stand a chance against trained men with guns. I couldn't stand it if anyone else got hurt because of my stupidity in inventing this system." Jasper looked at both of them with a sad smile and added, "Besides, if you stage a rescue and don't come back, I'm not spending the rest of my life as a ghostlike electronic signature. The chip works on so little energy that I could be around until my body dies of old age."

Tony replied, "Yeah, I think it would be a good idea to build some sort of autodestruct sequence into the chip in case it all tubes. But think about the talk-show circuit man! Because if you did end up like a ghost. You could make a fortune on T.V. dude."

Eight

Newt woke up to a sunny day, and air that was refreshed from the rainy night. She left her bedroom to seek morning coffee and saw electronic gadgets overflowing on the kitchen table, blanketing the countertops, and spilling down to the floor. Tony had Jasper on speakers, and they were tech-talking at such a fast rate that it didn't sound like they were speaking English at all. She knew they had been at it since the night before without a break, but both still seemed to be going strong. Newt knew that if you love what you do, the time just evaporates away.

As Newt cooked eggs, she listened to them talk. She realized that Jasper was telling Tony what to code into his computer to run a secondary program to enhance the projections once they were released from the globe. She thought they must be kindred spirits, because they sounded like two halves of the same brain; they even completed each other's sentences like twins or longtime married people did. It was weird to listen to, but from what she could glean from the fast-paced geek conversation, Jasper had insisted on programming the chip with a fail-safe feature before anything else was done to modify it.

The chip would overheat and melt down if it was used for anything other than projecting thoughts back and forth between

Jasper's and Emma's real brains. If the fail-safe feature was activated, even accidently, then it would be the end of Jasper's and
Emma's projections. Tony argued that the chip's demise might
result in damaging feedback to Jasper's brain, but Jasper didn't
care. He felt the sacrifice of his brain wasn't too big a price to
pay for keeping the chip out of the wrong hands.

Newt wondered what would happen to Jasper if the chip
melted—and what about Emma's life? No one vocalized what
they all knew: destruction of the chip would result in both of
their deaths at the hands of the kidnappers. They would awaken
if their brains were intact, and the kidnappers would try and
force Jasper to make another chip, but he would refuse. And if
they didn't regain consciousness, the bad guys would undoubtedly have zero tolerance for damaged people. Either way, they
would be killed. Tony had apparently argued to disable the chip
in a less drastic way, but it was Jasper's life and his decision in
the end, so Tony had reluctantly coded it into the secondary
program.

There was also a discussion about what caused the size of
the images. They all knew that Jasper would be more useful and
feel better if he were scaled up to normal size. Jasper said that
at home his projection had been full sized, so it was probably
the volume of the globe that had miniaturized the projection.

Tony's response to that reasoning was "Cool, so let's break
the glass and see what happens."

Newt was quick to express concern. "Wait a minute, guys,
there are a lot of variables here, such as the chip's distance
from his brain, that didn't exist before. Once the glass is broken, there's no going back if we find that it was important to
the projection after all. Maybe it protects, rather than contains,
the image." She considered that for a moment and then said,
"Jasper, how did you get the chip in there to begin with?"

He sighed because he didn't want to remember. "When I
arrived on the island, this witchy woman brought me Emma,
who she held out at arm's length because she had a soggy,

feces-filled diaper. It didn't look like anyone had fed or changed her since she was kidnapped. I was really angry, and Emma was screaming bloody murder! I'd brought her diaper bag with me, so I took out some supplies and palmed the chip. The witch showed me a bathroom where I could change Emma's messy diaper and mix up a bottle. An armed guard stood outside of the windowless room, so they didn't think I could do anything. Besides, no one could talk with a baby screaming and dripping a smelly diaper all over the floor, and I was yelling and waving her bottom in their faces. I didn't think it would be an opportunity to ditch the chip—I just wanted to take care of my daughter.

"I considered flushing the chip down the toilet, but I thought I might still need it to secure Emma's release. On the counter in the bathroom was a dish of shells and the fishing float for decoration. Along the base of the float there was a crack with a missing piece of glass just barely big enough to get the chip through, so I slid it in after wrapping it in a bit of rag to help conceal it. I sealed the hole with a wad of caulking I scraped off from around the sink. Then I folded the globe in the dirty diaper and put it in the trash, thinking most people wouldn't look inside a soiled diaper. I used the float because I didn't see any other place to hide the chip and I wanted to protect it. I didn't realize they would just quickly dump the smelly diaper in the ocean, and that the chip would float away in the globe with us projected inside. It was a dumb idea."

Tony shot back in support, "Not stupid but really smart, Jazz, because here you are, and now you've got help. Why don't we pick off the goo, take the chip out slowly, and see what happens. If you or Emma can't handle it, then we put the chip right back inside and find a plan B."

They all agreed to try it, and Newt held her breath as the chip slid out of the globe. The digital image of Jasper and Emma wavered a little and then held steady on the table. They were still miniature. Newt was enchanted by their small size; it was like Thumbelina come to life, she thought. Six-inch-high Jasper moved around the table, stretching his legs and holding an inch-long baby in three-dimensional miniature perfection. She had the urge to hold out her hand and have him sit in her palm, and only the scowl on his face prevented her from trying it out. Newt knew enough about men to realize that small size was not desirable in their eyes, so she didn't say anything about how cute they were.

After assessing the situation the men decided that because of the chip's distance from Jasper's brain, an additional power source would be needed to project Jasper and Emma to their natural size. The big hurdle would be preventing the kidnappers from backtracking the new programs. Eventually, their geek-speak was too much for Newt, and she went for a walk on the beach.

There was a short path from the garden gate through the dunes to the water. The dunes and their tough supporting grasses changed over time as they were sculpted by wind and water; she loved seeing their altered shapes as she walked the familiar sandy trail to the ocean. The storm from the night before had washed sea creatures up on the beach, and she spent time returning clear jellyfish and fuzzy gray sand dollars back into the ocean before they dried out and died. Then Newt stood still in the water, looking out to the horizon as the shallow waves washed ashore. She enjoyed the sensation that she was moving out to sea rather than watching the water come in to shore. It was a thing she had loved doing since she was a small child.

Seagulls called and fought over beached dead fish. Crabs scuttled away from her, and clam holes squirted water when Newt walked along. She filled the pockets of her gray hooded sweatshirt with shells and bits of polished glass, and she breathed in deeply the fresh salt air. The setting was peaceful, but her mind was arguing with itself; her cautious and practical nature was at war with her heart. Jasper's strong words of warning hadn't fallen on deaf ears, and she was scared because it looked like they could start working on a rescue plan. She had dedicated her life to helping people, but it was always at a distance with her medical research discoveries. This situation was a chance to help someone directly for a change. Sure, there was risk involved, she thought, but sometimes you need to take a leap of faith to follow your heart.

"On the one hand, no pain, no gain. But nothing ventured, nothing lost could apply, too," she muttered to herself as she turned back toward home.

Once she was back at the cabin, Tony told her they were on the final steps to enlarging the projection. While they were finishing up, Newt made a quick trip to the Ocean Shores grocery store and stocked up on food for simple meals like sandwiches, spaghetti, and tacos. The town's population was about 50 percent seasonal visitors, and the rest were year-round residents. It had two main roads that ran one way in each direction through town. The ocean side was lined with hotels, restaurants, and a casino; the town side was fun and filled with gift shops, an ice cream parlor, a family entertainment center, a kite shop, and other stores and amusements. She and Tony had always loved it, and she hoped someday to share it with her husband and children.

Once home, Tony told Newt they were ready to make the size transition. But he explained that there might be only be one chance to get it right because nothing was glitch proof and obviously it hadn't been done before. He said that they had both given it their best shot and that they couldn't think of another way to do it or of any possible problems they hadn't accounted for. Jasper had dictated his will to Tony and had given him a list of people to contact if it didn't work. That made Newt feel frightened, but she had to trust their collective genius. They were the best at what they did, and if they couldn't do it, no one could.

They did a verbal countdown from ten to one, and then Tony pressed "enter" on the computer. Small Jasper and Emma instantly disappeared from the table, but it took thirty seconds before their larger images flickered to life in the kitchen. At first Jasper was just a vague outline of multicolored static, and Tony desperately fiddled with his computer, trying to add more power. Slowly, Jasper's complete image came to life; he was clutching Emma to his chest. His hands, feet, and face looked semisolid, but his body was transparent enough to see the kitchen floor right through it. His arms, legs, and torso sparkled with fleeting bursts of colored static like a television on an inactive channel, and that gave him a constant fluctuation of density. He didn't look how Newt had imagined a ghost would—all misty and white—but he sure didn't look human either. It was cool, and creepy at the same time.

Once the projected images were as solid as Tony could make them, Jasper staggered over to the chip still on the table and put it in his pocket; then he collapsed on the faded living room couch, still holding Emma in his arms. He dry heaved a couple of times, gagged, and passed out; his face was slightly greenish, like that of a seasick sailor.

Tony trembled, and his face was pale and sweaty. "Man, Newt, I felt like Scotty on the *Enterprise*, trying to catch a fading transporter signal! I thought for a minute I wasn't going to pull it off. I was scared they would just fly apart and that would be the end of them."

Newt gave Tony a hug of support as he cradled his head in his hands. She said in a fake Scottish accent, "Yea gave it all yea got! I'm proud of you both for making it happen at all." She was shaky too.

They both stared at the couch. Emma looked a lot more solid than Jasper did, maybe because her static fluctuations were smaller and so less obvious. Newt guessed it might have been because her body mass was less to begin with, so there wasn't as much surface to project—or maybe Jasper's intense thoughts about Emma gave her more substance. She draped a blanket over them as they lay unconscious on the sofa, not because they could feel cold, but because while she was on the beach walk she had made up her mind to treat their projections as normal people. It was a difficult enough situation, and they didn't need to feel like monsters, too.

She was surprised when the light blanket outlined Jasper's digital form rather than settling down on the couch as if he weren't there. That meant his projection had some mass, so it was not just an energy signature as they had previously thought. Newt was excited because Jasper's and Tony's enhancements were now converting his thoughts into both energy and a little substance too! Fundamental to physics was the fact that energy could be converted to mass and visa versa as Einstein had described in his $E=MC^2$ formula. But she was seeing it right before her eyes, and she was astounded! The applications boggled her mind! Like Tony had said, it was the first step toward the transporter machine on *Star Trek* and "beam me up, Scotty."

She was eating celebratory ice cream with Tony when he said, "I'll call my team and have them take over all the upcoming jobs. There isn't anything they can't handle, and besides, they can call if something comes up. How about you?"

Newt scraped her bowl. "After this vacation, I was going to start writing grant proposals for next year's funding. Everything else is routine, and the project managers know what to do."

She thought a moment. "The sooner we get their projections back into their bodies, the better. Jasper is thin, and I've noticed his hands shake just a little. I think he's holding on by a thread mentally, too. We've got to get moving on a plan, or he's going to self-destruct, with or without the chip in his pocket."

She finished by saying, "I have some ideas. I'll talk to you both as soon as I can. I think it's better to wait until Jasper is ready to participate fully, and I need some time to mull it over anyway."

The next morning, Jasper seemed much better. He was sitting at the kitchen table staring at the chip in his hand when Newt walked in. She walked over, and he stood up and gathered her in his arms as best he could. It didn't feel like being hugged by a real person, she thought. He was taller than she had expected, and he leaned over slightly to place his cheek against hers. His arms wrapped around her back, and his hands rested on her shoulders. Newt could feel his face and hands slightly, but his arms and chest registered no touch at all on her body. She thought it was like a hug from a sock puppet—the fingers of the puppet's owner only animated its rubber head and hands, and the rest was just collapsed cloth. As weird as that sensation was, his deep gratitude transmitted itself through the hug directly to her heart.

Newt carefully tried to hug him back by placing her hands on top of his and squeezing gently, and there was a slight "zing" and a snap of static electricity in response.

"We're going to make this come out right, Jasper. Think how amazing it was that you escaped at all, let alone washed up here to be found by a person who just happens to have a brother with exactly the right computer skills you need. There's magic in that, so we should just trust the process as it unfolds. I know that sound kooky, but statistics will support my conclusion that it was unlikely to happen by chance alone, so maybe there's a greater design." She reserved judgment about whether that was true, but she wanted to give him hope, and there had been some unlikely coincidences.

After their hug and her pep talk, Jasper seemed embarrassed, so Newt walked over to Emma, who was still wrapped in the blanket and lying on the couch. She sat next to the baby and gently touched her small hands.

She looked up at him. "Can I pick her up?"

Jasper nodded "yes," so she carefully slid her arms under Emma's body and lifted her up. She was light, but she had a semisolid feel in Newt's arms like Jasper's hands and face had had. Newt cuddled Emma against her chest with one arm and looked down at her sweet face. She used her free hand to touch Emma's downy, soft hair and to stroke her pale cheek. The baby was just like a living doll. Emma was visibly breathing, but Newt couldn't feel any body warmth or resistance in her muscles. She knew from her undergraduate studies in child development that every day Emma wasn't awake and interactive, she fell farther and farther behind on important developmental milestones. Jasper said she already was speech delayed, but what other problems did she have that needed to be addressed by early intervention therapy?

Emma should have been trying to roll over and then crawl; she needed face time and play time and so much more. Newt rocked her gently in her arms as a huge wave of sorrow swamped her. It was so unfair! If she felt a fraction of what Jasper felt for Emma every moment since the abduction, then she was surprised he hadn't collapsed under the strain of that alone. Newt knew that no matter what, both of them were worth fighting for.

Nine

Jasper felt so disconnected from his body that it was becoming harder and harder to care about who he had been before the abduction, and that feeling frightened him. His mind and its thoughts were clearly projected, but no sensations came from his physical self to help bind him to where his body was. He was a brain floating free from any perceived connection to living tissue. In the globe, to counterbalance that disconnect he had reviewed the details of a typical day in his life before Emma's abduction. He had recited his birth date, his height, the members of his family, where he lived, where he worked, what he did, his favorite things, and so on until he had felt more like himself again.

But now freed from the globe, he wasn't sure that technique would help. Inside the float, he had felt weird, but when he had looked down at his body, he had been able to recognize himself. But back to his full size, he could see completely through his skin and his clothes to the floor below. What did that make him besides a freak show? He wondered how a real person is defined. Is it the ability to think? Jasper knew that when he was brainstorming with Tony the day before, he had done some of his best thinking ever. They'd made an amazing team, but even then he'd definitely noticed some changes in the core of who he was.

He was more paranoid, pessimistic, and angry—he really just wanted to smash the kidnappers in the face then destroy the damned chip, and to get it all over with. Jasper didn't feel like he could trust himself to make good judgments or decisions because he felt so messed up right now. He didn't even know what was real anymore. The whole situation could have been happening in a coma-induced dream state—or maybe he was already dead, he thought.

He had been on top of the world one day, sure of every decision he made, and the best at what he did; the next day, everything he had cared about was gone. After Emma's birth he had felt hope for the future and a zest for living, and now he dreaded shifting through the ashes of what had once been their life. How could anyone deal with this surreal situation, he wondered. Jasper felt rage most of the time, and when he wasn't mad, his life was packed in the gray insulation of not caring what happened to him anymore. He knew there was still color out there, but his despair painted everything in shades of black and white. Jasper felt like he had fallen into a deep, dark hole, and he didn't care enough to even try to get himself out. The lonely weeks of drifting in the ocean had taken their toll on him, and he knew he was a permanently changed man. If not for Emma, he wouldn't have been cooperating with Tony and Newt, because he had given up hope.

Jasper knew they were good people who were trying to help Emma and him, but they didn't realize how powerful an organization they were up against. He had seen the uniforms, the vehicles, the remote location, and the type of people involved. He bet neither of them had been held at gunpoint or knew what it's like to feel the world turn to mush as you look down the barrel of a gun. Maybe if he had grown up in a gang area he might have handled those feelings better, but he was from a small town where violence rarely happened. Newt and Tony had also grown up as insulated as he had. It was like there were two levels of reality: one was just gunplay on television, but the other shrunk your life down to a finger on a trigger.

Jasper's mind tracked around and around those same negative thoughts in a repeating loop. His only anchor was holding Emma, but that also generated a grave concern. How could he help her? Was she all right? What could he do to bring her back? Would she be permanently damaged even if they did rescue her? Finally, he realized that there was something that still made him the person he had been before the abduction, and that was his constant love for Emma. It remained strong and unchanged, and it was a bright beacon, guiding him forward no matter how freaky he looked and felt at the moment.

To Jasper's surprise, Tony turned out to be his ideal work partner. He was extremely smart, a straightforward thinker who was able to focus intensely on a problem, and had clear, strong ethics. Together they had accomplished what hadn't been done before: they had compressed electrical forces into layers so dense that he could interact on a limited basis with the physical world. The trade-off was that his projection's body had become less substantial, but it was great to be free from the globe, even though it intensified the helpless and negative feelings he had. He was still a projection with a tiny amount of mass, so although his situation had improved, his biggest desire was to go home with Emma and to live the simple and happy life he'd had before everything had happened to them.

The day before, Jasper had felt TNT's intense drive to make the situation right. Tony had told him in no uncertain terms what he would like to do to the bastards who planned to screw over Jasper and turn his outstanding chip into something bad. He'd made him feel like a mistake had been made elsewhere, not like Jasper himself was the mistake. Tony had "hero" written all over him, because Jasper wasn't sure he would have jumped in with both feet like Tony had if the situation had been reversed. Amazingly, he was beginning to trust both Tony and Newt. That was something he hadn't thought would happen, especially because he'd worked out that one of his friends must have told the kidnappers about the chip in the first place. The timing was too tight for it to have been anything else. That made trusting people he had recently met difficult, yet he had accepted the Newtons' honesty easily.

TNT was the brother he'd always wanted, but Newt was a light shining in his personal darkness. She was small but mighty, and she was carrying around the power of goodness and right seemingly unaware of it. She wasn't that far from the angel he had first mistaken her for, and in his eyes, she was beauty incarnate. Gazing at her short red-golden pixie hair-cut, her bright green eyes, and her cinnamon-sprinkle freckles made his burden lighter somehow. He even liked the nerdy black-framed glasses that slipped down her nose when she was reading. He heard her intelligence in every conversation, and she always had something important to say—no chitchat for Dr. Newt. Her amazing discovery of the globe combined with her fairy-tale looks made him believe—at least a little—that unseen forces might be working in their favor. But Jasper felt more than gratitude and admiration for Newt, because physical attraction also swamped him when he was in her proximity. And that just proved that sex is mostly in the head, as his body was miles away.

But the best part of Newt wasn't on the outside—it was in her heart. He saw its sweetness in the first instant their eyes met as she held the sign asking if she could help him. She had had a smile on her face and hope in her eyes for a person she hadn't even known. Since then, she had never acted like he was anything but a human being worthy of that help, despite the fact that he was only a projected image. She even cuddled Emma, and he could see that she really cared about his baby, too; it was like she shouldered some of his grief and worry, and that support gave him a little relief from his suffering.

Newt didn't expect him to take charge with a plan. She didn't even expect him to speak until he was ready. She found an old tablecloth and made a makeshift front pack for Emma, and they took a long walk on the beach together. He and Tony had enhanced the density of Emma's projection a little the day before. She remained comatose, but now had the weight and skin consistency of a soft rubber doll.

As they strolled, Newt gathered a small batch of sea glass and shells, and she told him about the jewelry she was going to make out of them. She pointed out the kelp that had washed up on the beach and talked about how it sometimes made patterns resembling letters or pictures. She remembered how as kids, she and Tony would pretend to read their fortunes in the kelp like tea leaves in a cup. Newt explained to him how the force of wind and water sculpted everything on the beach, from the shape of the cove itself to where the driftwood was deposited.

Jasper saw the beach in a whole new light; it had never occurred to him that there was a reason for what had appeared to be random. It seemed so natural and normal for him to be there with her that he relaxed for the first time since his ordeal had started. There was something about the sky and sea that grounded him back to himself and put things in better perspective, because they would still be there no matter what happened to him and Emma in the end. Although the thought might have been more soothing to Jasper if he hadn't been aware that the wind was blowing right through his body.

Jasper watched Newt interact with Emma's projection. She tucked one of Emma's arms back into the sling when it drifted out as if it might have gotten cold, and she talked to the baby as if she were aware and alert. Jasper noticed his feet didn't set off squirts from the clam holes and that sandpiper birds didn't run away from him as they walked along, but Newt didn't appear to notice any of that strangeness. She acted like he and Emma were completely real people, and that filled him with a welcome sense of peace.

Newt finally asked a question that had been bothering her. "Can you tell me about Emma's mother?"

After a long pause, Jasper responded because he felt she deserved an answer, even though he had never discussed it with anyone. "She showed up one night at my house, claiming she was pregnant and that I was the baby's father. I hadn't seen her since the one time we were together months before, when I 'd been drunk and feeling sorry for myself. I did make a mistake by not using protection, and there's no excuse for that. Anyway, when she showed up again she was broke and didn't have a place to stay, so I took her in. I doubted the baby was mine, but what was I going to do—throw her back out on the street? She looked terrible, and the whole time she lived with me she was sick from the pregnancy, so clearly she needed my help. But I think she grew to hate the baby because it made her so ill. I give her credit for sticking it out—she never threatened to get an abortion.

"Emma was born by C-section a month early because it became life-threatening to continue the pregnancy. Her mother never made breast milk or bonded with the baby because she stayed two weeks in the hospital after Emma was released to me. It was a surprise when the paternity test showed I really was Emma's biological father, but it didn't matter anymore to me by then. I felt like her father no matter what the test results were. When her mother was finally released from the hospital, she asked me for twenty-five thousand dollars and then signed off on her parental rights, and we haven't seen her again and probably never will. I'll always be grateful to her, though, because I got Emma out of the deal, and she's priceless to me."

Newt had to ask another stupid burning question. "Do you have a serious girlfriend?"

Jasper blinked in surprise at her question. He was attracted to her more intensely than he had been to any woman before her, and he knew her past crush on him made her curious about him too. But the circumstances seemed too screwed up to move ahead with any romantic possibilities between them—not just because he didn't have a physical body, but because any emotions were suspect due to their situation. He thought they needed to meet in the day-to-day world, have dates, and then see if they were still attracted to each other. But after all Newt had done for him, he decided to be straight with her.

"My family believes in traditional gender roles: men stay out of the kitchen, and women stay out of the garage. That way women were kept at a distance from the men. They were always talked to carefully and with respect, but any closeness was discouraged between the sexes. Women hung around with women, and men smoked and drank away from home. That upbringing has made me awkward with women all my life. I've had a few attempted relationships, but women eventually tell me I'm not open enough with my thoughts and feelings and because of that they can't develop true intimacy with me."

Newt thought for a minute about her reply as she adjusted Emma more comfortably in the sling. "I think it's stupid to limit people that way, because men who like to cook should cook, and women who like to fix things should do that, too. Putting labels on people, limiting their skills, and judging based on gender only creates closed minds. I believe people should develop naturally to be themselves and follow what their passion leads them to do. The world would be a better and happier place if we opened rather than closed doors, and that's how I was raised."

They walked along, enjoying the beach. Newt reached over and held his projected hand for a few minutes. Jasper knew that if she squeezed his hand very hard, the electrical matrix giving it stability would collapse, but she held it lightly with the right amount of pressure. She showed him where she had found the glass float in the sand, and they sat together on the driftwood.

He turned toward her with his heart full of gratitude because she'd found the globe, and he surprised himself by suddenly opening his heart to her. For once he wasn't shy and reserved; it just came pouring out from his soul. Jasper shared how deeply afraid he was and how vulnerable his love for Emma had made him. He felt that the choices ahead were all bad because he would be responsible if anyone died. He felt that no matter what they did, someone would be killed, rescue or no rescue attempt. Newt listened to him with a compassionate look on her face; he felt no judgment, just empathy, from her. It was like she created space for him to have his feelings, and he felt they were accepted and understood for the first time in his life.

That evening Tony suggested they watch a James Bond marathon, starting with the first one, *Dr. No*; they enjoyed four before Newt fell asleep at midnight. Jasper thought it was appropriate, considering the circumstances of "good versus evil" they were in, but unfortunately, none of them had Bond's skills, gadgets, or ability to dodge bullets. If one of them had, he felt they might have had a small chance of success.

Jasper didn't eat any of the popcorn Tony had popped for the movie viewing. He was afraid that after he went through the motions of chewing and swallowing it, the popcorn would just fall out onto the floor through his semi-invisible body. That picture was too gross to try eating anything. Sometimes, Jasper felt mildly hungry, but not enough to try to consume anything. He hoped the faint hunger pangs were his body signaling that it was still alive and not so damaged that eating was out of the question. He also kept a sharp eye on Emma for any changes that might have reflected what was happening to her body. He knew he couldn't do anything about it if she was in danger, but it made him feel better to see that her image was stable from hour to hour.

Ten

In the morning Tony repacked his equipment back into his truck, and Newt took it as a sign that Jasper and Emma's enlarged projections were as stable as they were going to get. So after shooting a warning glance at Tony to keep out of the conversation, Newt began gathering data to determine if a rescue plan was even possible.

"Jasper, do you have any idea who sold you and the chip out?"

"Not really. I've gone over and over who it could be in my mind, but I'm still not sure. I showed the chip to three people I trusted and considered my friends. I've known all of them for at least five years. We became friends when we realized that we program in similar ways. They knew about Emma's lack of vocalization and my struggle to communicate with her. I wanted to reassure them that I had solved that problem. All I did for the demo was have Emma wear the ear microprocessor, and then I showed them how her thoughts were displayed on the computer screen as images of objects. I didn't demonstrate what the system could do with my thoughts, and I never showed them the chip in my pocket."

"You met as a group in a secure place?"

"Yes, I picked a pizza place at random and texted its location to them less than an hour before the meet up. Two days later Emma was taken, and that can't be a coincidence. In the globe I had a lot of time to think about how it was so organized, and two days wasn't enough time to plan and pull off the abduction, so I think that lunch was the trigger for a preplanned operation. The informant must have had cameras in my home, because I hadn't told anyone about the chip, and that's what the abductors said they wanted. I mean, how did they even know what I was working on? I think, as much as it pains me to say it, one of my friends at that lunch was already spying on me probably to get a jump on my new game designs. Then whoever it was saw my thoughts projected and understood the system's potential to make money before I did. And they also knew Emma could be used as a lever to get my quick cooperation."

"I'm sorry, Jazz," Tony said after a quick apologetic look to Newt for interrupting. "But I agree that someone at that lunch must be your rat. And if we can find out who it is, then maybe we can use him or her to trace backward to where your bodies are located. Have you eliminated anyone yet?"

"I've narrowed it down to two guys, because money has to be the motivation, and the other one is already wealthy. They both work for SMART computer processing and do gaming design. That's how we met—I consulted on a problem in graphics they needed help with. But I still can't believe either of them would have sold me out, because we hit it off immediately and have been friends ever since. But I guess you really never know what people are like on the inside." Jasper paced the room as he spoke, clearly upset that one of them had betrayed him and put Emma at risk for money.

"I have an idea about how we can ferret out the creep!" Tony slapped the table. "I can get into SMART as TNT by suggesting some basic upgrades on a discount special. I've worked with them before, and their hardware definitely needs my help. They run on a shoestring, and anything that sounds like a deal will get their immediate attention. I can scope out their financial data while I'm installing hardware, and I can see if anything seems suspicious. If that doesn't work, I can ask a few questions about computer-brain interfaces and see who perks up."

Both Newt and Jasper spoke up at the same time. "Too dangerous!"

Newt added, "And a big time waster, Tony. The spy made an outside deal for money, and I doubt he would risk leaving hard evidence at his job site."

Tony shot back, "So how else are we going to find the rat? We have to locate the kidnappers because they have Jasper and Emma. Do you have another proposal, sis?" He crossed his arms and glared at her.

Newt did have one. "How about we hack into SMART and search their personnel files. We look at both people to see if one is money hungry, disrespectful of rules, not a team player, or lacking ethics. People like that usually have notes from management on their records."

They kicked around a few other ideas, but nothing had the potential of Newt's suggestion. Plus—as Tony said happily—it was always fun to hack something, even if it was easy because SMART didn't invest much in security. They looked for advance draws against future paychecks, multiple requests for raises, complaints by coworkers and clients, and suspicious items on expense accounts.

While the guys were hacking, Newt researched Jasper's disappearance. She found it amazing how little splash his and Emma's abductions had made. His bills were on autopay, and he didn't have regular connection with family or friends who might have reported them missing. The days of piled-up newspapers and overflowing mail letting others know that someone was away from home were gone, she guessed. She knew that Jasper did most of the care for Emma himself at home, but on that fateful day he had left Emma with a nanny for a few hours so he could testify in court. The elderly woman had thought the baby was safe and napping, but actually she had been kidnapped and spirited away shortly after the nanny had closed the nursery's door.

Jasper told her that when he arrived back home, he had been intercepted by two thugs and told of Emma's abduction and ransom fee, and then he had had only a few minutes to gather his things and go with them. To protect the nanny, Jasper had told her a concocted story and had dismissed her before she even knew Emma had been kidnapped. Days later when the nanny couldn't contact Jasper, she had filed a police report about the suspicious men she had seen him with. But given Jasper's reclusive nature, a lack of evidence that a crime had been committed, and the fact that he frequently traveled worldwide, her alarm wasn't taken seriously by the authorities, who were already under an avalanche of unsolved murders. Newt thought it was scary how a man and a baby could drop out of sight without anyone doing much about it.

When she mentioned that observation to Jasper, he said, "If I had it all to do again, I would try to elude them and would call nine-one-one if I could. But it was such a fast, slick operation, that I didn't have time to think it through, and I was so worried about Emma that I didn't respond like I should have. Somehow it never crossed my mind that I was getting sucked into a crime thriller, but I'm sure they had it planned that way. I didn't realize at first that they were even associated with the people who had kidnapped Emma. They just said she had been abducted, there was a ransom, and to go with them because they knew where she was, and I went with them. My mind was still spinning with images of Emma's empty crib, and I didn't connect the dots like I should have. Once I was in their limo, I realized my mistake, but it was too late by then because they had me at gunpoint. After that, they just repeated, 'Stay calm,' and said I would see Emma alive again, so I had no choice but to cooperate."

Suddenly Tony shouted out, "I've got you, you S-O-B! I know who you are!"

Newt and Jasper rushed over to his computer screen, and he said, "Jazz, I assume you know a Bert Robbins. He has a bit of a gambling problem, and his finances are looking grim. His cash-flow problem was recently fixed, according to a letter he sent to the power company, with a deposit of fifteen thousand dollars into his account, and it was made the same day you and Emma disappeared. I looked at a copy of the check he sent with the letter, and it wasn't a bonus from SMART. It was written by another company completely. I'm sorry, man, but he's your weasel, because the timing just matches up too well."

Jasper looked shocked. "But Bert's a good guy. He helped me move and gave Emma a Seattle Seahawks blanket when she was born. He likes Emma, and he's my friend. He wouldn't sell me out!"

Newt tried to calm him down. "I'm not trying to make excuses for him, Jasper, but sometimes people act out of desperation. Maybe he was assured no one would get hurt. He might have believed Emma wouldn't be involved and you'd give up the chip easily."

Tony interjected, "Yeah, when pigs fly, sis! Maybe he was ripped because you're a top-notch programmer, Jazz, or he hates your games. Maybe it's because you make a lot of money, and he doesn't. But probably it's because he's a psychopathic jerk. I mean, you've been gone awhile, but has he reported it? Why hasn't he turned in the kidnappers and made more profit from a rescue? That's a big negative for being your friend, dude."

Jasper said slowly, "Thinking back, he has acted strangely lately. He moved to a bigger condo overlooking Puget Sound, and I haven't seen much of him. He makes excuses for why we can't get together now. But to sell us out for money—that's unbelievably cold! Let's go make him tell us where Emma's body is being held!" He had a full head of steam now.

Newt got in his face. "What are you going to do, Jasper? Tie him to a chair and beat him with a hose until he confesses? Does that make you any better than him? You can't fight violence with violence, because it only makes things worse! We need to take the higher moral ground here. The best path to success is outsmarting and outmaneuvering them, and then after we have proof that he's involved, Bert will be charged as an accessory to kidnapping. But for now, we treat Bert the Creep as a clue and follow the money trail. I'm willing to bet he was stupid and made mistakes along the way that we can capitalize on."

Tony was on board with Newt's calmer approach. "Yeah, Jazz, we need to keep a low profile, or he might alert the kidnappers, and that would be bad news for your and Emma's survival."

Jasper took a few deep breaths, "OK, you're right, and Bert probably did make a few errors, because he always looked for shortcuts to avoid work. I bet he's out of favor with whoever wrote that check, too. Remember, they don't have the chip. I still do," Jasper added.

They Googled Bert and hacked into his computers, and what they found wasn't pretty. When he had met Jasper, he had been a young computer wizard, but over time he had chosen play over work. At first the decline had been gradual, but in the last two years multiple reprimands from SMART for missing deadlines, unsupported expenses that he had charged to the company, and generally sloppy work had appeared in his inbox. His private e-mail was loaded with pornography and details of nasty breakups with girlfriends for his cheating ways. Newt wondered if Bert realized there was a connection between the two things. Jasper seemed shocked at Bert's decline, because he remembered him as an innovative programming star. Newt realized Bert was the perfect patsy for someone who wanted to control him with money, as he was irresponsible and disconnected from the consequences of his actions. She thought that if he was ever confronted with the damage he'd caused, he would probably blame someone else for what had happened.

Bert's paycheck for ratting on Jasper was written by a corporation called MSR Industries. Newt discovered it was a dummy company because the listed address was bogus and the phone number was disconnected. The check had been drawn from a bank outside the continental United States, so they couldn't trace it back, either. MSR seemed be to a dead end, but Newt asked Tony and Jasper to ferret out as much information as they could about it anyway. While reviewing the resulting data she noticed that the attorney who had drawn up MSR's corporation papers had also done multiple legal filings for a medical manufacturing company called Medi-Help. All such legal documents are a matter of public record, but they're rarely seen once they're filed. However, several years back, Newt had worked with Medi-Help to develop a commercial test for them to market. She had read their legal papers before committing to the job, so the attorney's name rang a bell with her.

It interested her that on the board of Medi-Help was a Sir Reginald Reed and that his name also appeared on documents as an MSR corporate officer. She had never met him, but it seemed unlikely for him to be connected to both businesses in a leadership position without an underlying reason for it. Medi-Help was a legitimate business, but MSR was not, and that didn't make sense to her either. Newt had learned through the years that sometimes coincidences have meanings if you looked hard enough.

On further investigation, Sir Reed himself was a puzzle. There was nothing documented in their many searches to explain how he had received his knighthood. It was assumed by people that he'd had an exemplary military career, but she couldn't find that he'd ever served in any country's armed forces. And despite Tony and Jasper's prime hacking skills, they couldn't turn up a birth certificate, a driver's license, a work history, or any family ties. That seemed pretty suspicious to all of them, because legitimate and underground computer searching for a man who had appeared openly with celebrities and politicians should have turned up some history. They agreed he could be a candidate for kingpin of the kidnapping operation as he was secretive, wealthy and interested in technology.

Besides, as Tony aptly pointed out, "Reed rhymes with greed, and that's the underlying bad-guy theme here, 'cause it was all done for money."

Newt proposed a plan. "My lab is the biggest one in the northwest, so I've worked with Medi-Help before., and Sir Reed is on the board there. How about if I write a proposal for a product I know they'll be interested in and then present it to them? And while I'm there, I can finagle a meeting with Reed—or at least try to get some details about him."

Tony and Jasper were both vehemently against the idea. "If he's the man calling the shots, meeting him without knowing more could be suicidal, Newt! He probably isn't mentally stable, and the last thing we need is another person kidnapped," Tony reasoned.

Jasper agreed and added, "Let's do some more digging first. No one lives a completely private life, no matter how much they might want to. We need to flesh him out better without his knowing about it before anyone thinks about walking into his lion's den."

That night, Newt watched Jasper burn the midnight oil doing deep extensive searches on Reed. She was curled up on the couch cuddling Emma, and she watched his jaw clench and fire light up in his eyes as he looked for information on a man who was mostly mist. She much preferred the intensely focused, angry look on Jasper's face to the one of despair she had seen the first time he had looked up at her from inside the globe.

Eleven

The next morning as Newt poured dry cereal into her bowl for breakfast, she continued to gather data by asking Jasper to go over what had happened after he was kidnapped by the men in the limo.

He reluctantly continued his account. "There were two men that came to my house plus a driver. They all carried weapons and didn't speak unless it was necessary. When they did talk, it was robotic, like they didn't have human emotions. At first I tried to get some information about my daughter and where they thought she was, but they ignored me. When I put it together and realized they were associated with Emma's abductors, I got angry and uncooperative, but they responded by sticking a gun in my face."

Newt nodded. "Maybe they had orders to shut you up and not to talk to avoid giving something away. That must have been hard for you, knowing they knew where Emma was." Newt sat down next to him on the couch and touched his hand in sympathy; he was reciting the events as if they had happened to someone else.

"I figured it wouldn't do Emma any good if I got shot, so I cooperated. They drove about an hour to a small airport out in the country. Then I was loaded onto a private jet. The men came along, but the driver stayed with the limo. The windows on the plane were covered so I couldn't see out. We flew all night, maybe ten hours total. We landed at the far end of another airport, and they put me in a helicopter." Jasper spoke in a clipped way, his voice devoid of emotion.

"Could you see anything at this second airport that might help us locate it?" Newt asked.

Jasper thought back to that nightmarish experience. "I saw city lights in the distance, but no tall buildings."

"What was the air like before you got on the helicopter? Was it warm or cold or humid or dry?" She took down some notes as he spoke.

"I guess it felt tropical, warm, and moist. And in the helicopter I could see more than I could in the plane because the side windows weren't blacked out. The helicopter flew over what looked like an ocean almost the whole time. That trip took only thirty minutes or less. I could see we were going to land on an island. It looked like a big rock with steep sides and a flat top. The sun was coming up, so I could see a huge, ugly house on top. It reminded me of a castle or a fortress. We landed on a helipad next to it, and the men hustled me inside."

Newt wanted to get an idea of how many people they were up against on the island. "Did the same men go with you, and were there more of them inside?"

"The original two men left right away on the 'copter, but there were two more waiting to take me inside. I thought the first guys were big, but those new guards were huge, like ex-football players. They didn't talk to me either."

"What was the house like inside?" Newt asked.

"Big, ugly, and cold, and it screamed 'I'm rich and crazy.' Actually, I didn't pay close attention to it because I just wanted Emma! I saw video cameras and knew someone was watching, so I started breaking things and yelling for Emma until the guards restrained and threatened me. Then the witch woman brought my messy, upset beautiful girl. I changed her in the bathroom, and the rest you know already. But I don't see how this is helping Emma much." Jasper had picked up a pencil and was fiddling with it while he talked, and then he broke it in two with a snap.

Newt was surprised that his projected hands could apply that much force. She suspected it was due to the intensity of his thoughts as he remembered what had happened, so she handed him another one in case he needed to break that one, too.

"Actually, you gave me a lot of good information, Jasper. Now I can run searches on small islands of that description in tropical areas about ten flight hours from here. Also, I'll investigate who hires large numbers of personal security, but the best bet is to find the airports and look for flights logged. There were two plane and two helicopter flights in fairly quick succession, and they both left from the same place and traveled to the same destination. One for Emma and one for you. The flight plans were filed somewhere." She smiled at him to give him hope.

Jasper's opinion differed. "Those guys fly off the record, Newt. I didn't see an airport crew or tower at either place. And when you have that much money, you can pay people to look the other way or enter false information anyway."

Newt replied in a firm voice. "Trust me, all flights are logged. It's too dangerous to commercial flights not to log them, and it's the law. Also, every country protects their airspace. They want to know who is flying over and when. If an unidentified plane flies over US territory and the flight isn't logged, then fighter jets can show up. So flight plans were filed, I guarantee it, and I just have to find them."

She thought for a minute and then added, "We might be able to search for people who own private jets and helicopters, too. They're too valuable not to be insured, so I can look for that information also."

She paused and tapped her lip. "Maybe backtracking the ocean currents that floated the globe here would give us a starting point to look for the island's location. Also, all this traveling requires passports. Maybe you or Tony would consider hacking the US post office or homeland security for that info."

Tony had finished his second bowl of cereal, so he joined the conversation. "Forget that, Newt, it's too slow. Jazz, how about hacking into CIA files to find Reed? He fits our profile so I bet he lives on an isolated island surrounded by private security too. Just because Jazz didn't see him that day doesn't mean he isn't pulling the strings. He's on the shady side that's why we can't flesh him out because he's doing illegal stuff. I mean, he's not a celebrity, so why else? And he got all that money somehow, so he's probably a criminal, and the CIA would have records on him. I know it won't be easy, but we could try. Reed is our guy I just know it!"

Jasper and Tony looked at each other with similar glints in their eyes. Jasper rubbed his hand together and replied, "Might be easier to hack the USPS for passports, but it wouldn't be half as much fun as hacking the CIA!"

They spent the day monitoring the five computers set up around the room, running hacking programs. When one got stuck, the guys would rotate to fix the problem. Most of the time the computers searched on their own by trying various protocols to get into secure locations without tipping anyone off. Newt finally set a paper by each one so she could write down what each computer was doing, because it was confusing her. They printed any hard data and stacked the pages on the couch for future analysis.

Newt took a break when a headache threatened and drove into Ocean Shores. She picked up submarine sandwiches for lunch and then visited a local thrift store. There she bought baby items for Emma. Newt had been spending time with her, and she was convinced the baby wasn't totally unaware of her surroundings. She thought Emma was like a coma patient who appeared to be asleep but was actually tracking some of what was happening around her. Newt felt she could hear and see a little, because when she played patty-cake with her, there was a slight tension in Emma's hands during the clapping part; it felt like she wanted to clap along, too. Newt had repeated the song over and over until she was sure it wasn't her imagination and that Emma was actually lightly responding.

At the thrift store, Newt purchased a few cute baby dresses that she could put on over Emma's projected pajamas. It wasn't that the digital pajamas' image was getting dirty, but Newt thought it might help Jasper feel more normal if the baby looked different sometimes. Besides, it was fun to buy baby clothes, and she thought she would enjoy dressing Emma up.

Emma's projection didn't need any real baby care, so it was easy to let her lie for hours while they worked on computer searches, but that didn't feel right to Newt. She noticed that Jasper got visibly upset when he held Emma for long periods, maybe because he missed the real baby he remembered. So to give Jasper options, Newt bought a baby swing, a stroller, a front pack, and a crib. She thought moving Emma's projection around in the baby equipment would give him more of a feeling that his daughter was a normal sleeping baby. Newt added to her purchases some toys that made noise, books to read aloud, and a CD with fun kids' songs.

Back at the cabin, she sat on the porch drinking iced tea, and all the emotion about Jasper and Emma's situation caught up with her. It made her tearful, and she tried to hide it, but Jasper noticed through the cabin window. He came out and put his hands on Newt's shoulders to comfort her.

He said with sympathy, "Newt, I appreciate all you've done for Emma and me, but you don't have to do any more. I know you're getting attached to us, and I wish you wouldn't. The chances of us coming out of this whole again aren't good, and you're just setting yourself up for more pain." He turned and faced her. "Sometimes I think it would be better if we were still floating in the ocean. At least then you could get on with your life."

Newt looked into his sad, dark eyes. Hopelessness and pain were there, but she could see he was reaching out too. "Meeting you and Emma has been great, no matter what happens.

Remember, you're still my teenage hero, and you've always opened me up to what's possible. I never thought I'd meet you in person—let alone help you out—but I've always known you, and your games brought out the best in me." She tried to lighten things up. "If nothing else, my nose is sure off the work grindstone now."

He leaned over and gently touched his lips to hers. It felt a lot like it had felt to kiss the picture of him in her room when she was thirteen. Not a bad sensation, but definitely lacking in moisture or real touch, and there was an unpleasant snap of static electricity when he moved his lips away from hers. She actually felt her hair stand up slightly during their contact. Not the kind of sparks she hoped would fly when she had imagined him kissing her as a young girl.

Yet there was a real sweetness to the kiss, and it came from looking into his beautiful eyes. Newt could see into his soul, and his vulnerability was laid out for her; he concealed nothing of his real self because she was seeing directly into his thoughts. It gave her vertigo, like looking into the night sky and seeing the limitless number of stars with the depth of space around them. She could almost feel the earth spinning underneath her as she gazed into his eyes, and she lost her sense of balance for a moment. Newt responded to his lips by reaching out with her soul too and giving him back a kiss packed with all the attraction she was feeling, despite the slight electric shock to her mouth.

He must have felt what she was putting into the kiss because his response was to swear a blue streak, and that made her laugh. She understood that to meet then and to feel the chemistry they had together when he didn't have a body just didn't seem fair to either of them.

Twelve

Jasper occasionally touched Newt's hands after their kiss on the porch, because he craved the semblance of physical contact with her, even if the sensation only existed in his mind. When Tony noticed them touching, he raised his eyebrows up and down at Newt behind Jasper's back. She stuck her tongue out at him—also behind Jasper's back—because Tony knew that she'd had a thing for him as a teen, and as an adult, she was free to explore what her feelings meant no matter what Tony thought about it. Besides, until the rescue was successful, taking their romance to the next level wouldn't be possible anyway.

Newt knew Tony would have concerns about his little sister forming an emotional connection to Jasper in this iffy situation, but she was trying to live in the moment and hoping for the best. Those few moments when she looked into the eyes of Jasper's projection and experienced his unfiltered thoughts directly from his mind forged a bond between them that she could never explain in words. It impacted her like nothing had before. She saw his basic goodness, the emotional pain he was in, his deep capacity to love, and the loneliness he felt. He had reached out to her and she responded in kind, but none of it had been physical. It occurred on some level beyond that, and it continued to resonate deep within her.

They sat around the kitchen table compiling data from the prior day's searches, and especially from the CIA's documentation, and an unpleasant picture of Reed emerged. He had been a bad man for a long time and had stayed just out of the authorities' reach by letting others do the dirty work of actually committing the crimes. Like in the Mafia, Reed was the don of an organization with its fingers in many illegal pies, and people disappeared when they crossed him in any way. He didn't appear to be involved in traditional organized crimes like extortion, prostitution, drugs, or importing illegal immigrants. His reach was more worldwide than local, and it involved computer scams, stock market fraud, and stealing new technology. Newt realized that what he had done to Jasper and Emma was just a day's work for him, because Reed especially thrived on stealing revolutionary ideas in their infancy and then reaping the rewards when they hit the market. He was very rich, regularly ruined lives, and was virtually untouchable on his little island kingdom.

The CIA had compiled extensive files detailing all the crimes they thought that was Reed connected to. However, they didn't have the unshakable evidence they needed to take him to court and to get a conviction in a fight against his legal team, so they had been watching and waiting for years. Reed was like catching smoke blowing in the wind; he always had an air-tight alibi for when the actual crimes occurred. And apparently, people were so afraid of him that they committed perjury—rather than implicating him—even when the CIA offered to relocate them in the witness protection program.

When they finished reading the CIA files, Jasper said seriously, "Newt, TNT, you can't go to the island and meet Reed face to face. Did you see the list of people they suspect he's killed? If professionals haven't been able to take him down, I don't know how we'll be able to do it. I told you I thought a rescue was a bad idea from the beginning."

Tony and Newt exchanged a sibling look that said they weren't giving up yet, and she responded, "We know it's not going to be an easy task, Jasper, but I believe we can stack the odds in our favor so we're unlikely to lose. Tony and I think we need a plan that doesn't rely on help from the authorities, because if they don't have enough evidence to arrest Reed, they can't help us officially either. But I bet they'll be happy when we crack Reed's kingdom open for them to pick over. I know a person who can help us plan your rescue, and it's our cousin Angela. She's retired Special Forces, and I happen to know she's between jobs at the moment."

What Newt purposefully neglected to tell Jasper was that Angela had PTSD—post-traumatic stress disorder—and hadn't been able to do any kind of work in over two years. She'd been wounded in the Middle East and discharged from the military, and currently lived in a shabby motor home parked as far from civilization as she could get. Their family loved her dearly, but they had been unable to reconnect her with any normal life style after her military service was over.

Newt knew Angela had the right skills for this job, but she had serious issues, too. Yes, she had commanded a few rescue operations, but at this point in her life, Angela seemed overwhelmed by a simple trip to a movie theater. But despite the problem of Angela's mental disability, she was the only person Newt knew with any experience or training in what they needed done. And not many people would believe the situation with Jasper if Newt explained it in an e-mail, but Angela would.

Newt was annoyed that Jasper was still trying to talk them into giving up on him, so she let him have it. "OK, I agree that you have a right to decide what you want to do with your life, and I respect that. But if you decide to sacrifice Emma's chance of survival, then that could be called murder, and I'm not having a part in it."

She glanced at Jasper's shocked face and softened her harsh words, because she did understand his thoughts and had felt how scared he was for all of them. "Jasper, I do know why you want us to back off. No one should risk their life for an impossible goal, but I think it wouldn't hurt for us to get an outside opinion from Angela. I think she'll understand this complicated and likely dangerous situation, and then she can help us decide if it's doable or not. I promise you, if she says it can't be done, then I'll abide by that decision."

Tony also agreed. "Jazz, Angela is seriously cool, absolutely trustworthy, and she knows about this stuff. It won't hurt to get her opinion, dude, because if there's a chance this can come out right, I want to know about it. Then if we make the final decision to burn the chip, we'll know it was the only option open. Because once it's burned, then it's all over for you and the kid. So give us that before we commit you two to the fire, man."

Jasper reluctantly agreed to meet Angela, although he protested that just because someone was trained by the military didn't mean she was qualified to judge what could realistically be done in his situation. But Newt fired off a quick e-mail to her cousin asking for a time they could get together anyway. Then she and Tony spent the rest of the day carefully going over the data again so they would have a complete picture of the task for Angela to review. Jasper refused to join in, and instead he paced the beach with Emma in the front pack. Their minds were still faintly connected, so Newt knew he was tormented by thoughts of what the future would hold. Twice she went out to the beach to find him and stood with her arms circled around him—as best she could—to provide comfort. Once she saw his projection was visibly shaking as he stood knee-deep in the outgoing tide. She was afraid for a moment that he would just take the final decision about what to do into his own hands and keep walking out into the ocean until the chip in his pocket was wet; then it and the projections it was making would be swept away on the current.

Newt knew it wasn't her right to insist on a rescue; she had made her case to try loud and clear, but the final choice was up to him. So she closed her eyes and tried to psychically send him love and support through their connection. After a moment, Newt was startled when she felt him touch her hair and she breathed a sigh of relief. She had been unaware of his approach because his projection moved around without creating sound or air movements, but she happily took his hand, kissed Emma, and headed with them back toward home.

Newt suspected most—if not all—of Jasper's relationships with people had been superficial and that he didn't know how to handle the fact that they were willing to help him. Newt knew he was capable of deep love, because she saw it on his face every time he looked at Emma and she felt it in his thoughts; but he was accustomed to loneliness and isolation, and he seemed unfamiliar with group dynamics or the relief of depending on others for support. There had been several friends at the pivotal lunch meeting and only one had betrayed him, yet he didn't think about the others who were still trustworthy; instead, he focused on the one who had shattered his life. Newt knew he felt that it was Emma and him against the world and that he wouldn't easily open up to other people's good intentions.

Jasper's family had done things to isolate him from people at an early age, and the nature of his work was solitary, too. Newt's life, in contrast, was the opposite, because her family was too involved in what she was doing sometimes, and her work required a lot of human contact, both with coworkers and the donors who funded her research. It was hard for her to accept the way Jasper viewed the world, but she thought it was high time he had people he could depend on. She believed friendship had the power to enact amazing changes for good and that sometimes it only took one person who cared about you to make all the difference.

Thirteen

Newt knew that most of life's transactions are available to the public if you know where to look. It takes time, expertise, constant updating, and vigilance to protect information, so unless money or privacy is involved, people don't bother to do it. Networking was one of Newt's best skills, and it was necessary to obtain funding for her research projects, so she knew people who knew people from all over the world. Newton Laboratory had a pristine reputation and was the biggest such facility in the west. She did a lot of community service, served on prestigious committees, and wasn't above dropping names to move down the chain of command to the level where people knew how to get the information she was after.

She was quizzing a pilot who was the brother of one of her staff about airports that might operate on the shady side when he revealed that private jets large enough to cross an ocean were usually leased, not owned, for maintenance, liability, and insurance purposes. Also, that benefited the user by allowing frequent upgrades to newer models. Newt thought that logically a man in Reed's business would demand the newest and fastest get-away plane, so his was probably leased. From that assumption, it was easy to contact the insurance company that typically covered leased planes and to get a copy of Reed's documents. In order to do that legally, Newt enrolled him inabsentia in one of her pending research projects and explained she needed the information for his medical coverage, because if there was one thing insurance companies understood, it was the need for more insurance. Newt purposefully made her request open ended, and as a stroke of luck, it was passed to a low-level, recently hired office drone who faxed her Reed's entire file.

The documents were a treasure trove of information because Reed had insured many of his possessions, including the island itself. Newt wondered why an international criminal would bother with insurance, but apparently Reed was smart enough to understand that if he could steal from others, then people could steal from him too. The computer spreadsheet showed that Reed owned his island free and clear of debt; it was insured for one hundred fifty million dollars without the house, which was valued at another fifty million dollars. She wondered why someone would pay insurance premiums for an island, but maybe Reed was afraid a tsunami or other disaster might wash it away. The house contents, including art masterpieces, antiques, aged wines, gems, and collections of carved jade and ivory, rare books, and coins, totaled a cool one hundred million in value. It was obvious Reed liked nice things and lived an opulent lifestyle.

For vehicles, he insured a huge yacht, a speed boat, two helicopters, a small plane, and a private submarine in addition to the leased jet. He also had a number of vintage and high-end cars. Newt suspected he had more valuables that he hadn't declared for insurance purposes because they were still owned by the people he had stolen them from. It was interesting that he didn't list any firearms, but undoubtedly he had those, too. But Newt reassured herself that it didn't matter how many weapons he had, because they were't going to outgun him—they were going to outsmart and outmaneuver him.

From the insurance documents Newt finally found the location of the island, and so where Jasper's and Emma's bodies were housed. It was called Reed Island—when he bought it he renamed it after himself, of course—and located in the Caribbean Sea near the Virgin Islands. It had once been named in Spanish for its round shape, although when it was seen from the air it had more of an oblong contour. The island was the leftover core from an ancient volcano. Once a much bigger island after the original volcanic eruption, it had slowly shrunk as the ocean waves washed away the outer, softer rock, leaving the center pressure- and heat-condensed stronger rock. In the 1800s, fertilizer from bird and bat droppings had been mined there, but since then it remained uninhabited by people, abandoned due to its steep cliffs and lack of fresh water except for rain. Seabirds, bats, and goats had been the only residents until Reed had purchased it eight years ago.

The ocean waves had carved a large cave inside one end, but the rest of the surface was gently sloping grasslands atop sheer cliffs. It was about one mile long and one-third mile across at its widest point. The highest part on the island was relatively flat and had the steepest sides; there Reed had built his house, perching it on the cliff that overlooked the surrounding ocean. There was a helicopter pad next to the house, and he had leveled out a rough runway for his small plane following the island's long axis.

The closest island to Reed's was St. Thomas, which was part of the US Virgin Islands. The United States had purchased their large part of the island group from Denmark in 1917 for twenty-five million dollars. The price of islands had really gone up since then, Newt thought, considering what Reed had paid for his comparatively small rock. It was unclear to her who, or what country, had originally owned Reed Island and had then profited by selling it to Reed. But it looked like it was under the jurisdiction of the United States, although sometimes in the paperwork it was referred to as a micronation instead of as a US territory. She suspected Reed loved that term and ran his island like he was the king there.

There were drawings, blueprints, and measurements for both the island and the house in the insurance file. The company had originally disputed its market value and had later reversed its stand and used Reed's numbers to calculate the exorbitant premiums he paid. They had conveniently included a few photos of the insured property, too. The main cave had an open exterior harbor area; Reed had dredged it deeper, and then he had secured it from breaking waves by building large seawalls on either side of the entrance. The small port was where he kept his huge yacht and, Newt suspected, his submarine as well; the harbor was the only place, besides the air, where anyone could approach the land due to its almost vertical walls. There were some pictures of the steep rock that made up the cliff faces, and she observed that not even seabirds had enough horizontal space to build nests there. Reed had secured the harbor both because hurricanes were frequent visitors in the tropical climate and because the insurance company had insisted on it before they would insure his yacht; but even with the required harbor improvements, Newt thought his total yearly premiums would have been enough to feed a small country for months!

In the photos, Reed's house resembled a castle, with the ocean serving as a surrounding moat. The structure occupied forty thousand square feet divided between three stories. There was a big round tower on one end and two smaller towers at the end of connecting wings, so the house made a Y-shaped branching along the cliffs that surrounded the harbor in the middle of the V. The whole structure was made of large dark stone and masonry cement, and it lacked any ornamental detail, landscaping, or charm. The smaller towers resembled turrets, and the connecting wings had flat, dark roofs and balustrades. The few windows visible were slits like arrow ports, and she could imagine soldiers crouching behind them, ready to defend the fortress from an attack.

The overall appearance of Reed's home was dark and heavy, and it loomed on the edge of the cliffs like an ugly gargoyle. To

Newt, it clearly said "evil lair," not "hearth and home." She suspected he had designed it himself, because it shouted, "I am a paranoid criminal who has something to hide from the world." She thought Reed was probably the kind of person who would have supported the Great Wall of China as a workable idea—despite the fact that it didn't keep out the Mongols—because the general concept of that structure was reflected in his home.

Next Newt examined the blueprints of the home's interior. The lowest floor of the main tower had a round swimming pool and spa, and it was surrounded by a tropical garden. The pool area was the only space with large windows, and it extended out over the cliff's edge for a 180-degree view of the ocean. The floor above the pool housed an office complex, and the top third floor looked like Reed's private large master suite, which could be accessed from his office by a spiral staircase.

Next to the tower was an immense room with vaulted ceilings; the helicopter pad was almost on the same level, so it probably served as a grand entry-room. Across that great room, opposite from the tower, a long, wide hallway ended in a sweeping staircase that led down to the harbor. Off that hallway were multiple suites for guests, a media room, a game and entertainment area, a library, and some unspecified rooms. Just before the harbor stairs, the two wings branched off at forty-five degrees from each other; one led to the kitchen and servants' quarters, and the other to a living area for security personnel. There was no mention of dungeons or medical labs, but Newt knew they were there somewhere; it interested her that a second smaller hallway ran under the main one and was identified for servants' use.

Newt printed everything and enlarged all the blueprints; she also copied the pictures from the insurance files. There was a photo of Reed posing on the deck of his yacht, but he wasn't smiling or looking happy. Newt used a magnifying glass to examine the picture closely. Reed was far from handsome; he had a comb-over hair style and a paunchy middle, plus his jowls sagged, and his eyes were small and mean.

One each side of him were two young, beautiful women, but they looked sad and scared to Newt. They were dressed in small bikinis, and Newt could see the wind had blown the boat's rigging straight and snapped the flags out, so they must have been cold. Newt wondered if they had been paid to be there, or if they had been forced somehow—human trafficking?—because it was obvious from their body language that they were scared of Reed. Both girls had pale skin, unlike Reed, who was tanned to leather, so they must not have gotten out in the Caribbean sun a lot. So what had they been doing there when the pictures were taken? To her, the photo came across as looking like one of a lord and master with his concubines; Newt wondered if Reed saw that interpretation when he looked at the picture, and if he did, if that was what he had been going for.

Fourteen

Newt's mother, Sophia, came from a strong Italian American "put family first" background. In the family Sophia was considered the smart child, and her sister—Angela's Mother—Teresa was obviously the beautiful one. Teresa had used her beauty to marry into a rich and powerful family, as was the tradition for gorgeous Italian women. She and her husband had produced three beautiful daughters who were also expected to use their looks to find wealthy and influential husbands.

Angela was the middle daughter, and right from the start, she had rebelled against her family's plan for her. She refused dance classes, makeup lessons, and lectures on grace and protocol; she wanted karate, paintball, and gymnastics instructions instead. Her parents tried repeatedly to make a lady of her but washed their hands of the job when she enlisted in the Marine Corps the day after her high school graduation.

During three tours of active duty in the Middle East, Angela had been awarded four medals, had saved countless lives in combat, and had infiltrated enemy territory, although many of the operations she had been involved in were classified secrets.

Angela didn't dwell on the glory of being considered a hero; instead, her mind had slowly been taken over by repeating loops of the death of soldiers and civilians she had known, and the horror she had witnessed during combat. She had full-color flashbacks that included the sounds, smells, and sights of war, and she often couldn't shut them off no matter what she did. They occurred randomly and frequently and felt more real to her than what was actually happening around her. The primary emotion she felt was unrelenting grief for the soldiers she had commanded to their deaths. Over and over her mind played slow-motion videos, like the one of her crouched behind a dusty mud-brick wall, motioning her unit forward to die, and then getting covered by their blood spray. She knew the dead men well because they had shared pictures of their families with her and had read her funny e-mails from home; she had eaten meals with them and had laughed with them. They had respected and trusted her, and then she had pointed them toward blood and death. When it had become clear to her commanding officer that she couldn't do her job anymore, she had been given an honorable discharge and the country's gratitude and had been sent home to rejoin normal civilian life.

Angela had then endured multiple rounds of therapy and various medications. Yes, the pills stopped her torturing thoughts, but they also muddied all other feelings too, and she didn't want to be a robotic zombie for the rest of her life. Angela had tried to reenter normal life; first she returned home and listened to her sisters' chatter about men and babies until she couldn't stand it anymore, and then she rented an apartment and wandered aimlessly around stores looking for furnishings, supplies, and food to buy. Her entire family, including Newt and Tony, contacted her regularly, but she couldn't explain what was happening to her any more than she could fix it. They had been close in the past, but unless you'd been there, Angela believed you couldn't relate to what she was feeling. She wouldn't have wished her war memories on anyone and certainly wouldn't burden those she loved with her suffering, so she withdrew from her family's concerns and superficial conversations.

She felt like she was in a different world than everyone else—why didn't they see that life was fragile and could end in an instant? Why save for retirement, have a baby, or lease a car? A million things could happen in an instant that would turn you into nothing. Angela thought everyone was living with an illusion of permanence or a delusion of life as it really was; she was the only one who appeared to know life was temporary—everyone else was playing pretend.

Nothing seemed important to her anymore, and she couldn't make even the simplest life decisions like what to have for dinner. Her body always felt on high alert for danger of any kind; when drinking coffee in a café, she sat with her back against the wall so she could watch people coming and going through the door. She couldn't stop herself from carefully looking for people who might have had a concealed weapon or who were acting suspicious in any way; she was always looking around and never felt relaxed because adrenaline and cortisol pumped through her system constantly. Her doctor had told her that over time, those high-stress hormones would take a toll on her health, so she isolated herself from people in an attempt to relax.

One day Angela had had enough of living like that, so she took her gun, dressed in her best uniform, and walked way out into the woods to finally end the thoughts that plagued her. She'd rationalized that a bullet in her head was the only way to shut off the constant mental torture from her brain. She'd lain down on leaves under tall ancient trees and sobbed her heart out over the waste of her life.

But then a strange thing happened. Angela noticed patchy sunlight on the tree's leaves and on its rough-textured bark next to her face. Her crying slowly tapered off as she gazed up into the forest canopy, and then the trills of birdsong and the brush of the gentle breeze blowing had soothed her. For an hour she had lain there in peace, feeling connected with the forest and the earth underneath her, and her mind had finally quieted at last.

The next day Angela emptied her bank account and sold everything she owned to buy an old motor home and a piece of isolated, heavily wooded property. Her undeveloped off-the-electrical grid land bordered the Olympic Peninsula Rainforest, was fed by a mountain stream, and was as far away from civilization as she could find for sale in Washington State.

Living in her new forest home, she concentrated on being in the present moment and in constant harmony with her surroundings. When pouring a simple glass of water, she practiced awareness of the glass's transparency and hardness, of the sound and liquid texture of the water as she poured, and lastly of how it tasted as she slowly swallowed it and took it into her body with gratitude. She slowly created inner peace through the practice of distracting her mind from her bad memories by focusing on simple things in the present with thanks in her heart.

She spent most of her time outside, soaking in the quiet solitude of the ancient old-growth forest as she slowly healed. First the thoughts of death would leave for an hour, then a couple of hours, then occasionally for a whole day, and finally for a happy few days in a row. Angela worked hard to replace the old, worn brain pathways of war with her new thoughts of nature and harmony. She also rebuilt the engine of the motor home and lived simply on a healthy vegetarian diet. The birds, deer, squirrels, fish, and other forest inhabitants became her friends, and she strove to have a low impact on the environment by using water from the nearby stream, burying her waste, and recycling almost everything. She gave thanks frequently, and when she walked through the woods, she was careful not to disturb anything with her footfalls.

One day after about six months of living alone in her woods, she was shopping in Sequim for supplies when she noticed a man wandering around with a tormented look on his face. She recognized his expression as the one she had worn before moving into the forest, so she invited him to find peace in her woods, and he became the first of what she thought of as her band of unmerry men. Her property was over one hundred acres of forest, so her guests didn't bother her, and they met occasionally to share a potluck meal. They camped out near the stream and obeyed her rules, and most found what they were looking for. Some stayed for months, but she knew they all would eventually move on when they could handle it mentally.

Angela did sometimes interact with the people camping on her property when problems and needs came up, and they treated her with respect and showed an urge to protect her similar to the one adult children had toward a beloved mother. Mostly she lived her solitary life and let the woods do the work of healing everyone's PTSD; sometimes she thought she heard the ancient spirits of the old trees whispering to the campers—as they did to her—"let the pain go, because the past is gone, and the future is unwritten." She knew living in the current moment with awareness was the key to finding the peace they were all seeking.

Angela had lived in her woods for over two years when Newt's text arrived on her phone. That was unusual; she kept her phone active only for emergencies, and her family tried not to upset or bother her unless it was important, so they rarely used it. She had asked the communications wizard from her old unit about how to get cell reception in the rainforest because her mother had been upset about her being completely isolated, and he had used a helicopter to install a small transmitter-receiver using one of the tallest trees as a tower. She used a solar panel for the small amount of electricity she needed to power it

Newt's text read: "Tony and I need your help to rescue Jasper Higgs & daughter, they're in trouble. Remember the Smoke and Mirrors game? Can you come right away? Prepare for weird!"

Angela sat down hard in shock. The Newt she knew was a successful scientist and well grounded in reality; the text didn't sound like her at all! Angela knew Jasper Higgs had been Newt's teen crush but that Newt didn't really know anything about him as a person, especially now he was an adult man. Angela had always been suspicious of him because his secretive life sent up big red flags to her. What the heck was Tony thinking, helping that guy and involving Newt too? It sounded to her like it was the other way around and that her cousins needed to be rescued from Jasper Higgs! She was going to Ocean Shores locked and loaded for this scammer—no one messed with her family if she could prevent it!

But before she fired up her motor home for the trip, she walked down to the camp to tell the guys that she was leaving due to a family emergency. It surprised her when five of the men quickly began to pack up their tents after hearing the news.

Angela loudly protested their actions. "Wait a dang minute! What are you guys doing? Someone has to stay here and mind the store! I'm only going to be gone a little while, and I don't need you to come along."

The one called Hook replied, "The store has been minding itself for hundreds of years. We're coming with you Angela."

She snorted. "What makes you think you're all invited?"

He said firmly, "I've known you for six months, and I've never seen you so up in arms. You're moving fast with spit in your eye, and you're ready to charge off to battle. You've never expressed any strong emotion since I've been here. So we're coming along."

She fumed. She paced, and then she gave in to the wall of men with crossed arms and determined stares. "All right, it's your time to waste, but I don't need your protection. And how am I going to transport your tents and stuff?"

Hook smiled, "If we put it in the motor home for now, then we can stop in town and get my trailer. It'll hold everything, and the motor home can tow it."

She grumbled but didn't know what surprised her more— that he had a trailer in town or that he wanted to come. And who had made him the spokesman for the group, anyway?

"All right, apparently you don't have anything better to do, but it makes no sense to me. It's only boring family stuff, and I bet you'll wish you never came along!" Angela was irritated that she would have company on the trip instead of solitude, because she thought that it would only make it harder for her to cope with life outside of the woods.

Hook looked around at the other men who were agreeing with his decision and eager to go with her too. "We'll take that chance. Load up, men." He grinned at her grumpy face before turning to collapse his tent.

Fifteen

Newt spotted Angela driving up the road to the cabin and quickly ran out to intercept her so she could prepare her for the shock of seeing Jasper's and Emma's projections. The motor home's vintage engine purred with health, but the exterior was ugly; the entire outer surface was covered with what Newt called natural camouflage. It was composed of peeling dark-green paint, dirt, algae, grease, plant pollen, and other unidentifiable things. But the outside appearance didn't concern Angela at all, and Newt knew she never even noticed it was dirty. Today Angela was hauling a medium-sized enclosed white trailer that was a lot newer—and cleaner—than the motor home itself.

Angela jumped out of the driver's door as soon as she stopped, strode up the walk at a fast pace, and gave Newt a two-armed hug while patting her back with both hands at the same time.

"Hey, Newt, good to see you. Been a while." Then she continued her greeting as if no time at all had passed since she had seen Newt or had received her text. " Of course I remember Jasper Higgs, but why after all this time would he have contacted you for help? And please tell me he hasn't moved in here with you."

Newt knew Angela was physically tough on the outside in a way she envied, but she was emotionally sensitive on the inside. Most people only saw her military persona because she shared her inner self only superficially, even with her family. She played down her looks by never wearing makeup or styling her hair. She preferred a simple appearance. She was from the pretty side of the family, and Newt had always thought she was the most beautiful of the three sisters with her thick, straight raven-black hair and hazel eyes. But Angela became embarrassed if anyone referred to her beauty, and she downplayed it whenever she could. Moral character was far more important than physical appearance in Angela's world. So she didn't hide her appearance, but she didn't play to it, either.

Newt knew she had deep mental pain associated with her time overseas and that therapy and medication hadn't seemed to help much. The family worried about her because she didn't communicate often and spent most of her time alone in the woods.

Angela continued in a strong voice, "So what's going on cuz? How do you know this guy is who he says he is? Have you checked any identification? And how do you know his appeal for help isn't just a scam—why is he targeting you here and now? There're agencies set up to assist people in trouble, and they have the training and the proper equipment you don't. Why hasn't Tony stepped in to stop this? I know you have a soft heart, sweetie, but some sort of a rescue attempt? That's crazy. You're a scientist with no background for stuff like this!"

Responding to her negative attitude, Newt moved away from her and folded her arms over her chest. "Thank you for coming, Angela, but give me some credit here. I'm a thinking adult, not some pushover kid!"

"But how do you know it's him, Newt? From that one picture by your bed when he was, what, seventeen?" Angela tried to tone herself down and to use a more reasonable voice. She was quite aware of how stubborn and focused Newt could be, especially when someone disagreed with her.

"It's him, Angela, and he is here! Why don't you reserve judgment until you have all the facts? I promised him that if you say we can't help him, I'll butt out, but at least you should meet him."

Angela continued as if she hadn't heard her. "First I need to tell you that I brought some men with me. Actually I didn't invite them, they insisted on coming, and they'll need to get out of the motor home and stretch their legs. But I may need them backing me up to get this guy on his way and out of your life."

Newt was incensed; what did Angela think was happening here? Some kind of illegal operation that she needed some extra firepower to clean up? She took a couple of deep, calming breaths because she could feel the heat of blood pressure rising in her face and knew they needed Angela's expertise for any rescue plan. She reminded herself that Jasper and Emma were her primary focus at the moment and that her main goal was to help them. Angela would soon see what they were up against and change her tune.

Suddenly, she was distracted from that goal by the implications of housing and feeding extra people. She knew that it was too late in the day to drive back to the woods where Angela lived, so she said in a worried voice, "Angela, you know the cabin is small, and it's already filled up with three adults and a baby. So where am I going to put more people?"

Angela smiled because her cousin was always grounded in practicality. "Don't worry, the trailer is full of their stuff. They usually camp out and cook their own food."

Newt sputtered back, "But I have to ask Jasper. He doesn't look normal, and he doesn't want to involve more people. I need to talk to him about this first." She felt things were snowballing out of her control, and her voice again elevated in volume and pitch.

Angela advanced until her nose was two inches from Newt's nose. "The men are with me, so if they don't stay, I don't stay. They're my people, end of story. So deal with it, cousin, or else I'm headed home right now without helping you." She was worried about Newt's situation, but she had drawn a line in the sand and wouldn't cross it. Also, she wanted to establish whether Newt would respect her position, because without that, her advice wouldn't mean much anyway.

While they were arguing, Angela's men had slowly exited the motor home and were huddled together near the trailer's ramp, waiting to be noticed. Angela motioned them forward, and Newt saw as they came up the walk single file that they all were disabled in some way. Each man paused in front of her one by one, thanked her for her hospitality, and asked how he could be of service to her. They reminded Newt of knights of old kneeling in front of their lady and swearing allegiance to her with their lives before riding off to war, carrying her colors. Newt could practically hear the clank of their amour and the hoof beats in the distance. She couldn't help herself—she fell in love with them on the spot; her eyes stung as she looked into the faces of those men who had sacrificed so much in military service but were not sure they would be welcome in her small cabin.

Angela introduced them. "This man, we refer to as Stubby, because he lost both legs in an explosion. The guy without most of one arm, we call Hook, because he prefers a hook to his other prosthetics. The tall one with the eye patch is Hawkeye, and the one who limps is Half-man, 'cause he lost half of a man-part to shrapnel. Last is Melt, who got his name because of the burn scars, and also because he can melt away like he's invisible."

Newt thought it disrespectful to refer to people by their injuries rather than by their real names, but she didn't say anything. Instead she vowed to get to know each man's given name, and their individual story as soon as she could. She shook their hands and welcomed each man warmly, and she sent Angela a disgusted look at the same time.

Then Newt took Angela aside. "I want you to meet them, but I have to warn you that Jasper and his daughter don't look like normal people, so it might be shocking. And I want to talk to him about involving more people in this before I do."

Angela still thought Jasper was a con artist with something to gain from Newt. "Don't worry, cousin, the military trains you to expect the unexpected. But I'm going to know how he does this deception, and then I'll get rid of him for you."

Jasper overheard Angela's comment, and he was angry that she thought he was dishonest and taking advantage of Newt. He decided his best defense was to show himself, so he opened the screen door and walked on to the porch, holding Emma in one arm.

He said loudly, "You're right, Angela, I'm not the real Jasper Higgs. I'm his digitally projected thoughts."

His appearance was greeted with total silence; Newt could hear the seagulls calling from the beach but no other sound. She looked at Angela and saw that her jaw had actually dropped open in shock. Newt moved to Jasper's side and took his free hand in hers; Tony also came out of the cabin and stood behind Jasper to show their solidarity of support for him. Tony could clearly be seen through Jasper's semitransparent body, and it must have seemed unworldly to the surprised observers.

Angela slowly recovered her senses and her voice. "Wow. I guess I owe you all an apology, so I'm sorry. Sometimes I don't look before I jump to the wrong conclusion."

Jasper inclined his head in agreement. "I appreciate that you're here because Newt wanted your opinion, but I think you should know I'm completely against a rescue plan of any kind. I don't want someone hurt on my behalf. You may think that I'm trying to convince Newt to help me, but it's the other way around, and I'm trying to talk her out of it. So I hope you can put some sense into her."

Angela laughed. "Yeah, I know how Newt is. She's talked me into lots of things good sense was against. I think the best approach here is to just look at the facts and to get the lay of the land first."

Then she walked up on the porch and around Jasper slowly; she especially focused on the sleeping baby, and from her expression Newt saw it broke her heart to see a child unnaturally limp like that. After making two full circles around him, she took her index finger and poked it completely through his arm, and as she removed it, the snap of electricity was audible to everyone. One of Angela's talents was quickly grasping a situation and then drawing critical conclusions necessary for decision-making. She knew no one could have possibly faked that test, thus, he really must be Jasper Higgs; so the rest of the story must be true too, and he and his daughter really did need her help. Plus, having a small child in trouble changed everything for her, because she was a sucker for kids in general.

After her thoughtful pause, she tried to lighten the situation by saying, "OK, I guess having a body like yours would be handy if you were shot at, because the bullets would pass straight through you."

Some of the men laughed at Angela's comment, and the tension was broken for everyone. Surprisingly, after that the men gathered around Emma like a bunch of mother hens, smiling and asking questions about her. Newt chuckled at the warriors' transformation, but she suspected she would have to beg for time with the baby after this. Clearly they were all a bunch of softies under their hard, manly exteriors.

Newt took the men down to the beach to find a suitable campsite while Angela positioned and unhooked the trailer. She listened to the talk among them as they walked, and she knew they loved the fresh salt air and the beach's scenic view. The men agreed to set up in a sheltered area by a stable rock formation above the high-water line. They quickly unpacked and pitched a small tent city. Newt was impressed at their speed, efficiency, and cooperative goodwill. They ribbed each other a little, but it was nothing meanspirited or off-color—at least when she was present—and no one commented on Jasper's strange appearance or the difficult situation ahead.

Then after the tents were up, they unloaded a gas grill from the trailer and made everyone a meal of hamburgers and grilled veggies. Newt relaxed about having extra guests when Angela offered her motor home as an extra latrine and kitchen prep area. The sunset was fabulous, and everyone basked in its purple-and-orange glory as they sat around a campfire making s'mores and talking about the task at hand.

Newt passed out a summary of their hacked data, including maps and pictures. Then she gave a short verbal synopsis of what Jasper and Emma had gone through, who they thought was responsible for their abduction, the description of the island where they were located, and the goals of the rescue operation.

Then, looking at each face individually, she expressed her feelings. "I want to rescue Jasper and Emma, but I don't want anyone killed on either side."

Angela snorted. "Girl, be real. Did you listen to what you just said about Reed? The jerk doesn't care how many people get hurt as long as he gets rich. He's like corporate America. Who cares if people lose their jobs or homes? It's all about the profit."

She took a sip of cocoa and continued. "Look, if someone wanted to do this rescue, it would be like any other hostage situation. There are three basic approaches: the first is to surround, threaten, and make the criminal give up the hostage. The second is to negotiate with something the criminal wants to trade for the hostage, and the third is to use stealth and surprise to overwhelm the criminal and to take the hostage back before the criminal knows what's happening. looking at this situation logically, we can't surround Reed, because he lives on an island and has a getaway submarine. We don't have anything to negotiate with besides the chip, and giving that up would defeat the purpose. So that leaves only option three, which is stealth and surprise. On the plus side, that approach usually results in more unharmed hostages than the other two methods combined—not that any of them have a great rate of success, you understand."

Newt said happily, "So you're going to help us get them back, Angela?"

Her cousin snorted. "I'll help you to make a plan, but unforeseen things happen to all plans. Complicated situations like this require constant reevaluation, and things are more likely to go wrong than in simple operations. Our plan would need to be fluid, because even big missions are scrapped or modified at the last minute because of new intelligence or changing environments. But in every case the bottom line is if the hostages are threatened, you abort immediately. It sounds simple, but it won't be easy to do on an isolated island when we're outnumbered."

Newt was still encouraged because it sounded like Angela was going to do more than just help them make a plan. "So you think it's possible to rescue Jasper and Emma?"

She replied, "Most things are doable if you assume the risk and commit to it, but don't think that means it'll come out fine in the end. And we have a lot of things against us. One of them is that part of the potential team is totally untrained." She pointed at Tony and Newt.

Then she smiled. "But Reed also seems like a pompous ass, so he thinks no one would dare attempt to breach his island, and that works in our favor."

Tony and Jasper both started talking at the same time. They loudly protested her comments because they weren't OK with what had started out as a discussion about a possible plan turning into speculation about training a team! Angela folded her arms, and her men sat quietly, looking at the ground.

After the noise settled down, she explained, "If we're going to attempt this rescue—and that's ultimately up to you, Jasper, Newt, and Tony—then you must accept that I'm the leader. You'll follow my orders immediately without question, no matter what I ask. Not because I'm always right, but because any operation is more successful with a clear leader. There'll be no arguments or discussions over procedure once we set a plan into motion. Whether we go ahead with this or not, you'll need to accept that first."

Newt knew that her statement was also a test of loyalty and that if they were going to question her every decision, Angela would back out before things got rough.

After another sip of cocoa and a thoughtful pause during which Angela listened for protests about her leadership, she continued. "My plan includes gathering information directly—blueprints aren't accurate enough—and hinges on providing a good distraction that buys us time to secretly infiltrate the island for the rescue. We'll use a tried-and-true distraction ploy, which is sex. This man, Reed—I know Tony calls him "Greed," and I think that's a better name for him—obviously has a liking for finer things, and I bet that includes beautiful women. If he's fully distracted by his testosterone, then it will be much easier for the rest of us to sneak in under his nose and to gain the upper hand. This has worked well before, and it will work again if we stage it right. The time frame for the mission itself will be a few hours only, and I'm hoping the preparation can be done in less than a month."

Newt objected. "But Angela, if you're distracting him with your beauty, how will you be the leader at the same time?"

Angela smiled, because this part of her plan was another test of her command and their loyalty. "Not me. You, Newt, will be the womanly distraction."

Newt gulped. "But I'm not pretty or sexy! You know I've never been sexy in my life!"

Jasper started to protest because to him, Newt was the definition of gorgeous, but Angela stopped him with an arm gesture. "You will be that hot woman, Newt, and you'll also dangle the prospect of making a lot of money in front of him. He'll be so distracted by your beauty and charm that he won't know what hit him when we show up. That's my plan. Take it or leave it, cousin."

Newt was gulping like a fish out of water, but she didn't say a word because she understood how serious Angela was when she tossed out that kind of ultimatum. Then she rationalized that Jasper and Emma came before any cleavage she might have to reveal to creepy old Greed.

Angela chuckled as she looked at Newt's face. "I have a dear friend who'd love to do the glam thing for you. He's a drag queen named Dee Light. We met in a Seattle club before my first tour of duty, and I guarantee you're going to love each other. Plus, maybe he'll stop trying to give me a makeover for a while."

Then, while Newt was still in shock over that, Angela turned to Jasper and Tony. "You're supposed to be software and hardware geniuses, so get us a communication system that's stealth-quiet and small. We need to know at all times where the other members of the team are located and what they're doing. We'll also need some type of weapon that knocks people down and out without killing them, which will make Newt happy. It needs to be quiet, accurate, and able to fire at a distance. Then if you could hack into Reed Island's security so we could see what's going on from their perspective, it would be very helpful."

Angela ended her rapid-fire command sequence by saying, "The things that are going to make the biggest difference in this mission's success are training, planning, communication, and timing. We'll start working on those tomorrow. Dismissed."

Sixteen

Hook rapped sharply on the motor home door. It was after midnight, but he knew Angela was still awake, because the pale light from her lantern shone through the front window. She opened the door abruptly, and he had to close his eyes for a minute. She was so damned beautiful, it was physically painful; just the sight of her was like a hit to his solar plexus. Her hair was rumpled, and she was wearing a worn-thin sleeveless nightshirt with barely there shorts. The lantern illuminated her like it was candlelight; it glinted off her dark hair, softened her features, and cast shadows with the planes of her face. Hook glanced away from her when he noticed she wasn't wearing anything under the pajamas, because that knowledge tempted him to fold his arms around her and kiss her like he had longed to do for months.

The romantic atmosphere abruptly broke when she tersely spoke. "It's late—what do you want?"

He responded in the same tone. "I saw your light, and I needed to say some things."

She stepped back and gestured him inside. He'd been invited in a few times before, and it struck him again how severe the interior of her motor home was; it was compulsively organized, Spartan in furnishings, and completely lacking in color.

It resembled a barrack in almost every way possible. There were no pictures of her family, artwork, or personal items visible. Hook had never decorated a home, but he thought a couple of brightly colored pillows on the couch would have been nice. Then there would be something for the eye to look at besides ubiquitous brown-and-olive drab.

She sat down at the foldout dining table and motioned for him to sit, too. Papers covered the table's surface from the file Newt had given her earlier. He saw that Angela had been highlighting and making notes in the page margins, and he figured they were her ideas for a more complete rescue plan.

Angela looked at him with an impatient expression. "I'm busy. Say what you have to say so I can get back to it."

Hook had planned to approach his topic gently, but her tone irritated him, so he growled back, "I think it's stupid to take civilians on this op. It reduces the chance of success and increases the risk to every other person there."

He could see her jaw clench before she responded. "I take it that means you're in, then. So what do you suggest, Hook? Sneak off in the middle of the night?"

He ran his good hand through his hair in frustration. "Angela, you're talking about risking your own cousins' lives, and you're planning on using Newt as bait. Think about that, for God's sake!" Hook tried to reason with her, but his voice was angry instead of solicitous.

She picked up a pencil and made a note on the paper in front of her. "If you don't like it, then train them up to reduce the risk."

"Angela! I can't get them up to speed in a couple of weeks! Tony's a geek and Newt's a scientist—not to mention the invisible man and his baby. Even if I did have time to work with them, you know that you can't train someone to make split-second decisions about things like whether running left or right has the best chance for survival. No communication system, weapon, or training can substitute for combat experience. You know that!

They're the weak link that's going to get someone killed on the mission—and it's probably going to be one of them."

She slammed her hand down on the table, and the papers scattered. "I didn't ask any of you to come here with me or to do this either! If you don't like my plan, then go back to the woods, Hook."

He sighed heavily and calmed down. "Well, maybe you can just explain to them why they should stay home, or I can talk to them. You know I'm right about this. Be the voice of reason and clearly explain to them that staying here while we do the rescue alone is best for everyone involved, including Jasper."

She laughed without humor. "You've no idea how stubborn and single-minded Newt is. And she's in love with him, so I guarantee she will not listen to the voice of reason. She'll offer an alternative hypothesis with supporting arguments and fully document it with footnotes included! Besides, we need female bait as a distraction for Greed, or we won't even get close to that island. I can't lead the rescue and be the bait at the same time, and she's the only other female available for the job."

He shoved himself to his feet, knocking over the folding chair he had been sitting on with a crash. "Don't you get it? You're probably sending her to her death! And how does that benefit true love?"

"In or out, Hook!" Angela remained calm and started to gather the papers from the floor so she could continue planning. As far as she was concerned, the discussion was over.

He paced around the small space, but he couldn't think of anything else to say that would change her mind. Finally he said, "Crap, I don't like it, Angela. But it's your family you're risking, so why do I care what you do?"

She didn't even glance up at him as she worked. "OK, then, you'd better start deciding what training everyone needs, especially Newt, since she's going to face Greed alone. I think you're going to find her stronger than you imagine. She didn't get where she is professionally without brains, persistence, and a backbone of steel under that sweet exterior."

Hook sat down again. "Another thing—what about your PTSD? I know it was bad, and another combat experience might make it so entrenched that the woods won't be able to help you beat it back anymore." He and the other men had watched her daily struggle with admiration because they knew how tough it was to dig out of that particular hole. Watching her cope had earned their loyalty and support, which was why none of them had questioned coming with her to Ocean Shores—or on the rescue mission either.

Angela was straight with him as she finally looked him in the eyes again. "It'll probably come roaring back. I know that. I haven't gotten rid of the thoughts permanently, but I can hold them at bay for a while now, and I'm not going to let my family do this without me."

She put her hand over his. "Promise me that if I go off the deep end, you'll take over command. I'm already damaged, but Newt and Tony are whole. Try to make sure they come home OK. Please, Hook. I won't ask again, or for anything else, because their safety is the most important thing to me."

"I can't promise you that, Angela, but I'll do my best." He had thought she didn't care about her family's welfare, but suddenly he realized it was the opposite. She was endangering her life to help them do what they needed to do, even if it cost her everything.

"Damn! I can see you've thought this through and that nothing I say will change your mind. And you think Newt is stubborn! The mission is crazy, Angela, no matter how you plan to do it! No trained unit would ever take this on under any conditions." Hook shook his head, trying to deny the reckless decision she had made.

"No trained unit loves their family like I do, Hook. I have to try it, or I'll regret it for the rest of my life. Newt loves Jasper and has since she was a girl, and there'll never be another man for her—I know it."

She rubbed her face. "I can't look into her sad eyes as we age, knowing I didn't even try to save him. My training and my love for my cousins make me the best person to do this rescue. I don't want them to try it alone or to hire someone who's not as invested in the outcome as I am. I'm willing to risk my mental health and life for it, but you don't have to, Hook."

He smiled. "Before I came here tonight, we all discussed the rescue plan in camp. I gave everyone the chance to decline with honor. They almost laughed at me for asking. Everyone is eager to risk their lives again and to rescue Higgs and his kid, for some crazy reason."

"What about you, Hook. Are you all in?" She was visibly relieved that she would have the men's help.

"I guess I'm coming, too."

He stayed until one in the morning, helping her to refine the plan and going over possible approaches to the island. Angela was in favor of splitting up the team and doing a multipronged air, and sea attack. She felt that tactic increased the probability of their success, because if one group was neutralized, then another could press on to the goal. Also, Angela thought that Greed wouldn't expect several sets of intruders at the same time and that if an alert was triggered, he would send all his guards in that direction, giving the other teams a better chance to complete the rescue.

Hook understood Angela's strategy, but pointed out that if Greed neutralized one group it meant that some team members would be hurt or killed in the process. He felt the chances of coming out with Jasper and Emma intact and no deaths on their side were incredibly small. He knew that hostage rescue operations of that scale typically had a calculated amount of acceptable losses to achieve their goal. In fact, the military made charts of percentages to expect—how many predicted injured and how many would be killed for each mission. Maybe that predicted risk seemed fine when he was twenty, felt indestructible, and didn't truly understood what it meant. But he was older and wiser now and understood it was the death of people he cared about or injuries that lasted a lifetime. Maybe after all he had experienced it made him care too much about the probabilities and statistics of human losses in combat.

While those thoughts were going through his head, Angela stopped talking and looked at him was if she understood what he had been thinking. She said, "Look, I of all people will understand if you don't have the stomach for it anymore, Hook. You know that to be a good leader, it's important to concentrate on the job and to distance yourself from the cost of the mission. Maybe I'm still emotionally shut down enough to deal with it, and maybe you aren't. That's OK, too."

Hook stood up suddenly, tipping over the chair again in the process, and slammed out of the motor home door, saying nothing to Angela in response to her statement. He paced the beach, trying to control his emotions. Yeah, she was shut down emotionally, because that's how they all dealt with the crap that happened in the Middle East. And if she hadn't been numb, she might have noticed she was wearing next to nothing and that he was practically drooling all over her—she was completely oblivious even to how he felt about her.

He just couldn't let her go into danger alone, because that would kill him. He needed to be there to help her if something bad happened, and it was clear she was going no matter what logic he threw at her. Maybe he could talk to Newt and Tony separately about the risks; no, that would be undermining her behind her back, and he wouldn't do that. He knew Greed was an evil man who needed to be taken out by someone—her cousin's research clearly proved that. But why did it have to involve civilians? He worked possible options again and again in his mind, but Hook couldn't find a good alternative to moving forward with Angela's plan.

After pacing back and forth on the moonlit beach, he finally decided that all he could do was try to plug the holes in her plan and get everyone up to speed with intensive training as best he could. Angela was a good leader, so he'd let her lead, but that didn't mean a strong second-in-command couldn't make all the difference in an operation's success. The bottom line was that everyone would need to be 100 percent invested and ready to work the plan, and that included him.

It was well after four in the morning before he crawled into his tent and wrapped himself in his sleeping bag with some peace of mind about what they were going to do.

Seventeen

Newt was heading to bed after sitting by the campfire and listening to the basic outline of Angela's plan when Jasper stopped her by taking her hand. Her head was reeling. Angela had had made it perfectly clear that she was to put up and shut up, but Newt had always had a hard time doing that without asking questions. She knew Angela was key to making the mission a success, so she was trying to roll with it by mentally releasing any control she thought she might have had. She was desperate to rescue Jasper and Emma, and she trusted Angela's expertise, so she quietly repeated a mantra to do everything asked of her—and more if she could.

Jasper said, "Sit with me on the porch, please, Newt."

He was fighting with himself to stay calm and reasonable. "I like Angela's men, and she seems like the right person to pull this off if anyone can. So thanks for setting it up for me." Jasper looked toward the bright campfire still burning on the beach. He missed the smells of wood, smoke, and salt air that he knew scented the twilight breeze. "But I don't want you to be bait. If we follow Angela's plan, you'll be with Greed by yourself. No communications, no weapons, and no safeguards. I don't think that's a good idea at all! She needs a different plan."

Newt sighed. "I know you have reservations, and so do I. But neither of us is in a position to change things, because you're a projection without a body and I can't do what needs to be done without her help."

Newt lightly touched his face. She would have leaned back against his chest, but she had tried that once on the beach and her entire head had accidently sunk into his body until she had felt electricity snaking along her face. She wasn't doing that again. It hadn't been a pleasant experience, and it had freaked her out a little because colors and shapes had bloomed in her vision, and she had heard a whisper of thoughts that hadn't been hers. Ever since Jasper's release from the globe, she'd been conscious of his mood and of the direction of his thoughts, and she found that interesting and useful. But sinking her brain into his projection and having his actual thoughts speak into her mind was horribly like possession by another entity, and just remembering it gave her the creepy goose bumps.

However, she was working on building a relationship with him despite the fact that he wasn't there physically, so she continued to try to win him over. "I think we need to trust Angela, and I have time to get some training before we leave. I've worked with Medi-Help before, and that gives me an inside track with Greed. We need that in order to get on the island without detection. She hasn't told us her whole plan yet, so let's wait and see, Jasper."

He was not satisfied. "How much training can you get in a couple of weeks? You're a doctor, not a fighter."

Newt didn't know if she should laugh at his unexpected *Star Trek* reference or be insulted. "Remember, I copied his CIA file. I know he just snaps his fingers and people die. I get that! But I have waited my whole life for you, and if I can help get you back, then I'm doing it!"

He was frustrated. "I've waited a long time to feel like this too, but I want you alive and healthy. What if I come back and you don't? I want to really hold and kiss you. I want to make love to you! We need a different plan that doesn't put you up as bait."

Newt was close to tears at his words, but she stood firm. "We're all going to take risks no matter how it's played. Everyone else has useful combat skills, and I don't, but there is an important part I can play. Being the distraction is the way I can help, and I'm going to! What would you have me do? Sit at home as the little woman and wait to see if my man returns from battle or not? What if I can make the difference that means you're whole again and we can be together in every way? I need to do this for me and for us, Jasper, and I will do it no matter what you say, and you can't stop me." She stood up and entered the cabin without looking back at him.

She had pretty much the same discussion with Tony the next morning, only it was a lot louder, so everybody heard it. He threw in a few additional good arguments, but he stopped short of threatening to involve their mother. That was good because she knew her mom would not be in favor of either one of them going into danger under any circumstances and she would give Angela hell for having planned it. And it would be the end of any real hope of rescue for Jasper and Emma

Newt was scared, too. She understood their concern, but she believed everyone was needed on the team for the most effective rescue. What they wanted was the modern equivalent of "leave the women in the village while the men go off to defend the borders," and she wasn't all right with that outdated concept. She knew she wasn't taking on any more risk than the others were. Sure, she was short on fighting skills at the moment, but everyone else was going in with some disadvantages, too. Most of the men had physical disabilities, so how was that different from her perceived lack of fighting skills? And she intended to quickly make up for her shortfalls and then face her fears with courage and the pure stubbornness she was known for. She had learned long ago to listen to her gut, and it was saying loud and clear to go to the island. There was no way she was going to stay home, biting her nails and waiting for a text.

After facing down Tony, she was grumbling and stomping up and down the beach in her yoga clothes when Hook caught up with her. "I heard from Angela that you'll need training to make sure you survive this little adventure she's planning."

The morning sun was burning off the mists that were drifting in from the ocean, and she breathed the air deeply to find some inner calmness. This was her chance to prove to everyone she could be useful in a fight. She turned to Hook with a determined look on her face.

"I do have skills, just not the skills they're thinking I need."

"OK, what do you have?" He thought she had the soft body and mentality of an untrained person, but he was willing to hear her out.

She thought a minute. "I have logic, I have a quick grasp of situations and possible solutions, I have words, I can sway people with reason, and, if Angela is right, I will have sex appeal, hopefully."

Hook didn't discount those attributes, but when push came to shove, would they be enough? He didn't think so. "OK, but how about we work on developing some other things today? Because when you're facing down an armed guard, you may not have time to use those particular tools."

Hook started her training with a discussion of blades because sharp objects were readily available and easy to conceal. He demonstrated the concept by picking up a shell from the sand, breaking it in half, and holding it to Newt's neck for a moment.

He then said, "There are basically two types of blades—long and short. Both require you to be close to your opponent to use, unlike guns. With a long blade, you can slash or stab big openings for serious injuries or a quick death. With a short blade, you need to go for a large blood vessel, or the target will take too long to die, so think of cutting the throat or femoral artery. I'll demonstrate."

Before he could begin, however, Newt slid to the ground, her face as white as snow. She gulped several times. "I appreciate the help, Hook. But there is no way I can stick a knife into someone and bleed him to death. Even if it was Adolf Hitler and killing him meant saving millions of lives, I still don't think I could do it. Just the thought of warm blood running out over me—I would throw up or pass out! Let's try something else, please. I want to learn to fight, just not this way."

That only confirmed what he had said to Angela the night before about civilians being a liability, but he gave it another try. "How would you feel about a little target practice with Hawkeye? He's the best shot I know. You can't take a gun in with Greed because they're bound to search you, but maybe you'll find one once you're in his house."

He considered a moment. "Also, a little hand-to-hand combat with Angela would be helpful. She's tough and won't play nice with you like the men would."

Newt agreed. "Maybe I can't take in an obvious weapon, but could I have a hidden device, like in James Bond movies? You know, her face powder is really an explosive, or the lipstick is a flamethrower—like that?"

Hook laughed; she was charming in her naïveté. "It's harder than you think to fool people with hidden weapons. And if they do find them, then it immediately makes you the enemy. You'll need to appear completely authentic and innocent to do your part. Greed and his guards will be alert for anything that feels even slightly off to them."

Hook pointed her toward the nearby sand dunes where the men had set up a target range. There, Hawkeye lent her a small pistol, and she shot round after round. The recoil was the biggest problem—that and the fact that she was afraid of the gun. The sudden explosion of gunpowder next to her face didn't give her a sense of power like it did some people; it made her want to avoid squeezing the trigger again. So it became an exercise in mind over matter, and she forced herself to do the job. Out of the corner of her eye, she saw Hawkeye motioning for people to stay far away, probably because he thought she might injure someone with friendly fire. Both of them were equally relieved when he called it quits for the day. Newt resolved to practice frequently until she could at least hit the targets most of the time.

During their practice Newt learned Hawkeye's real name was Phillip. He had spent his childhood jumping from one foster home to another because no one wanted to adopt him. Sadly he couldn't remember one day while he was growing up being treated as a valuable person by anybody. At eighteen he enlisted in the military and became one of their top snipers. After his tour of duty he had been headed for Olympic gold because he qualified as one of the best marksmen in the world, and that recognition had finally given him a sense that he had value.

But three weeks before his release from military service, shrapnel had hit his face and he lost one eye, his depth perception, and his future in the Olympics as a marksman. He had been honorably discharged and then drifted around in an alcoholic stupor for over a year until Angela invited him to stay in her woods. He had been sober since then and was trying to get a grip on his life.

He told his story to Newt in a monotone as if it had happened to someone else; he didn't express any emotion about the loss of his eye and his Olympic goals. In his own mind he was a washed-up has-been, and while he was happy to teach Newt, he told her that because of his handicap, he wasn't a good shot anymore.

That negative attitude made Newt both angry and sad for him. She saw he was still an amazing shooter, and more than that he was the best teacher she had ever had—and she had been in a lot of classrooms. Hawkeye had unlimited patience and a natural gift for the sport. She believed he could still have a future in precision shooting if he could gather any self-esteem and accept what had happened to his eye. The man just didn't know how to use lemons to make lemonade, she thought!

He admitted to her that he had a cosmetic glass eye—paid for by the military—but that he always wore an eye patch so people would be put off by him and leave him alone. He reinforced that stay-away look with a shaggy beard and mustache and long, unkempt hair. Newt thought all he needed was a parrot to complete his bad-pirate look. She suspected he really cultivated his appearance for self-punishment, because every time he looked in the mirror and saw the patch or the empty eye socket, it reinforced his belief that he was damaged beyond any value. That was all horse manure, she knew, and she intended to point that out to him after the rescue was over. His victim mentality had to go—she would make that a personal goal—but there was no point in rocking the boat now; there was just too much going on already for that challenge.

And at the moment he was helping her see that she should never carry a gun, because she was ten times more likely to shoot herself than anyone else. Newt realized all her academic studies hadn't taught her to coordinate multiple body parts at one time. She could direct her hands or her feet or her body or her head—just not more than two of those at the same time. Hawkeye decided it would be best if he stored the gun for her in between practice sessions, because once when she had been carrying it with her to check the target patterns, the gun had accidently gone off and had almost taken his good eye out; that had had a sobering effect on both of them.

After lunch, Angela showed up wearing sweats to practice some self-defense moves with her. Normally, soft mats were used for training, but instead they practiced in shallow ocean water to break their falls. Of course, Angela never hit the water once, but Newt was soaking wet and covered with sand and bruises in no time. Newt was the kind of person who would take mental notes for later identification if she were mugged, not the kind who would throw the man over her back when he grabbed her. The Pacific Ocean in the Northwest was very cold most of the year, and if she hadn't been working so hard physically, she would have been at risk for hyperthermia, because Angela threw her into the water again and again.

Eventually, Angela took pity on Newt's panting and her bruised cold body, and halted their session; she knew Newt's stubbornness wouldn't allow her to give up until she was physically unable to move.

Angela was only wet from Newt's splashes and warned her that the next time they would practice on the sand instead of in the water. Newt intellectually understood that if any of Greed's guards grabbed her, no amount of last-minute training would save her, no matter how hard she tried to learn. Because it wasn't just her lack of experience—she also didn't have the height and weight advantage to take on a bigger trained man. Angela was closer to her size than the average man, but even with a good grip, and the momentum Angela was always harping on, it felt like she was trying to heave a hundred-pound rock around rather than just her cousin. Newt understood the physics involved and she consoled herself that if she tried to make force instead of mass work in her favor, like using a lever to shift a big load, it might ultimately balance the scales in her favor.

Newt knew that learning to fight was serious business, but she was who she was; she couldn't turn into Wonder Women in a few weeks. She believed her advantage would be using what she already had going for her: her brain and her ability to think on the spot. She could problem solve, predict outcomes, and analyze options at supersonic speed. Obviously that wasn't going to do her much good if she was shot, but many a tense situation had been defused with a little rational thinking. All she had to do was convince the other team members that mental agility was as good as any physical skills they had, because if it came down to fighting, that's all she really had to offer.

Eighteen

"**F**ocus, Higgs," Jasper scolded himself. He had his head resting in his hands and his elbows on his knees as he sat dejectedly on the driftwood where Newt had found the globe. But since he didn't have skin, muscle, bone, or nerves, his sensations were only a projected memory of what it had felt like to sit in that position; things got confusing quickly when you didn't have a body.

It was a beautiful day—the sun sparkled off the water, and seagulls flew and called overhead. But he didn't see or hear any of that. He didn't even notice a small crab carefully climb up his energy-dense shoe only to fall completely through his more transparent projected leg back down to the sand and then scuttle off. Emma was resting in his lap and appeared to be sleeping as usual.

He'd been trying to hold it together for days. He'd thought it was bad enough to involve Newt and Tony, but now six other people were going to be putting themselves in danger because of him. He could hear distant gunshots as Newt practiced target shooting; that was a skill she wouldn't have needed if he hadn't entered her life. He had always liked being self-sufficient and had prided himself on never needing anyone; now that was gone, and it made him feel weak and exposed.

He continued his mental list of complaints. He was sick of living half of a life as a projection, and seeing Emma day after day in an almost-dead state tore huge chunks out of him. He felt responsible for everything that was happening, because he had created the damn chip. It wasn't fair that one day he had been living a happy, quiet life—just he and Emma doing whatever they wanted—and the next day they had been turned into the living dead.

He'd been trying to roll with the punches, but everything was coming to a head with a stupid plan where good people were going to get shot at and probably killed. The others hadn't seen Greed's operation; they didn't know what a well-oiled, evil machine it was. But he had looked into the hard eyes of a guard pointing a gun at him—a man it seemed who was just waiting for Jasper to make a wrong move so he could shoot him and then casually watch him bleed to death while he smoked a cigarette. He wouldn't have wished that on anyone, not even on the friend who betrayed him and ruined his life to begin with.

He had finally found the woman of his dreams in Newt, who was beautiful, smart, and kind, but she was as far away from him as she would have been if he'd never met her. He could talk to her but only touch her briefly, and what kind of a relationship was that for a man and a woman nurturing new love? It sucked!

On top of all he was dealing with, Angela had commanded him and Tony to invent both a new high-tech weapon and an advanced communication system in just weeks; each of those complicated designs normally would take years—not days—of research and testing. His mind was so tormented that he couldn't even focus on the moment, let alone get into an inventive state on orders from her!

Suddenly Angela strode into view and added to Jasper's black mood with more bad news for him. "Hey, Jazz, I want to let you know that you should be prepared to shrink down again for transport to the island. I think that's the best way to protect and conceal your projections." She took one look at his glowering face and tried to further explain her decision. "You'll need to carry the chip and Emma, so you aren't much use as a fighter anyway. When we have control of the situation, you'll be converted back to full size, and then hopefully you can track your computer's signal to locate your bodies."

He stood and loomed over her, his face contorted in distress. "You don't understand how impossible that is! I almost flew apart the first time, but twice in a row, I don't think I'll stay intact. And what about Emma? It's too hard for her! You're asking too much of us, Angela!"

She sat quietly and just let his emotions wash over her. When he sputtered to a stop, she said quietly, "What, too much for you, Jasper? Then we'll just call it off and all go home. But wait, you can't go home, and neither can Emma, so what should we do? We could toss the chip into the fire next time we make s'mores and end both your projected lives. Newt could be restrained while we do it, but I'm not sure of the long-term impact on her from seeing you and Emma destroyed right before her eyes."

She paused and then added calmly, "I've watched that girl moon over you for years, and frankly, I don't see what she finds so special about you. She's a beautiful, bright, clean spirit willing to risk everything she is for you, and I don't see you appreciating that at all."

Jasper sat down again and groaned. "How am I going to deal with all of this?"

Angela didn't respond to his statement directly; instead, she asked a question of him. "Do you know what courage is? It's not running through enemy fire to help a wounded soldier just because you can. It's being scared to death to do it and doing it anyway—that's courage. It's knowing that a task is hard and dangerous but finding the inner strength to do what you need to do." She paused to reflect. "A hero for me is a little harder to define. Sometimes it's living or dying with courage, and sometimes it's pure dumb luck that you didn't die after all and people just think your a hero."

"I'm so angry all the time."

She snorted. "Is it anger, Jasper, or something else? I think with your smarts and early success, you've been able to hide from things that make you uncomfortable. But unfortunately, it's the difficult things that make you grow and strengthen as a person. Hiding from life isn't living life, you know. You've been in your ivory tower, thinking you aren't subject to shame, regret, guilt, and fear like the rest of us, but you are."

She picked up a stick and traced a circle in the sand. "Those people who say 'it's all good' are delusional. It isn't all good—there's suffering, destruction, and death everywhere, but it's part of life too."

"But I can't control anything anymore!" He turned his face away from her.

"Controlling life is an illusion, Jasper. Life just happens to us, and we play the cards we're dealt as best we can. Because there's only two things you can ever control: one is how you prepare for a moment, and the other is how you respond to that moment when it happens, but you can't control whether the moment happens or not."

"I just want my life back the way it was! Is that too much to ask? I never wanted this or have hurt anyone so why am I being punished?"

"Jasper, I hear whining in your tone." Angela spoke harshly. "The past is the past, and there's no changing what's happened to you. Fighting what you can't change only causes more pain, so your only choice is to move forward."

She added rays around her sand circle, which made it appear like a child's picture of the sun. "Actually, I've never met anyone with so much damn luck. But then again, maybe it's not luck. Maybe the universe is somehow giving things a push." She smiled. "I mean, what are the chances of us sitting here and talking after you hid the chip in the globe thousands of miles away? Pretty amazingly small, I think."

"I just don't see how any of the dots connect in my favor, Angela. But I do know what I'm feeling for Newt is love and that I couldn't stand to see her hurt because of me." Jasper looked at Angela, and she could see the honesty of that admission in his eyes.

She suddenly realized that Jasper might end up in her family and that he needed to hear some plain talk and to grow up a little. "OK, if you feel that way, then you've got to let her live her truth. She needs to be free to do her best for you and Emma. Don't protect her and assume she isn't up for the challenge. Let her be who she is, and celebrate it."

"But I'm just a freak, and you guys are all taking on too big of a fight to save me! Someone will get killed!" Jasper continued his appeal to abort the rescue or to at least keep Newt out of it.

"Believe me, I understand the risks! I've sent people I cared about to their death, and that's why I live in the woods and suffer for what I did. I think about what I was responsible for every day, even though no one blames me but me."

Jasper started pacing back and forth on the beach. "We can't win—the odds are too stacked against us!"

Angela was getting annoyed. "No man is an island, Jasper. We as a species depend on each other, and that's something you don't seem to understand. If we function as a team, then we can shoulder together what would break one person alone. That's why I'm dividing the jobs into smaller manageable parts, and you can be sure we'll work through problems as a group when they come up." Angela heaved her drawing stick out into the ocean with force and walked down the beach toward the cabin without ever looking back at him.

Jasper sat back down on the driftwood. He suddenly noticed the sparkling water and looked up to the distant horizon where gray ocean met blue sky. He felt more inner peace than he had since Emma was abducted, and he understood that Angela was trying to tell him to get his head in the game. And that's all he really was at this point—a disembodied head—but his head had a good brain, and he could use it to help with the rescue. She was right: It was mostly fear holding him back, and if he could convince his head that the things Angela wanted were doable, maybe they would be.

After further thought, Jasper decided he could bring some unique skills to the rescue because he was a projection and not a physical man. For one thing, as long as the chip wasn't damaged, his projection couldn't be injured either. And weren't the abilities to change size and survive bullets superhero skills? He had others attributes too, because he didn't need to eat, drink, sleep much, or breathe, either. Finally, Jasper realized he had talents he could bring from his former life; he had studied and mentally practiced military moves and strategy for his video game designs, and that might be very useful during the island assault.

Yeah, thanks to Angela, he had his head in the game finally, and it felt much better to be moving forward than to be stuck spinning his wheels, wishing things were different somehow. For the first time in his life he wasn't alone, and that felt great, too.

Nineteen

As Jasper approached the cabin feeling much lighter—if that was possible—TNT intercepted him and said excitedly, "Let's go brainstorm, dude. This is going to be great! We're the dream team of inventing techno-machines, and that's what we get to do, man."

Jasper didn't feel excited about the tasks, but Tony's enthusiasm was contagious, and he had been looking forward to working with him, so he said, "OK, but you know Angela's asking us to do the impossible. But I guess it won't hurt to discuss some ideas at least."

Tony invited him into his work truck, a place Jasper had wanted to check out since it had first arrived. He'd been hesitant to ask for a tour before Tony offered one voluntarily, because for him, a work space was personal and almost sacred. And he didn't know if Tony had a clean room and needed to avoid contamination. Clean rooms were essential for manufacturing computer chips because even the smallest particle of dust could affect the final product's function. Jasper had one in his home in Seattle with precise airflow, filtration, and a special air shower.

They entered the plain brown nondescript truck through the driver's door, and Jasper saw it had a walk-through behind the seats to the back of the vehicle. The cab area was deluxe, sporting leather seats and real teakwood trim. All the gauges were housed in tarnished brass fittings, and the numerous edge accents were brass, too. That gave an almost nautical feel to the dash, seats, and door interiors. The truck's length was similar to a large U-Haul and was separated from the cab by a locking solid-steel roll-up door. And once Tony opened the door, the working space was revealed.

As he looked around, Jasper wasn't disappointed—it far exceeded his expectations. The center area had a long work-table with a comfortable chair on each side. The chairs ran smoothly on tracks the full length of the table. Tony could sit and quickly glide from end to end as he assembled computer components spread out on the surface. The walls were lined with drawers containing parts and cubbyholes with pullout baskets. There were keyboards, screens, hard drives, and a lot of other disassembled computer hardware Jasper didn't even rec-ognize filling all the available storage spaces. Even the ceiling had magnetic boxes stuck to it with small parts inside.

Jasper noticed a small sink, a coffee station, and a micro-wave in one corner. Natural light flooded in from two overhead locking skylights that Tony said were made from bulletproof plexiglass. Then Tony gleefully demonstrated the motorized coverings for the skylights, an almost theater-sized video screen that rolled down behind the closed steel doors, and a rock-ing surround-sound music system. Everything was controlled remotely from his phone or computer.

The center worktable had a cover that fixed projects in place and then flipped over to become a comfortable double bed, and one of the corner cupboards held a small shower and toilet. There was a small fridge under one of the front seats, and under the other were sheets, towels, and food storage. Everything was precisely organized with identifying brass labels, so the space didn't feel small or cluttered to Jasper. The drawers, cupboards, appliances, and table were all made of stainless steel. The floor was cushioned by a colorful carpet in an abstract pattern.

Tony explained that power to run the electrical equipment came from roof top solar panels. Water for showers and cooking, and septic waste were completely self-contained in units under the truck. Fresh air constantly circulated, but the skylights opened and the rooftop had pull-down steps for easy access on nice days. Adjustable halogen lighting from the ceiling bounced off the semi-shiny metal surfaces, and Jasper thought that made the space feel roomier.

After taking in the whole space and looking at Tony's proud expression, he said, "I think just calling it a work truck is an understatement, TNT."

Tony laughed. "It's my home away from home, Jazz. If I really need to think, then this is the space for me to do it in. Something about how it's closed up with all my stuff handy gets my creative juices flowing. I just turn off the phone and get in the zone."

Jasper could feel it himself, as energy practically hummed through his projected body. "Let's do it then, and try to come up with the designs Angela wants."

They sat next to the table on the chairs opposite each other, and Jasper discovered they comfortably reclined, too. "Any ideas about the weapon we're supposed to invent?"

Tony laced his arms behind his head and crossed his legs. "It would be a lot easier to make one if Newt didn't care about killing somebody, because that effectively eliminates penetrating projectiles."

He opened a nearby drawer, took out two snack bags of chips, and gave one to Jasper. "I thought about rubber bullets or a bunch of microprojectiles hitting the target at one time because neither one is likely to kill, but they won't stop someone determined to hurt us, either."

Tony talked between crunching. "I even considered caustic liquids, gases, and other chemicals because they're not usually fatal, but I don't think that stuff is reliable enough to go against actual bullets. And I bet Newt wouldn't like them, either."

Jasper thought for a minute about those options. "OK, that leaves energy, if you aren't using a force made from mass of any kind."

He thought it was nice of Tony to offer him chips, but no way was he going to try eating them in public; and besides, he didn't have taste buds to appreciate their salty flavor or teeth to crunch with anyway. "What about something like a stun gun? A stun gun can incapacitate without killing if you use it right."

Tony reached over and grabbed the second bag of chips with an apologetic smile for Jasper. "Yeah, but a stun gun uses electricity fired down wires that stick to the target with barbs. That seriously limits its use to close targets, and Angela wants our weapon to fire from a distance, which is safer for us anyway."

Jasper threw out some other energy types they might use. "So how about microwaves?"

Tony grimaced. "Gross, man! That's going to heat up the water in the skin and eyeballs and cause pain and burning. Newt would have a fit!"

"How about sound, light, or radio waves? Maybe a sonic boom focused down to a small point. Would any of those have enough power?" Jasper was having fun tossing around ideas with Tony.

Tony walked to the small fridge and took out a soda. "I don't think there's a way to limit things that travel by wave action through the air, Jazz. Because all waves spread out quickly once they leave the source, and that again reduces the effective target distance."

Both men rocked back and forth in their chairs—Jasper using his hands to push off from the table—thinking deep thoughts. Finally Jasper said, "That, my friend, limits us to electricity, and we're back to the problem of how to direct it to the target without wires."

Tony said, "How about Tesla coils or lightning? Those aren't directed down a wire."

Jasper picked up a pencil and twirled it around in his fingers. "No, but with those the electricity is attracted to a target made of conductive material—that's how lightning rods work."

Slowly an idea formed in his mind. "But maybe we could fire a conductive pellet or something not connected to a wire first, and then it would pull the electricity after it to the target."

Tony shook his head back and forth. "Not reliable enough, Jazz, because there's bound to be something bigger and more attractive—like any bigger piece of metal around—that the electricity would rather go to than a pellet small enough to be fired out of a gun. You know it's hard to predict where lightning will strike, even with all the science we have."

What followed was lots of shuffling feet, flipping pencils, and staring off into space. Finally Jasper suggested a practice to generate ideas that had worked for him in the past; he turned off conscious thought and let his mind drift so his subconscious and creative right brain could work on the problem without the louder chatter of his logical left brain. Tony agreed to try it because a similar technique had worked for him; Newt called it "goofing off," and he freely admitted that's usually what it was. But thanks to Jazz, he actually had an explanation and justification for extended lollygagging, and that was so cool!

After about twenty minutes of drifting and trying not to think, Jasper threw out an idea. "Could we make a path for the electricity using an ionized channel from a laser light?"

"What do you mean by that?" Tony asked slowly.

"Well, lasers are light given off by excited electrons and other atomic particles. You know that the resulting charged light ions can cut through delicate tissue—or thick material, too—by focusing the light's path out from the laser device. So what if we could fine-tune a laser's light, making a channel of its charged particles through the air to draw the electricity after it? Then it would reliably direct the electricity to a target."

Tony was excited. "Not only that, man, but the light beam would also show the shooter where to aim, and I know if the light is bright enough, you can temporarily blind people with it; its called dazzle."

Both men got to work on assembling materials for a test weapon that would use a laser at a low power to direct the electricity where it could deliver its punch. They figured out the kilovolts needed to neutralize an average man without any real injury. The voltage necessary to knock a person down depended a little on body size, clothing, and moisture level—especially sweat. Nothing would be foolproof, they knew, but they rationalized that old people with heart conditions probably wouldn't be shooting at them. So the level they chose would knock down a big man, but just in case, and for safety reasons they limited each firing time to five seconds unless the trigger was pushed again. That way if somebody froze on the trigger it would automatically shut off. A five-second two or three hundred–kilovolt blast would disrupt a firing muscle without harming a heart's electrical activity. They calculated that the voltage might or might not cause unconsciousness but that the target person would fall down and be unable to move for the few minutes needed to tie him up securely.

Tony had some lasers of various sizes in stock, so they assembled a small weapon for testing that looked like a science fiction movie blaster. They whooped in elation when it actually worked, firing an impressive crackle of blue-white light directly at the target with an ozone smell afterward. Then they fine-tuned it to the proper kilovolts by building another target composed of sensors to record the amount of energy delivered by each firing. They knew eventually one of them was probably going to accidently take a hit, but they could outfit vests with similar sensors for practice drills. At the end of the long day's work, both men had had fun, and each was satisfied with the gun they nicknamed "the Zap."

Tony had the final word when he said, "The Zap will spring the trap for Greed with speed!"

Jasper laughed, because after a day of working with Tony, he realized that TNT had the same subtle bulldozer approach to life that his stubborn sister Newt had. Both worked full bore on a problem until they solved it, and they never lost their sense of humor. He and Tony and had been in harmony all day, and Jasper could see what problem solving with Newt would be like in any future relationship—if they got the chance to build one, that is—because even disagreements with Tony had been entertaining for both of them.

Twenty

Jasper gently laid Emma on Newt's bed and kissed her cheek. With sadness he remembered the days when laying her down had started a game of blowing raspberries on her tummy and chewing on her toes to hear her laugh. She couldn't talk, but her smile and giggle more than made up for it in his mind; plus he only had to look in her eyes to see the person looking back was aware and intelligent. And of course the desire to communicate with that precious being had landed them in the mess they were currently in. Why couldn't he have left well enough alone?

Now he stroked her hair and said, "Baby, I promise I'm doing all I can to get us back home again. Everyone's working hard to help us, so just hang in there a little longer, sweetie."

He looked around Newt's small bedroom where he and Tony had set up a cutting-edge computer workstation. Jasper was going to adapt the chip's design to function for communication during the rescue by eliminating the part that projected images. The communication device would collects thoughts from one brain and transfer them to other team members as words only. He knew he was taking a risk by recycling even part of the code he'd used before, so he built in a meltdown sequence and traps for anyone who was trying to work backward to figure out what he had done. It had taken a lot of soul searching to conclude that good communication was more important to the rescue than his desire to destroy all of the chip's technology, so he was moving forward and trusting the team to keep his invention safe.

Newt was on a trip to meet Angela's friend for a makeover, and he felt a little lost without her around. Jasper liked Newt's appearance the way it was, but he understood that anything that improved her chance of survival—and consequently the success of the rescue—needed to be done. He just hoped she didn't change too much, because he thought she was beautiful both inside and out already.

Newt's bedroom was simple and homey with older wooden furniture, and a colorful vintage patchwork quilt on the bed. His eyes were drawn to a large collage of family pictures on the wall. They had all been taken on the beach by the cabin at various times during Tony's and Newt's childhood. Jasper saw their mother and father for the first time and noticed they had had a yellow Labrador dog that adored fetching sticks out of the ocean. Their loving, close, stable relationships were obvious in each picture; they had fun together, they cared about each other, and they were a family unit. Jasper thought about how lucky they were that their childhood was a world away from his upbringing where loving words, kind gestures, and silliness never happened.

He suspected a lot more kids grew up emotionally empty like he had, than filled with family love like Newt and Tony had; a stab of jealously and envy touched his heart. Kids don't get to choose who they get as parents—and at least he'd had food and a roof over his head—but children need more than the physical necessities, he thought. They need to be loved and cherished for who they are by their parents or guardians. It was water under the bridge for him, but he vowed he was going to fill Emma up with all the love he had every day—if he ever got her back.

Jasper wandered around the bedroom, touching Newt's few personal items that were sitting out; he paged through a mystery book she was reading, sniffed some scented body lotion, and stroked a blue worn but still serviceable terrycloth bathrobe. He missed her and longed for a future with her and Emma where they were safe, normal, and living somewhere homey like the cabin. He thought Newt would create the same kind of family she had been raised in—laughter instead of angry shouting and hugs rather than spankings given out generously. He and Emma both needed that kind of a family, too.

Finally Jasper reined himself in and booted up the computer. The new design he was creating would have the advantage of instant direct brain-to-brain communication, and so wouldn't have the risk of misunderstandings that spoken language did. He would scale it down and combine it with the ear thought-collecting microprocessor and run it from a program on his tablet. Then instead of a chip like the one he kept in his pocket and the tiny earpieces his and Emma's bodies were wearing to collect their thoughts, there would be only once device small enough to hide in an ear—unless an otoscope was used to look in the ear canal during a body search.

He added some filters so that the chip only projected strong thoughts specifically thrown to it by the wearer's brain; Jasper didn't want stray thoughts or memories to be disruptive in the heat of battle. He would ask Tony to mold a soft waterproof material around the chip so it would sit comfortably in each person's uniquely shaped ear canal. The device would both project the wearer's thoughts and collect thoughts directed to it by other devices, thus leaving one ear free to hear surrounding sounds.

He removed the chip he carried from his pocket, placed it on the desk, and stared at it. Jasper had written the program code and had constructed the chip in his clean room at home. At that point, he'd thought he knew exactly what he was doing and how the chip would function to communicate with Emma because he had worked it all out first. Sure, he knew that new programs and microprocessors have expected glitches and errors. But he never could have predicted the chip's ability to project a functional 3-D digital image in real space. That still boggled his mind; and because he didn't understand exactly how it was doing it, suddenly he was afraid that if he copied the chip's code directly, it might fatally disrupt the projection supporting him and Emma.

So he decided to scrap his original plan of uploading the chip's data and working with its original program; instead he started a new design from scratch, coding from what he remembered he'd done. He put the original chip back in his pocket for safety, even though he didn't understand how his projection could have a functional pocket to put it in. He had accepted that some things in his situation defied rational explanation, but maybe he would work out the how and why in the future—if he had one, that is.

He outlined the requirements in his head for the new device. It would need to collect thoughts from several sources and transfer them to one or more of the other team members as needed simultaneously. It also had to project the thoughts over distances and through a variety of materials, including through solid rock. Jasper decided that the meltdown system would destroy the devices after a preset time period or with a verbal- or thought-activated command. Then if a device was captured by Greed, he wouldn't have it long enough to decode it before it self-destructed. Because even though the communication device wouldn't be the actual chip Greed was so desperate for, Jasper had to use some of its design for the new device; he didn't want the enemy to get even one tiny clue about how he had made the original chip.

Jasper limited the thoughts drawn and transmitted to the left side of the brain's cerebral cortex only. In most people, that area was generally responsible for number computation, language, and reasoning. He hoped that would take emotions out of the mix of projected thoughts. Jasper reasoned that a cool head was an important asset in combat and that emotions like

fear and anger only muddied the waters of quick, logical decision-making. He also knew that traditional education taught
people to concentrate on left-brain skills, so he thought the
team members would more easily learn to send out thoughts
from that area.

Finally, he added name recognition, which was the only
thing he could think of for directing people's thoughts to the
desired recipient. So if Jasper thought a person's name, then
the thoughts would automatically go to that person, and if he
thought "all," then everyone would receive the thought. Jasper
figured the team would need to practice as soon as possible,
because things could get complicated quickly if stray thoughts
were accidently sent to the wrong person. Jasper laughed at the
possibilities; Angela was going to have some challenges training
with the new communication system!

After he finished designing the new device, Jasper wiped
everything from the computer's memory except what was on
the hard drive—that he removed and took to Tony. The plan was
that Tony would go to the clean room in Jasper's house since
he didn't have a clean area in his truck, and he would build the
devices there. Then he would test each one and destroy the hard
drive when he was done. They could Skype with each other if
problems came up during the build.

Jasper reminded Tony to suit up completely and to then
use the air shower in the gray room before entering the clean
room to assemble the devices. Jasper's clean room reduced
the number of particles in the air from thirty-five million per
cubic meter to about twelve; it did that by maintaining positive air pressure in the room—constantly pushing air out of
the room and using an advanced filtration for the air coming
in. It also employed a laminated air-flow system that directed
air in a linear pattern to prevent particles from settling out in
the room.

Jasper had originally thought he might have trouble trusting Tony enough to hand over the hard drive to him, but after

working together on the Zap, it wasn't an issue. What he did worry about, though, was Tony and the hard drive being abducted, because he thought Greed might still be watching his house. So he asked Angela to send Hook and Half-man along for guard duty, and that gave him some peace of mind.

Twenty - One

Newt stopped in to see her mother, who was working that week at Tacoma General Hospital, before lunching with Angela's friend Dee Light. She, Tony, and Angela had met privately that morning to discuss what to tell the senior Dr. Newton about Jasper and Emma, and despite the dishonesty inherent in the omission of important facts, they all agreed the best approach was to act as if nothing unusual was happening in their lives. That was because Sophia was a force to be reckoned with on a good day, and as they understood the astute woman well and loved her—they voted to keep her in the dark for as long as they could, despite any future consequences of that decision.

Historically, if Sophia suspected that any one of her chicks was in danger, she would swoop in and take over completely; they had all been recipients of her scathing lectures that usually begin with her calling them Theodore, Angelina, and Abigail. They were afraid that once she knew of the situation, she would spend the next six months figuring out her own way to rescue Jasper and Emma—while their bodies faded away to nothing.

Plus, Newt knew her mother didn't respect or like Jasper Higgs. As a teen, she had endured many lectures about suitable role models for a girl with a future in science; her mother always insisted that such a role model was not a computer game designer, no matter how skilled or inventive he was. Computer games were only for leisure time, and they were not a respectable way to make a living in Sophia's world. It was Mother-Daughter Talk Number Fifteen, and Newt still had it memorized word for word. Tony knew it too, and sometimes—when he really wanted to antagonize her as payback—he would start the lecture and then run away laughing as she chased him. She knew her mother wouldn't waste any time before separating her from Jasper Higgs if she could; Newt was afraid Sophia still had the power and the resources to make that happen if she found out about what they planned to do.

Newt, Tony, and Angela all knew that Sophia would learn what had happened at some point and that then she would undoubtedly be hurt and upset that they had left her out on purpose; however, it seemed the only good option when a quick rescue was necessary. Hopefully, Sophia would understand and forgive in the end. But if—heaven forbid—one of them was killed, she would follow him or her into the afterlife, shaking her finger, crying, and yelling at him or her for all eternity. Sophia could be very scary, and they all knew family came first for her—it always had and always would—and she acted out of love, even if it was tough love.

Newt wore exactly what her mother would have expected to see her wear while she was on vacation: jeans and a crisp white shirt. They were meeting for coffee in the hospital cafeteria where her mother was consulting on a difficult case.

Her mother breezed in wearing a white lab coat and a welcoming, warm smile. "So good to see you, dear. I hope you're enjoying the beach." They kissed each other's cheeks lightly.

Despite Sophia's disarming smile, Newt knew she was taking in every detail and looking for signs of stress or unhappiness in her daughter. "Mom, you're beautiful as ever. The cabin is great. Tony and I are having a good time, so we extended our vacations another two weeks."

Sophia lifted her glasses up and took a close look at Newt's face. "Really? That's unusual for either of you, and you haven't taken that long of a break in years."

Newt thought quickly. "Well, Tony has his truck at the cabin, so he's still working, and I have a lunch meeting today with an important person who might be heading me in a new direction."

Sophia looked skeptical. "That sounds mysterious and exciting, dear. What new direction is that?"

Newt carefully kept her face neutral. "I'm looking at brain-computer interfaces and their applications." She hedged her statement with enough truth thrown in to sound credible. She wondered how her mom would react if she knew her meeting was with a drag queen.

Suddenly there was a loud page for Dr. Newton, STAT, and they stood up together, almost bumping heads—and then they laughed at themselves because it wasn't the first time both Dr. Newtons had done that. Newt hugged her mother and watched her hurry off down the wide hospital corridor to help a sick child. Then she breathed a sigh of relief that their meeting was over and she didn't think her mom suspected anything unusual was happening. Newt was an honest person, and she hated to deceive anyone—especially her mother—but Jasper desperately needed her help, and for the time being, that came first. She would pay the price for her deception later, and she hoped that it wouldn't be dire. Sophia wasn't the only one with a precious child to save and little time to do it in, because Emma's life was at stake too.

Newt drove to the Tacoma waterfront to meet Dee Light at the Harbor Lights restaurant. It was beautiful driving along the edge of Puget Sound; she could see part of green tree-covered Vashon Island and several huge cargo ships slowly moving on the water. As she drove, she pondered what had happened to her regimented life. First, she had found out she was still in love with a man who was currently a projection, and now she was lying to her mom! Where was the constantly working and scientifically grounded Newt? She had sprung from one reality to another in a matter of days, and it made her head spin just to think about it. How could her mother not have noticed such a dramatic shift? Newt felt like a completely different person than the one she had been before she found the globe.

Newt knew Dee Light had actually been born Don Liam Jacobson, and meeting him was another shift in what she was familiar with. No, meeting *her*. Angela had explained that when in drag—or even while transforming—the proper gender pronoun was female. Only when Dee presented as male would it be proper to use the masculine pronoun. Newt didn't want to offend Dee, so she hoped she could get it straight.

Newt knew the moment Dee entered the dining room—all heads turned to look at her. It was impossible not to, because she was the most beautiful woman Newt had ever seen and her glamorous looks attracted the same attention as a movie star's would have. It made Newt feel like a brown sparrow in the presence of a peacock displaying his glorious tail feathers.

Dee was dressed like a 1940s pinup girl. Her pale blond hair was swept up in a complicated bun at the back with the bangs rolled up in front. She wore a tightly fitted coral-colored suit and a pencil skirt with a kick pleat in the back. She wasn't wearing a blouse under the short fitted jacket, so she displayed quite a bit of flawless cleavage. Her full lips were stained a dark coral, and her gorgeous eyes were beautifully highlighted with smoky makeup. Dee's smooth skin was a warm caramel color, and her finger and toenails were painted an exact color match to her suit. Large round pearl earrings, a pearl hair clip, and open-toe high-heel strappy sandals completed her look.

Dee sat gracefully down at the table and examined Newt closely. "Hey, girl, Angela said we're going to be roomies for a few days."

Newt felt star struck, but she replied, "Are you sure you want to take me on? I don't think there's much to work with. I've never worn makeup, most of my clothes are casual, and I get my hair cut at the beauty school." She paused and then added quietly, "You're so beautiful, Dee, it takes my breath away, and I'm not even pretty."

Dee gently took her head. "That's not true. And even if it were it's all the more fun for me, sweetie. You have the beautiful creamy skin of a natural redhead, and just wait until I get a push-up bra on you. It'll be dangerous curves ahead. Hand over your credit card, dollface, we're going to have the time of our lives!"

Later, after six hours of shopping, Newt decided Dee was a drill sergeant in a dress and heels. She had not only selected a drop-dead gorgeous outfit for Newt to meet Greed in, but she had also revamped Newt's entire wardrobe. Up until this point, Newt had ten basic outfits in two categories: casual stuff she threw a lab coat over and professional, dark-toned, serious looks for meetings. She felt that most people only needed one outfit a day and that as long as she could go from one laundry day to the next, she had more than enough clothes. But when she explained that to Dee, she just shook her finger and said with a look of pity, "Honey, we can do better than that. Trust me."

Dee made it quite clear to Newt there was never any excuse for not looking her best at all times; her motto was " it feels good to look good", and people judge on appearance—even if that isn't a fair thing to do. Newt had always divided her wardrobe into comfortable and not so comfortable clothes, but another one of Dee's core beliefs was that good shopping always results in flattering and comfortable clothes. Newt quickly became a believer in Dee's philosophy, and she learned it was all really about careful shopping. Dee never settled for anything less than perfection—no matter how long it took to get there. In the past Newt had frequently bought the first thing that would cover her up because she just wanted to get out of the store and on with her life; but as Dee pointed out, that attitude had resulted in an unflattering hodgepodge of clothes. Eventually

Newt's eyes glazed over as she tried on item after item for Dee until the stores closed for the night. In the end she had little idea of what Dee had finally purchased or how much it had cost—and she didn't care. She was embarrassed that she had never even considered what colors and shapes looked best on her body. But with Dee's help, Newt discovered that jewel tones like emerald, ruby, and sapphire complemented her red hair and pale skin, while white and yellow washed her out. And for the first time in her life she showed some skin on her back, chest, and midriff, and it didn't make her uncomfortable because she knew she looked good.

In the stores Dee was treated like royalty by the staff and customers, and they often asked her for fashion advice. Newt got over being embarrassed when Dee adjusted her breasts and clothes for just the right look. And after shopping for clothes, they bought accessories, fancy underwear, and pretty nightwear, too. Newt had never shopped with a girlfriend before and discovered it was fun to laugh and talk about purchases. They made jokes about the things that didn't work and sighed with pleasure when they did. At 4:00 p.m. precisely, they had high tea with little fancy cakes and sandwiches as a break from shopping. Newt couldn't remember having such a great day or being so tired! She would never look at clothes shopping the same way again.

After the stores closed, Dee had one last trick up her sleeve, so she took Newt to a twenty-four-hour shoe store. Newt tried on her first pair of high heels, but when she took a cautious step, she fell into a tall stack of shoeboxes.

She wailed, "Dee, I can't walk in these things!" Newt only wore flats, rain boots, or athletic shoes. "Let's skip wearing heels, because I'm not going to make much of a glamorous impression when I'm falling down."

Dee said sternly, "Girl, it just takes practice and technique to walk in them. And without heels, no man is going to sit up and beg for you. Heels shape your legs and add strut to your walk and sizzle to the whole look. Angela told me your life may depend on va-va-voom, and you're not getting it without wearing heels—I guarantee it."

"OK," Newt said in a small voice.

Dee gave her a quick hug. "Don't worry, sweetie, put one foot in front of the other, swing your hips, land heel first, and balance on the ball of your foot. Here, I'll walk beside you so you don't fall."

Dee chose ten pairs of shoes, sandals, and fancy boots for Newt. Not all of them were stilettos, but they all had significant heels. Newt was determined to practice walking in them daily. When they finally finished shopping it was 1:00 a.m., and she went to sleep by falling across Dee's guest bed fully clothed and still clutching her shopping bags.

The next day was almost as strange as the day before. It started with a facial and a full-body massage; Newt had never experienced either one before, and at first it was uncomfortable, but then it got better and better until she felt like her bones had melted away. Next she got wavy, color-matched, human hair extensions for her short hair that were just long enough to brush the tops of her breasts. Dee said most men liked long hair and that it could be styled several ways, unlike her former six-inch locks. Dee scheduled a haircut for the extensions later in the day with her own stylist, because he was the only person she trusted to cut them properly.

And then Newt was waxed—ouch—had sassy nail extensions applied, and had a spa pedicure. She didn't understand why Dee wanted to do all of that stuff on a regular basis, but she now understood that it took time, was occasionally painful, involved a lot of work, and was expensive to be glamorous. She was willing to do it for a short time with an important goal in mind, but to keep that up as a long-term lifestyle choice would have been impossible for her. Newt's current morning routine was five minutes, tops: she washed her face, combed her hair, and brushed her teeth, and she was done. She had always envied the fact that men could look good with only a little effort and time expended.

Dee took Newt to the friend she called her "hair genius" for the final cut and style of her hair, which included the added extensions. He added subtle gold highlights and cut it so that it would fall into a sexy, slightly messy shape when she shook her head. The concept of her with sexy hair made Newt want to laugh—but to be polite, she stifled it with a cough.

Dee took her to the dinner theater--where she did drag shows--for makeup lessons. The lighting and tables were perfect for revealing any flaws in makeup application. First Dee took off all her own makeup so she could demonstrate how she did her own face; to Newt's amazement, a slender, attractive young man appeared. First he closely shaved his beard, and then he showed Newt how Dee's beautiful drag look was created. She concealed her natural eyebrows by covering them with white school glue that dried clear. Then she covered the dry glue with foundation and painted on new eyebrows higher up on her forehead. She contoured and highlighted her cheekbones, nose, chin, and forehead, skillfully shading to sculpt her face into a more feminine form. Dee added extensive eye makeup using multiple colors, shading, liners, and artificial lashes. She did one eye and left the other natural so Newt could compare them. In the end Newt understood why most women used makeup, because what a difference it could make to a person's appearance!

Newt decided now she was wearing eye cosmetics, she would use her contacts regularly--ditching her thick glasses most of the day--so her eyes could be seen clearly. After a lengthy discussion and trying out various products, Dee designed two looks for Newt: one for daytime wear and one for nighttime glam. It took Newt hours to master the makeup application process, but when she was done, she took a good look at the final product and was totally shocked. A screaming-hot babe looked back at her from the mirror! She blinked her eyes and fluffed her hair, and then she smiled. Greed was going to trip over his tongue—she really could do her part in the rescue plan now!

The last part of the makeover was the hardest part for Newt; she had to learn to project sex appeal, because in the end it was all about that. The walk, the talk, the voice, the body language, and the silhouette all had to say "come and gets it, boys—if you can." Surprisingly to Newt, it didn't seem to matter if the hips were shaped with foam rubber and the breasts were a latex sculpture as they were in Dee's case, because if it looked sexy, then apparently men would flock to you. Dee could demonstrate that anywhere and anytime; when she turned it on, people noticed her. Mostly men were attracted—even though drag queens weren't necessarily gay—but women too reacted with interest to Dee's hyperfeminine persona. They wanted her opinion on clothes, asked questions about makeup, and wanted to stare at her just like the men did. Newt tried and tried to be alluring like Dee, but even though she looked the part, she was embarrassed to be noticed and felt silly flirting.

Finally, Dee decided to give Newt a drag name because, according to Dee, one of the great things about doing drag was that it freed the suppressed parts of people's personalities. Drag queens could openly express what was often hidden away by less outgoing personalities; the reserved people became fierce, the shy became extroverted, and the quiet people spoke up. A drag name usually went with the larger-than-life looks and personality of queens. Often the drag name was a play on words or used a part of their given names. Dee knew queens named Ginga Snap, Barbi Wire, and Frada Cat. She played around with drag names for Newt using Abigail as a springboard for the name; she considered Abby Sin and Stormy Gail, but she eventually settled on Absinthe after the pricy licorice-flavored liqueur.

As Absinthe, Newt suddenly felt free to express her sexuality; she moved slower with more sway and purpose in her movements, her voice became a little deeper, and she smiled more. She consciously scaled her big vocabulary down, stopped

talking in complete sentences, and tried to project her femininity instead. Hand and eye movements became a bigger part of
her communication than words were; every small body movement was calculated to draw attention to her—especially from
men. Newt mentally visualized making them want to take a sip
of her Absinthe because it was so desirable and delicious.

It surprised—and saddened—her just how easy it was to
deliberately influence people. Appearance counted for a lot
more than she had thought it did. Some men were attracted
enough to Dee and Absinthe that they approached them after
only a five-second stare at them and a slow smile from Absinthe.
She knew at least some of them must have been married, and
the old Newt wanted to surface and give them a stern lecture on
fidelity. But with a little practice—and Dee's help—she learned
to switch Absinthe on and off at will.

The final test was a trip out to dinner together, but that time
in the restaurant she attracted as many admiring stares as Dee
did. Newt suspected Dee had played herself down to make that
happen, but she didn't care because it was an amazing feeling to
know she was pretty and desirable. And the best part was that
she could go back to being Abigail whenever she wanted; but
she wasn't sure if she would ever be just plain Newt again after
feeling the heady power from channeling sexy Absinthe.

She said good-bye to Dee with tears in her eyes, but it wasn't
farewell, because Abigail knew she had found a true friend. She
was grateful for all she learned about being a woman in such a
short time.

She sneaked back into the cabin and prepared to make a
dramatic entrance while everyone was sitting around the table
eating dinner. For her reveal, she wore a bright blue halter top
sundress that left a lot of her back bare, wedge-heel sandals,
hoop earrings, and a wide gold belt to accent her small waist.

Her dramatic new appearance caused a few seconds of
stunned silence that was followed by stamping, clapping, and
whistling. She flirted with everyone—including Tony—but had

eyes mostly for Jasper. He gave her smoldering looks, and she wanted to sit in his lap and give him the best kiss of his life, but she knew she would sink right through his projection. So she placed his hands on her hips and wiggled a little side to side while looking at him through her lashes with her head cocked. In reaction both he and Tony groaned, one from desire and the other from knowing just how complicated life had gotten for a protective big brother.

Twenty - Two

Jasper walked with purpose up the path to the cabin with Emma in his arms—or at least he thought he did, because it was hard to tell if he was actually walking when the sand under his feet didn't move and there was no sound of footsteps. Abigail was sweeping off the porch, but as soon as she saw him, she met them partway down the path and kissed him and Emma with delight.

The awkward stiffness Jasper always felt around women suddenly took hold of him. "You look beautiful." So beautiful, he thought, that she was totally out of his league; he was crazy to have believed she would ever fall permanently for a nerd like him.

Abigail felt his reserve instantly, and she remembered how he was raised to respect and to keep a distance between himself and women. It was ridiculous that when she looked like one of the guys, he relaxed around her, but now that she was clearly the opposite sex, he felt she was off limits as a pal to him. How stupid was that!

"I'm the same person, Jasper. Dee just added fake hair, fake nails, face paint, and new clothes. But under all that I'm still me, and I feel the same way I always did, especially about you."

He considered that a moment and then shook his head back and forth. "I don't think so. You're different deeper than that, too, somehow. You've changed inside, and I noticed it right away at dinner."

She knew it was true, and she had recognized it when she had looked into her own eyes in the mirror; amazingly, Jasper had picked up on it almost before she had realized it herself. She believed that when Dee had forced her to tap into parts of herself that were more feminine, and it had caused her to change somehow. Looking back, Newt saw that she had been so involved in school and then in running her laboratory that it must have delayed her emotional development. And the few days she had spent with Dee had suddenly blasted away tomboy Newt and had replaced her with a grown-up Abigail. Until then, her focus had been outward on doing things, and not inward on how she felt emotionally or on how she expressed herself as a woman. To be honest, she thought she had consciously rejected expressing her sexuality. Maybe because the scientific community was dominated by men and she wanted to be treated as an equal, thus she had down played her gender to the point that it almost hadn't existed anymore.

Now she felt more mature but awkward in her own skin, especially around Jasper. She was trying to cope with the internal shift herself and had no idea how to help him adjust, too. So after several false starts trying to explain the new awareness of her femininity to him, she gave up.

"Well, my transformation isn't as extreme as you becoming a projection of yourself, Jasper. And some people—like my mother—would say this change was long overdue. Believe me, I'm fundamentally the same person I was, and we'll work through this together. Besides, as soon as we have Greed in the bag, then I'm getting these annoying hair extensions and long nails off, I promise." Then she wheedled him. "Can I hold Emma, please?"

Jasper relaxed a little because she at least hadn't changed her mind about Emma, so he might still have a shot with her. "Tony said Dee told him not to call you Newt anymore. Is that true?"

They sat down on the porch swing together so Abigail could rock Emma. "Newt is a nickname that goes with a tomboy image, don't you think? And Dee wants me to be womanlier, at least until this is over, because I have to appear attractive to Greed so we can spring the trap. She thinks a name change will help me do that. It's like actors who stay in their parts even when the camera isn't rolling, and I need to do everything I can to make your rescue a success." She kissed Emma's forehead and asked him, "Is switching to calling me Abigail too much for you to cope with right now?"

He avoided eye contact with her. "It sounds too formal. Like I just met somebody new. It makes me feel weird around you, and I miss the Newt I knew. Because then I was comfortable talking to you, and now I'm not so sure what to say."

She knew exactly what he was feeling, because she got the same sensation when she looked at herself in the mirror. "OK, I get that, but has it occurred to you I might feel the same when I meet the real Jasper reunited with his body? Then I might be overwhelmed by you as a physical man because I was accustomed to talking to your projection. We'll both have to adjust to new images of each other."

He smiled about that hopeful eventuality and moved his eyebrows up and down. "Me in my physical body meeting you looking like this? Wow! It'll be worth any adjustment we both have to make in the meantime."

She grinned. "OK, here's something else to process: my drag name is Absinthe."

"What?"

She laughed. "Dee gave me a drag name and a sexy persona to go with it, and she's called Absinthe. Just wait till you see me really turn it on as her." She gave him a flirty look through her lashes. "It's strange how dressing the part and a new name can transform you into a different person. I can't explain why looking hot frees your inner sexy somehow. Maybe Dee could put you in drag—then you'd see for yourself!"

"Not in a million years, Abby!" He was astonished and horrified at her suggestion.

She pointed a finger at him. "Ah, calling me Abby feels comfortable for you. I'm fine with that too, and it's a good middle-ground name." She sent him a sexy smile. "But I'm telling you, Absinthe has some great lingerie. You don't want to miss out on that!"

He suddenly looked very interested. "Really? I can't wait until this is over and you can model it for me as Abby or Absinthe—I won't care."

They both had similar speculative glints about the future in their eyes when Angela approached the porch and asked to see Jasper in private. Abby reluctantly returned Emma to him, and then she picked up the broom and started sweeping again. As they walked away, Jasper turned around to wave at her, and she blew him a dramatic kiss—like a drag queen would have—and he smiled back at her. Abby thought he would grow to love Absinthe, given time.

When Angela walked up to the cabin's porch, she'd deliberately ignored Emma—as she always did—because she knew exactly why she'd been sucked in to this crazy mess to begin with and why she was staying. It was because of Emma. Emma was the glue holding everything in their situation together; she was like a tiny sun, and all the adults revolved around her. Angela loved kids and hoped someday she would be a mother, but the war had taken that, along with her other plans for the future, so she snubbed kids in self-defense. Jasper might have been a good guy—and at least her cousins thought he was worth saving—but Emma had to be saved. There was no question about that in anyone's mind.

Angela had originally traveled to Ocean Shores to scope out the situation because it had sounded crazy; she'd wanted to make sure her cousins weren't being sucked in to a scam or something worse. Then she had taken one look at the baby and had fallen hard for her. Since then she'd never looked directly at Emma again and had stayed as far away from her as possible, because she knew she was an unstable, crazy person who was not qualified to hold a precious, innocent baby—or probably to even look at one. What she had inside her mind was a dark fog of negativity, and maybe she was being too cautious, but better safe than sorry when a baby was at stake.

At the cabin she tried to cope by numbing her mind with constant white noise playing loudly into her ear buds and concentrating on the rescue plan, but that was getting harder and harder to do. And her only hope was that she could hold it together long enough for the rescue and then never leave her woods again.

She'd been known as a fearless solider and leader, but the new communication system frightened her. Yeah, it sounded great and might make the difference between success and failure on the rescue mission; but her mind was filled with horror, and she didn't want to share that with anyone in a brain-to-brain way. At first she had hoped she could somehow bury her negative thoughts, because Jasper had said only dominant thoughts would be projected and that if thoughts weren't dominant, no one would hear them; but talk around the dinner table had convinced her that it wouldn't be possible. So she knew that her thoughts would leak through the communication chip—no matter what she did to control them—and that her memories would affect everyone's ability to function on the mission and contaminate their minds with her horrible memories.

After walking a bit with Jasper on the beach in silence, she suddenly said, "I don't want to wear the communication device during the op."

Jasper suspected the reason, but he quietly replied, "OK, but you're the leader, and if we can't use the device, then we need to come up with a different plan for communication." He looked at her with kind eyes as seconds passed, and then he asked, "What's really up, Angela?"

Angela squirmed inside, but she knew he was her only way out of wearing the device and spilling her guts to everyone. So maybe if he understood why she was asking, he could fix it.

"I got into some bad situations in the military, and I don't want to share them with the team."

"Angela, I don't think that'll be a problem. The communication device picks up only strongly projected surface thoughts and not deeper past memories. You'll be safe wearing it." Jasper waited patiently for her response. He understood that she rarely revealed anything about her inner self.

She walked away from him, fought with herself mentally, and came back. "You don't understand! Those memories are the most real thoughts I have. I can't bury them deep or get rid of them permanently, so you'll all be having them too, over and over. What's the point of rescuing you but filling the team's brains with crap like my thoughts?"

"I've read a little about PTSD, Angela. Have you thought about therapy? They're working on some new techniques because many people who have experienced trauma have trouble getting it out of their minds. It isn't just an issue with the military."

"Look, just get me out of this brain share thing, because I'm not doing it, Jasper!" Angela was retreating to her fallback emotion of anger.

"It's a repeating loop of bad stuff, right?" Jasper remained patient and understanding even though the full energy of her formidable anger was directed at him. His projected self could almost feel it physically spark against his body's image.

"That is the biggest understatement in the world!" She had been stupid for even thinking he would understand the situation, because no one who hadn't been there ever would.

He'd hoped he wouldn't have to use this option, but he could see there wasn't a choice. "I've been thinking about your PTSD,

Angela. I suspected you might feel like this, so I had Tony make a special chip for you when he was at my house."

Jasper had struggled with the idea of making a chip for that purpose, because it came too close to the original chip he had in his pocket, which projected thoughts as images. But for him to change her thoughts, he needed a digital image of them he could work with on a computer screen. He'd vowed to himself never to use that type of code again, but it was the only way he could think of to do it without risking a brain-to-brain connection—and he wasn't sure his projection could do that anyway.

He explained. "The chip would project your dominant memories like a series of flowing images onto my computer, and then I could tone them down by overlaying them with something peaceful but stronger and fresher. I don't think I could completely delete them, but I should be able to make them a distant memory rather than dominant in your brain, and I think that might help you. And it would only take a few hours to do. But you'd have to trust me to modify the right ones, Angela." He tried to sound positive, but he wasn't sure it would work very well, because playing with somebody's brain was scary and unpredictable.

She laughed cynically. "Don't worry, Jasper, you'll know the ones to fix because they're going to show up on the screen in bold black dripping with blood. But are you sure you want to do this?" She didn't want even one person to experience her traumatic thoughts if it could be avoided.

"Angela, you're important! I know you're risking your life to help me and Emma, but that isn't the only reason why I want to do it. You're a hero who has given almost everything in service to the rest of us. You deserve a happy life free from tormenting thoughts you can't change. So let's try to make your bad thoughts a faded past memory." He took her hands in both of his, and suddenly he felt like she was the sister he had missed in his life.

Angela was overwhelmed by his offer. She hadn't believed that a door would ever open to save her from her punishing mind forever. What would it be like to be happy? To live a normal life, to help other people, and maybe even to have a baby of her own someday? It had seemed impossible before, but she was going to grab onto the chance that Jasper had given her with all she had.

She wished she could give him a hug, and she said gratefully, "Let's do it, and let's do it now! Thanks, Jasper, for even trying to do this. You might be my lifesaver, and I mean that!" She air-kissed him on both cheeks and did a happy dance in the sand.

Soon Angela relaxed on her bed in the motor home while Jasper hooked up the chip. It was a comparatively crude system compared to the one projecting him and Emma, but her thoughts flowed on the computer screen without a hitch. It only took an hour because the terrible memories were repetitive and prominent. But once he softened them by overriding them with woodland images and the sounds of nature, he was amazed at the complexity and sweetness of the thoughts they had hidden.

Afterward, Angela sat on the beach by herself, adjusting to the dramatic change in her mind's thought patterns. She was stunned and grateful for what Jasper had done to give her inner peace. Her overall feeling of despair was gone, and she could see the brightness of life all around her, but it was a little overwhelming because her senses had been suppressed for so long by her pain. Her war experiences seemed like a bad movie she'd watched, and she felt like the movie had finished and she'd walked out of the darkened theater and into the daylight, squinting in the bright sun, very glad the movie was over so she could put it behind her and get on with her life.

Twenty - Three

Everyone sat around the camp table enjoying a fresh straw-berry shortcake Half-man had made from ripe berries grown locally. Angela was late to join the group, and when they saw her smiling face, questioning looks—and a few raised eye-brows—were exchanged, but no one said anything about the dramatic change to her normally dour expression.

Jasper stood and called for attention. "This afternoon I used a special chip I made to suppress some of Angela's negative combat memories. I'm going to burn the chip and destroy it, but before I do I want to offer the same process to anyone else here who wants it. You only have to look at her to see how much bet-ter she feels."

Angela also stood up. "I'm not newly prettied up on the out-side like Abby. Instead, it was an inner beauty makeover for me. I feel much better now that my memories are staying in the past and can't hurt me in the present anymore. I'm grateful to Jasper for helping me." She made eye contact with each of her men individually. "It's not weak to ask for help, you know, and I'll make a more focused team leader now." She sent a sultry glance to Hook, who looked like he'd been hit with a poleax because of her amazing transformation; she practically glowed from the inside out.

Jasper then passed out a communication device to each team member. He demonstrated the on-and-off sensor at the end of the housing, and he pointed out the two active areas. One area collected incoming thoughts projected by other devices and then made them audible in the wearer's ear; the other area collected the wearer's thoughts and projected them to the other team members' devices.

Jasper individually checked that each person's device was fitted correctly, so it was almost invisible, placed deep into the ear canal, with plenty of contact to the surrounding bone. "I'm going to turn most of this demonstration over to Tony, as the devices won't receive my thoughts because they're already projected to the original chip I carry. That means Abby and I will be the only ones out of the communication loop while we're on the mission."

With a serious tone, he added, "I've included a timer, which I'll set once we start the rescue. It self-destructs the device five hours after the first communication is sent. I did that because I don't want the technology to fall into the wrong hands, as then Greed will have some of the information he wants even if I'm rescued. I'll also give you a code word that can be thought or spoken to instantly destroy the device you're wearing and can also be projected to destruct all other devices, too. It won't affect the soft housing, only the electronics, so your ears and hearing will be safe even if it destructs."

Tony stood up and said, "OK. Let's play, boys and girls! There's a ten-hour battery life on one charge, so we can have lots of fun before they need to be docked again. The device is activated when you consciously send a message to someone. Every message must start with a short name to direct it to that recipient. If you want to send it to everyone, then think, 'All.' The name-directing feature can be overridden in case of emergency, so thinking, 'The house is on fire!' would send that to everyone automatically. To send a thought, you must push it out with some emotional force. Keep your messages simple and direct.

If you see a hot girl and you project it intensely, that thought, along with details you might like to keep to yourself, will go out to everyone. It's going to be worse than having a kid sister spy on you and your girlfriend and then tell Mom about it!" He grinned at Abby, who stuck her tongue out at him in response.

Tony laughed and continued. "The kinds of messages we want are like this: 'Ange, have arrived at harbor entrance,' or 'All, one guard passed going north in main hallway.' Things like that. The names of the team members need to be kept short, like Hawk instead of Hawkeye. Any questions? No? OK, break into pairs, and communicate with each other. Let's keep it as clean as we can, people."

At first it was serious practice, and then it deteriorated into fun. They figured out that there was a hole in the system—the sender of the message was anonymous. That meant that insults, ribald comments, speculation, and crazy observations could be sent without retaliation. So as long as the sender maintained a straight face, no one knew who the thought had come from, because every thought projected into the wearer's ear sounded the same.

All, why does Tony need a double bed in his truck? Is it to show the girls his hard drive? Tony carefully examined faces to see who had sent that thought, but he laughed with everyone else when the answer came back: *All, no. It's to give them a place to sleep after he's bored them with his techno-talk.*

Hook wasn't as amused when a moment later the thought was about him. *All, Hook has an umbrella attachment for his arm stump so he can fly around like Mary Poppins does.* Angela was the only one to guffaw, and everybody else quickly suppressed snickers as Hook glared around at their faces.

Angela ended their teasing with a scavenger hunt that used clues delivered by thought communication only. Everyone started from different locations, and she sent out directions via the device. It was good practice for her to keep track of where everyone was located without seeing them directly. In her mind, the task was like a chess game; each man had moves to make from his starting place on the board. She just had to keep track of where they were at any given time, and where she wanted to move them to. After a few mix-ups, she got the hang of it, and there was a mad stampede to the finish with their collected items. The prize was total control of pizza toppings for the next night's dinner, and no one wanted Melt to add anchovies.

After dark, Tony decided they should go to the practice grounds and run a simulated mission using thought communication only. The practice grounds were a complex maze—cleverly built by Melt and Stubby—on a part of the Newton's property composed of a half-mile square of rocky outcroppings, sand dunes, and cliffs. They had been enhanced with added difficulty by driftwood, brown tarps, and shallow foxholes. In an adjoining area, the men created a full-size model of the ground floor of Greed's fortress using PVC pipes, wood, cable ties, and tarps. It had a main hallway, doors made from tarps, and a simulated stairway down to the harbor entrance. The helipad, Greed's office, his guest suites, the grand room, the staff quarters, and the guards' living space were all crudely represented. Everyone had practiced in the day light, but after dark it seemed impossible to negotiate through until Tony handed out the night-vision goggles they would use on the actual mission.

Angela divided them into two teams of three people each. Each group would work together to get from one side of the fortress to the other, with Jasper, Abby, and Tony acting as Greed's guards out of the communication loop. The team that finished the course without detection would win a second helping of shortcake for their group.

Tony knew they could act as a team when staying together but that that wouldn't require thought communication, so he started each member of the group at a different point on the practice grounds. Then they needed to locate their team members, keep track of them, plan an assault, move through the fortress, keep the location of each of the opposite team's members clear, and watch out for the enemy all at the same time. In addition, each person would be moving all of the time, so it would take good knowledge of the terrain, three-dimensional visualization, and superior communication to make it work successfully. They learned that if you goofed around or sent long messages, it would throw your team members off their game. So it was obvious to everyone that short messages containing only the basic facts worked the best. And conversations, descriptions or explanations were just confusing.

After three hours of intense practice, Melt was the only one who had made it across the course without being tagged by the guards in the fortress. But even though there was only one winner, every single person learned to use the communication system well, and each appreciated how it tilted the odds of the mission's success in their favor. Angela declared the device was as good as any weapon for protecting the team members from harm. Melt divided his winnings evenly, so everybody had a small second helping of strawberry shortcake, and Stubby pointed out that telepathy was a great superhero power to have.

The next day Tony introduced the Zap to the team. Abby personally thought the weapon looked like a compact hair dryer, but she didn't say it out loud. Tony had made all the adjustments that he could to lengthen its range, but the Zap still didn't have much accuracy past twenty feet, even with the laser guide. If the guide was turned off, a bigger area could be zapped—both farther away and wider—but it was like discharging a lightning bolt. It just sprayed undirected electricity ahead of it for about one hundred yards, and it couldn't be aimed.

Tony had modified workmen's vests for everyone. The vests contained sensors that registered the number and force of hits from the Zap. He explained that the trigger could be pressed for up to five seconds, and then it stopped firing unless the trigger was pressed again. The time limit was a fail-safe to prevent freezing on the trigger and delivering too large an electrical dose, which could potentially kill someone. The vests covered the wearer's torso, but if the wearer was hit anywhere else, he or she would be disabled by the Zap's electrical shock.

Hawkeye had previously evaluated each person's skill on the shooting range and had decided to use just the laser sight without activating the Zap's power for Abby and Tony; then they wouldn't hurt someone if they missed targeting a vest. Both of them had been practicing, but they still weren't as good as the ex-military team members.

The others decided to practice with fully active Zaps, but they agreed that they wouldn't shoot unless the laser guide showed a clear shot to the vest. Abby wondered how anyone would enjoy the chance to take a disabling electrical hit, but she guessed their attitudes were why they had chosen to enlist in the military to begin with. She could see they obviously relished shooting at things.

Practice with the communication device and the Zap continued for many days. And everyone had a lot of fun despite knowing soon it would be serious business involving bullets aimed at them by people hoping to inflict pain and death.

Tony showed them that before they headed to the island, the vests' practice sensors would be removed and replaced with protective Kevlar sheets. Each vest had multiple pockets to hold the Zap and other essential mission items; Abby wondered if there would also be a spot for hope, prayer, and fairy dust, too.

Twenty - Four

At lunch Angela revealed that her master plan for Jasper's rescue was two pronged; there would be an ocean assault by scuba divers and a simultaneous attack by people scaling the cliff face. Tony didn't have any experience rock climbing, so she assigned him to the scuba team, where she thought there were fewer risks for a newbie.

The idea scared him. He didn't have any experience diving deep below the water's surface, where he knew only an oxygen tank would stand between him and death by drowning. And although he loved the ocean as a dear friend, he purposefully only went as deep as one lungful of air would allow. He liked to fish, drop crab pots, and boat; he relished surfing the waves, jet skiing, paddle boarding, waterskiing, parasailing, and just about everything else done on top of water. He swam like a fish, but he had always hated the idea of sinking deep under the water's surface and depending on canned air to survive. He also knew the Pacific Ocean off the Washington coast was cold, murky, and filled with some scary things like giant Pacific octopi and orca whales—also known as killer whales for a reason, he thought.

Tony met Hook at the local dive shop and tried to convince him that scuba diving off Ocean Shores was a bad idea. But Hook was as immovable as Mount Rainer, because in Hook's world what Angela wanted, Angela got. She wanted Tony on the dive team, so that was where he was going to be and they were practicing today. Tony had worn a wetsuit before—any activity involving getting completely wet in the ocean in the Northwest required one, as fatal hypothermia could occur in minutes, even in the summer.

Hook had already selected all of the equipment they would need, and he pointed to the pile directing Tony to get ready. The rubberlike wetsuit Tony squeezed into covered most of his body, including his head and hands. It was called a wetsuit because it allowed a small amount of water to leak inside of it. Tony remembered that the initial sensation of leaking cold ocean water against skin was unpleasant. But once the water pressure inside the suit equalized with the ocean, the body heat warmed up the water inside, and the temperature felt OK after that—not nice and warm, but not critically cold either.

Tony discovered that Hook was a focused machine who never seemed to tire or lose his cool. He had adjusted amazingly well to losing an arm, and he had a number of nifty tools that snapped onto his stump in place of his usual hook. He even had a battery-powered propeller to speed him through the water— Tony thought that maybe he did have an umbrella like Mary Poppins!

Tony also realized that Hook had a serious thing for Angela; it was a combination of hero worship, total devotion, and feelings maybe deep enough to last forever. Hook seemed oblivious to the fact that he frequently referred to things Angela said like he was quoting from the Bible; it was clear to Tony that Hook would sacrifice himself to save her if she were in danger. Tony thought Hook loved her, but Hook was careful not to use that word. And Tony certainly appreciated how scary loving someone like Angela would be—and using the L word induced fear in most guys anyway!

Tony learned that Hook's real name was Mark Stevens and that he had been born into a multigenerational military family.

All the males in his pedigree—back to the Spanish-American War—had served their country in the armed forces and were heroes to the rest of the family. So Hook hadn't had any choice about what he would grow up to do, and during his childhood, the softness had been drilled out of him by the constant pressure to be a man. Even when he was a toddler first learning to walk, falling down was fine, but he wasn't supposed to cry about it—"be a man, son!" Every gentle emotion had been carefully eliminated while anger and aggression encouraged. Hook had been systematically groomed to be a soldier and nothing else.

Hook's family was proud that he had been wounded in combat, but they never saw past his service record to the good man that he was. Sadly he believed they would have been even prouder of him if he had died in action, because they seemed to lose all interest in him once he couldn't serve and make the military his career. To Hook, their love was all about the image, and not about the person he was. After he was wounded and honorably discharged, his family's main interest shifted to his brothers' military lives. When he visited they seemed remote and he felt his physical handicap embarrassed them, so he went home only about once a year.

Tony listened closely, as he suspected it was rare for Hook to share his history. Clearly Hook had walled himself off from his feelings for years—probably first as a childhood survival tactic and then from force of habit. He recognized that Hook believed he wasn't worthy of love—especially Angela's—and that his injury made him less than a whole man somehow.

Tony saw that the opposite was true, because Hook could have passed for a comic book hero. He had a large muscular body topped by a handsome craggy face, and he radiated power and energy. Hook clearly had goodness, honor and a strong moral compass; leadership sat on his wide shoulders, and dignity and compassion shone from his eyes. He might have considered himself damaged goods, but Tony had never met anyone who projected all the best a human could be like Hook did, all without seeming to be aware of it.

So as Hook checked the scuba equipment, Tony tried to reason with him. "Look, man, you're awesome, but have you ever dived around here? Not that many people recommend it for a reason, dude. The visibility sucks."

Hook replied firmly, "I've dived in every ocean on the planet, and this is the one we have available for practicing in today. I won't let anything happen to you, so don't worry."

Tony chewed on his thumbnail. "How deep are we going?"

"Deep enough."

"Man! Can't you be a little more specific?"

Hook placed his hand on Tony's shoulder. "What does it matter, Tony? You can stay home and not go on the rescue if you want. But if you want to come and not be in the way, then Angela said you'll need practice today. On the real dive, people with guns will be trying to shoot you. That's why you need to have some experience in deep water—so you don't get hurt." He made intense eye contact with Tony. "So, my man, are you in or out?"

Tony shuddered as he thought about what he was committing to. "When you put it that way, I guess I don't have a choice, dude. OK, then, let's swim to win."

Hook carefully explained all the gear and how to use it, going over everything slowly twice so it was clear. Tony had snorkeled in shallow water in Hawaii, but he had never used an oxygen tank and a regulator, so Hook promised they would take it slowly to begin with. Hook explained that it was important to learn to dive deeply because the clarity of the water around Greed's island would expose them as they approached the harbor entrance if they were in shallow water. He added as an afterthought that the Caribbean Ocean was warm, so there would be sharks to deal with too—yeah.

Surprisingly, Hook believed that the reduced visibility of the Northwest's coastal waters would help hone Tony's senses to sharp awareness; without vision to depend on, the variations in water movements, surrounding temperature, suspended particle density, and other things could register more clearly. He said that some people have claimed that they have fishlike abilities to sense electrical fields and sound waves in murky water. Hook promised Tony that he would stay close to him at all times and that if he freaked out, they would surface together immediately.

They entered the ocean off the dock near the dive shop; as Hook lowered himself into the water, Tony's fear amplified the slapping sound of the gray waves against the dock's pilings. His one coherent thought was that he so didn't want to do this! Once in the cold water, they stayed near the surface awhile, clearing their masks and acclimatizing to the temperature. Then Hook signaled by pointing down into the water, and they descended slowly. At first Tony hated it. All he could hear was the rasp of his own breathing—which was fast because he was slightly panicked—and the air bubbling out of his respirator. He couldn't see more than a couple of feet in front of his eyes, so it felt like he was trapped in a cave; the claustrophobic feeling was awful, and he started to panic. Suddenly, Hook tapped his shoulder and pointed down. Tony could then see the rocky ocean floor and a moray eel sticking its alien-looking head out of a small cave. Once Tony could orient himself by looking at the sea bottom, he began to calm down and breathe more regularly.

Tony discovered it was peaceful and quiet under the water—it was so different than on the noisy surface. Small pushes with his flippers glided him along, and he began to understand what Hook meant about developing his other senses. With his sight, hearing, touch, and smell blunted, he reached out with something else: an awareness of his surroundings not dependent on what he was used to sensing. It made Tony feel totally cool and like he was part of the water itself. All he needed was a cute girl in a small bikini swimming next to him, and he would actually be happy, he thought.

Tony found he liked the neutrally buoyant floating feeling the weights around his waist gave him, because it felt almost like he was flying over the ocean's floor as he swam along a few feet above it. He grabbed onto Hook's leg for an effortless ride, as Hook used his arm's propeller attachment to speed them along. Tony even began to have fun. What had initially seemed like a lifeless, alien planet began to unfold its beauty right before his eyes. He saw colored starfish, sea anemones, and sea cucumbers, and small schools of silver fish swam away, avoiding them.

The allotted two hours went by in a flash, and Tony couldn't wait to dive again. Hook smiled at his enthusiasm and said the next time they would carry the approximate equipment load and cover about the same distance they would swim for the rescue.

Angela greeted them warmly when they returned to the cabin; seeing her big welcome smile, Hook practically choked on the water he was swigging. She them sashayed up to Hook, grabbed his hand, and dragged him off toward the beach. Tony watched her tow him away hand in hand with a smile on his face and envy for them in his heart.

Once they were alone, Angela asked Hook directly, "So I have a question. Do you want to have sex?"

Hook froze and sputtered, "Why are you asking this now?"

She replied firmly, "I've wasted a lot of time sunk in PTSD, and I want a new life from now on. Maybe I'm wrong, but I thought you might be interested in me, so I'm asking you if you are or not."

He sighed deeply. "I'm interested, but I can't do it cold like this. I do want you, but I want more than a quick turn in the sheets, Angela."

She was astonished. "Like what? Romance and stuff?" She curled her upper lip.

Hook sighed again. "Yes, romance and stuff. Sex with the mental parts of us involved too. Kissing, hugging, talking, bonding, all that." As he spoke he moved closer to her and removed the clip that held her soft, glossy hair up in a tight knot; it cascaded down her back in a black satin fall. He threaded his hands through it, pulled her up on her toes, and then curled them under with a deep, tender, electrifyingly long kiss. Then he looked in her dazed eyes and said, "You'll find it's a lot more fun and satisfying that way."

Angela cleared her throat. "You may be right, so let's go to my motor home and find out."

Hook was rocked by the kiss too, but he spoke firmly. "It's not every day a man gets that kind of an invitation from a beautiful woman, but I'm not cutting to the chase and making it just about sex, Angela. I've waited for this, and I'm going to do it right, even if it kills me."

She was stunned by his rejection, but she licked her lips slowly to entice him. "Suit yourself, cowboy. My door is open. Come anytime." She swayed her hips as she walked away, and then she flipped her hair back and blew him a kiss over her shoulder when he stood there clearly not following her lead.

Thus began the courting of Angela. Hook sent her flowers and bought a few pretty things for her motor home. He wrote her fanciful poetry, delivered jewelry trinkets, and complimented her openly and often in public. The whole team got into the spirit by deliberately leaving them alone together and speculating on when he would crack and take her to bed. Hook established a personal rule for himself: he would never enter Angela's motor home when she was home alone, because he knew he would cave and ravish her once he was inside with the door shut behind him.

In retaliation for that rule, Angela made a point of answering her door after dark wearing minimal clothing. Once it was just an oversized T-shirt with nothing underneath, and the next time her shirt was unbuttoned and open to her waist. It almost became a game for both of them, and it slowly inched up the sexual tension. But after three days of teasing him she suddenly gave in and surrendered to the process by accepting the pace he set. She gave up trying to control the "where" and "when" of their relationship and started to think about her true feelings and where her life was headed after the rescue was over.

On the fourth night Angela met him at her motor home door simply wearing her normal worn-thin pajamas. Hook was empty-handed—he hadn't brought her a gift for the first time since their battle of wills had started.

Angela looked at him and calmly stated, "I love you, Hook, and I have for a while. I just didn't realize that's what it was."

He stepped into the motor home, swept her up in his arms, and finally took her to bed.

Twenty - Five

Angela and Hook were still in bed at noon the next day, enjoying a brunch of cinnamon-raisin toasted bagels. They were trying to discuss the rescue plan without being distracted by each other again, but Angela's mind kept wandering to what had happened between them. For Angela, sex with Hook was as different from her previous experiences as night was to day, because copulation had always been hormone driven for her. Mostly she ignored the itch, but sometimes when she couldn't stand it anymore, she would find a willing male and have an impersonal quick release. She was always careful and discrete about it, and she'd never lacked for a suitable partner in the predominantly male military organization. She would explain in advance that she wanted no emotional involvement, so afterward they would go on with their separate lives. She never chose the same partner twice and always selected from outside of her unit. Angela had always hated how superficial and animalistic the sexual act was, and that was why she rarely gave into her urges to mate with a man.

In dramatic contrast to her previous experiences, sex with Hook was a slow, serious, focused, intense business. He insisted on her total involvement in the moment and her full commitment to their intimacy together. He asked questions about how she was feeling and what she liked, and he volunteered information about what he was feeling, too. It made her squirm in embarrassment despite the circumstances; showing him her naked body was so much easier than unclothing her emotions and feelings for him.

At first, Angela just mumbled or made noncommittal sounds in answer to his questions, but he was persistent and sneaky about touching, stroking, and asking until he found out what he wanted to know. Then he played variations on that theme until she wanted to scream out "stop" or maybe "don't stop"—it wasn't clear in her mind at that moment. He moved slow then fast and traveled her whole body until she was at the breaking point again and again, awash with glorious sensations. Lovemaking with Hook was almost an out-of-body experience for her; it felt like her mind floated above the bed on a cushion of pleasure while he was in charge below, making magic happen.

Not that he was unaffected, she thought; he even growled at her low in his throat and gently used his teeth. It was moist, sticky, engorged sex, where every part of him connected with every part of her. It was so far removed from her past almost-clinical experiences with men that Angela had no choice but to give herself completely—body and mind—during their joining, and she knew Hook had given himself the same way to her. So now the question in her mind was, how were they going to deal with it?

Angela marveled that she felt sensitized to his maleness after their intense experiences together; it was almost as if a magnetic field of attraction was still connecting them together. She was aware of his bare skin, his woodsy scent, his eyes on her, and the rustle of the sheets as he moved to pick up his coffee cup. She sighed because she knew her life had changed forever last night, and she hoped they were both ready for it.

Hook broke into her thoughts. "The weak links are still Tony and Abby. Do you think they'll be ready to fight when the time comes?"

"Yeah, Tony isn't the total geek he likes to pretend he is, and we'll need tech support once we get there anyway. But with Tony, there might be something unexpected because he just thinks differently than other people. He lives in his own universe sometimes."

Hook nodded in agreement because he had experienced that while scuba diving with him. "What about Abby, then? Is she ready?"

"She seems like a soft girl, Hook, but remember that she's very smart and motivated. You don't get double PhDs at a young age and then start and run a very successful, complicated business without being tough. If anyone can confront Greed, she can."

Angela thought for a minute. "What we really need to do now is gather detailed intelligence. There's so much stuff I don't know, and that makes it hard to formulate a final plan. I want to know things like, does Greed do regular submarine patrols around the island? Because that affects the water team's approach. Also, how many guards are in residence at any given time, and what's their movement pattern? That's crucial to the fortress assault. Plus, I need to know where Jasper and Emma's bodies are being held. Because maybe if they're easy to access, we can just blast in and out, and the plan won't need to be complicated at all."

Hook shook his head. "It's going to be complicated, Angela. Greed built that whole setup and hired guards to protect what he wants to keep, and that includes Jasper."

Angela sighed with pleasure when Hook reached out and began to massage her feet. "So what do you suggest doing, Hook?"

He laughed, and his eyes glinted at her, but she said quickly, "OK, other than that! Work now, play later. We're running out of time here."

"All right, play later. It's a deal." Then he added, "I think you're underutilizing the men."

"What do you mean by that?"

"They have good skills, and I know they're champing at the bit to get more involved. So far Hawk has done some shooting at targets, and the others have built a training range, and that's all they've contributed. Send some of them on a reconnaissance mission and get the intelligence you need that way."

"You know their abilities better than I do, so who do you suggest sending and why?"

"Stubby for sure—he can build or modify about any piece of equipment. He's already talked to me about flying a drone over the island as a surveillance tool."

Angela's face lit up. "That sounds great! Just what I need! Who else?"

"I would consider Half-man. With his theater background, he can be anyone he wants to. Once he did a miniplay for Hawk's birthday, and he played all the parts. I'll never forget it because in thirty minutes he was the Queen of England, a Scottish pirate, a wealthy widow, an inventor, and an angel, too. It was amazing. He's perfect to go undercover on St. John—the closest land to where Greed is."

She rubbed her hands in glee. "And how about Melt, too? I've heard he can make himself almost invisible, so maybe he can actually sneak on Reed Island ahead of us and look around. Then he can report on the setup before we even get there."

Hook shook his head. "I don't think that's a good idea, Angela. If Greed discovers him on his island and then figures out we're coming to rescue Jasper, the whole mission will immediately go up many levels of difficulty."

They spent the next two hours making plans and scrapping them. Angela wanted detailed views of the cliff faces around the island's perimeter because she and Hook would be climbing up from the water and she wanted to take the right equipment for the climb with nothing extra to add weight. Her main worry was getting from the boat to the cliff face without strong waves smashing them against the rocks. She thought if she had detailed views of the cliffs, she could find a small sheltered area to land an inflatable rubber raft, and then she could place a carabineer in the rock as an anchor point for climbing. But she needed pictures of the cliffs in order to finalize a climbing route.

Hook wanted to know how much of the surrounding ocean Greed's surveillance covered. He reasoned that fishing boats must go close to the island regularly and that they might be able to conceal their divers by using a vessel Greed routinely ignored. He also wondered how detailed ocean observation was from the island. Were there visible markers warning the fishermen to stay back? Did Greed run boat patrols around the island, scaring tourists off, or was the security all done electronically? He hoped to find a blind spot in Greed's surveillance coverage, and then they could approach unseen from that location.

Angela wondered how Greed was viewed on St. John by the locals; undoubtedly they watched, speculated, and gossiped about him. Maybe Half-man could find a disgruntled employee who would leak details about the guards' schedules and the location of any booby traps. Angela suggested they might buy a Reed Island staff member's service as a double agent to spy for them. But Hook pointed out that idea would risk involving someone they didn't know who might rat them out to Greed to collect a second payout. He speculated that anyone who worked for Greed had to be of poor character and thus likely to betray them.

They both thought it was important to know where Jasper's and Emma's bodies were being held to expedite their rescue. Angela speculated that Greed might have a medically trained person to care for their comatose bodies and that he probably had computer personnel working with Jasper's laptop, too. Did Greed's staff regularly come and go by helicopter, they wondered? And if so, surely someone would realize it was wrong to hold an unconscious baby and her father hostage.

Hook knew the feds didn't have enough evidence to lock Greed up, but why didn't the local authorities care about Greed's activities? Surely he had a parking ticket or something that could be used as a springboard for investigation. In fact, who were the authorities, and would they support their rescue operation? About that last question, Hook was pessimistic because he thought they must be on Greed's payroll, too. And if they weren't, why hadn't something been done to shut down Greed's criminal operation before Emma's kidnapping had even happened?

Angela and Hook made a list of the questions they wanted answered by the reconnaissance mission. Then they drew up a list of supplies and equipment each person would need for the operation. The men would need to bring most of their gear with them because buying spying stuff locally was sure to arouse suspicions; each team member would also require a fake identity with supporting papers, like a passport. Finally, transportation had to be arranged, and everything needed to be done as soon as possible!

They kissed deeply a few times, and then they got dressed and walked hand in hand to the camp to talk to their team.

Twenty - Six

Stubby looked up from the gadget he was working on as Hook and Angela approached. "You're a couple now?"

Angela nodded. "Who won the betting pool?"

Stubby grinned. "Tony. He said Hook was too much of a gentleman to rush in. What was your bet?"

"Twenty-four hours. I was way off, but I tried my best to tempt him."

"Oh yeah, everyone could feel the sparks." Stubby winked at her.

Hook was flabbergasted. "You were all betting on when we would have sex?"

"Sure, you want in for Abby and Jasper?"

Hook shook his head. "I don't think private relationships are for everyone to speculate on." Angela had to hide her smile; who knew that a manly man like Hook could sound as prim as her grandmother?

"Suit yourself. It's the same prize—an expensive bottle of wine. Winner's choice." Stubby tightened the last screw and gathered up his tools.

Hook changed the subject by calling out, "Will Melt and Half-man come over here for a meeting, please?"

But instead of just those two, everyone—including Abby and Jasper—gathered around. Hook explained that they needed Stubby, Melt, and Half-man to travel ahead of the rest of the team to St. John on a fact-finding mission. They would send back the critical information Angela needed to make final adjustments to the rescue plan before the main group arrived. Stubby could fly drone missions to Reed Island from St. John, and Half-man could use his acting skills to chat up the locals.

Melt spoke up. "I know I could get on Reed Island for a personal look-see."

Hook spoke firmly against that idea. "I don't see how you could do that safely, Melt, because the only back-and-forth traffic is by helicopter, and they're hard to stow away on. Angela and I discussed that idea, and we decided that it's better to play it safe, because even if you get on Greed's island, we won't be able to back you up if you run into trouble. Also, how would you pass on to us any information you gathered there without them possibly intercepting it on their surveillance system? It's just too risky to even consider going there alone! But we appreciate the offer."

Jasper spoke up. "Leave the communication between St. John and here to Tony and me. We can come up with something protected by scrambling its code. That way, if Greed is monitoring the airwaves, we can gather information safely."

Stubby had an idea. "I've worked with the helicopter Greed listed on his insurance documents as his commuter. I built a small compartment in the tail of one. We used it to transport booze, and once"—he coughed and looked around sheepishly—"a lady of the evening for the men in the barracks. The brass never knew the compartment was there."

Abby was shocked. "That's horrible—multiple men and one girl!"

The other men looked embarrassed, but Stubby said, "Hey, she volunteered and made a ton of money in one night, so don't judge how some people need to make a living."

Angela considered his idea. "So, Stubby, can you make a similar compartment in the tail of Greed's helicopter? Would it be big enough for someone to hitch a ride to Reed Island and back undetected in it? Won't the pilot notice the extra weight or that the balance is off or something?"

"Nah, it's right at the base of the tail so it balances fine, and a small person could fit easily. Hey, I could get in there without my legs on, and I could place a bug in the cab so I could listen to the talk inside the helicopter."

Hook exchanged a glance with Angela to make sure they were both in favor of the idea. "All right, Stubby, see if you can make a similar compartment if the helicopter is there when you're on St. John. But if it's guarded or stored in a hangar, scrap the idea, because it'll be too dangerous." He sent Stubby a look that meant he was serious about that condition. "Now let's figure out how you three are going to get to St. John. Should we hire a private plane, Angela?"

Half-man entered the discussion. "If we make a big deal out of it with fancy transportation, then Greed will know something is up. He'd be stupid not to keep track of unusual flights coming his way. He probably has a paid informant at the St. John's airport. I know I would if I were him."

Angela asked him, "So then do you have any ideas for getting there? Air or sea is the choice, but a ship would take too long."

Half-man replied firmly, "We go as tourists. Many arrive and depart every day because St. John is a popular tropical getaway. Stubby, Melt, and I can go as a family group enjoying a vacation. Then when they think we're eating a nice room-service dinner and watching a pay-per-view movie, we can slip out as different people to do our spying. We could even double-book the rooms, one for each of our identities. No one is going to check the flight passenger lists and notice that only three tourists flew in but six checked into hotels."

Angela was excited. "That sounds like a great plan, Half-man! I assume you can create a backstory and disguises for all of you." She turned to Jasper and Tony. "Can you make fake identification papers for them, like a driver's license, passport, and credit cards?"

Tony replied, "Jasper and I hacked the CIA files, so we can do almost anything. We could even access the department of motor vehicles and make driver's licenses for them. But even better than fake credit cards is a real bank account. Half-man could open a checking account here in Ocean Shores using his tourist identity, as Abby can vouch for him at her bank where she's golden. Because when there's money in a real account, it's easy to attach a debit card and credit card to it. Then if anyone does check, it'll all be legit, and they can use it for vacation expenses while they're there."

Angela smiled. "Make it so, number one."

Abby laughed. "I guess my aunt Ethel just moved to town and needs a good bank for her money—and then a tropical vacation to relieve the stress of moving."

The meeting broke up as meal preparations began. Stubby grabbed Abby's arm and pulled her over to Angela and Hook. "I've got some ideas so this sweet girl doesn't meet Greed unarmed."

Angela cautioned, "She'll be searched, Stubby, and anything that even resembles a weapon will blow her cover and put her in danger. They'll be looking for a lipstick Taser or a pepper spray key chain."

"Well, they aren't going to strip-search her before the deal is made, and if they do, then the jig is up anyway, because that means they aren't planning on sending her home. Besides, no one but me and her are ever going to know the weapons are there. I guarantee it."

Angela considered his suggestion carefully. "All right, Stubby go ahead, and I'll feel better if she has something to protect herself with, anyway."

The group went over the list of supplies and equipment. The dive team needed wetsuits, oxygen tanks, regulators, and underwater scooters; Hook added antishark devices and a bubble dispersion system so they could go undetected in the harbor for as long as possible. For cliff climbing, Angela had a long list, including a low elongation rope, harnesses, ascenders, a sling, nuts for wedging into rock cracks, camming devices, and finger boards. Tony and Jasper added electronics for jamming the security system, tapping into Greed's computers, and extending the drone's capabilities.

After everyone had finished adding essential items, Angela stared glumly at the final equipment tally, knowing the things they needed would weigh hundreds of pounds and that they would never get that amount of baggage into St. John undetected. So the team spent a fruitless hour trying to cut the list in half without affecting safety, effectiveness, or versatility.

Suddenly Abby had an idea. "I bet Greed is expecting me to travel to a brief business meeting in my own jet. After all, time is money, and that's the way he travels. We could easily put all that stuff in a small plane, and if we got the right pilot, no one would know."

Hook liked that suggestion. "I've got a friend who owns a small business flying rich people around the world. He'd be perfect for the job, and he might already have hangar space on St. John. Then the rest of us can go as crew on the plane."

That plan cheered everyone up, and they dispersed with various jobs to do. The reconnaissance team planned to leave in five days, spend a long weekend on St. John transmitting data to Angela, and then wait for Abby to arrive. Abby needed to create a product that would entice Greed enough for him to quickly arrange a meeting with her on his island. That meant there was a lot to accomplish in a short period of time for everyone.

Twenty - Seven

Abby knew it was time to start reeling Greed in, so she called Medi-Help and made an appointment to see the operations manager, Gilbert Douglas. Two years before, Douglas had hired her laboratory to develop simple tests for detecting five genetic diseases. He had insisted the tests be inexpensive to produce, but afterward, Abby had seen a journal article advertising them for sale, and Medi-Help's markup had been over a thousand times what she knew it had cost to produce them.

It made her angry that he and Medi-Help made lots of money while the people who really needed the tests couldn't afford to buy them—especially after her lab had worked so hard to keep the price reasonable. Abby had vowed never to work with Douglas or Medi-Help again, so she felt scamming Greed through Douglas was fair payback, because Douglas had even snowed her with double-talk convincing her to donate some of her lab's services to his project as the tests would help so many people with low incomes. Abby felt what goes around comes around, and she was just the person to knock Douglas off his high mercenary perch while aiming for Greed.

Abby started preparations by calling Dee Light for fashion advice; she didn't want to be too specific about what she needed—and possibly involve Dee in a dangerous situation at Medi-Help—so she made her request vague.

"Hey, Dee, I need style guidance. I'm going to see a man about a horse, so to speak. There isn't a horse, but he needs to be convinced that there is so he'll put me through to the head horse buyer. And then I can take both their evil butts down."

Dee paused only a moment because she caught on quickly and Angela had prepped her on the situation when she had asked her to makeover Abby. "OK, standard problem of how to get a man to do what you want him to do, so standard solution: show some skin, do some doublespeak by implying sex is on the table but never putting it into words, let him do most of the talking, don't let him touch you in an intimate way, and walk away leaving him drooling and wanting more. I'm not saying it's right to manipulate that way, but it's a time-honored tradition, and it usually works."

How could you not love her, Abby thought. She was so fierce! "Noted. Now what should I wear?"

"You need to look totally professional, so wear a suit that's very upscale New York. Only when you lean over or cross your legs do you show enough skin to stop his thoughts. You show skin when he asks too many questions about the horse you don't have, understand? Of course, slutty high heels are required. Never put yourself behind a locked door or in a car with him alone, Abby, just to be safe. Because remember that you aren't dealing with a nice man here. Take a concealed weapon that will pass through a metal detector, honey. Some men believe they deserve to take what they think has been offered, even if it hasn't been."

Abby was grateful for the sage advice. "I love you, Dee. You're awesome! I've got your number on my phone, so it only takes a touch to call you."

"Then you give me a ring, sweetie, if there's any trouble. I've got beefy friends in Seattle who can get there quick. I love you, too! Ta-ta."

Abby choose her black designer suit. It had concealed lace panels in the skirt, so when she was walking no skin showed, but when she sat just right, the lace inserts showed her thigh almost to the panty line. Normally she wore a contrasting red underskirt with it, but she decided leave it off to show skin if she needed to. Under the fitted jacket she wore a see-through lace blouse with a fancy, barely there bra. Usually she paired the blouse with a matching camisole, but she left that off so she could unbutton the jacket or take it off as needed to distract Douglas. She sure hoped she didn't need to take the jacket completely off, because if she had to expose that much skin to prevent him from asking questions, then she was in big trouble!

Abby took a good mental look at what she was planning to do: deliberate deception with sex and manipulation for gain using her body. It was wrong—she knew that—and it went against all she stood for as a woman and a person. It made her feel sick inside. After a long moment of staring with self-loathing into her own eyes in the mirror, she decided it was time to call on Absinthe.

You use what you have to fight with, the Absinthe part of her thought. Then she gave herself a pep talk: Get over it, girl, because sometimes two wrongs do make a right. And it's good practice for Greed, when much more will be at stake—Jasper and Emma's lives!

Abby knew she needed to play her part well for her own safety and so Jasper and Emma would have a future. She styled her hair carefully and then fluffed with her hands so it was slightly messy. She boldly highlighted her eyes and added the fake eyelashes that Dee had said were essential for natural redheads with pale lashes. Then she outlined and painted her lips a deep red. Just as she finished, there was a knock on her bedroom door.

Abby took a deep breath because she knew who it was and had been hoping to sneak out without him noticing her sexy look. "Come in, Jasper."

He took a good long look, and then he whistled in appreciation. "You're drop-dead gorgeous, Abby! Tony told me you're meeting with the head of Medi-Help so he can set up the meet with Greed Is that true?"

She squirmed inside knowing that he knew she was going to deceive someone on purpose and use her body to do it. "Yes, you know I don't have a device to show yet, but I can start setting the trap now. Then when the men get the information Angela wants from St. John, we'll be ready to move ahead with the rescue."

Jasper put his cheek against hers, and his voice was grave. "I'm worried about you dangling yourself as a lure without any backup. It's dangerous!"

She kissed him gently. "I need to do this by myself, Jasper, and it's good practice for my role with Greed. You know what my job will be on the island, and this isn't as big of a deal as that will be. I'll be alone then, too, and we both need to get used to that."

"I know, but I don't like it. Can't you at least take one of the guys with you today?"

"It's a simple business meeting Jasper. I've always had them in the past without an escort, so bringing someone else along would seem suspicious. I'll be fine." She tried to sound sure of herself even though she wasn't.

He walked Abby to her car. "Call and let me know how it goes...Oh man, I wish I could be there as a real person! I hate letting you do this for me!" Jasper wanted to shred something with his bare hands!

"If you were there Jasper, it would blow the single woman, hot and available, so-tell-me-everything effect I'm skillfully creating." She slid into the car carefully to avoid revealing her skin through the skirt's lace panel and waved good-bye to him with artificial cheer.

In downtown Seattle's Pioneer Square, she used valet parking and took the elevator to the top floor of the Hoge building. It had been built in 1911, and she thought it must have depleted the entire white-with-gray-vein marble supply in Italy. Not only were the floors completely covered with marble, but so were the walls, windowsills, and trim too. There was a large fancy staircase in the middle of the building—also sheathed in marble—that traveled the full eleven stories, and it spoke of a time when people actually used the stairs instead of the marble-covered elevator. Medi-Help occupied an entire upper floor, and she was buzzed in the front security door by an assistant who led her to Douglas's office.

They walked down long rows of busy people in small cubicles working on computers. It was hard to tell what they were doing, but Abby noticed they were all dressed in black suits with white shirts; apparently, there was a strict office dress code. There wasn't a plant, or any paper clutter in sight. The desk cubicles didn't have personal items of any kind, and the people in them were like hollow-eyed drones. She couldn't imagine working there day after day—she would go crazy! And it was a huge contrast to her lab's environment, which was brimming with creativity and individuality on purpose; her people were happy working there, and it showed in their productivity and loyalty. I bet he has a high staff turnover, Abby thought smugly.

Douglas's office was a big contrast to the stark cubicles. It was luxurious with dark wood, plush carpets, and expensive antique furniture. As Abby was shown in, Douglas moved out from behind his expansive desk to shake her hand. His grip was just a little too firm, and he held her hand a little too long on purpose. She knew from her past experiences with him that that was a control move on his part, so she didn't let it affect her. Let the show begin, she thought!

He opened with, "Dr. Newton, so nice to see you again. My, my you're looking beautiful today. I'm curious, what prompted this visit to my humble office?"

Abby air-kissed his cheek but thought about what a jerk he was. His office was far from humble, and he knew it. "You've done me the great favor of a visit to mine several times, so I thought it was time for me to visit you in your office. Besides, I have a proposition for you." She held the word proposition a little longer than necessary to bring to his mind another meaning entirely.

He smiled. "Well, I'm always interested in a proposition from an attractive lady. Let's sit and have refreshment and then discuss it. But I think it's time for you to call me Gilbert, Abigail."

She perched at the edge of the chair to avoid showing skin too soon. He brought out a repulsively sweet sherry and poured two small glasses. Abby wet her lips, pretending to sip it. "I wanted to offer this opportunity to Medi-Help first due to our past lucrative partnership. If you aren't interested, Gilbert, then I will open bidding to other companies."

She gave him a slow intimate smile. "My staff and I have designed a medical instrument that will take the delivery of health care to the next level. The device my lab created will soon be used in every clinic and hospital worldwide. There's a lot of profit to be made easily, Gilbert, and with very little investment overhead. I am confident you will love this product, and it's a game changer. You'll see." Her smile was real that time, because she certainly intended to change the game—just not in the way he expected.

He gave her a used-car salesman's smarmy smile. "What is this new device, Abigail? May I see it?"

Abby slowly unbuttoned the first button on her jacket to distract him. "Well, Gilbert, I didn't bring it today. I want to show it only to the moneyman himself, Sir Reed. He has the resources to stop copycat marketing, and I don't at this time, and that's why I'm here today. Because once the device is available, then everyone will want...a piece of the action." Her hand lingered on her cleavage to draw his attention there.

Gilbert looked astonished. "How did you know about Reed's ownership of Medi-Help? That's confidential information!"

Abby sat back in the chair and crossed her legs deliberately with a sensual smile on her face. His eyes immediately went to the large swath of creamy skin behind the black lace. "My mother, Dr. Sophia Newton—you must know of her, Gilbert—travels in high circles all over the world as a medical consultant, and she knows Sir Reed."

He cleared his throat. "But Reed won't see you. You'll have to show the device to me." His eyes never left her bare leg.

She stood up. "So sorry then, Gilbert. I guess my business here is done."

He was desperate. "Wait a minute, Abigail, maybe I could send him an e-mail about it."

Abby shook her hair and unbuttoned another jacket button. "Tell him I will fly to Reed Island at his convenience. I'll bring the device and demonstration materials and show its potential to him. I'm only asking for five million dollars to turn it all over to him, and I'll finalize the paperwork right there in his office by releasing the patent to him. I know he'll be pleased with the deal, and so will I, Gilbert." She moved closer to him and bent over at the waist to say good-bye; he was still sitting down, sipping his sherry.

He craned his neck to look down her cleavage as far as he could. "Wait, Abigail. Maybe I can come with you now! How about dinner tonight?"

She moved toward the exit door, swaying her hips so his eye went to the rear of her skirt. "So sorry, Gilbert, but I'm in a relationship at the moment." Abby knew Gilbert—the swine—was married with three small kids. "Send the e-mail to Sir Reed promptly, and after I meet with him, I'll consider your offer of a dinner date and possibly more." When hell freezes over, she thought. "I'll see myself out. Don't bother to get up, Gilbert."

She closed the door in his face as he came after her, and then she walked quickly out of the building. All in all, a successful gambit, she thought. She had noticed sweat on his brow and dribbled sherry on his white shirt; hopefully he was already sending the e-mail to Greed. Abby sat in her parked car for a moment and called Jasper to tell him she was all right and coming home. Her hands shook a little as she held the phone, and she wanted a hot shower. She felt dirty even though only his eyes had touched her; it had creeped her out—it was like filthy hands had followed his eyes to her skin. She guessed it just wasn't in her nature to be the femme fatale.

Twenty - Eight

Sir Reed finished reading the e-mail from Douglas at Medi-Help. He tapped his recently manicured and clear-coated nails on his huge desk as he thought about the request. So the bitch wanted to come and beard the lion in his den. How interesting, he thought. He was aware that most people would have avoided visiting his little kingdom regardless of the cost—and for good reason—so her desire to meet him in person on his island was intriguing but naive.

He pulled up her file on his computer. She had made him money in her past venture with Medi-Help—thirty million dollars to be precise—so her proposal was worth considering. He remembered meeting her mother long ago at a black tie charity function. He had disliked her immediately. She was a perfect example of why advanced education should be limited only to men. The senior Dr. Newton had an inflated opinion of herself and had made the mistake of talking down to him in front of other people—he had as much understanding of medicine as any doctor alive! Usually the apple didn't fall far from the tree; it might be fun to take the daughter down to the level where she belonged with an educational experience her mother must have missed. Perhaps it was already too late to help Abigail Newton see the light of male mastery, but he could try to teach her and it would do the world a favor too.

Reed kept careful track of his holdings through technology, so he viewed the Medi-Help security tape and watched the beautiful redheaded Newton walk through the office work space at Medi-Help scanning the cubicles with a look of disgust. Apparently she disliked order; how could a scientist operate a prestigious laboratory without insisting on a tidy work space and efficient workers? Yes, she had a thing or two to learn from him!

Douglas told him that the part of the tape that had recorded his face-to-face meeting with Newton had been accidently erased, and Reed doubted that story. It sounded like there was something that Douglas was trying to cover up, and if there was, he would pay the price for that deception. Reed closed his eyes and took a couple of deep breaths to calm himself, and then his gaze returned to watching Newton walk out; she was certainly beautiful, but she had the superior, haughty air of her mother. Someone needed to spoil her delusion that she was special in any way!

He had been bored and restless in the last month, and he was frustrated by his inability to locate the computer chip that was crucial for his future wealth acquisition. His usual fun distractions weren't helping either. He had completely dominated his staff with fear, and the women he sported with no longer reacted with terror when they were brought to him. The only bright spot was the usual joy of tallying everything he owned. There was so much that it took a long time, and that was gratifying.

He begain by examining the gems and checking their etched identification, weight, and clarity against his log. Then he counted and stacked all the currency. Next he carefully scrutinized his art objects and looked up an estimate of their current values, and finally he checked the stock market and calculated the worth of his stocks and bonds. When he was done, he carefully recorded the amounts in his spread sheet, because money was protection from being used by anyone. He believed that someday he would have enough wealth to be completely secure on his isolated island. No one would ever again sell his body to get money for drugs like his parents had time after time. For Reed, sex, money, pain, and love were intertwined in his damaged mind, and he justified every criminal activity in terms of his survival and escape from abuse by others.

While he was counting and recording his assets, his mind returned to the decision he needed to make; maybe Abigail Newton did have a device to make him more money quickly. Could he afford to bid on the open market for her invention and to potentially lose easy profit and market share to others? No, that route was unacceptable because she had offered it to him first, so it was his already. But he was suspicious that she might be up to something else, because he knew with certainty that absolutely everyone had a hidden agenda against him. Should he chance accepting her visit even if she wasn't completely honest with him about it?

But what risk did he take inviting her there? He had a small army of guards and total control of everything on the island. What could she possibly do to harm him? Douglas had written that she would be stupid enough to bring the device and the patent release with her on the visit. So once she signed everything over to him, then she could have a helicopter accident on the way back to the mainland, and he would have the device free and clear without paying her a single cent for it. Then all of the profit would be his—just as it should be.

As a plus, his helicopter was insured, and because of the shark-filled waters around the island, no one would expect to find her body after a crash in the open ocean. He chuckled. He could keep her down in the caves and educate her about the superiority of men. He crossed his shiny shoes at the ankle and leaned back in his chair as pleasant daydreams of tearing that sexy business suit off her filled his mind.

Later, he went down to the caves to see how his current pet project was going; he had to take many deep breaths to control his rage when again no progress had been made toward obtaining the chip. Higgs still lay there like a wax figure, and the valuable computer chip was still missing! How could this have happened? He had planned the kidnapping so precisely, and he had been sure of the favorable outcome. It astounded him that Higgs had been on the island less than ten minutes when the chip had disappeared and that his body had lain almost lifeless since then.

None of the experts he brought there had any explanation for what had happened—no matter how many threats he made against them. He could see Higgs's computer was still active and that it was running a program with some chip-related sequence of numerical code they said they were trying to decipher, but it was taking so long! And since the program was linked to the chip, it was active somewhere, but where?

Reed knew it had been in Higgs's possession in the helicopter, because his guard had checked for it during the flight and had transmitted a picture of it to Reed as he had been ordered to do. Then it had disappeared sometime between when Higgs'd disembarked on the helicopter pad and had used the restroom he had stupidly been allowed access to. Everyone on his staff had searched Higgs's path again and again, and his rages grew every time they came up empty-handed. He knew Higgs hadn't discarded it in the ocean, because he had been closely escorted by the guards, so he must have hidden it somewhere his moronic staff hadn't looked yet. In retrospect, he should have had it confiscated as soon as he knew Higgs had it, but he'd been hoping to win his cooperation and had been planning to bargain for his help with its applications. He wouldn't ever make that critical mistake again!

Reed walked up to the comatose Higgs. He had inflicted pain by various methods to try to wake him up, and it soothed Reed's anger a little to see the results of the trauma on Higgs's body. He also noticed Higgs was thinner and had a slight yellowish color, and he pointed those developments out in a loud voice to the nurse. Without making eye contact, she explained how difficult it was to maintain the health of a comatose person over time and said they were doing everything possible. In a cold voice, Reed reminded all of them that if Higgs died before the chip could be found, then one of each of their family members would suffer for his loss. The penalty applied to all of the people working on the important chip project, because Reed believed in an eye for an eye—and he conveniently forgot that none of the people had joined the group by choice.

After Reed left, the nurse folded back the curtain hastily drawn around Emma. Reed had apparently forgotten about the baby, and they hadn't wanted to remind him after they'd witnessed him torturing her father. Higgs hadn't felt any pain, but it had turned their stomachs when Reed had touched himself and moaned as the blood dripped from Jasper's comatose body.

After seeing that, they made a pact that they would string Reed along—hoping for a miracle—until they had no other choice but to save themselves. The computer guys knew that the chip was active because it was communicating with its computer program. They had tried repeatedly to send Higgs a message through it but with no luck. The more times they failed to decipher the code, the more respect they had for the man who had created it; twice a day they prayed as a group for Jasper Higgs to reanimate and save them all from Reed's mad obsession with obtaining the chip.

After the fruitless trip to try and wake Higgs again, Reed enjoyed a satisfying session of verbally abusing his house staff to demonstrate his total power over them, and then he called his business manager to schedule Abigail Newton's visit. He made some menu choices to make sure Dr. Newton was properly welcomed and enjoyed her trip to his tropical paradise. Then he e-mailed Douglas and said that Newton must come alone and that she would only be allowed to bring the device, demonstration materials, and the patent release. He said that all legal papers must be sent at least two days ahead of her visit so his lawyer could review their completeness and approve the binding nature of the text. After sending those demands, he enjoyed a lunch of lamb chop grilled rare and began cataloging his wealth once again.

Twenty - Nine

Half-man's real name was Jim Osborn, and he was an actor just like the rest of his family. For most of his early years he had worked in the theater, playing childhood roles alongside his parents. Some plays opened and closed quickly, but others traveled around the country and were a more permanent means of employment for actors. His parents mostly followed the traveling shows, and they had taken their only child with them on the road to learn the theater craft. They were both completely self-centered people; it had been all about their talent and the parts they were playing or the next important roles they were auditioning for. They had never gotten around to marrying, and Half-man had been accidentally conceived in a drunken opening night celebration.

In his parents' lives, a child was a distraction they had never wanted or paid much attention to, other than providing him with food, clothing, and shelter. Half-man's real family had been the theater, with its colorful costumes and changing, bigger-than-life characters. Slowly his parents had drifted apart, joining different troupes to play plum roles that demanded the most from their respective skills. Jim had happily stayed with the core of the group he had grown up with as his parents had come and gone, honing their talents.

When Jim was eight years old, his father had been sent to prison because of his profitable side business of stealing wallets from the theater patrons. His mother had been gone five years by then and had refused to take her son back, saying it would disturb her concentration as an actress too much. So Jim had continued to be cared for and educated in a hodge-podge fashion by anyone in the troupe who had had an hour of spare time to spend with him. The group had moved from town to town frequently enough to confuse the authorities about his parentless status, and whenever it was questioned, someone would play his mother with convincing skill.

Consequently, Jim's extensive acting experience—and the natural talent he had inherited from his parents—allowed him to easily become anyone he wanted of either sex. He believed gender was a continuous spectrum from supermale qualities to superfemale traits, and he moved fluidly throughout, blending one into the other. Traditionally, Hollywood celebrated people who were extremely masculine or feminine, but he recognized that most people's sexual identities were in between those points. Based on that observation, Jim could convincingly play anyone no matter who they were.

Given his talent and upbringing in the theater, everyone in the troupe was surprised when, at twenty-one years old, Jim had found his life shallow and lacking in real meaning. He wanted to know who he was as a real person, and not just as character in a play; he'd played so many varied parts over such a long time that he didn't know himself at all, and the one part he couldn't play was Jim Osborn.

With no formal education or job skills useable in the real world, Jim hadn't been able to find a conventional job, so he'd enlisted in the army. He'd decided that if he couldn't connect with who he was during dangerous combat missions, then he probably didn't exist at all. But in an ironic plot twist, Jim had been assigned by the government to use his acting skills for classified spy missions, so by the time he was discharged, he felt like he'd only played the part of a military man after all. He hadn't found himself until he'd spent months in the quiet solitude of Angela's woods.

Jim was nicknamed Half-man when he lost part of his inner leg muscle and one testicle to shrapnel when patrolling with Hawkeye. Coincidentally, they'd met during basic training, had been assigned to the same unit, were wounded together, and patched up in the same hospital. Both ended up trying to recover emotionally by living in tents in the same forest with Angela. In boot camp they had been buddies hanging out together, but it was by talking in the quiet dark of emotionally painful nights in the woods that their true friendship had been forged. And even though sharp flying metal had wounded them both, Half-man's injury hadn't changed his view of himself the way Hawkeye's had. He believed it hadn't changed his self-perception because he hadn't had an intact personal identity before the attack, so it wasn't altered afterward. His identity only came after inner stillness and isolation finally peeled away the layers of each character he'd played and revealed the deep core of who he really was.

Now Hook and Angela were asking him to again assume a part for another play, and this one had life-or-death consequences for a lot of people. He had wrestled with the risk of losing himself again if he acted, but his inner identity had solidified with the time he'd spent in nature. He knew who he was as a person, and he could play from that strength finally. And that had the potential to make him an even better actor than he'd been before. He thought now he would return easily to himself when any part was over—or at least that's what it felt like.

Half-man considered the task requirements: Three people needed to get themselves and their equipment thousands of miles away to where they would gather information without being detected. Then they would reunite with the rest of the team for an assault on a heavily protected small island; they would do all of that where Greed and the authorities could plainly see their activities. Then they would assemble as a team and rescue a man in a coma and his unconscious baby daughter and finally transport them to safety. It was a ridiculously hard, daunting task by anyone's measure!

First Half-man dealt with the equipment that they needed to bring. Stubby would have both air and water drones for spying and also the tools and materials needed to make a concealed compartment in Greed's helicopter. Melt had volunteered to get as close to the island as he could underwater and to look for anything that might be a problem for the team entering by the harbor route; therefore, he needed scuba equipment and underwater tools. They also had to bring a computer to track the drones and to communicate with. All of that was a lot to carry on a regular commercial air flight, especially because they were going to be posing as innocent vacationing tourists.

Slowly an idea took shape in Half-man's mind. If Melt traveled as an invalid in a wheelchair, they could attach the scuba gear to it and say it was necessary oxygen equipment, and the computer could be concealed as a monitoring screen. A lot of the other equipment could be disguised as part of his wheelchair or as necessary stuff to maintain a disabled person. Melt wouldn't like it, but showing his burn scars would add authenticity to the invalid storyline, and he wouldn't need a disguise or any acting skills either. Then at night he could sneak out the hotel beach access door in the dark, slip into the water, and swim to the island to do his job. Both his skills at melting into the shadows and his melted-looking face would be put to good use on the mission. All Half-man had to do was convince him to show his vulnerability, and that was no easy task for most men.

Half-man knew that Stubby didn't have acting talent either, so like Melt, he could only be himself. He'd also noticed that under pressure Stubby sometimes stuttered, and that would be a tip-off if he tried to play two different people. He wouldn't be visible when he directed the submersible drone, because it was maneuvered by remote control under water. But the air drone was different because it was too fast to guide by hand, so it would fly in a preset pattern gathering data, and Stubby would have a long antenna pointed at the sky.

He decided that Stubby would be an avid fisherman and that the air drone's communication antenna could be disguised as a fancy fishing rod. Stubby could even rent a boat and fish at night; that would conceal their activities near Reed Island. The locals might shake their heads at the crazy night-fishing tourist, but it would make spying on Greed so much easier and safer.

Half-man would play the loud, exuberant, and offensive Ethel. The backstory he decided on was that she and her husband, Stubby, would have both a second honeymoon and a fishing holiday while taking a disabled family member on the trip to St. John he'd always wanted. Half-man then would assume an alternative male identity for trips around town snooping. Ethel would be so loud and overly friendly that no one would likely remember what anyone else in the group looked like; and then the only person needing a separate room and identity would be him. Simpler plans always had a greater chance of success, he thought, and things were less likely to go wrong when the others were just playing themselves. He worked the idea in his mind, looking for problems, and after discussing it with Angela, she gave him the go-ahead.

Half-man borrowed Abby's car and drove to the thrift store in town. He bought several huge tent-like dresses, a brown medium-length poodle-permed wig, orthopedic shoes, opaque stockings, quilt padding, and a huge bra and panties. He used shoe polish to add gray roots to the wig, deciding Ethel was at the time of her life when she would grow the gray out. He used the padding to make a body suit and held it together with duct tape so he could easily take it off and on. Half-man created swollen ankles, a large muffin top, and generous thighs for Ethel; she had upper arms that stretched the dress sleeves and huge sagging breasts that strained her buttons and drooped to her waist. Half-man thought it was fortunate for St. John that Ethel didn't own a bathing suit and would spend most of her time in the hotel room caring for her disabled brother. In addition, Ethel's unattractive personality would be the obvious reason Stubby spent most of his time fishing.

His alternate character was a single Australian man looking for both female action in the nightclubs and an exotic setting for the murder mystery he was writing. That cover story would be an excuse to talk to the locals, to move around the town, and to poke his nose in any activities he thought were suspicious.

Half-man laughed as he thought that maybe he could even talk Stubby into renewing their marriage vows on the fishing boat. Then they could use it as an excuse to anchor near Reed Island and to use a camera—with a telephoto lens—to take pictures of the special event with the island in the background. He was sure Stubby would be thrilled with that idea! Maybe he would get a wedding dress for Ethel just in case—if he could find one big enough!

Thirty

Ethel visited the team after dinner. Abby was awestruck, or star struck, but probably a combination of both. Nothing about Ethel resembled Half-man, but Abby knew he was in there somewhere. Half-man was a tall, thin man with aristocratic features. He wore his long, straight blond hair scooped back from his widow's peak and tied at the nape of his neck with a leather cord; he had a sharply pointed nose and prominent cheekbones, and his intelligent gray eyes scanned the environment at all times. Abby had always mentally pictured him as a French nobleman wearing a lace-trimmed blousy white shirt, tight breeches, and tall riding boots. He looked to her like he would challenge a rival to a duel with fencing swords because of an insulting glove slap on the face. Even his speech had a cultured tone as if he had come from royal blood, and she thought that was due to his Shakespearean training. But she had never seen him as anyone but himself, even though she knew he was a stage actor.

In contrast with Half-man, Ethel was morbidly obese and wore a tent-sized flowered mu-mu dress. Her cheeks were plumped with fat, she had a broad flat nose and double chins, and her skin was white and pasty. Half-man had shown her the process of sculpting a facial mold and casting a silicon mask that was feathered at the edges to blend seamlessly into the wearer's skin with makeup. But she was still surprised how transforming it could be, because Half-man was unrecognizable.

Ethel patted the beads of perspiration from her brow and fanned herself with a grubby handkerchief. Then she carefully positioned her bulk and sat down hard in the chair next to Abby with a groan. "It's getting harder and harder to move around these days. Doctor says I'm obese, but honey, I don't pay him no never mind. Got anything bad for you to eat, dear?" She spoke with a nasal twang and a slightly southern accent, and she made smacking motions with her lips.

Abby offered her a dish of healthy green salad, and Ethel brayed a loud laugh. "Now, honey, how am I goin' to keep up my girlish figure by eatin' rabbit food? Got any chips or cook- ies?" She reached into the chip bag on the counter and literally smashed a handful into her mouth and chewed noisily. Chip crumbs fell out of the sides of her lips and down the front of her dress and joined the other food stains already there.

Abby couldn't help but snicker. "Half-man, how are you going to fit in an airplane seat in that outfit? You're huge!"

Ethel patted Abby's hand with her slightly sticky one. "Well, bless your heart, sweetie pie, thinkin' about me. We're taking my brother, Dwight, on his vacation wish. He's so skinny after the fire and all that I'm just goin' to take up the part he don't need for my other butt cheek." She spoke in an unpleasantly loud voice as if Abby were partly deaf and sitting across the room instead of right next to her.

Abby shook her head in admiration for Half-man's acting skills as Ethel struggled to her feet and lumbered down to the beach camp to introduce herself to everyone else. When Ethel passed by, Abby smelled a faint trace of body odor under her heavy rose-scented perfume. Abby marveled at how detailed and clear Ethel's character was; no one would ever suspect that she and Half-man were the same person. She could even clearly hear

Ethel's loud braying laugh and grating voice blessing everybody's hearts on the beach which was almost a city block away.

Jasper, Tony, and Stubby were working in Tony's truck, busily customizing an older wheelchair they had bought at the thrift store. They installed a monitor screen to display Melt's heart rate, blood pressure, and oxygen saturation. Under its surface display of changing medical data, Jasper had hidden the technology they would need for the reconnaissance mission, and that included a protected communication system, the drone programs, hacking tools, and other spyware.

The display was carefully designed to make Dwight look disabled enough to need a support person with him, but not so handicapped that he couldn't travel safely on the airplane. He had to be mobile enough to get to his own seat and to use the bathroom with some assistance. Otherwise, the airline wouldn't let him travel, because it would be worried about the liability risk of a medical crisis occurring in flight without an attending doctor present. Airlines collapsed and stored wheelchairs during flights and then made them available again after landing. So the extra gear the men needed had to be simple, look like a normal part of the chair, and be collapsible, too.

They made the portable oxygen tank removable and designed the scuba regulator to appear as if the oxygen flowed through a nasal tube. They purposefully booked a night flight to St. John so Melt only had to act disabled for the short periods he would be awake.

At first Melt had been resistant to his part in the plan. He didn't like it when his scars attracted notice from people. But Half-man convinced him to participate by explaining that playing a part was just another way of using camouflage to conceal himself. Half-man also added a brain injury to Dwight's physical disabilities. That way Melt could avoid looking at and speaking to people outside of the team. And with a little acting practice, it was scary how Melt could empty his eyes of intelligence on a moment's notice.

They had planned to conceal Stubby's tools by incorporating them in the wheelchair back or seat, but try as they might, the tools either prevented them from collapsing the chair or were too visible. They were standing around, scratching their heads about it when Ethel slowly huffed up the steps and squeezed through the truck's doorway. They explained the problem to her, and she came up with a solution. She stripped down to her huge bra and panties, and they concealed the tools in duct-tape pockets in her fat padding.

Ethel couldn't let the moment pass without a comment. "It's not every day a girl of my size gets half-naked with her husband and two other good-looking guys while they insert their tools in wherever they can." She did a shimmy dance around the truck, shaking her large bosom and rear end to see if anything would fall out.

Jasper shot back, "Well, cooperate then, Ethel, because unless we add some special shielding, the airport security scanners are going to see the tools, do a complete strip search, and then haul you and your fat suit off to jail!"

Things got serious after that. They knew that in addition to X-ray machines, there were metal detectors and full-body scanners at some airports. The fat suit shielding had to look like there was a real person under the dress—nipples and all.

Half-man's other character—who was named James—made an appearance later that night. In contrast to Ethel's appearance, James had fiery-red short curly hair and a bushy mustache to match. His skin was tanned from the sun of the outback, and he had fine lines around his eyes and mouth. He had a pronounced Australian accent, a jolly attitude, and wire-rimmed glasses outlining his shocking blue eyes. James was a man's man and loved the outdoors, sports, sun, and travel. He smiled a lot, stood a bit too close to others, and physically touched other people often. He wore Hawaiian shirts in loud prints, khaki shorts with lots of pockets, white socks, and hiking boots. He walked with a slight limp and carried a wooden cane to support his bad leg—which fortunately happened to be the same leg Half-man had injured in the military. Like Ethel's character, Half-man had created James to stick in people's minds; then their personalities would occupy center stage, attracting all the attention while the scenery shifted behind them without anyone in the audience noticing it.

Abby liked him immediately. "James, what are you going to do on your trip to the Virgin Islands?"

He smiled, showing white teeth against his tanned face. "Find a nice Sheila, I hope. Take in the local color, meet blokes, and have a great time in the sand and sun."

"I understand you're writing a mystery and the setting is in St. John."

He laughed and pulled a chain with a huge shark's tooth on the end out of his pocket. "Not so fast, little lady. I haven't put my pen to paper yet—just researching, that's all. But let me tell you a story about when I took this tooth out of the great white's mouth. That was quite a dip in the ocean, I can tell you!"

Whereas Ethel deliberately put people off, James purposefully drew them in. He was fun, friendly, and a good listener, and he had lots of great stories to tell. Abby could picture him chatting up the local shopkeepers; his body language conveyed he was a nice, honest, trustworthy guy.

Abby asked Half-man how he generated that friendly perception, and he explained. "Keep your arms and legs open, because crossing them makes a barrier. Sit tilted to the side, but not collapsed. That signals you're small and safe to approach. Smile wide often, and keep your eyes soft and a happy expression on your face. Look at people almost like you've recognized a friend, and speak like you would to someone you have known for a long time. Laugh and include the people around you. Talk to everyone, and be an extrovert. Even closed-off people respond when treated like that."

She marveled, "You do it so easily. Like that's who you really are."

"I've had lots of practice, and in that moment it is who I really am. Half-man doesn't exist for me anymore. I didn't hurt my leg in combat, because a crocodile actually bit it."

Abby gave him a big hug. "You're Half-man, always, to me. I love you exactly as you are—not you playing a part, but who you really are inside. No one is as special as that!" She kissed his cheek.

He looked away with a lump in his throat and tears in his eyes. He had waited his whole life to hear someone say that they saw him, and liked him, for who he really was—that Jim, the real person, had value just as he was.

Thirty - One

The hotel in St. John gave Ethel and Stubby a little welcoming party for their twenty-fifth wedding anniversary when they checked in; a staff of three popped the cork on a small champagne bottle, presented them with a gift basket of local goodies, and produced a halfhearted round of applause. Ethel simpered and sent suggestive looks to Stubby. And Stubby shifted on his feet, looked embarrassed, and moved slowly away from Ethel. Half-man thought it was a perfect way to establish their characters quickly. Melt playing Dwight, let a small drip of drool string out of the corner of his mouth; Half-man almost laughed, spoiling their opening act.

In their beachfront hotel suite, they unpacked their equipment, checking to make sure it hadn't been damaged during transport, and then set up the computer to run the encoded communication device program that would link their thoughts together. Ethel lumbered to housekeeping, where she insisted in a loud voice that absolutely no one was to enter their rooms ever. She said that her disabled brother was not to be disturbed and that he had delicate medical equipment that could easily be ruined by cleaning fumes or vacuuming dust. She left fifty dollars to seal the keep-out deal and put her demands in writing for the management.

Stubby drifted down to the docks to rent a boat that was outfitted for night fishing and had a cabin to conceal their spying activities. They ordered dinner served in their suite: two full portions for Ethel, a normal meal for Stubby, and gruel for Dwight. Luckily for Melt, a generous Ethel shared half her double dinner with him, and the gruel went down the drain.

At dusk, James Dun from Australia checked in to an economy room at the same hotel. His room opened onto the parking lot rather than onto the scenic beach as Ethel's did, but it was easy to enter and exit without detection because Stubby had strategically damaged several video cameras. James had arrived by ferry and carried only a worn duffel bag. He immediately went out looking for a drink at a local nightclub, and once seated there he scanned the room, looking for a local person who might be short of cash and willing to exchange information for booze. He zeroed in on a man nursing the last of a tall drink and having an intense conversation with the bartender.

He strolled over and slapped the man lightly on the back in a friendly way. "Hey, mate, what's the best local buzz-drink to take the dust from a traveling man's throat?"

The man looked him up and down and then said, "Rum brewed on the island...mate."

James stuck out his hand with a disarming grin. "James Dun, glad to meet you. Bet the island rum packs a punch, eh!"

The man didn't offer his name, answer the question, or shake James's hand in response. That rudeness didn't affect James at all. He sat on the stool next to him and continued, "I'm a writer looking for a setting for my mystery book. What can you tell me about Reed Island? It's caught my eye, and it seems spooky enough for my purpose." The bartender set a small glass of amber liquid in front of James and then leaned back with his arms folded to listen to the conversation.

The man finally responded by saying slowly, "If you have any sense, stay away from that place. Reed doesn't allow visitors or like attention. Take my advice, and choose somewhere else for your story, mate." Then he stood up abruptly, tossed back the rest of his drink, and strode away.

James addressed the bartender. "Friendly sort, ain't he? You agree with what he said about Reed Island?"

He curled his lip at James's question. "Everyone who lives here is going to feel the same way as him. People have disappeared over there, so take care you don't, too." He turned his back and started polishing glasses.

James took two sips of the very strong rum, tossed a twenty on the bar, and cut his losses. He tried two more night spots with similar unfriendly results. The tourists didn't seem to know anything about the island, and the locals weren't talking if they did. That response alone told him something because people usually like to talk, especially if they're telling you something they know and you don't; it strokes their ego to know more than you, and that for that moment, they're smarter than you.

The next day, James decided, he would check out some books from the local library. Then Ethel could read Dwight some nice books about the area, and hopefully he would find ones with detailed maps included. He was sure Dwight would love to know more about the ocean currents, rock formations, and sea life of the area. James would also do some shopping and make inquiries for a room to rent as if he were staying awhile. That would send up a red flag to someone. A curious writer settling in the area who wanted detailed information about Reed Island for publication—he was willing to bet Greed already knew through the grapevine that James was there, and was making plans to encourage him to move on to another location. And if Greed focused on James, he would be less likely to be aware of the team's other activities.

Half-man decided that the next night they would try to check out Greed's helicopter and possibly install the hidden compartment. They knew his helicopter made frequent flights back and forth to Reed Island, carrying water, food, and other supplies; the island had no fresh water except rain, so it all had to be transported from St. John. It took a gig power plant to remove a volume of salt from seawater and a large space to house it in, and there was no evidence in Greed's insurance documents that he had invested in desalination technology. He knew Greed had a staff on the island and that they probably all ate three meals a day and drank lots of water in the hot climate; therefore, the helicopter trips had to be at least daily or every other day. Water weighs eight pounds per gallon, which would limit how much could be carried on one trip. And Half-man bet Greed insisted only on fresh water to clean himself, and that would up the total volume needed considerably, even with the rain-catch storing system he had.

Back at the hotel suite, Stubby had the flight drone ready to test. Abby had done an amazing job of making it look like a real-istic local seagull by creating a surface decal from a picture she had found in a book, carefully gluing it on, and covering it with sealant. Tony had installed a noise-concealing unit because it was going to fly close to the island and its inhabited guard-rich fortress. The unit disguised what little noise the drone's electric motor made with a repeating sound loop of wings flapping and bird calls. Half-man had teased Tony about installing a bird-pooping unit they could aim at Greed, and it had given them all a good laugh in the middle of a serious situation.

Stubby planned to fly the drone-bird at dawn and dusk when the gulls were naturally the most active and vocal. Most of the air drone's passes around the island were preprogrammed, but Stubby would still monitor it from the boat and would be able to make last-minute corrections, recall it if necessary, or add addi-tional passes if Angela wanted them. All recorded data would be immediately downloaded from the drone and sent to Angela—not stored either in the drone or on the boat in case they were discovered—and the drone would completely destruct by burn-ing if it crashed on land or melting if it fell in the water. Judging by the number of pesky seagulls flying around, Half-man thought it was not likely that anyone would notice one more bird.

While Stubby assembled the air drone, Melt gathered his scuba gear and double-checked the oxygen tank, regulator, and other equipment he needed. He planned to swim alongside the underwater drone as long as he could safely remain undetected, and then he would send it alone into the harbor to finish its job. Stubby would use the remote with Melt's help to place several surveillance devices as deep in the harbor as possible. The concealed electronic bugs would then send audio and video feed from the harbor directly to Angela.

It was an ambitious plan, and there was risk involved in each part of the operation, but good brains had worked together to plan the mission. The only thing left to do, Half-man thought, was rest until dark, at which point they would visit the heliport as a team and, hopefully, install Stubby's hidden compartment.

Thirty - Two

Stubby was high functioning on the autistic spectrum and a savant of gadgets with genius-level skills in that one area only. He usually disconnected from normal life because people confused him and overloaded his senses; he preferred to live mostly with machines, which he understood better. To him, even complicated mechanical things were straightforward compared to the intricate complexities of human beings and their lives.

Stubby could build almost anything from spare parts. A trip to the grocery store overwhelmed him with choices and sensations, but a trip to a salvage yard opened him up inside and created design possibilities. The unique machines he made were usually a mix of pure genius and inventive thinking.

Stubby had been born Edward Smith—the last son of seven—to a multigenerational farming family. His parents had called him retarded, kept him out of school, and hid him away in embarrassment when it was obvious he would never be like their other children. It wasn't that they didn't love him, but they'd been busy and hadn't known what to do with a growing child that needed special care. So at ten years old, they had sent him away to live in a group home, and slowly their visits tapered off and then stopped. Stubby mostly lived in his own world, and if that included parts that could be assembled, then he was happy pretty much anywhere.

Stubby might still be living in that group home, but his mechanical genius had come to the attention of the US military. They had contracted him to design and build new spyware and robotic weapons. Sometimes he came up with amazing new ideas, but mostly it was a frustrating experience for his coworkers—who had no training in working with an autistic person—to try to figure out what he was doing and how to work with him.

One day he'd been tinkering with modifications to a bomb-disposal unit when it had exploded and had taken off both his legs below the knees. Stubby had been compensated for the loss of his limbs by the government as no one had explained to him that he should first check if there was a bomb inside before opening the unit, and because he hadn't been adequately supervised at the time. Stubby had taken the loss of his legs in stride and had built himself a number of artificial legs that were more useful to him than his natural ones had ever been.

His monetary settlement by the government was enough to support him for the rest of his life—because he was a simple man with simple needs—but he hadn't had a home again until Angela invited him off the streets, where he had been wandering alone for months. She had seen past his smooth boyish face to the old-looking, disillusioned eyes hidden beneath his thinning hair.

Stubby enjoyed living with Angela in the woods, mostly because strangers left him alone there. He hadn't been in combat, but his legless status made him a military hero for some people, and it confused him when people he didn't know came up and shook his hand and thanked him for his service. Eventually he avoided everyone, but Angela was persistent about becoming his friend. Stubby was finally happy and part of a family again when Abby, Jasper, and Emma entered his life.

He loved Abby because she gave him big hugs and talked to him like he was a real person, and that made him important again.

But when he held Emma in his arms, his life finally focused for a moment, because he felt real, normal, and alive then instead of out of sync with people and drifting alone through his days. Then Jasper clarified his world further by adding a special program to Stubby's communication device. The program filtered out most sensory stimuli and simplified incoming thoughts to a standardized clear meaning. When he was wearing the device, he could mostly understand what people were telling him and could respond appropriately for the first time; it had changed Stubby's life for good. Jasper explained that designing a program for Stubby actually benefited everyone because it helped clarify communication for the whole team. Stubby knew he would be Jasper's buddy forever, and now he enjoyed being with people rather than shutting them out.

Stubby was proud when he wore his device, because no one treated him like a child and talked to him in a loud voice as if he couldn't hear them. People understood that he was smart—very smart—and that he just processed things in a different way. Finally he was on the same communication wavelength as the others, and he could focus and do his job easily; he still wasn't very educated, but he could help Emma and Jasper as an important part of the rescue team.

All three men dressed in black for the mile walk to the airport where the helicopter was located, and they stayed to the side of the road freezing in a crouch when a car passed them. Half-man discovered that Greed's staff placed their orders in local shops--after examining the merchandise--stayed overnight in a hotel, and then loaded the delivered stuff in the helicopter and flew it to Reed Island the next day. The helicopter crew usually included a cook, the pilot, and one security guard. The owner of a local bakery had told James that the cook selected only the best produce, meat, seafood, and staples available. The cook always came along because the menu was designed on the spot as she shopped for what was freshest that day. Anything not perfect—down to the last grape—was rejected and sent back the next day for a full refund. The money Reed spent on St. John greatly helped the local economy, so everyone put up with his excessive demands. But despite the influx of money Greed's shopping habits further distanced the local people from him. And Half-man thought the fear and anger Greed's demands generated might be a potent mix in the team's favor. Plus, Greed's shopping schedule was perfect for their purposes because the helicopter was left poorly attended as its staff visited the local bars and slept in their hotel beds between flights.

The team had night-vision goggles, so unless they made a lot of noise, no one would know they were modifying the helicopter tail. They carefully approached the darkened heliport by cutting through the chain link fence surrounding the airport and squeezing through the opening. Runway lights were visible in the distance, and a few planes landed and took off, but they were in a different section of the airport that was reserved for private air transport only, so it was poorly lit and quiet.

Greed's helicopter was secured to the tarmac with cables, and the doors were locked for safety. Half-man was amused because the locks wouldn't have stopped a thief with any ability at all. Stubby quickly slid under the tail section and started removing bolts. He had explained that helicopters with tail blades or fans wouldn't have enough room for a compartment in the tail but that this model would require only a little modification and rerouting to make a space for a small person to curl up in comfortably. Stubby was careful not to disturb the surface of the metal with any marks that might draw attention to it. He moved the wiring and hydraulics over to make space, and then he added support to the metal skin of the tail using struts made of carbon fiber reinforced with aluminum. The additional supports would help hold the hidden passenger's weight during flight. He installed a strong lock and padded the compartment with towels and a pillow borrowed from the hotel laundry. Half-man had assured Stubby that they would pay for the laundry lost when the hotel bill was settled—otherwise Stubby would have refused to use them. Honesty was important to Stubby, and Greed's deceit was one of the many reasons Stubby disliked him intensely.

While Stubby modified the helicopter tail, Melt installed the bugging device, and Half-man stood watch for anyone approaching. The bug would allow the person in the hidden compartment to listen to the conversation in the cockpit. The helicopter already had a sound system, so Melt hid the bug in one of the speakers, and there it looked like a normal part of the system. The bug was operated by battery power, self-contained, and wireless.

Stubby tested the final compartment for strength and then practiced getting in and out of it quickly. As he had predicted, only the small collapsible set of legs he was wearing would fit inside with him, and then only if they were detached from his stumps. Half-man thought that even if the compartment was discovered before or after they used it, no one would suspect it was big enough to transport a person in.

While Stubby modified the helicopter, Half-man used the night-vision goggles to scan for potential threats. He also looked over at the far lights on Reed Island. He thought about Jasper and Emma's bodies, so close but so far away, too.

He sent a thought message through the communication device: *Stub, Mel, wrap it up. I can see dawn breaking.*

Stubby picked up a handful of dirt and rubbed it over the compartment edges and surrounding helicopter tail to conceal any marks he'd accidently made and missed seeing in the dark. He knew that small errors might collapse the whole rescue and that they had to be extremely careful, because no one—except Abby—wanted to bring Emma and Jasper home more than he did.

Thirty - Three

The next night, the three men took the fishing boat out before dawn to fly the air drone missions, and they anchored it clear of the buoys off Reed Island. Stubby was the only person who would be visible from the island, and he was fishing from the boat's deck and using the drone's antenna remote control disguised as a fishing rod. Melt lay concealed under a tarp on the stern's bench seat with small but powerful binoculars pointed upward at the air drone's flight; Half-man sat on the floor of the dark boat cabin monitoring the data as it came in from each drone pass on the laptop's screen.

For the first programmed flight, the drone carried infrared sensors to pick up heat signatures. Infrared, the longest wavelength of the visible light spectrum, gives off a red light, but its energy is mostly detectable as heat. Infrared light bulbs are used to warm things like French fries and baby chicks. When the air drone's sensors registered infrared energy, it meant living human beings were present and radiating heat. Half-man watched as signature after signature appeared overlaid on the fortress's floor plan, which was already displayed on the computer's screen. Some were gathered together—at a meeting or breakfast, he speculated—while others were horizontal and probably still in bed. He watched as guards patrolled the hallways and the kitchen staff moved around cooking and serving food. But he didn't see the tiny baby Emma heat source he wanted to find, so he knew she was either cold, dead, or deep enough in the rock that her heat signature was blocked. Half-man knew that the infrared scanner wouldn't be able tell them anything about people inside the caves, but he had hoped to find Emma anyway. He was disappointed, but at least now they had a head count of the fortress occupants, so they knew how many people they would be up against during the rescue.

He waited until he got the signal from Angela confirming she had received the infrared data, and then he sent a thought message to Stubby through their communication devices: *Stub, call in the bird for the switch.*

Stubby landed the air drone gracefully in the boat, so he could change its equipment. The next sensor pass would register the structural density and material composition of the fortress. Jasper and Tony had taken equipment used by miners to find oil and marketable minerals underground and had modified it to fit on the light drone's body. The second flight would be a short series of patterns mostly around the fortress and harbor area. They already knew the geological composition of the island itself because that hadn't changed in hundreds of years. But Angela was checking the building and cave entrance for alterations since the blueprints had been filed by Greed's engineering firm. She wanted to find any hidden rooms, reinforced walls, secret passages, or traps to avoid any surprises if possible.

On the flight, Stubby was hoping to locate Greed's safe—they knew his dirty money had to be kept somewhere. Tony had hacked Greed's financial records extensively, and they only showed a typical pattern of money taken in from legitimate businesses and money paid out for reasonable operating expenses, with a modest salary for himself as owner of the businesses. Greed had listed a charitable donation of fifty thousand dollars a year as an income tax deduction. The team had had fun with that item on his return by suggesting charities he might have donated to, such as Megalomaniac School or Thieves-R-Us. But eventually Tony had traced his donations to a nonprofit agency owned by Greed, and the recipient was Greed himself, so the deduction made sense after all.

What was not revealed in any financial record were his ill-gotten gains, and the team speculated that they must have amounted to hundreds of millions of dollars a year. The total amount was hard to estimate because Greed's fingers were in so many illegal pies. Abby reasoned that if the authorities could have tracked the dirty money to him through financial records, then Greed would be behind bars. Thus, the money must not have been traceable electronically and so it was probably kept in the fortress as cash or goods. And because most thieves didn't trust easily, a large safe somewhere on the island was a good bet.

They further reasoned that protecting a huge treasure stored on his island explained some of Greed's paranoia and excessive security for a home that was already isolated enough to be secure in most people's minds. The team had all agreed that if they had time after the rescue, they would find Greed's wealth and use as much as they could carry away for good in the world. Beyond that vague agreement, they had not defined exactly what good they would do, but everyone had ideas about how it might be spent to balance the scales of justice that Greed had tipped toward evil.

They decided that if a safe was found using the drone's imaging, Stubby would to try to open it after Jasper and Emma were rescued. He enjoyed safecracking as a hobby. Most of his gadgets were made of recycled materials that had to be deconstructed before use, and that included numerous types of locks. And while wandering around scrapyards, he'd found enough discarded safes and security hardware to continually test and sharpen his skills. It was fun for him to solve the puzzle of a safe's lock and to open it, and he was very, very good at it.

The plan's timeline included thirty minutes—maybe a little more—for Stubby to crack Greed's safe, assuming everything went as expected. Angela had warned him sternly that if there wasn't enough time for him for him to unlock it, then too bad, because everyone had to leave when she said so with no arguments. But Stubby was absolutely sure he could do it in thirty minutes or less with no problem because he understood locks on a level only another gadget savant would have understood. It was almost like Stubby was one with a safe's mechanism, and he was sure it would open for him when he asked it to.

The drone's data on material composition flowed across the computer's screen superimposed over the fortress plans they already had. If Greed had made structural changes to the original architect's design Angela believed it would be for a reason, because reinforcing walls or changing things around wasn't easy when you lived on an island and had to transport materials and workers over ocean water.

Tony had tried to add a sensor for electronics to the drone, but he had been unsuccessful due to weight issues. He had hoped to find all the surveillance cameras and security control rooms before the rescue happened. He knew they would discover them once they were in the fortress, but that carried more risk for the team than knowing the locations beforehand. In the end the drone was just too small to add the necessary detection hardware on a flyby, so he had to scrap the idea and hope they could gain the information another way.

Just as the sun crested the horizon, Stubby sent the drone on its last and longest mission. They needed daylight to take digital photographs and video of the fortress, cliff faces, harbor, and airstrip. In addition to video, the small camera mounted underneath the drone was programmed to take one still photo per second, and the drone's flight path would cover every surface from at least two angles. The program started by flying the drone over the least inhabited areas of the island and ended with pictures taken directly into the fortress windows.

Tony doubted anyone would see anything other than a flying bird—even if they were looking out the window as the drone flew past—because it was fast and most of the fortress windows were small. Nevertheless, the last passes carried the highest risk of discovery, so Stubby made a big show to distract anyone watching from Reed Island by pulling a large fish—one they had purchased at a local market—out of the water. Stubby planned to land the fish and then to scatter bird food liberally on the deck to attract gulls. That way, he could land the drone safely among them. The happy fisherman would then take his boat back to St. John to show off his catch to his family. It was designed as a choreographed play of deception for the island's inhabitants, and they hoped it would be a safe exit strategy, too. But once they put the plan in motion, there was a scary moment they hadn't counted on. A speedboat containing several of Greed's uniformed, armed men circled around them close to their fishing boat. When they saw the speedboat approaching, Melt froze under the tarp below the deck's rail, and Half-man crouched down in the cabin behind its tinted windows. Stubby was the only one exposed on the deck, and he tried to look as innocent as possible by waving at the unsmiling men as they circled and by pointing at the fish dangling from his line. The men held their guns in sight as a loudspeaker on the speedboat repeatedly warned them to stay behind the marked buoys and away from Reed Island. The show of security would have been enough to scare any tourist away, and Half-man wondered how Greed got away with terrorizing innocent fishermen without legal consequences.

In addition to hearing Greed's numerous warning buoys clanging as though they were telling him to keep away, Half-man had known exactly when the dawn's light had become bright enough to see the fishing boat because the satellite dishes on the fortress roof had suddenly swiveled around and had followed them constantly after that. He'd been watching the fortress through his night-vision goggles as the drone made its final passes, and the sudden satellite tracking showed him Greed's equipment needed daylight to see boats; that was good information to send to Angela for her final timeline.

Luckily, when the dishes spotted them they were almost done, so only the final drone landing and the fish show was visible, as they had planned. Stubby had anchored the boat away from the island's harbor entrance and well back from the warning buoys on purpose, yet they had triggered Greed's alarms and speedboat goons anyway. So that meant that when they came back for the rescue mission, the scuba team would need to enter the water farther away from the island than they had originally planned to. That was more good data for Angela's plan.

As they approached St. John, Half-man donned his fat suit and became Ethel, and Melt settled into the wheel chair as Dwight for the trip back to their hotel room. The toolbox, air drone attachments, and laptop computer disappeared into a fishing bag that looked suspiciously like the duffel James Dun had checked in with. They all enjoyed the fresh fish Stubby had caught for lunch, which was cooked especially for them by the hotel chef.

Thirty - Four

James Dun was enjoying a beer when Greed's business manager walked into the hotel bar and grill; even if he hadn't seen her picture in Greed's CIA file, the black-and-gold uniformed escorts would have tipped him off to who she represented. He thought the group was overdressed for a warm tropical evening, and the Hitler-Gestapo look had been done before and just looked dated.

He sent a quick thought message: *Stub, Mel, Greed's wicked witch has arrived. Stay tuned for possible change of plans.*

She brushed off the approaching waiter and strode directly to his table. He noticed there was a dramatic drop in bar noise as the locals turned their eyes away but tuned their ears in to hear the conversation. She sat at his table, but the two guards remained standing behind her at attention with their legs slightly spread and their hands clasped behind their backs.

He asked, "Hey, pretty Shelia. Can I help you, I hope?" James gave her his friendliest smile.

He observed that she was beyond pretty and well into beautiful. Her looks reminded him of a classic Italian movie star who was playing the part of a Mafia girlfriend. She had thick, wavy black hair cascading over her shoulders and carefully plucked, arching, heavy eyebrows to match. Her upper eyelids were accented with hard black lines ending with wings on the outer corners, and her lipstick was a dark killer red. Unfortunately, the eyes the makeup highlighted were as blank as shark's eyes; the black irises blended seamlessly with her pupils, giving them a flat, cold, expressionless, and emotionally empty look. He wondered why completely black eyes looked sweet on a puppy but were chilling on her. He felt like they might suck him into a dark place, so he looked up at the guards instead of at her face.

James asked, "These guys your friends?"

Instead of answering his question, she got right to the point. "I understand you have been making inquiries about Reed Island. I am here at Sir Reed's request. He wants you to stop your questions, or he will file a restraining order against you and have you deported."

"Whoa, lady. I just needed a setting for my book. No harm, no foul." James knew her threats were unenforceable and she was just blowing smoke at him.

"My employer, Sir Reed, is a very private man. You will stop immediately and leave the area, or you will be sorry. I promise you that." The guards shifted their hands to the front of their bodies, and James saw the flash of brass knuckles.

He looked at her and saw she was smiling and relishing the power over him she thought she had. He realized that she was hoping for the excitement of his refusal, because then she could make good on her threats. Maybe she wanted to watch—and would become aroused—as the robotic guards beat him bloody on her orders. Jasper had nicknamed her "Witch" within moments of meeting her, and Half-man understood how well that name fit; he marveled that someone hadn't dropped a house on her yet.

Time to take the wind out of her bloody plans for the evening. "I'd like to forget Reed Island to make you happy, beautiful lady, but my publisher beat you to it today. He changed the setting for my book to the big city of Chicago. He's already sent me tickets to fly there next week."

He watched her process through that information, checking for holes in his story. James noticed she was much older than she had first appeared to be. She had had several cosmetic procedures done by a good plastic surgeon, but he was an expert on stage makeup and faces, and he could see where she had concealed the faint scars from multiple facelifts.

"If it would make you feel better, pretty Sheila, I can show you the tickets back in my hotel room." He said it with an obvious sexual leer and winked. "The guys have to stay outside, though. It's not my thing. You understand, baby."

That was blatant enough to convince her he was sincerely moving on to Chicago. James knew she was aware of his status as a single guy looking for action with the ladies, and he played on that.

She replied with so much frost that he could almost see it in the tropical air around her. "If you are not gone within the week, my next visit won't be so pleasant. That is my thing, you understand."

"Read you loud and clear, honey, and I'm sorry I caused an upset on your island. Now can I buy you a drink to make up for it?" He smiled his best smile at her, but somehow he couldn't make it reach his eyes. That would have been a telling acting mistake if she had been looking for it, but thankfully she didn't pick up on it. She was one creepy lady, and he almost felt his skin crawl just sitting across the table from her.

She stood abruptly, leaned over, and bared her teeth at him. "When hell freezes over, Mr. Dun. Good-bye." As she strode away, James heard her call him an insect.

James let out a relieved breath as they left; hell was going to freeze over for Greed and the witch soon. He was looking forward to taking her down personally, because she belonged safely behind bars. He gave the mental order to stand down to Stubby and Melt, finished his drink, and started back to his room across the beach-themed hotel lobby. Time for James Dun to make his last curtain call in St. John, he thought.

In Greed's helicopter, Madam La Ruhr, as she was currently calling herself, fumed about the insect Dun, who she had been ordered to threaten. Reed had no business sending her on such a low-level errand; it was definitely time for her to search for another job! Reed personally kept a careful tally of his safe's contents and of the household expenses down to the last dime, but he had no real involvement in managing his many businesses because that was her job. He occasionally asked for a financial review with profit and loss statements, but mostly he left the routine management decisions in her hands. Meeting with Dun should have been assigned to a guard, not to his business manager! She had enough to do without menial tasks like warning a letch off because he was stupid enough to ask some questions!

La Ruhr had been carefully siphoning off money from Reed's businesses into her own accounts for several years. She knew he was mentally unstable—and would kill her unpleasantly if he ever found out—but she was smarter than he was, and she had spent a great deal of effort on covering her tracks. But all good things must come to an end, and she knew it was important to get out just before that ending time. She had always listened to her survival instincts, and they had been clanging "get out" for months. So slowly, she had switched two of Reed's guards' loyalty to her with sexual favors, and soon, with their help she would disappear to where she couldn't be found.

She easily exploited Reed because he—stupidly—felt safe on his little island and rarely left it to go anywhere. That might have been security for him, but it created a weakness that she had capitalized on. She did make sure that his businesses were all running smoothly in her capable hands, but only because it benefited her directly; as Reed had given her more and more responsibility, she had embezzled more and more of his money, too.

Her temper was cooling a little, and she realized that it wouldn't be good to rock the boat over Dun. Instead, she would let Reed believe all was safe and sound in his world until she disappeared in a week or so. After all, she knew timing was everything in the world of crime.

When James was halfway through the hotel's lobby, a police officer stepped in front of him and snapped open his identification wallet. "Mr. James Dun, would you please accompany me to headquarters? We have some questions for you."

James sighed and went willingly, but he sent another thought message. *Mel, Stub, night's not over. Headed to the police station—something is up.*

At the station, James was directed to the head man's office, and there a smartly uniformed officer stood up and shook his hand. "Welcome to St. John, Mr. Dun. I hope you're enjoying your stay with us."

James stayed neutral in his tone and glanced at the name plate on the battered desk. "Hell of a nice rock, mate. What brings me to your office tonight, Chief Lawrence?"

The chief tapped his fingers on his desk and carefully said, "It has come to my attention that you met this evening with a woman we are interested in knowing more about."

James laughed. "She met with me, not the other way around, and then she put the verbal strong arm on me about my interest in Reed Island, leaving nasty threats behind her."

The chief measured Dun with his gaze and decided to lay all his cards on the table. "You might like to know that yesterday we ran the prints that you left on a bar glass. What we found was very interesting. There wasn't a match for an Australian man named James Dun, but it turned up a very distinguished military service record for a Jim Osborn who was a match. Actually, much of your record is sealed for national security reasons, but it's clear to me that espionage was your specialty."

The chief then leaned over his desk and spoke quietly. "The woman you met is very bad news, Mr. Dun, but like Reed, we can't pin anything on her yet. We believe they're holding some missing girls on Reed Island, but we don't have enough evidence to get a search warrant. Can you help us find the girls? You're my last hope, because believe me, we've tried everything else!"

James considered the request, but he said nothing. He'd seen posters with the girls' information around town, and it made him sad they were missing, but the chief apparently didn't know for sure they were with Greed.

When James didn't respond, the chief sighed. "We've been spinning our wheels for years, knowing Reed Island is a hub of illegal activity, but we haven't had enough hard evidence to shut it down. Now at last you might give us a possible opening to do that. I know you aren't working alone, and I know your intention is to get onto Reed Island somehow. I don't want to know when, how, or why. I just want the girls back, and any evidence you have after it's all over, so we can lock the bastard up good and tight."

Half-man finally said in his real voice, "Are you offering to help?"

The chief shook his head reluctantly. "I can't do that legally unless you send a distress signal from the island. I don't want to risk Reed getting away for improper procedure. So I'm sorry, but I can't be involved with you now. But here's my private number, and call me if you need advice." He grinned. "No one else knows about the fingerprint match, and I recorded it as 'no match' for the record. And no part of this meeting has been recorded, either." He stood and stuck out his hand again. "It has been nice meeting you, Mr. Dun, and good luck with the rest of your vacation."

Half-man shook the policeman's hand with appreciation this time. "Nice meeting you too, Chief Lawrence, and believe me when I say that I will be in touch. So be ready. There's much more wrong on Reed Island than you know, and it's going to end very soon."

Thirty - Five

Melt felt secure under the ocean's surface because no one was staring at his scars and the job at hand was the only expectations for him to meet. He glided silently along the ocean floor in the dark water, but he could see clearly, as his night vision goggles were concealed behind his swim mask. A faint red light glowed from the head lamp banded around his diver's hood, and he swept it back and forth as he swam and looked for man-made objects around him. In the fishing boat's cabin Halfman tracked Melt's progress toward Reed Island on the laptop's screen, and he occasionally adjusted his swimming course with a thought through the communication system.

In one hand Melt carried a long blunt club to poke sharks away with, and in the other hand he had a tether attached to the neutrally buoyant underwater drone. He swam slowly toward Reed Island, looking for sensors or nets protecting the harbor from divers, and occasionally he probed at the seafloor with his club. Melt's oxygen bubbles were sent through a dispersion device that broke them into a fine, barely detectable stream, and what was exposed of his pale face was covered with a black oil-based cream. As he swam he was virtually invisible in his black wetsuit, gloves, flippers, goggles, and hood. Even the ocean predators seemed to avoid him and the submarine drone he towed along behind him; they were just two more dark-colored fish swimming deep in the ocean.

Melt was the only child born into a wealthy family who firmly believed children should be seen and not heard. His parents were rich from several generations of accumulated money made from logging old-growth forests in the Northwest. During Melt's childhood, his self-absorbed mother had been active in social circles and charity groups, and his father had had lofty political aspirations. It had seemed to him growing up that his only purpose was to be trotted out for display at parties. Then after the viewings, he would be reburied in the nursery in the care of a revolving staff of nannies and tutors. He had always been called "the heir" and never had been addressed by his real name; in fact, his name was his father's name with a "junior" at the end, and it had never felt like his at all. He had been ordered to call adults "sir" or "madam," but mostly he was supposed to keep his mouth shut at all times. It had been a lonely childhood, and it had produced a man who felt more like a ghost than a real person.

At twenty-one Melt had joined the army just to get away from home, but he had pulled two fellow soldiers out of a burning building just six months into his first tour of duty. The burned men had lived, but Melt suffered extensive facial, arm and torso burns; so despite skin grafting and ten cosmetic surgeries, when he looked in the mirror he saw a version of the Phantom of the Opera. Unlike the movie's phantom, he still had hair on his head, and his nose was intact, but one side of his face was thick with ropey scars and patchwork repairs. In addition, his left ear was small and curled, and his lower eyelid, nostril, and lips all drooped slightly on that side. So he looked a bit like a wax figure that had gotten too close to a flame melting one side of its face. His injuries only intensified his inner feelings of disconnection from people and normal life.

Due to his childhood training to always be quiet, Melt usually felt uncomfortable when people noticed or talked to him, but now it was worse because strangers stared at his scars. That unwanted attention—often delivered as negative comments about his monster-like appearance—made him even more reclusive. At the time of his discharge from the military, he had spent more time in government hospitals than in service to his country. He was publicly awarded for saving lives, but by then he hadn't even wanted positive attention; he just wanted to be left alone!

Melt returned home from his extended hospital stay to find that his parents had died in a multiple-car pileup on the freeway. He had immediately fired all the servants he had hated growing up; and then he had been informed by the lawyers that his family's wealth was spent a decade ago. His parents had frittered away all the money maintaining appearances and their old mansion. Melt realized that after most of the ancient old-growth forests had been cut down, his family had lived without any real source of income.

And even though his parents had known that their lifestyle had consumed all the money, instead of adjusting how they lived, they had continued spending using credit until they were deeply in debt. His father had spent lavishly on political campaigns that he didn't win, and his mother had financially supported obscure charities that had never made sense to Melt. He had come home planning to finally confront them with how they had neglected him as a child, but instead he had found out that they had lived an empty, shallow life that had been worse than his was. He had wanted to shout at them that they had made him a fake child who had grown up to be a fake adult. But it now all made an ugly kind of sense--they were fake people, so of course they had raised a fake kid. For them, appearances were always maintained as a priority, even while the center of them rotted out until they were empty and hollow inside just like he was.

Melt had sold everything his family owned to pay off as much debt as he could, and then he had declared bankruptcy. He had walked away with only the clothes on his back and some army surplus camping gear. He hadn't taken anything from the mansion—not even pictures of his parents; the stuff hadn't meant anything to him when he had lived there, and it sure didn't mean anything to him after.

He had camped in the rainforest alone for months and had grieved the irreplaceable ancient trees his family had cut down to buy a meaningless life. He had lived apart from people for almost a year before he made his presence known to Angela. Melt had watched her from behind the trees for weeks, and he had recognized her deep love for the forest too. One day he just sat down beside her while she was meditating, and the next day he moved his tent into her campground. He still spent a lot of time in solitude and drifting around unnoticed, but he became part of something human again because of Angela's obvious love for nature.

Melt felt good in Angela's camp because he could talk, or he could ignore everyone if he wished. None of Angela's other campers had ever mentioned his burn scars except to razz him about them, and they all had disfiguring disabilities, so he could razz them back. In a way, being there made him whole again because he was important to a group, so he counted for something. They hadn't asked him to come along on the rescue mission—they had all just assumed he would because he was a valuable person to them and a team member with skills to contribute. Melt knew Jasper, Emma, and Abby needed him, and that was all it took for him to risk his life again.

As he swam along in the dark tropical ocean water, he felt fully alive, like he had when he had known that the only way to rescue his teammates was to run through fire. The clarity of tonight's purpose had burned away the numbness he normally used to shield his feelings. Melt hadn't even been aware of how numb he had become until it was gone and he felt alive inside again. He marveled at the emotions bubbling up; some were good and some were bad, but they all were his true feelings and were important to him. He was Melt—not a shadow man or a ghost of a boy—a real person with substance who was valuable to the rescue mission and to his friends.

Suddenly the sonar on the submarine drone pinged a warning, and he stopped swimming and sent a thought message. *Half, how far to the harbor? The drone pinged something ahead.*

Mel, about fifty yards. Send the drone out, and I'll activate the camera. Stub, start the remote control.

The drone suddenly switched on its red headlamp, and its propeller activated quietly and moved it forward in the water. Melt then trailed behind it at the end of the tether; Half-man had made it clear that the drone was expendable but Melt wasn't, so it had to be in the lead as they approached the harbor entrance.

Mel, sonar picking up some barrier across the entrance dead ahead.

The drone came to a slow stop, and Melt cautiously swam to a fence structure. It was made of stainless steel chain link and ran from one side of the harbor entrance to the other. It was attached to floats at the surface and ran along rails anchored to the seafloor; it completely closed off the harbor entrance with strong netting. Melt was close to one side of the entrance, and he saw that the chain link was securely bolted to the rock boulders—which shielded the island from waves—with strong u-shaped bolts and cables. The fence was in two portions that joined in the middle like halves of a huge gate, so it could swing open to allow boats in and out of the harbor.

Melt thought that opening and closing the fence was probably done electrically from Greed's command center. And he knew that where there was electricity, there was potential for the whole fence to be dangerously charged with voltage; any disruption in the electrical field could set off an alarm and alert security guards to his presence. So he swam along the fence, looking for a way to deactivate it, to open it for the drone, and to secure it safely for the water assault team when they came back for the rescue. Finally he risked crawling out on the jetty rocks and traced the electrical supply conduit back from the fence on land. There he found a clearly labeled emergency shutoff box and thought that you just had to love construction codes sometimes.

He reentered the water and swam to the center gate opening. At the bottom on one side, he saw the fence had been bent backward when it had been closed against a large rock embedded in the seafloor. Melt smiled because somebody hadn't been making maintenance checks like he or she should have, and the handy opening was just big enough to slide the drone through without touching the fence.

Half, Stub, fence preventing forward progress, space to slide drone in. Can you take it from here?

"*Mel, affirmative. Release drone and wait.*"

Stubby manually guided the drone through the harbor's waters by watching the feed from its nose camera on the computer screen. They saw a series of six large underwater compression cannons on either side of the rock barriers leading to the main harbor where Greed kept his small submarine and ostentatious Yacht moored. He and Half-man exchanged concerned looks because the cannons were there to send out massive sound waves designed to disrupt and disorient divers, and they knew brain damage could be a result; so somehow, they would need to disable them before the scuba team swam through on the rescue mission.

The submarine drone's task was to plant bugs to try to gather surveillance data from the caves. They had maps of the original cave's structure from before Greed had bought the island, but they knew he had done extensive structural modifications; the rock for the fortress walls and the jetties had all been excavated by extending the cave deeper under the island's surface and enlarging the harbor's width and depth. The air drone's equipment hadn't been able to penetrate the rock's surface, so the bugs were their best chance to see what the harbor team was up against.

The submarine drone had several thin robotic arms that extended from its torpedolike body. One arm came out of its top like a periscope, and it had a video camera mounted on it that swiveled and could film three hundred and sixty degrees around as well as up to the roof of the cave. There was a similar camera mounted to the bottom of the drone that filmed the sides and bottom of the cave. There was a risk that someone would see the top camera because it extended two inches above the water's surface, but Angela thought the intelligence gained by filming above the water was worth the small chance of discovery. The drone filmed continuously until it reached the end of the u-shaped harbor, and then Stubby turned it around to place the bugs. Half-man was pleased to see that Greed had installed a number of night security lights around the cave walls and on his yacht's deck too. The extra light was helpful because the harbor images flowed perfectly clear from the top camera, so he sent the video feed directly to Angela.

The drone placed five surveillance bugs with Stubby's guidance. One on each side of the harbor's entrance, one at the far end, and two on the yacht. Each bug was slightly above and slightly below the water line and had both audio and visual capabilities. Abby had gone to great lengths to make them look like clusters of small barnacles native to the area. Half-man tested the feed from each one to make sure they all were working, and then he signaled Stubby to send the drone back to Melt, who was waiting on the other side of the harbor fence.

Once Melt and the drone were safely back on the fishing boat, the men opened a bottle of wine and had a late dinner on the way to the hotel. Soon Abby would arrive with the remaining team, and she would distract Greed while the rest of them rescued Jasper and Emma. The risks they had taken on the recognizance mission were mild compared to the danger they knew they would face on the next step of the operation.

Thirty - Six

Abby refused to just sit around looking pretty and to define her whole contribution to the rescue mission as bait. Warrior princess she was not, but she did have a good brain and was not afraid to use it. She had completed university-level classes in inorganic chemistry, organic chemistry, and biochemistry, so surely somewhere in her head was usable information for rescuing Jasper and Emma. She started brainstorming for an idea by reviewing the information she already had. She knew that Reed Island had been formed by an ancient volcano erupting under the ocean and then shaped over eons by waves wearing away the softer rock, leaving a flat top, steep sides, and caves carved into one side. It didn't have a source of fresh water except for rain, so Greed had all the drinking water flown in by helicopter from St. John.

That was a weak link she thought she could exploit, because everyone needed drinking water to live. What if she poisoned the water? No, not poisoned, because that might kill some people. But how about adding some sleeping powder? Then the team could just walk in over snoring guards to scoop up Jasper and Emma and get away clean; easy peasy. However, the downside was that that result would require everyone to drink the correct amount of drug for his or her body weight at the same time and then fall asleep before the team arrived, which was unlikely at best.

But maybe if she found a safe compound and only put it in bottles of the same size, it might work. Theoretically, large people would need more hydration and would drink more water, and smaller people would drink less. Also, there was probably a pecking order for a necessary commodity like water, so the guards—who were likely heavier too—would drink before the kitchen staff, and that would naturally make the most dangerous people fall asleep first. She pondered the idea. It wasn't without risk, but if she could take a few guards out of the fight, it would skew the odds of success in their favor.

Abby suddenly had a horrible thought: what if the tainted water was given to Jasper or Emma? Would a sedative kill them in their weakened state? But they were comatose, so oral liquids probably weren't used due to the risk of aspiration; they likely gave them liquids through an intravenous catheter from a sterile source. Although if they fed Jasper with a stomach tube or used the bottled water to mix Emma's formula, a sleeping potion could create a problem.

She chewed on her bottom lip while she thought. What were the chances of the top few bottles of tainted water making it to the caves before the rescue team arrived? Jasper and Emma had to be at the bottom of the hierarchy for resources, and it was very unlikely that they received fresh water from the newest lot the same day it was delivered. So many other things could go wrong way before the water made it to the top of the risk list for Jasper and Emma, and she gave herself the go-ahead to proceed with the idea.

Abby considered how to time the distribution of the adulterated water for the best results. If she used next-day shipping to get the sleeping powder to Stubby on St. John, he could inject it into the water bottles already loaded on the helicopter before he hid in the helicopter tail's secret compartment. Then the water shouldn't be distributed on the island until thirty minutes or so before the team arrived; the guards unloading it would probably have first dibs, and then the rest of the staff would have some, so the timing would be perfect. And if Greed, being the top dog, drank two bottles off the top, that would be a big plus for her part of the mission.

What drug could she use? Traditionally, barbiturates were the choice for sedation, but because they were a controlled narcotic, the DEA would need notification, and there wasn't time for the red-tape clearance required. Next she considered antihistamines like Benadryl because they often made people sleepy. But their bitter taste in water might alert people to the fact that it was tainted, and that wouldn't be good, because then guards would be suspicious when the team arrived. That bad taste was also the problem with over-the-counter sleeping aids. Abby paced the kitchen and thought some more.

OK, how about chloral hydrate, the compound called knock-out drops used during the prohibition area? Illegal, yes, but so easy to make. It was just chlorination of ethanol in an acidic solution, and it worked quickly, too. It was perfect for the job!

She could even ship it as a powder, and then Stubby could add water to make a solution and inject a measured amount in each water bottle. If he used a syringe with a small enough needle, the hole would be undetectable. The drug was clear and tasteless—it was absolutely the perfect drug for the job. Abby had a moment of regret about breaking the law, but the whole rescue pushed the envelope of legality—in for a dime, in for a dollar, she thought. And besides, it was probably too late to think about ethics. She would run the whole idea by Angela for her approval, and nothing they had planned was totally risk-free anyway. Yes, someone might have a drug reaction or something, but she thought the benefits outweighed the chances of that unlikely outcome.

Abby paced the kitchen, looking for supplies and generating a list to send to her staff for the chemicals and equipment she would need to make the sleeping powder. She owned a research lab, so she had a fully stocked chemical pharmacy in Seattle, and her aids were accustomed to their boss's unusual requests for projects she had in development. They had sent boxes by currier to Ocean Shores before, as she sometimes worked on new projects in the peace and quiet of the cabin.

Abby started the chili she had planned for dinner and suddenly thought about making her own pepper spray. The main ingredient was capsaicin, the chemical that caused the spicy burn from hot peppers. She knew different kinds of peppers had different amounts of capsaicin and that it was located in specific parts of the pepper pod. To make the spray, capsaicin was harvested, concentrated, and suspended in propylene glycol for delivery as an aerosol crime deterrent. She didn't have any fresh hot peppers available, but the cabin had different strong hot sauces and powdered hot pepper spices in the kitchen cupboards. She wanted it strong enough to incapacitate a guard for a few minutes—just until they could cuff him—without doing any permanent harm.

She decided to ask Jasper to measure, stir, and pour the pepper mixes because concentrated capsaicin could cause inflammation to the nose, throat, and eyes; temporary blindness, uncontrollable coughing, skin burning, vomiting, body spasms, and collapsing. As a projection, he would be the perfect assistant, as the pepper wouldn't have any physical effect on him. Plus, she cherished the smiles he gave her when they were together. Normally they spent a little time in the mornings and evenings getting to know each other, but most of his days were spent with Tony working on projects for Angela, and she was a little jealous of that. But she could spend a few precious hours with him today, and Tony couldn't commandeer him back, because her project was for the rescue too.

After he arrived, their conversation naturally turned toward the men on St. John. "I'm worried Greed will see the air drone, Jasper, because even though I made it look like a gull, it's bigger than a real bird and doesn't flap its wings." Abby frowned.

He shook his head, "The total time for the daylight passes is less than ten minutes, and it will only be visible from the fortress for four minutes. I don't think there's even a small chance someone will notice."

"Thanks for telling me that, Jasper. It makes me feel better." She lined up supplies on the kitchen counter. "Then I guess it's really Half-man who has the most risk of being discovered." Jasper didn't respond, because he was deeply worried too and couldn't reassure her about that possibility.

Abby continued. "I've grown to love them all like family, you know. And I feel so bad that almost all of them came from a sad childhood." She thought for a minute. "But probably that, and the war, is why they ended up with Angela in the woods."

"Post-traumatic stress disorder can happen even to people who were happy growing up, Abby, and all families have ups and downs because they're made of imperfect people." He didn't want to remember his own dysfunctional past.

"Yes, but that doesn't change the fact that kids deserve people who care and will stand for them." She touched his clenched fist because she knew what he was feeling. She lightened the mood by saying, "But I guess then you might end up with a mother like mine who has a hard time letting go, even though we're all grown up."

Jasper also revealed something that was bothering him. "I hate that Half-man uses that name. He's a whole man and a complete hero for what he's doing for me and Emma."

"I think it's OK for now. He'll find a name that fits better at some point, and I think when he openly declares what some might see as a fault, he becomes more of a man in a strange way."

Jasper wasn't sure he saw her point, but he nodded. "I care about them too, and it's hard to see them risking it all for me."

"It's their choice, and even though they're disabled, I've always said mentally strong trumps physical strength any day."

Jasper snorted. "It's better to have both, and I should know."

They had reached the stage where the pepper was diluted into a solution for spraying. Typically, propylene glycol was used so the pepper solution couldn't be easily washed off with water and so the burning would last for hours. Abby wanted a shorter duration spray, so she used a water-based compound for the mixture and planned to deliver it in a narrow stream of spray, which would limit splash back. She thought that maybe a water sprayer would work because it would spray bigger droplets and there would be less of a chance of the spray drifting back to the shooter than there would be with the fine mist of aerosol pepper sprayers. She wanted exactly the opposite delivery system from the paintball-type gun that fired pepper spray into riots for crowd control. How to test the knockdown strength of her pepper product was a problem. Maybe Hawkeye or Tony would be willing to place a small amount on his skin or lip and grade the burn reaction for her. Abby suspected the chili for dinner would end up spicy!

Pepper spray and sleeping powder were fine contributions to the weapon arsenal, Abby thought. All it would take was a solid day of work once the chemicals arrived and she would have enough chloral hydrate to ship to Stubby, and she already had ten pepper solutions for Hawkeye to try. Not bad for just a pretty face, she thought. And she had dinner almost ready too!

Thirty - Seven

In the beach cabin the remaining team took turns watching the live feed from the bugs that the water drone had placed in Greed's harbor. Mostly it was boring, and there was little activity, but someone's eyes monitored the screen around the clock, and currently it was Angela's turn. Everyone was enjoying an excellent apple crisp topped with vanilla ice cream when Angela jumped up and swore violently.

"That f—¾ motherf¾¾ bastard!"

All eyes turned to her when she shouted, and she pointed to the screen. "Hook, rewind the feed. That ball of slug slime does have the missing girls Chief Lawrence told Half-man about!"

Everyone gathered around and watched the few minutes when two girls were led from the stairs down the cave's hallway until they were out of sight. Their images were detailed and clear because the camera at the end of the waterway had recorded them. Both girls were wrapped in small blankets, with bare feet, and legs showing. Neither had visible clothing, and they held hands, giving each other silent support. Evidence of multiple beatings were clear on both girls because fresh wounds and bruises on their faces, arms, and legs were layered over healing scabs. The smaller girl had tear tracks visible on her face, and she limped; both were thin and dirty with tangled hair. Hook stopped the playback, and in the quiet room afterward Abby could be heard crying, so Tony went over and put his arms around her as comfort.

Angela took a deep, calming breath. "OK, everybody, this changes everything. We start by modifying our plans to include rescuing at least two more people besides Jasper and Emma. We can't assume those girls are the only additional victims on the island. Greed might have more that also need medical attention. The second helicopter—the one Greed keeps on his island—will have to carry them out, so the scuba team should be prepared to swim back to the boat if needed."

She strode around the room and pointed to the screen that was then continuing to stream live data from the harbor. "I want all the background info on that man"—she pointed to one guard—"that man and that man," she said while she pointed to the others returning back from the cave without the girls. "I want to know everything about them. What are their skills? Where did they come from? I want to know about the girls we saw. How old are they? Were they healthy before capture? Can they survive until we get there?" She pointed at Tony. "Your job."

Tony replied in a loud voice. "Why don't we just send that video to Chief Lawrence? Now that there's proof Greed kidnapped the girls, he can go and get them, and then we can just ride along and pick up Jasper and Emma."

Hook lifted a finger when Angela started to speak. "Let me tell him how it is. Not only isn't that proof that Greed did it, because I guarantee he will claim one of his men had them without his knowledge, but that evidence was also obtained illegally and will be thrown out of court, so he will get off and not pay for any of his crimes. And when the chief approaches his island, he will immediately feed the girls, Jasper, and Emma to the sharks. A complete lose-lose situation for our side."

Angela continued as if Tony hadn't interrupted her. She pointed to Jasper. "You figure out how the fortress gets its power. Maybe we can shut down his surveillance and make things easier for us by cutting off his electricity. Then hack into whatever you can and see what passports were issued for his staff. Be sure to check for expired visas. Maybe the chief could ship some guards home—which would help shift the odds in our favor—before we get there."

She spoke to Abby. "I'm approving all your projects and ideas, but we're running out of time to make the medical device you promised to show Greed. Work on that now."

Finally she turned to Hawkeye. "Calculate the maximum weight both helicopters can carry, because we may have to leave some stuff on the island. I would prefer there isn't a trace of us after we leave, but that may not be possible if we need to carry extra people so have to leave equipment behind. Then make up a medical kit: pain relief, portable power for Jasper and Emma if they're on a ventilator, and whatever else you can think of that we might need for them and the girls. Add that weight to what we already have for supplies." She did a fake laugh. "No thirds on apple crisps for anyone tonight!"

Angela grabbed Hook's arm and pulled him toward the door saying over her shoulder. "We're going home to finalize the rescue and to add in the new prisoner release part." Hook could tell she was upset but trying to control it, so he put his arm around her as she continued. "Jasper made a video game of the proposed fortress assault. It's three dimensional, and each player will play first person as themselves. It's going to feel like we're really on Reed Island creeping around the fortress and zapping guards as we go. Tonight we'll load it up and run simulations of the current plan with the girls added in. Half-man, Melt, and Stubby will join online from St. John. We can work on various alternative approaches that include this new information so we'll be prepared if—or more likely when—something goes wrong with the first plan. No speaking during play, so use the communication device only. Jasper will patch it through to St. John. A dollar for every guard down, ten for La Ruhr, and twenty for Greed. Bring your money, boys and girls, and let's take him down tonight every way we can!"

She and Hook walked to her motor home, but once the door was closed, Angela had a good cry in his arms. She knew the stakes had just gotten much higher. There were more people to rescue, and clearly Greed was more than a scam artist; he was also a sexual predator who liked to beat women up. She sobbed to Hook that she was sending her sweet cousin Abby right into his jaws dressed like a tasty treat for him to gobble up!

Abby, Tony, and Jasper were arguing back in the cabin about the very same thing. "This does change everything! I don't see why Abby has to be involved at all now. The risk to her has gone way up. Angela should just send Stubby in the helicopter, do the land and sea assault as planned, and then take Greed out once the fortress is secured," Jasper said.

Abby protested. "But I want to be involved, Jasper! Greed needs to be distracted while the teams get in place. He's already agreed to see me. I can do it, so just give me a chance!"

Tony backed Jasper. "Now that we know the kind of man he is, we can't risk sending you in there, sis. You might not just be a distraction anymore. Instead, you could be a sacrifice to a monster! Think about all the things that could go wrong. You would end up like those poor girls. Angela has got to change the plan!"

Hawkeye jumped in loudly. "Abby's right because we've run the plan's chance of success with and without her, and it's a much better op if she's there."

Tony shot a mean look at Hawkeye. "Look, man, she isn't your baby sister! We can do it without her. Jasper and I will do better work without worrying about whether she is getting beaten and raped by Greed!"

"For gosh sake, he's not going to get that far! I'm not a helpless girl, so give me some credit for once! Besides, Stubby will be right there on the helicopter pad if I need him," Abby shouted back.

Tony wasn't convinced. "How's Stubby going to know if you're in trouble? You won't be wearing a communication device or carrying weapons." Tony tried to reason with her.

She stayed strong. "Stubby made me a couple of awesome defense pieces that'll be well hidden. Greed won't know what hit him if he tries anything bad with me."

"Hidden weapons aren't easy to deploy, little sister, and he may have armed guards in the room with you at all times. You aren't going to take them and Greed out at the same time using less force than they have available."

"I've thought about that possibility, and I don't think he'll keep guards with me. If Greed thinks sex is pending—and you know Dee set me up so I can use that as bait—he'll want me alone. And I'll look like such a small threat that he won't be thinking 'danger.' I'm just another weak woman for him to dominate, so why keep guards?"

"Remember the video, Abby! It looks like he gets off on inflicting fear and pain. Do you really want to go there alone? Or maybe he likes to let the guards watch and will keep them around for the show. You just can't predict what'll happen."

She was really angry then. "Back off, Tony! I'm Dr. Newton, and he wants something from me very badly. He hurts me, and I won't sign the papers to make him lots of money. Plus, people will know I'm visiting the island, so he can't just make me disappear."

Hawkeye slammed his fist on the table and ended the argument. "You guys don't like the plan, take it up with Angela. She's the leader, and she has the final say. Abby is important to her, and if she thinks the risk is too much, she'll change the plan." He left the cabin, slamming the door behind him. Hawkeye didn't want to put Abby at risk either, but he trusted Angela's experience. What did two computer geeks know about a combat-rescue mission anyway?

The two geeks looked at each other in surprise. Hawkeye was usually so quiet and calm. He had always told them that emotions ruin the sniper's chance of success, so a clear, cool head must be maintained at all times. When he was shooting, he even controlled his breath, and they joked that he stopped his heartbeat for a moment too.

After a moment of silence Abby offered a compromise to the men. "How about if we play the video game tonight with and without me? If you trust your simulation's accuracy, Jasper, then it will be obvious to everybody if the rescue plan is just as successful without me. And if it's the same either way, then I'll stay home. I promise."

They agreed to let the computer decide, so everyone poured a fresh cup of coffee and went about the tasks Angela had assigned with fresh determination. Dr. Newton would soon pack for her trip to Reed Island; already, there were piles of climbing gear, scuba equipment, and other stuff Abby didn't recognize filling up most of the free space in the cabin.

If she were honest with herself, Abby would have admitted that she didn't want to face Greed alone, but logic told her that the plan was weak without her involvement. She loved Jasper and Emma, and she wanted to do everything in her power to make a life with them a part of her future. But because she had seen the suffering girls, it was even more important that the rescue plan worked. Greed needed to be locked in a prison cell permanently, even if that meant she had to take a personal risk and put herself in some danger.

Thirty - Eight

Hawkeye was upset, and he ranted to himself as he paced up and down the beach. He felt Angela's plan was ridiculous considering that they knew what Greed was capable of. There was only one way to run a rescue mission like this against a man like him, and it was done with a sniper. He was just the man for the job. In then out, absolutely quiet and quick; just one kill shot, and then exit the scene before anyone can even comprehend what has happened. Leave kids like Tony, Jasper, and Abby at home where they belong, safe and sound. Send an expendable man like him to kill Greed with a single well-placed bullet to the brain—to blast him out of existence with a splatter of gore like he'd done many times before.

Hawkeye strode the beach at the waterline, oblivious to the waves wetting his shoes. Why were they messing around with nonlethal weapons like the Zap? He only had one eye, and that limited his depth perception, but he still had skills, and no one was more motivated to do it than he was. What Greed had done to Jasper and Emma was bad enough, but kidnapping and torturing innocent girls was inhuman; he would be the judge, jury, and executioner, too! Suddenly he noticed that Abby was walking calmly beside him, and he stopped in his tracks.

He snarled at her, "What the hell are you doing here, girl? Angela gave you enough to do for three people, so go do it."

"I thought you might need a friend." Abby looked at him with understanding and no judgment in her eyes.

"I don't need you. I don't need anyone, so beat it. Now!"

Abby looked at his face; it was twisted in hatred and despair. She put her arms firmly around him but said nothing in reply to his asking her to go away. At first Hawkeye held himself rigid and tried to shrug her arms off with his shoulders, but when Abby continued to hold him, he slowly relaxed and rested his cheek against her hair.

"I want to murder Greed so bad! I've killed people who deserved it less than he does. The marines made me a lethal machine, so Angela needs to let me go and do my job. No one else besides Greed will get hurt, and you can all stay home safe. A nice head shot, and Jasper, Emma, and the girls he has will be OK again, I promise."

Abby drew back and looked him in his one good eye. "Hawkeye, no matter what you say, you're not a killer! Killers enjoy their work, and I can see how much it hurt you to do it in the military. You're one of the sweetest people I've ever known. You're so gentle and kind that I doubt you would even smash a bug biting you." She knew Angela's other men had also killed and suffered for it, too, but Hawkeye didn't seem to register that fact. She realized he saw himself as a damaged person incapable of releasing the label he'd taken on under orders.

Abruptly he caved and hugged her back. "I've worked hard to put the memory of the people I've killed behind me, but I want to take him out so bad. He'll hurt you, Abby, so please stay home!"

She kissed his cheek. "You're part of a team this time, Hawkeye, so we'll all share responsibility for what happens. Everyone will work Angela's plan together, and Greed will pay for his crimes. Have faith in us as a group. If someone does die, then we will all bear the responsibility and the sadness because none of us is alone anymore."

She toyed with his pirate beard. "Besides, don't think Angela hasn't considered a sniper-hit plan. Greed hasn't left his island in five years, so you'd have to get close to the fortress alone, hide, wait without being discovered, and then get a clear shot at him through shielded small windows. You might be able to make that work, but you could also wait months for the right moment to shoot, and we don't have that kind of time. Even with your amazing skill, a single sniper shot isn't a good plan, Hawkeye."

They started walking back down the beach toward the mostly empty camp—with Stubby, Melt, and Half-man in St. John and Hook living with Angela, he was the only person currently in residence—and he linked their arms together. He quietly confided in her.

"I went to live in Angela's woods because death seemed more real to me than life. The thoughts of what I had done occupied my mind day and night. I couldn't stand it anymore, and she offered me some peace!"

He stopped walking and looked at her like she should run away from him, but Abby stayed put firmly. "I killed only under direct orders, but I watched my shots hit home in the rifle's scope. I saw the blood and destruction magnified that way. The brass ordered the shots, but I pulled the trigger, and I watched them die. In my mind I see it over and over again. I don't know why they had to die, because I never knew who they were. I don't know why I did it without questioning my orders, and that makes me a bad person, Abby. Just like Greed." His voice choked up.

She put her arms around him again. "I'm so sorry that happened to you, Hawkeye. You've always seemed controlled about your shooting, but you are nothing like Greed. He enjoys hurting people, and you never could, believe me."

"I'm not controlled. That's just my training."

"No, it's not. When you were teaching me to shoot, you were so patient with me and explained technique again and again. You didn't flinch even when I shot wild and almost hit you."

"I have to keep everything tamped down tight, Abby, or I might accidently kill someone when I'm angry."

"That's not true!" She turned and yelled at him and kicked the sand in frustration.

"I'm a trained killer, and that's what I do. You all need to accept that. I can't limit myself to zapping someone—not when I could shoot him and get it over with for good."

"No, Hawkeye. Trust yourself to make the right decisions even when you're angry. You're a good person. You may want to kill Greed, but there is a big difference between wanting to and acting on that impulse. How many parents say they want to strangle their kids for throwing a tantrum in the store? Does that make them bad parents? Just thinking about it isn't a crime, because only acting on that thought makes it bad."

"Only I have the skills and the high-powered rifle to do it," he said grimly.

"Hey, I have the skills and the chemicals to kill half the population of Seattle. Doesn't mean I'm going to do it when I'm mad."

They reached the rock barrier at the cove entrance and headed for the cabin. Hawkeye wasn't pounding the sand with his feet or clenching his fists anymore, so Abby took that as a sign that he was feeling better. She felt tender toward the man who took orders and did what he was told even when it damaged him inside. She remembered that he had been lonely as a passed-around foster child but happy once he had found his talent for shooting and had received recognition as an Olympic-level marksman. How awful it must have been for him to turn the skill he thought finally gave him value into a destructive killing force.

His good heart had been broken by the pain of rejection in his childhood and further damaged by the trauma of his military service. Abby knew he played down his good looks with shaggy hair, an unkempt full beard and mustache, an eye patch, and glowering facial expressions. That off-putting surface was all a shield to keep people away from his sensitive feelings and tender heart, she thought. It was time to talk to Jasper about making a chip to tamp down Hawkeye's memories, because she knew he wouldn't reveal his pain and ask for it himself.

Abby continued her lecture. "All that control while you're boiling with emotion isn't good for you, Hawkeye. You may feel like it holds the inner killer at bay, but none of the good stuff in life is getting through to you either. Life is short, and it's filled with emotion, both bad and good, for everyone. Maybe when you're shut down you don't feel like you want to kill anybody, but when is the last time you felt joy?"

He considered her point as they walked along. "Even as a kid I never had joy. I'm not even sure what it is."

"Oh, Hawkeye! It's recognizing and embracing those small moments that make you feel good. It's a sunset, a smooth stone, a bird in flight, a great cup of coffee, or anything you appreciate. Take a deep breath and purposefully open yourself up to the experience, and take it in with gratitude. Believe the good is there for you and that you deserve to enjoy it, and you'll find it's all around you."

He scoffed. "If you're happy, then something bad will come along right after it and knock you down lower than before."

"Well, no wonder you don't experience joy, then! That's not true, and even if it were, those happy moments can sustain you through the bad times. You need them, Hawkeye. Look for them, because those precious, wonderful, simple moments are everywhere—I promise."

Abby resolved to put Emma in his lap at dinner. She'd noticed that he had deliberately stayed away from the baby, and she finally knew why: he believed bad things would follow being happy. Emma might appear to be always asleep and unaware, but she was cuddly and warm and had a calm, angelic presence.

She noticed that Emma was a magnet for upset people—and there were always willing arms to hold her—because she made people feel happy in some mysterious way. Emma was soothing magic, and most of the adults orbited around her small body with love bubbling in their hearts. Maybe it couldn't be scientifically measured, but it was a daily observable phenomena.

"Why do you care if I'm happy anyway?" Hawkeye grumbled.

"Here's a news flash: I like you. I see so much to respect and admire when I look at you. You're a great guy under all that facial hair, and I want to be your friend for a long time." She laughed and squeezed his hand.

They stopped in the center of the camp where beef stew was simmering in a big pot over the fire. Hawkeye put his arms around Abby again and gave her a long hug. "Thanks, I want to be your friend, too."

As Abby walked away from him, she realized that that was the first time he had touched her voluntarily—outside of positioning her body on the firing range. He had always stayed on the periphery of the group, too—cooking and serving food but not sitting with everyone else to eat it, and attending meetings but not saying anything. She had thought it was shyness, but now she understood it was his perceived lack of worthiness to be with others on the team.

Probably he thought killers didn't eat with the group or have anything important to say; who wanted to sit with a murderer or be a friend to one? She remembered he had even pitched his one-man tent away from the group. Well, she was going to make it her mission to change all of that. Abby's definition of a friend was one who stood by you and treated you as an equal no matter what. Hawkeye had a friend in her, and he had better get used to being part of a team rather than just the lonely, damaged sniper he thought he was.

Thirty - Nine

Abby wore gloves, a protective apron, goggles, and an air-filtration mask as she poured the potent capsaicin-rich pepper mixture into the sprayers. She capped the containers and thought about the design of the medical device she would need to distract Greed during the rescue. He didn't have any scientific background, so it needed to be simple and understandable to a layperson, and its monetary value in sales had to be self-evident. She cynically thought he wouldn't see easing suffering or curing disease as valuable in itself, because it was all about the money it would make for a man steeped in greed like he was.

Portability of the device was necessary because she would carry it on the helicopter with her, so that meant no large attachments or special requirements for its operation could be involved. She wanted it to be a unique, new idea in medical equipment with universal appeal and a flashy look to catch his eye. Putting all those requirements together was a tall order, especially since she had limited time to produce a finished product. Greed undoubtedly would require a working demonstration, and that alone made it complicated because there wasn't any time for testing and redesign. It had to work the first time and every time after without fail, or her life might be in danger.

Abby could picture Greed throwing it across the room and then insisting it still work perfectly.

She played around with some ideas as she worked. How about a new diagnostic tool that measured joint degeneration? No, that was just too complicated in the short timeframe she had. What about a computer assisted device for people with memory loss? No, Greed couldn't have cared less about helping people. So how about a cure for cancer—lots of money there! Yeah, like she could make that happen. This wasn't the first time Abby had thought about the device. She'd been mentally going around and around with ideas and discarding them even before her visit to Medi-Help, but nothing had jelled for her. She decided to ask Tony and Jasper for ideas because those two minds were the definition of out-of-the-box thinking, so she paid a visit to Tony's truck.

It was a little uncomfortable for her because playing Jasper's rescue game made it clear to the team that she had to be part of the plan for it to succeed, and neither man had talked to her much after that. Abby knew they weren't mad at her and that they just felt bad about the extra risk she'd be taking. She found them leaning back in their chairs, twiddling their thumbs, and talking about their favorite episodes of *Dr. Who*. Most people would have thought they were goofing off, but Abby knew serious mental work was taking place behind their relaxed appearances.

"Hope I'm not interrupting, but I need some help thinking of an idea for the medical thing I'll tempt Greed to buy." Abby listed her requirements for the device.

Tony dismissed most of them. "It doesn't really have to work, sis. It doesn't have to do anything. It just has to look cool and to appear to him like it can function."

She objected to his casual attitude. "But Tony, I need to believe it works so I can put my heart into selling him on the idea. Otherwise he's going to smell a skunk right away. You know what a bad liar I am!"

Tony wasn't convinced. "No, magicians don't have to believe in their own magic for it to work. They just have to convince the audience it's real. Besides, he isn't going to take your word for it anyway. As a sharp businessman he'll only believe what he sees with his own eyes, and not what you tell him, so all we need to do is make it look real."

Jasper was concerned about what Tony was proposing and sided with Abby. "No, TNT! It has to be real, or she's in danger! Greed isn't going to be easily tricked. He's expecting fraud because he's paranoid. Otherwise he wouldn't live in that setup of his."

Abby tried to get them back on track. "OK, let's just brainstorm some ideas and see how far we get with it, guys. We don't have a lot of time to get this done."

Tony got up for a soda and chips, and soon the truck was filled with the sounds of him slurping and crunching. Just when Abby was about to start screaming with impatience, Jasper said, "You know what I hate about doctors? All those needles they want to stick in you all the time. What's up with that, anyway?"

Tony agreed. "Yeah, bro! I hate them, too. Either they want to put something in you with one or to take something out of you with one."

Abby thought about that for a minute. "Actually, that's a good place to start, Jasper. Simple and universal because pretty much everyone hates needles. Greed would understand the appeal of a needle substitute and realize that it's a chance to make lots of money because every hospital, clinic, and lab buys syringes and needles regularly."

Tony laughed. "He would be a hero, and famous for sparing people needle trauma, and would make lots of mullah at the same time. What's not to like?"

"But how would we do that? You'd need to inject something as a demonstration, wouldn't you?" Jasper asked.

Tony replied, "No, we don't, Jazz. It just has to appear to Greed that something was injected."

Abby thought about transdermal patches as a delivery system because no needles were involved in that application. But only a limited number of drugs could pass through the skin barrier, and the total dose received depended on variables like the skin's thickness, so a redesigned and universal patch wouldn't be convincing if Greed knew anything about them.

"How about the air gun vaccine injector used by the military for recruits? Maybe we could put a new spin on that device." Jasper asked.

Tony scoffed at that idea. "I heard those hurt as much—if not more—than needles. Besides, if you demonstrate on Greed, then it can't hurt, or he won't buy it. It's well known that bullies can dish it out, but not take it very well, so it's got to be painless for sure."

Abby defined the problem to help them focus. The device needed to get a volume of material through the skin and into the muscle without damaging tissue or activating nerves because that was what created pain.

Jasper had researched anatomy and physiology extensively for his game designs. He pondered her criteria out loud. "How about an electrical pulse to numb the area and then lots of tiny holes for the injection? Then the liquid would slide between the tissue layers rather than cutting through them and activating nerves."

Abby was impressed with his knowledge but explained that there were problems with that idea: nerves run on electricity, so they would react to an electrical pulse by contacting nearby muscles, which would register pain. Also, she reminded them that even a small electrical shock isn't fun and that muscle fibers overlap, so there wouldn't be a way to slide in between them without creating damage.

As she was telling them why Jasper's idea wouldn't work, it occurred to her that Greed wouldn't know any of that information either, so it actually wasn't important to the design after all. And she could easily tech-speak the idea in such a way that Greed would be convinced it would work. It had certainly sounded possible when Jasper had suggested it, so she could use a lot of big medical words in the explanation and then follow up with a great demonstration, and he might believe it. After all, Dr. Newton had credibility, and why would she lie about such a thing? Greed would understand it was a big breakthrough in technology and had the potential to change the delivery of medicine forever.

Abby suddenly high-fived Tony and happily said, "Actually, I like your idea, Jasper! And I can work it with Greed. But how are we going to convince him that it injects when it really doesn't?"

That problem required a refill of chips and an in-depth discussion about which was the best *Transformer* movie made so far. Abby tried to be patient, but she fidgeted and mentally recited the periodic table of the elements down to their atomic numbers while she waited. She understood that Jasper and Tony were occupying the left critical-thinking side of their brains with trivia while the right creative half worked on the problem. Even knowing that, it was hard to be quiet and to let them work. She solved hard problems in a different way by making lists, looking things up, and planning in detail on paper. Their system drove her crazy!

Jasper finally said, "One day about six months ago when I was at the park with Emma, I watched this little girl feed her doll baby a doll bottle. The bottle had milk in it that disappeared when she turned it upside down to feed the baby doll, so it looked like the doll actually had drank it. Her mom let me look at the bottle, and I could see it only contained a small amount of white liquid and that most of the bottle's volume was made up of a clear cylinder. It just looked like it was full of milk to begin with because the small amount of white liquid was squeezed between the cylinder and the bottle wall. But when it was turned upside down, the white liquid flowed into the bottle cap and disappeared from sight, creating the illusion that the doll had drank the milk. Turned upright again, the milk flowed back into the bottle's small inner space for another pretend feeding."

Jasper sketched on a piece of paper. "Overall, it looked pretty convincing, so what if we used a variation of that idea? Push the plunger of the syringe, and the liquid disappears like it was injected. Instead it was only a small amount to start with, and it went into a hidden chamber. The result would be an absolutely pain-free shot because there hadn't been an injection at all."

Tony slapped his hand on his knee. "Absolutely genius, man!"

Abby kissed him. "Make it so, number one, but make it look cool, too."

Tony laughed. "So how about a *Star Trek* design? Dr. McCoy's sensor scan thing was pretty cool. Medical and awesome at the same time, but I think they modified a saltshaker to begin with."

Abby did a brief happy dance. "I'll get some B12 vitamins for injection because they're a bright red color, so Greed will be able to see them easily in the syringe. I'll take the bottle with me, and he can watch me draw them up from the actual container. Plus, he might know B vitamins sting on injection.

"Maybe I could take a real needle and give him a comparison shot. Too bad I can't use a nice anesthetic to sedate him. It would be so much easier to rescue people if he were unconscious," she added, her lip curled in an expression of disgust.

"Unless he wanted you to demonstrate the anesthetic on your own arm, because then you'd be in trouble, sis," Tony said.

Forty

Angela called a team meeting to review the results of her latest assignments; the men in St. John were joining them by video conference.

"Tony, what do you have to report on Greed's staffing?" she asked.

"You're not going to like this, Angela, but officially, all he has for employees is a business manager—La Ruhr—a cook, a housekeeper, a helicopter pilot, and a ship captain. He hires some extra crew when he takes his yacht out, but his total staff on record is only five people."

Angela protested. "How can that be, Tony? Stubby recognized at least twenty heat signatures in the fortress, and I'm sure there are more down in the caves, too."

He smiled. "Well, those are all that are listed for official payroll deductions when he files his taxes, but I didn't believe it either. So I had Half-man ask around on St. John, and it turns out every six months he orders new uniforms for his staff from a local company. I guess Greed's vain and wants the people who represent him to look sharp in his black-and-gold colors even though most of them aren't seen by the public. I printed his last uniform purchase invoice." Tony passed a copy to Angela.

"Good work, Tony." She fist-bumped him. "Not only does it give us how many sets he ordered, but also the sizes, the embroidered names, and the titles too. Did you get background checks for anybody on this list?"

"They're mostly an invisible presence because they all stay on the island except for a few who do the supply runs. No one, apparently, gets vacations or travels at all, or at least they haven't been seen on, or leaving, St. John by the locals. It reminds me of how many illegal aliens or people who have been victims of human trafficking live. But sometimes the supply run guys get in trouble with St. John residents. Drunk and disorderly, that kind of thing. Complaints were filed but then withdrawn later in every case I saw."

"Any complaints other than 'D and Ds' that I need to know about?"

He shuffled through a pile of computer printouts. "Here's one from a fruit stand in the market." Tony read from the paper. "Complainant claims Mr. Smith frequently walks through the market and takes fruit from his display without paying for it. He then allegedly takes a few bites, throws the fruit on the ground, and complains loudly that it tastes bad. In the past, he has also tipped over garbage cans, kicked them around to spill the contents, and then walked away, leaving other people to clean up the mess. Mr. Smith also grabbed and kissed the complainant's fourteen-year-old daughter without permission and then dropped her to the ground and complained loudly that she tasted as bad as the fruit from his stand."

"A jerk who thinks he can do whatever he wants to anybody at anytime. It shows that Greed picks them mean and stupid too!" Angela hissed.

"Greed probably cleaned up after the incident, because the complaint was suddenly withdrawn after a suspicious fire started in the man's fruit stand."

"That must have chapped the chief's butt!" Angela shook her head in sympathy for him. "So do any of the people Greed acknowledges have valid passports? Did you do any criminal background checks on the ones he openly has on staff?"

"The five people on record are all clean as a whistle. All totally nice, law-abiding citizens, and that means the paperwork is fake, because Mr. Smith is one of them."

"So where did all the rest of the people on Reed Island come from, and who are they?" Hook asked.

Tony looked around the room. "Well, Jasper and I have a theory about that. We think Greed moves people in and out on his submarine. Ships can be tracked and flights have to register a plan, but submarines are hard to follow deep under water. I'm willing to bet that's how he gets the girls there, too."

Angela thought for a minute. "That makes total sense, Tony. Maybe some of Greed's workers aren't there voluntarily. They're like shanghaied sailors: once they're on Reed Island, there's no way out, and his guards make sure they behave."

"Cuts down on overhead to have unpaid labor. It would appeal to his greed. No costly wages, pesky withholding taxes, or trouble with unions, either," Abby added.

"Don't think that if that's true his people will be on our side in a fight! They won't recognize us as a rescue team, and Greed's power probably has scared them enough to kill us on sight just to save their own skins. We won't have time to convince them we're the good guys and win them over. The chief will have to sort them out after the rescue is over and we're on our way home," Angela said.

Tony poured coffee refills around the table. "But maybe if they see us as a chance to escape, they'll cut and run rather than fight us."

"Don't bet on it, anyone! Even pausing a moment to see how they feel about Greed will give them a chance to kill us. We have to consider everyone on the island an enemy and Zap them on sight." She glared at each person on the team until they nodded in agreement and then continued. "So if I count the uniforms ordered—looks like even the cooks wear his colors—that makes twenty-five against seven, not counting Greed, La Ruhr, or anyone else who didn't get a cool new outfit this time. Assuming Abby, Jasper, and Emma won't be Zapping anyone, then each of us has to take out at least three and a half people."

Abby and Tony exchanged concerned looks. It was a sobering thought to take down one person, but it seemed impossible to take down more than three without getting injured. She took Jasper's hand and squeezed it gently, because she knew he wouldn't consider rescuing Emma and him worth the risk of those odds.

Hawkeye chuckled to relieve the sudden tension he felt in the room. "We'll have fun dropping them, so I love those odds. I can't wait to engage the bad guys in a good fight! I don't know about everyone else, but I'm pumped to do this and bring little Emma home."

Angela made a settle-down movement with her hand toward Hawkeye and changed the subject. "What did you find out about the kidnapped girls, Tony?"

Tony took a deep breath. "You're not going to like this either, Angela, but the two we saw are just the latest in a series of missing girls. I did a search for reports within two hundred miles of Reed Island by sea when I saw the way the girls were kept together and acted like a team. I wondered if that was an abuse pattern for Greed—usually criminals repeat their methods. So I looked for two girls taken at the same time, and there were five reports for a total of ten girls—or an abduction every nine months. There might be more if I look farther away or if there are some who haven't been reported as missing to the authorities."

Abby gasped. "Oh God!"

Tony touched Abby's shoulder, and Angela said with vehemence, "I swear that the girls we saw are the last people that bastard ever takes. If the rest he kidnapped are there, we'll get them out somehow. And if he's already killed them, then we'll at least give their families some closure about what happened to them." Angela was so mad that she wanted to kill Greed right then with her bare hands! Because after seeing the suffering girls on the video, no one had any doubt that Reed Island was the destination for all of the missing young women.

Hawkeye cleared the lump in his throat and then spoke. "Angela, given this new information, I think some of us should be armed with lethal weapons. Greed didn't abduct people by himself, so he has accomplices on the island who'll fight hard to avoid a prison sentence."

He turned to Abby. "I know you didn't want to use guns, but this is a much more serious situation than we had originally thought."

"You wouldn't use them unless there is no other choice but to kill someone?" Abby asked quietly.

Hawkeye answered, "No. We're not killers. Remember our talk, sweetie?"

"Then I think you should take whatever you need." She looked in each person's eyes one by one, including the men on St. John. "I'm not limiting you to the Zap anymore. I'll be sad if someone dies on either side, but you're far more important to me than they are, so take what you need to be as safe as possible."

"Melt, Stubby, and Half-man, given this development, do you want to add any additional supplies to what we're already bringing? If so, send me a list pronto," Angela said to the computer screen.

She consulted her notes. "OK, Jasper, can we shut down power to the fortress during the rescue?"

He shook his head and replied, "No way to do it, Angela. Greed has multiple solar panels and a second system where ocean waves turn generator turbines. He stores all the power he doesn't use immediately. We can't shut off all the sources at one time, and each one automatically backs up the others. They get a lot of hurricanes there, so he has everything covered by multiple systems."

Angela sighed. "Win some, lose some" She tapped her clipboard. "I want supplies double-checked by each team tomorrow because I don't want to get there and find some important piece of equipment is missing. I need everything on the master list brought to the cabin, and I will review it before dinner." She glared around the room to make that important point clear to everyone.

She continued. "Everyone will be issued a unique predistressed fishing vest. Unlike Greed, I don't want us all to look the same. A casual lost-tourist appearance might make Greed's staff pause for a critical moment before they shoot, and that would give us the advantage. Also, after Hook and I jam the monitors, the guards may not connect that a team effort is in play at several locations on the island, because we'll appear to be individuals.

"The vests are lined with Kevlar and have pockets inside and out. Please become familiar with where everything is located so you can get to it fast. Practice drawing and returning your gear quickly. Each vest will be equipped with two Zaps, two communication devices, two dozen pairs of nylon cable-tie cuffs, two pepper sprayers, a knife, and other important items. The harbor team has special waterproofing on everything. Vests have already been sent along with the sleeping powder to St. John for the guys there."

She grimaced at Jasper. "Lastly, Jasper, you and Emma will need to shrink back down tomorrow. I know it's hard on you both, but you know it has to be done for the plan to work best. Meeting dismissed. I think there's barbequed pulled pork sandwiches for lunch, so let's eat."

Forty - One

Madam La Ruhr was finalizing her plans to escape Reed Island. It had been a lucrative job, but the risks clearly outweighed the benefits. The day before, Reed had called her into his office to review the financial statements for his Medi-Help corporation; he was trying to decide if he should market Dr. Newton's device through them or create a new company especially for that product. She had embezzled seven million dollars out of Reed's Medi-Help profits, but she wasn't worried about him discovering it, because she had carefully covered her tracks through creative accounting, and she was an expert at it. Ruhr knew only a forensic accountant would notice anything amiss and that if he did catch a glimpse of her activities, he could never trace the money back to her. She had made sure Douglas would take the blame long before a single dollar was tracked to her bank.

What she was worried about was Reed's slow but steady downward spiral into psychosis and violence over the last few years. When he had first hired her, his mind hadn't been strictly normal, but it had functioned. Lately darkness seemed to occupy most of his thoughts, and she thought it wouldn't be long until his kingdom collapsed into madness. La Ruhr planned to use Dr. Newton's visit as a cover for her own disappearance. Reed hadn't allowed a visitor to his island in years, and she intended to take advantage of everyone's distraction to escape. Once she was far enough away, she would assume a new identity; everything was already in place, and she only needed to set it in motion.

One of biggest factors for her decision to leave was the girls he kept for playmates. Of course La Ruhr knew about them—and it had been fine by her—but the time between acquisition and discard was getting shorter and shorter. He had had his latest pair for less than ten weeks, and he was already losing interest in them; she knew that because he was directing more of his violence to the staff instead. So they probably weren't giving him the intense reaction to fear and pain that he craved, and soon they would be tossed off the cliff to the sharks like all the others had been, and then he would want new ones immediately.

Reed's disgusting hobby was especially dangerous to her now because he had taken the last girls from St. John, and not from his usual distant hunting grounds. That was the stupidest of moves because La Ruhr knew Chief Lawrence saw Reed as a person of interest in their kidnapping. Two more missing girls would result in a search warrant, and then they would all go to jail. She didn't intend to be on the island when that happened.

Reed was also getting suspicious that she was stealing from him somehow. Two days before he had asked to see the inventory list of his small jade figurines. When it had tallied correctly and he had carefully inspected each one, he'd dropped one on the floor and had asked her to pick it up. But when she'd reached for it, he'd stepped on her hand and held it on the floor with his full weight crushing her fingers.

Then with a cold smile on his face, he had said, "Never take what's mine, madam, or I will take what's yours, and it will hurt a lot. And I'll enjoy that immensely."

She'd been careful not to show him any pain or fear and set off his psychosis so had answered calmly and firmly. "No, Sir Reed, of course I won't."

Later, she thought that experience had been like being in a room with a tiger who really wanted to rip your throat out but was barely restrained on a leash meant for a small dog. The tiger knew the leash could be broken, but it was waiting for just the right time to do it. La Ruhr had never had such a chilling experience. She knew at that moment that she could easily end up like his playmates if she made the wrong move at the wrong time. She was lucky he hadn't broken her hand, but she was even more grateful that she'd been able to remain calm!

She had taken many items from his priceless collections, but she wasn't stupid. She knew he prized the ancient jade figurines, and she had drooled over them; but the chance of getting caught was too high, so she had left them alone. Instead, she had slowly replaced large gems with look-alike laboratory-grown synthetic stones that were identical down to the etched numbers and valuable paintings with specially commissioned copies. She had ordered gem replacements based on Reed's careful documentation of clarity, color, flaws, and cut, and hidden them in her undergarments until she could make a quick exchange. And when the paintings were sent out for cleaning and restoration, duplicates had been made, then exchanged for the masterpieces and shipped back in the original frames.

She knew Reed wasn't a gemologist or an art appraiser, so unless he imported experts to his island for an analysis, she was home free. He might find out someday, but by then she would be long gone into a new identity in a different country. It had certainly paid off to have connections in the criminal world and money to pay for the best copies possible.

As La Ruhr iced her hand, she sighed sadly because it had been a good job, netting her at least four million a year for the three years he had employed her, plus what she would make by selling his stuff once she was off the island. If she added the standard salary Reed had paid her to the free housing, meals, utilities, and transportation, it hadn't been a bad gig for an ex-pornstar from New Jersey with a talent for cooking accounting books.

La Ruhr's exit plan utilized the submarine and a pair of twin Russian American brothers who had been dishonorably discharged from the United States Navy. They operated the submarine when Reed did his kidnappings, but she'd won their loyalty over to her by planting seeds of rebellion and then watering them with sex; finally, she'd promised them lots of money to transport her off the island. She planned to hand over the cash once she was safely away, and after they let her off, she would allow them to take the submarine. They talked about getting rich by doing drug runs from South America with it, and she encouraged their big dream while thinking how stupid it was, because once the cartel had the submarine, why would they give the brothers a big cut of the profits?

Dr. Newton was supposed to arrive that night, and La Ruhr could tell Reed was full of maniacal excitement. She had seen him like that before and was willing to bet that the good doctor would end up in the cave, like the girls, before morning. Reed was too far gone to realize that kidnapping a person of Newton's status was a very bad idea; if he did that, it would bring in the authorities, and his whole house of cards would tumble down on his head. She thought it was only in his deteriorated mind that he believed he could get away with it.

La Ruhr had distracted him by playing it cool all day and by showering him with compliments and attention. He had preened with delight over her words and had never considered that he was a just another mark to her. Maybe he had been smart once, she thought, but those days were long gone, and he was just a decaying carcass she was picking clean.

After lunch she wandered down to the harbor to see the brothers. She never wrote anything down that could incriminate her, so she whispered her final plans to them while carrying on a loud conversation about fishing to confuse the ever-present monitoring.

"Tonight, be ready. When the visitor arrives and he takes her into his office, I'll use the staff hallway to bring my stuff. Prepare the sub to take it out for an engine test. I'll forge his signature on an order for that and give it to the commander once Reed is occupied."

They nodded in agreement; she trusted them to do as she said because she knew they hated taking orders from Reed—that was why she had selected them in the first place. They both thought Reed wasn't worthy of commanding a vessel or of giving orders to them. They complained that he didn't look like an officer and that his obvious mental sickness made him unstable and inferior. She had a slight worry the brothers wouldn't convincingly conceal their true intentions, because neither man had acting skills or was very bright, but she knew it was a risk she had to take. Hopefully, the excitement of the doctor's arrival would cover any change in their body language.

Reed had posted all the guards at their stations for Dr. Newton's visit, and the kitchen staff was busy producing a fancy dinner. Under the guise of preparing everything perfectly for their rare guest, La Ruhr would add more demands and spread conflict wherever she could. Then when everyone was running around doing extra chores, the confusion would give her additional cover to make her final trip down to the submarine safely.

She would take only one bag, the money to pay the brothers, and the clothes on her back. The bag contained the data she needed to move all of Reed's money into accounts controlled by her. She had a power-of-attorney authorization signed by Reed himself, because when he had thought he was signing a cover letter, she had slipped it in, and he had signed that instead. She had his account locations and numbers, his PIN identification codes, and his passwords. But even better than those was the fact that she had made herself known as his business manager at his various banks for years, so no one would question her activities. La Ruhr had chatted up officers and tellers alike, and she had moved money for him in the past, so they wouldn't question her authority to do so then.

It was all a matter of timing, so when Newton disappeared, the authorities would swoop in, and Reed would be imprisoned. Then she could clean him out at her leisure. And as insurance that he would be incarcerated for a long time, she had planted evidence that he was responsible for kidnapping and killing all the girls he had taken. It was such a sweet plan, and heaven knew she deserved the money more than psycho Reed ever had.

Her beauty wouldn't last forever, and she planned for this to be her last job where she had to obey a boss. From then on she would be the boss with all the power—and toys—she wanted!

Forty - Two

Hook stood behind Angela in the motor home's bedroom, slowly brushing her long black hair in the dim lantern light. It was one of his favorite things to do. Occasionally, he brushed her hair to one side and kissed her neck with passion, but on that night she didn't respond; she seemed pensive and withdrawn into herself.

"Do you want to share what you're worried about with me?" He met her eyes in the mirror with a question in his.

It took a long time for her reply; finally, she simply said, "I don't want to use protection tonight, Hook."

He paused his brushing for a moment and then continued stroking the silky strands. A lot of questions ran through his mind, but he didn't let them show in any way. He had seen the expression on Angela's face during the rare times she held Emma, and the longing there had cut into him, so he already knew they would start a family sometime. To deny her what she wanted so deeply was impossible for him; he loved her, so what she needed, he would give to her if he could.

He calmly asked her, "Why now? Why tonight?"

She looked away from his eyes, which were reflected in the mirror. "I need to go on this mission believing I might be pregnant. You could be killed or I could be killed, and I want that very slim chance that it might have happened already. I need fierceness and a hope for the future to carry me through what I need to do this time."

"But Angela, you've done harder rescues than this one all alone, and wouldn't you be putting our baby at risk if you do get pregnant? Remember: I'm not leaving your side for a minute. We're a team, so we'll be strong together and get the job done."

Again she was slow to respond. "The possibility of conception is remote, but if it does occur, the embryo would only be a few cells along. At that stage, most women wouldn't even know they were pregnant, so they wouldn't change anything they were doing to protect it. I'm not going to feel any different physically, Hook, just mentally stronger." She tried to explain it to him so he would understand. "In the past before an important mission, I always chilled and disconnected completely. I worked better that way—just clear and cold with no emotions at all. Whatever happened, happened, so even if I died, it was OK. If one of my squad was killed, then it was meant to be, and I moved on to the next step. It was my job, and death was the cost of doing business. Obviously it did impact me or I wouldn't have ended up in the woods, but I could put myself in that space for awhile and operate efficiently to get the job done."

She lowered her head into her hands. "But I can't do that anymore. I've tried, and it scares me because this rescue is so important. I don't have bad PTSD now, thanks to Jasper, but I'm feeling too much emotion to be a good leader, and that's going to get someone I care about killed. I can't be cold and detached anymore, so I feel like I need to be mommy-bear fierce!"

Hook was concerned about her distressed tone. "Angela, that mental numbness was bad for you! It became a way of life, and it took you over completely. You might have disconnected to do the job, but you also didn't care if you or anyone else lived or died, and—bottom line—that wasn't good for you or for the mission, either."

Angela slammed her open hand on the dresser and then took a deep breath to calm her feelings. "See, I'm awake and emotional now, and that's the problem here. My military record proves that numbness worked, because the operations were successful. But I can't get back in the mental freeze zone anymore, and that means I might not do this job right! I can't focus like I did, and I need that to be successful. How do you think I survived so many rescues anyway?"

Hook turned her to face him and enfolded her in his arms. "I think you can bring your new emotions and passions on this mission, even without being pregnant, and be every bit as successful as before."

"That's not what the military trains into people." Her voice was muffled against his chest.

"Well, they can't have lots of young people going off to war full of intense emotions about it. They want soldiers who are predictable and easy to direct." He stroked up and down her back in a soothing motion. "But look back to the Revolutionary War against England. One of the reasons we won was because the colonists were committed and passionate about the cause they were fighting for—like how you are passionate about Abby, Emma, and Jasper."

"It's not how I work best, Hook!"

"Caring about the outcome is even better than being numb. Trust me on this, Angela. You haven't done it like this before, that's all, but I know it'll work fine. Besides, I'm not letting you freeze yourself up again."

"I never felt scared before, but I am now, and I don't know how to handle it."

"Fear can give you an edge. It makes you cautious and extra-aware of your surroundings. It's not a bad thing if you don't let it take over. Fear was survival for cavemen, and it still works like that. Every one of us is going to be scared on Reed Island, and that will only help us win. Greed is confident that he's untouchable on his island kingdom, but we're going to prove him wrong.

No one is above the law, and he'll pay for what he's done to innocent people."

"Hook, you don't understand! That numbness was my security, and I could handle anything like that. I just put one foot in front of the other and depended on my training and instincts, and I got the job done right every time."

Hook spoke firmly. "No, you just didn't care what happened, and Angela, you must see that wasn't right! What's the point of living if you're an emotional zombie? Isn't that exactly why you put that gun to your head and prepared to pull the trigger? Aren't you glad you woke up and started to feel things? I know I am, honey!" He kissed the top of her head gently.

She began to cry quietly against his T-shirt, overwhelmed by love for him. It felt wonderful to have someone she could depend on to be by her side no matter what. "Does that mean you don't want a baby ever?"

"Of course I want kids! I'm planning on making a family with you, sweetie. I'm just not sure tonight is the right timing for this step."

Angela rose on her tiptoes and placed her lips on his. She gave him a series of small tear-salty kisses both on his lips and all around them. "It's the right timing for me. No matter how this all turns out, I know it's the right time to do it. I want to hold hope for the future inside of me, Hook. I want this so bad!"

He kissed her back. "OK, then let's try to make a baby before we take Greed down. But you know it's another thing for me to worry about when we're fighting on the island."

"You can handle it, big guy. We're a team, remember?"

"Let's see if you can deal with this then. Jasper, Tony, and I were talking about how the communication device could be used in the bedroom setting." He gave her a hopeful look.

She laughed loudly. "I can just picture that situation! How are you going to prevent my 'oh baby, right there' from going out to the whole camp? You know I'm going to project loud and clear—I can't help myself when we're in bed, because you're just that good, Hook."

"Do I detect a slight tone of sarcasm? I might just have to prove to you again that I am that good."

"Oh baby!"

He sighed in disappointment. "All right, Angela, we can skip it, but Jasper made a modified version for us as kind of a honeymoon deal. It only projects in a three-foot diameter around the wearer. I can tune into your thoughts and know precisely what you want, where you want it, how long, and how hard. I'll know the best position, the best rhythm, and every fantasy you're having without your saying a thing. I guarantee that information will earn me more than an 'oh baby.'"

Angela stopped running her hands under his shirt and stared at him with her mouth open. His pupils were dilated, and he had a slight smile on his handsome face. She could feel the heat coming off him, and they were still fully dressed. Her every fantasy? That could get weird! She wondered if it would only pick up thoughts she projected to it directly, or if it would transmit everything she felt.

Hook watched the emotions cross her face. "Don't overthink it, honey. You can hear all my fantasies, too. He winked. "So, do you know how to belly dance?"

Angela smiled and batted her eyelashes at him. "OK, tough guy, let's go play with the new chip. Maybe if we're very lucky, we'll make a baby while we're at it, too."

Forty - Three

Abby and Jasper walked hand in hand on the beach at dawn. Emma rode in the front pack strapped to Abby's chest over her oversized purple University of Washington sweatshirt. The emerging sun bathed the stratus clouds in a pink-and-gold radiant sunrise, welcoming the new day. Abby held Jasper's hand gently and was careful not to pull or swing his arm. She knew he still had strong objections to the rescue; he didn't think they were worth risking more lives for. The discovery of the kidnapped girls had at least overruled that ridiculous idea, and he had stopped throwing verbal roadblocks at her participation. That was a relief, but she still knew he wasn't supportive of the mission to retrieve his body. He said he would prefer floating in the globe for eternity rather than sending anyone to the hell of Greed's island—especially her. His feelings about rescuing Emma, his computer program, and the kidnapped girls were torn between fear about leaving them there and the huge risk the team was taking to go and get them.

Abby forced cheer into her voice. "Today is the big day, Jasper, and it looks like Mother Nature is pulling out all the stops this morning." She understood how much he hated being miniaturized again for travel, because then he would lose what little control he had over the situation and his life.

"I know. I guess I'm glad it's going to be over one way or another, but I still wish you weren't coming along. I want you safe here. It sucks that I met you at the end of my life and that you never had a chance to see Emma awake."

Abby stopped and turned with fire in her eyes. "I can't believe you just said that! Have you ever heard of a self-fulfilling prophecy? It means you subconsciously make the outcome you predicted happen. It occurs all the time, especially if you think it over and over again. Spend energy dwelling on things like, 'I'll probably lose my wallet,' and it's bound to happen because you've already mentally lost the connection with it. Think positive, Jasper! Hold in your mind the clear intention of winning against Greed, and it'll be more likely to happen. Athletes psych themselves up like that all the time. They review in their minds every detail about how they're going to win and picture themselves winning. It works."

Jasper considered her point. "I guess it's like the placebo effect. If you believe it's the right medicine, then it can cure the disease even though it's only a sugar pill."

"Yes, like that. Right makes might, we're a fabulous team, and good always wins over evil. Play those thoughts in your mind, and believe them. Think of all the preparation we've done and of the great people we have on our side. We're going to get you back safely, and I firmly refuse to let any other possibility enter my mind!"

Jasper saw tears in her eyes. "I do believe the team will take Greed down eventually, Abby, and I'm happy about that. I'm just not sure Emma and I will survive to see it. Let's be honest about that. I know you've seen how I'm fading a little every day, and it's worse than you know, because I've been hiding it as much as I can. Now Angela is asking me for three more transformations: shrink back into the globe again today, then back to a full-sized projection when we get to the island, and finally quickly back into my physical body before we leave there. I don't think I have the strength for all that, and who knows what Emma can handle safely? And it's not really my projection that's fading, because I can feel my real body on the island is ill. Maybe that's due to being comatose or having half my brain here—I don't know. I just know that I feel sicker daily and that my projection is getting weaker.

"And even if everything does all work out and I get back here again, will I be the same person still? Will I remember who I am and who you are? Can a biological brain survive all this stress intact? I'm scared for Emma and me and for everyone else, too."

She put his hands around her waist. "You haven't hidden anything from me, Jasper. I clearly see your projection's deterioration, and that's why today is a good day to get started on Angela's rescue plan. Maybe once you're little again, the chip will draw less energy from your brain, and you'll feel better. I know visually your projection isn't as stretched-out looking when you're smaller in size."

"I don't think my projection's deterioration is about how much power I draw. I bet on the island I'm slowly dying—or that's what it feels like to me anyway."

Abby leaned forward and placed her head against his. He was semisolid in so few places that it limited her ability to be physically close to him, and what he'd said frightened her, so she needed to touch him. "OK, so that's another good reason to get going on the rescue."

Her tone was deliberately positive, but his words had hit her like blows, and she felt the pain of the truth she had been avoiding. What were his chances of returning as the man she had adored since girlhood and then was in love with? Probably not really good, but she was determined to put a favorable spin on their time together. Maybe it was all they had left, so she was going to make the most of it.

"On that happy note, I have something for you." She reached into her sweatshirt pocket and took out a box wrapped in brown paper. "I hope you take this the right way, because it was the best I could do on short notice."

They sat down on the same driftwood bench where Abby had originally found the globe, and he slowly opened the wrapping paper. Jasper's hands worked well on a computer keyboard, but for other things, he struggled with his finger dexterity. When he finally got it opened, he was astonished to speechlessness. Abby had found a rectangular clear glass jewelry box at the thrift store and had outfitted it for his travel to the island with doll furniture. She'd put in a bed, a lounging chair, and a crib for Emma. There were blankets, pillows, and miniature writing materials clipped to a small desk.

"I glued everything down so it won't move around when you travel." Jasper continued to stare at it and still said nothing. "If you don't like it, I can find something else. Probably it was a stupid idea anyway." She was embarrassed suddenly.

Jasper cleared his throat; it felt like there was a big lump preventing him from speaking. "No one has done anything this nice for me, ever. It's going to make the size transition much easier this time. I'll think of you, and of what you did to make me comfortable, during the whole trip, Abby. Thanks—it shows the kind and caring person you are."

She breathed a sigh of relief. "I thought for a minute you were mad at me, but I couldn't stand to see you go back into the globe. Some guys would be insulted to live with pink doll furniture, but unfortunately Barbie didn't have any man-cave stuff."

"Hey, those guys didn't spend weeks in a glass ball, sitting on a computer chip! This'll be so much better. Even though I'm a projection and can't actually feel anything, I was physically uncomfortable because my brain told me so, I guess. Kind of like the phantom limb thing where you feel pain even though the body part isn't there anymore."

Jasper put his hands on either side of her head, gazed into her eyes, and said sadly, "I want to court you, Abby, and to kiss you until your head spins, but I can't even put my arms around you properly. That's just not fair!"

She smiled back at him. "Given the situation, I think we've done the best we could to get close to each other. Besides, it's your mind I was attracted to as a girl, and it's still that way, Jasper. I'm not saying I wouldn't love to get physical with you, but bodies change, and I desire who you are as a person. The rest is frosting to me. So my feelings for you are progressing just fine even though you're a mind projection, and I hope you feel the same way, too."

How lucky he was, Jasper thought, to have found someone who cared about him even as a projection. "I also have a gift for you." He smiled as her face lit up. "It's not much. Half-man found it when he was gathering stuff to be Ethel, and I had Tony fix up the inside when he was at my house." He reached into the front pack alongside of Emma, and pulled out a small box topped with an extravagant bow and handed it to her. "I bet Ethel wrapped it, because it's so pretty!" Abby carefully opened the box and revealed an ornate antique silver locket on a matching chain. She opened the locket and saw that one side had a picture of Jasper with a grin on his face and that the other side had a picture of an animated Emma with her eyes open.

"It's wonderful, Jasper! Just to see Emma alert and awake is amazing. She looks so connected and happy, but so do you. You're relaxed and happy, too." She peered closely at the pictures. "You both look so different, and that brings home to me how hard this has been for you."

"Yeah, it's almost painful for me to see how we were. It feels like they're photos of a different man and his daughter. I'm not him anymore. I'll never be him again."

Abby kissed him gently. "He's still the core of you, Jasper, and I know that hasn't changed. Everyone gets stronger from life's challenges, even when it doesn't feel like it at the time. I'll treasure the locket and wear it to remind me to be strong, too. Thank you." She fastened it around her neck and tucked it in her shirt.

They walked back to the cabin where Tony had set up a small ceremony for Jasper's shrinking. Jasper shook everyone's hand, and they wished him well.

"See you on the other side, guys," he said.

Jasper placed his chip in the glass box Abby had given him, kissed her with as much passion as he could, held Emma close, and nodded at Tony to stop the add-on program that had been projecting him to a larger size. And despite a lot of self-talk and mental preparation, it still felt like he was going through a paper shredder alive. He woke up in his original small size vomiting air from guts he didn't have, and swearing a blue streak. Jasper struggled to his feet, made the thumbs-up sign to reassure everyone he was OK, laid Emma in the tiny crib, and thankfully passed out again on the pink plastic dollhouse bed.

That night, Abby slept with the glass box containing Jasper and Emma cuddled up to her in bed. In the morning, Tony hooked up the microphone communication system again and told Jasper where he had spent the night. Jasper was sorry he'd missed it.

Abby modified the front pack she had used for Emma to hold the glass box securely for transport. Tony would carry it and the tablet computer sealed in a waterproof bag as he swam with the harbor assault team.

Unbeknownst to everyone but Tony, Jasper had hidden in the tablet another program that could run his chip's brain projection. They knew Jasper's computer was currently working, because it was projecting him, but they didn't want to risk damaging his brain if his body was suddenly reanimated by Greed shutting down the original program. Since Jasper's laptop was in Greed's possession, they couldn't predict what would happen once he knew the island was under attack. His first move might be to shut down the chip, and if that happened, it would immediately activate the second program, which would sustain Jasper and Emma as projections.

The hidden chip projection program would self-destruct seventy-two hours after it was activated. So unless Jasper's laptop was recovered and was still running the original program, they had three days to return him to his body before the backup projection program terminated for good. No one knew if Jasper's body could house his mind anymore, and he wanted his projection to die if his mind and body couldn't be functionally united again. Jasper felt everyone had the right to determine whether they wanted to go on living or not. People refused cancer therapy and signed living wills to prevent being hooked up to machines to sustain their lives, and he insisted that he had that right, too. He had contemplated the horror of existing as a projection if someone else controlled the program and his body was kept alive artificially. He didn't want that to happen to him or to Emma, no matter what.

He had also given Tony strict instructions to save Abby and Emma—in that order—if the rescue went badly and his body had to be left behind. He had written letters to his family saying good-bye and giving directions for disposal of his and Emma's physical remains. He had made a list of his outstanding debts to be paid by his insurance policy—although he wasn't sure if there was a no payout clause for death by evil villain—and he had put his assets in trust; after his death, they would be awarded equally to the team members who'd risked their lives to rescue him. Finally he left a love note for Abby hidden in the cabin where she would find it eventually if he didn't return; she was the love of his life and he wanted her to know it.

All he had left to do--now that he was miniaturized again-- was to rest and think the positive thoughts Abby believed would help the team to succeed on their mission.

Forty - Four

Angela gathered everyone in the cabin for one last meeting. She spoke quietly but with authority. "We'll be on the airplane to St. John in less than six hours, everyone. Most of the flight will be at night so you can catch up on your sleep then. I'll be meeting with each of you individually on the plane to address any last-minute concerns you might have."

Angela was every inch a commander in charge, and any doubts she might have still had were buried deep inside. "Halfman, Melt, and Stubby are joining us again by video conference. I would like to introduce my good friend Dee Light, who some of you haven't met in person. Dee has generously volunteered to help us. As you know, Dee is responsible for Abby's new look, and she has been completely briefed about Greed and our mission. Dee's varied skills make her uniquely qualified to be our ground support in St. John, and you can trust her completely. And Dee is responsible for the nice flight staff uniforms most of us will wear on the trip."

Dee broke in. "In addition to the fabulous hats, I have given you all team colors. Greed is black and gold, so I made you white and silver. It's the avenging angel look with nice silver accents."

Angela quickly continued because she didn't think her men cared much about silver accents, and she knew how Dee loved to elaborate about fashion. "Thank you, Dee, for the professional-look on short notice. But moving on. During the rescue, Tony, Hook, and Stubby will check in with Dee every twenty minutes by thought messaging her a prearranged signal. Tony represents the water assault group, Stubby, Greed's helicopter, and Hook, the climbers. If she doesn't hear from each of them within five minutes of the scheduled time, or if they ask for immediate help, she will send the chief an alert requesting his intervention. That means she must have contact with all three groups regularly, or else she will send in the authorities, pronto."

She paused a moment to make sure everyone understood how serious her next statement was. "We all know Greed can dispose of us long before any helicopter can fly to his island from St. John, so if we have to ask for the chief's help, then it means we need him in order to survive. I've also given Dee press releases to send out to the media if for some reason we don't return. The statements explain about Jasper and Emma's kid-napping—leaving out any references to his technology and to the purpose of our mission. Also, she will release the video of the girls and evidence we have of Greed's illegal business prac-tices. So one way or another, Greed is getting shut down, even if we don't come back. I hope you've all considered the risks of this operation carefully and are one hundred percent sure you want to come along."

Half-man tried to lighten the tone of Angela's grim state-ments. "Once our flight lands in St. John, there'll be only a few hours to check your equipment and to get into your assault position before Dr. Newton—we should get use to calling Abby that—boards the helicopter for Reed Island. The minute the team waiting on the fishing boat sees her helicopter approaching the island, the climbers will be dropped off and the swimmers will enter the water. Our excuse for all being on the boat near the island is that Ethel, Dwight, and Stubby will spontaneously invite the entire flight crew for a fun night of fishing to celebrate the last day of their romantic vacation."

Angela corrected him. "Make that Ethel, Dwight, and a fake Stubby, because the real Stubby will fly with Dr. Newton in the hidden compartment of Greed's helicopter. Dr. Newton will have approximately thirty minutes to distract Greed before Hook and I reach the top of the cliff. During that time, Stubby will jam the security system, let us know how many warm bodies we need to neutralize, and be backup for Dr. Newton."

Tony complained. "I don't see why one of us can't go with Abby, excuse me, Dr. Newton, as her assistant. That seems a safer plan to me."

Abby answered with a snort. "We've talked about this before, Tony. It's because I'm distracting him with the fake syringe and the anticipation of sex. If I have an assistant, that means he'll have to have a guard present to balance the numbers. And then he'll be more apt to notice the device doesn't really work, because the sex will seem less likely to him. That puts me in more danger than if I just went in alone."

"Trust our Absinthe to make a really hot smoke screen, big brother," Dee added with a wink of her eye.

Angela continued after she rolled her eyes. "After the climb, Hook and I will work our way through the fortress, neutralizing guards as we go. Our main job is to reduce the number of people the harbor team has to fight with. I think most of the household staff will be in the kitchen preparing dinner, so we hope to barricade the door and lock them in. Same deal with the guards' quarters. Once nonsecurity people hear there's fighting in the hall, they will probably lie low anyway. If we run into serious problems, then we may take the hidden hallway instead of the main hall to the harbor. That's after we find the control room, open the harbor access gates, and neutralize the compression cannons so the swimmers can get in. Communication will be key throughout the op, so we all need to know what the other teams are doing all the time."

Tony suddenly objected in a loud voice. "That doesn't sound like a plan, Angela! That's a sketchy idea about what will happen!"

Angela jumped up and got in his face. "Well, civilian, here's news for you: detailed rescue plans don't work! They just distract soldiers with what the plan says they should be doing, so my plans are a framework that can be adjusted moment to moment depending on what's happening. There are always too many variables to predict exactly how things will play out once you're on site. I say keep alert, communicate, be flexible, and survive. Things always go wrong, things always change, and you must be able to adjust instantly with or without a plan in place!"

Hook took the floor to give Angela time to settle down. "Once Dr. Newton's time is up, then Stubby will go to the office, subdue Greed, and open the safe if there's time."

Angela continued on her tirade as if Hook hadn't spoken. "During a rescue, you don't think with your logical brain, Tony. There's an animal part that takes over, and you operate from instinct. It makes faster and better decisions than you do when you take the time to think it through and follow a specific, preplanned pattern. Always go with your instincts because the fight-or-flight part of your brain is rarely wrong. It's been sharpened for millions of years to protect your life. Anyway, the bottom line is either you trust my leadership, Tony, or you stay home. Because I know what I'm doing on a rescue, and you don't!"

Tony said contritely, "Yes sir, Angela. I'm sorry, sir."

"I am the leader. I've spent most of my time here working on every possible contingency that might occur while we're on the island. I've lots of alternative plans stored in my brain, and depending on how things evolve moment to moment, I'll use them. So if you're in a tricky situation, contact me right away, because I have the knowledge and experience to guide you to the best next step. But if you can't contact me, trust your instincts to tell you what to do."

Hook sighed. "Can we get back to the plan now?"

She poked her elbow in his side. "The harbor team is the most important part, so it has the most members. Once the harbor guards are secure, then you will divide into teams of two to explore the caves looking for Jasper, Emma, and the girls. Stay alert, because we don't have much information about what's in the caves or the number of additional guards that might be stationed there. Mark every turn or cave division with the chalk provided in the vests. The mark should be small and only visible if you're looking for it, because you don't want to make a big arrow pointing Greed to where you're located."

"What do they do when they find Jasper and Emma's bodies?" Abby asked.

"I don't know what kind of physical shape they'll be in, so I've decided not to shut the projection off if we don't have to—at least not until we get a medical opinion on the health of their bodies. The chip is working for them now, so let's not fix what isn't broken. Half-man will be packing a battery to run any life support machines they need during transport. Melt will have a collapsible stretcher to get Jasper's and Emma's bodies to the second helicopter on the airstrip. The two girls will probably have to fly with Stubby and Abby because I don't think there will be enough room on one helicopter for them, Jasper, the rest of us, and the medical equipment. Hook, Stubby, and Melt are all trained to fly copters, and if there are other people to rescue, I'll figure out what to do depending on the extra weight and what kind of shape they're in."

"So when do Emma and I go back to full-sized projections?" Jasper asked via the microphone from his glass box.

"I don't know at this point. I'll leave it up to Tony to decide based on how things play out. But in general, your projection is safer and more portable in a smaller size. And I've seen how sick you get when changing size, and that makes you vulnerable to attack while you're recovering. I don't want to give them any chance to hurt you, so unless we really need you big, I think you and Emma should stay as you are now."

"After it's all over and we're in the air flying away, then what?" Abby asked.

"Dee contacts the chief, who sends in his forces, they take the Zapped, handcuffed guards to jail, and then his forensic people gather evidence to convict Greed for life. If we have injured people aboard, we fly directly to the closest medical facility. If not, we crack open a bottle of bubbly and fly home."

"OK, that's not real! How do you actually think it will turn out, Angela?" Tony asked.

She and Hook exchanged a glance. "It will be hard and messy. Some parts will be better than expected, and some, worse, because it always goes like that. We just need to capitalize on the good things and minimize the bad things. The trauma center is probably where we'll end up. There'll be injuries, and some will be significant. Remember that Greed likes booby traps, so he won't go down easily. We'll be outnumbered by armed guards, and we'll be taking them on in their home territory, so they'll have an advantage. On the plus side for us, we'll have surprise and a wicked-awesome communication device to help us succeed."

"We have more than that really. We have people committed to doing the right thing and lots of practice and preparation. His guards are motivated by fear and money, and I think that's not as powerful as what we have on our side," Hook added.

Angela looked at each face one by one. "I'll understand if any of you want to bail out now. You've all served others and have given more than most have to do what's right. If we do end up opening the bubbly, it very well might be in a hospital room or even in the morgue, so think carefully about whether you want to come."

She walked around and touched the hands of everyone who was physically present. "If you decide to take part in the rescue, pack your stuff in the motor home or trailer and be ready to go four hours from now."

"This stewardess will be serving gourmet in-flight meals. You're just going to love them, I know you will!" Dee added in a lighter tone.

Forty - Five

Abby opened the sliding glass door of her St. John beach-front hotel room to let Stubby in. It was dusk, and he was dressed in black with his face concealed under dark paint. Soon he would walk to the airport to inject some of Greed's water bottles with her chloral hydrate knockout solution, and then he would hide in the helicopter compartment.

He gave her a peck on the cheek, and with a slight stutter he said, "Break a leg, kid. I'll be right behind you, so don't worry about anything. If Greed tries to mess with you, I'll be there to kick his butt ASAP."

Abby thought it was nice of him to say that, but she knew a lot could go wrong that he couldn't fix for her; however, she swept that thought out of her mind and replied, "I'm really only worried about Jasper and Emma. I want them to be OK, Stubby."

She reconsidered. "All right, maybe I'm a little worried about my magic trick fooling Greed."

"He'll buy in to it, don't you worry, kid. That expression 'blinded by greed' fits him to a T, so all he'll see is dollar signs. You got all the protection stuff I made you tucked away?"

"Yeah, he's never going to suspect the push-up pad in my bra contains tear gas." She grinned at him as he blushed.

"Well, I'll be happy if you don't need any of it. I'll Zap him as soon as I can get there—twenty or thirty minutes, tops. You can easily stall him that long with your big scientific words."

"Everyone else on the fishing boat and ready to go?"

"Yeah, Ethel transferred the scuba and climbing equipment from the plane to the boat in wheelchair loads. A blanket and a hat over the top, and it looked just like Dwight was sitting there. Angela made a passable me after Half-man worked his stage makeup magic. They'll be swimming toward the island once you're in the air."

Abby looked at her watch. "I've got to get ready, Stubby, so good luck. See you in Greed's office later." She gave him a big hug.

She dressed in a white suit with black trim and black accessories, and she added rich solid-gold antique jewelry. Dee had personally selected the look to awaken Greed's desire for her. The white linen was virginal on purpose because he was attracted to young girls, and the black and gold made her part of his team. Dee explained that it was a subconscious appeal designed to focus his thoughts away from the injection device and onto her. The suit was cut low in the front for a cleavage view as she leaned over, and the skirt was so tight that she needed the kick pleat in the back to walk. The black detailing consisted of a velvet collar and matching trim around the lapels, cuffs, and hems.

Abby added shiny black thick-toed sky-high heels and a black-and-gold beaded belt she had made herself. Abby thought Dee's makeup instructions were over the top—that they were OK for the stage but too much drama for a business meeting. But she changed her mind when she looked at the final result in the mirror, because a hot babe with sexy red hair definitely looked back at her. The hairstyle was simple—all she had done was bend down and fluff it. Dee explained that it was supposed to look like she had roused from a nap and had stepped out of the bedroom just moments before. All in all, Abby thought she was walking a line very close to slutty and that Dee would have been proud of the finished product.

She had just kissed Jasper's and Emma's pictures in the locket for good luck and had secured it in the hotel safe when there was a loud knock at the door. She repeated her mantra in her head—"channel Absinthe, channel Absinthe"—and then she opened the door.

Two men stood at attention in the hotel hallway, and they were dressed in uniforms she thought should have had swastika motifs. Her first instinct was to say "at ease, men" to them.

One man stepped forward stiffly, and without emotion he said, "Dr. Newton? We're here to transport you to Reed Island."

Abby picked up her purse and the case with the syringe prototype, which were the only things she was taking with her. The purse was small, shiny, and black, and it contained very little. She knew it would be searched at some point, so she'd made it easy for them to riffle through it. The men led her to a long black limo under the hotel canopy. A limo? Really? It was walking distance to the airport, she thought. He liked ostentatious, for sure; good thing Dee had taught her how to get in and out of a car in a tight skirt gracefully.

At the airport Abby saw that the men had already loaded the helicopter with supplies for the island. One of the men was obviously the pilot because he began the preflight checks, and the other one helped her into the copilot seat and then sat behind her. Soon Abby's stomach was in her throat as the ground tilted away and they flew out over the dark ocean.

A few minutes later her heart leaped in her chest when the man in the back offered her a bottle of water from the top of the case she knew Stubby had drugged. She declined politely but was horrified when the pilot accepted one and drank about a quarter of the bottle in one swig. She knew the water contained knockout drops because it was from the top of the stack, but she wasn't sure how much chloral hydrate the pilot had ingested or how long it would be before the drug took effect. They could all end up in the ocean if he passed out before the helicopter landed!

Thinking quickly, Abby touched the pilot's upper thigh to distract him, and then she took the water bottle from him and pretended to sip.

Abby alerted the hidden Stubby to what was happening by saying through the bug, "Sharing a drink with a handsome man is one of my favorite things to do. Even though it's only plain water and not wine, the view from here is magnificent."

She was looking at him as she said it and not out the window, and she saw him preen in response to her comment. That made her want to gag, but she suspected most of the male guards were starved for female companions on the isolated island; judging by the two in the helicopter, Greed picked men with plenty of testosterone but not much brain power.

Abby looked out the window to hide her disgust and saw the lights of Reed Island approaching. Somewhere down there in the dark, Hook and Angela had started to climb the cliff and the scuba team approached the harbor gate.

She breathed a sigh of relief when the helicopter safely touched ground on the pad next to the fortress's tower. Madam La Ruhr stood by the door with a clipboard in her hand.

"Welcome to Reed Island, Dr. Newton. I will escort you to Sir Reed's office." She used a walkie-talkie to tell the staff to unload the supplies from the helicopter quickly, chop-chop.

The two men from the helicopter walked through the door ahead of them, and Abby heard one tell the other he felt dizzy and wanted to lie down. That was at least one person out of the picture, she thought—a point for their side! La Ruhr led her down a short stone staircase descending from the helipad and through the great room. The fortress immediately reminded Abby why most people didn't choose to live in castles anymore. The floor was marble tile in shades of gray—it looked like there was an acre of it—and the wood-paneled walls were a dull dark brown. The sparse furniture was large and heavy to suit the huge space and also done in dark colors with some kind of geometric pattern.

An ugly giant iron chandelier hung over the room's center, and large paintings in ornate gold frames lined the walls. The artwork was also dark—mostly done in the old master's style—and featured people long dead and grim men on horseback. The room was cluttered with small tables completely covered in fancy knickknacks of some kind. The whole effect, Abby supposed, had been designed by Greed to convey that he was rich, powerful and intimidating. Instead, it felt cold, damp, gloomy, and oppressive. She had been in some old museums and supposedly haunted Victorian mansions that screamed "welcome" in comparison to Greed's place. She knew Greed was watching her on his video surveillance system, so she made sure to "ooh" and "ah" as she looked around and to swing her hips seductively as she walked.

La Ruhr led her past an iron-railed balcony that overlooked the pool and tropical garden in the lower level of the largest tower. Then they ascended a spiral flight of stairs to the upper level of the same tower where Abby knew Greed had his office and personal suite of rooms. They stopped at a double door with carved wooden dragons and gilt around the edges. La Ruhr knocked twice, waited a moment, opened the door, and almost pushed Abby inside. She closed it quickly behind Abby and left them alone in the large office.

Greed rose from behind his desk and gestured with one arm sweeping upward. "Welcome to Reed Island, Dr. Newton, and to my humble dwelling. May our ongoing association be profitable for both of us." He licked his lips with lizard-like tongue movements and looked her up and down. "I understand you have brought me a device of great financial interest."

Abby glanced around the room and felt overwhelmed and claustrophobic. It had large floor-to-ceiling red velvet drapes with heavy gold fringe and tassels. The huge, shiny dark-wood desk was elevated on a two-foot-high red pedestal, undoubtedly to make him seem taller and more impressive when he sat behind it, even though it actually dwarfed him. The entire office was crammed with stuff occupying every surface, including most of the floor. There were antiques, paintings, sculptures, and collections of all kinds. It looked more like a hoarder's lair than a space for working, and rather than highlighting his wealth, it cheapened it and made it look like a poorly maintained junk shop.

Abby carefully crossed the cluttered room like Absinthe was walking the runway and leaned over slightly to reveal some cleavage as she took his slightly damp and clammy hand in both of hers.

"Quite a fabulous place you have here. Thank you for meeting with me. I confess I've wanted to meet the mysterious Sir Reed for some time." She used a breathy deeper voice and gave him a slow smile.

Once she stood closer to him, Abby could see how short he was. In the insurance photos he had appeared taller; he had probably been standing on something, she thought. He had a careful comb-over hairstyle, a rotund waist, and an overbearing, pompous manner. He was formally dressed in a light-blue three-piece suit and a tie that she suspected was made from a polyester blend. He might have been laughable, but she could feel menace radiating off him. His eyes were cold and small, and although he smiled at her with his mouth, it didn't change the mean expression in them. She had a sudden mental picture of him carefully taking off and folding his jacket to avoid the risk of getting blood on it when he hit the girls. Abby camouflaged her cold shiver with a tinkling laugh. She realized that she wasn't going to distract this man with small talk of any kind, so she'd better dive right in with the magic show.

"Let's get right to the demonstration, Sir Reed. I can't wait to show you the injection device. My lab would market the device but we just don't have the resources to do the manufacturing or the product promotion or to keep copycats at bay. I had a great experience with Medi-Help, so I wanted to give you first shot at it." Greed didn't know that her experience had been terrible, but he'd made money off her lab's work, so why would he have cared anyway?

Abby laid the injector case she was carrying on the desk. The pilot had made her leave her purse in the helicopter, so it was all she had with her. Tony and Jasper had outdone themselves by modifying a velvet-lined black-leather flute case to hold the device and a bottle of injectable B-complex vitamins. She opened the case and took out the device. The guys had crafted it in black and gold with a phallic shape that would appeal to him immediately.

She continued. "I have the design specifications and testing data in the report I prepared for you." She leaned over slightly again and handed it to him because he hadn't even done her the courtesy of moving out from behind his desk. "I have also included a detailed cost comparison to traditional syringes and future sales projections for the next three years. It shows that the device can easily be marketed at fifty times what it costs to produce." Abby tried to channel the tone and manner of the sales representatives who visited her lab to hawk their new products. Greed spent a few moments closely studying the report—and her cleavage.

She forced herself to stand closer to him for the demonstration, and she could actually feel her skin ripple in revulsion. "You turn this dial to adjust for the viscosity of the liquid to be injected. A separate inexpensive disposable sterile shield is used for each patient. You just hold it against the skin at the injection site and push the button for a quick, painless experience. First, there is a microsecond-long electric charge to numb the area, and then the liquid is sent through two thousand microscopic ports. Together, they result in absolutely no cellular damage or pain caused by the material entering the body." She didn't push the injection button yet, because she wanted to show him only once. More than that, and he might catch on to the trick.

Greed took the device from her and examined it closely. "If this works as you say, it will revolutionize medicine. I'll call it

'Reed's Injector'—named after myself, of course. May I see it work, please?"

Abby thought Greed would roll up his sleeve and test it on himself, but instead he used an intercom to call a servant who appeared in less than a minute. The small older man was winded from running and looked only at the floor the whole time he was in the office. Abby felt pity, for it was clear he expected something horrible was going to happen to him.

Greed said, "I would try it on myself, you understand, but one can't be too careful these days. What with my international status, anyone could have substituted something else for the vitamins when you weren't looking, my dear."

The egotistical jerk! Abby thought. He was worried about possibly injecting poison, but he was quite happy to let his servant try it instead. She knew he believed people were disposable, but it was sickening to see it play out in front of her.

She carefully pantomimed using a needle to draw a small amount of red vitamins from the bottle into the device; but instead of pulling the plunger back, she pushed a hidden switch that allowed preloaded color-matched water to enter the device's visible chamber. Next she showed Reed that the red solution had entered the device. Then Abby reassured the servant that the liquid was only vitamins, and she made a show of placing an alcohol-saturated, sterile-wrapped shield against the servant's arm. She pushed firmly against his skin with the end of the device and clicked the button. It snapped audibly and quickly forced the liquid back into the device's hidden chamber. Finally, she showed Reed the empty device to prove to him that the injection had happened.

Greed examined the servant's arm at the injection site closely and questioned him. "Did you feel anything?"

"No, sir. Nothing at all, sir," he replied. He sounded amazed and relieved, too.

Greed dismissed the servant with a casual wave and sat down again at his desk, thinking; he slowly flipped through her report, and then he asked, "You have the legal release for the device with you today?"

"Yes, I thought it would expedite things to have it all signed in advance." Abby leaned way over the desk, showing a lot of skin that time, and directed his attention to the legal documents stacked at the end of the report. She breathed a mental sigh of relief because it looked like Greed had bought the magic trick hook, line, and sinker.

He stood up, walked around the desk, and reached out to shake Abby's hand with a smile on his face. "I guess we have a deal, Dr. Newton, but I won't be paying your asking price."

Then in a quick practiced move he broke her right ring finger just above the second knuckle with a snapping sound. Abby screamed and fell to the floor, clutching her wounded hand to her chest.

He gloated. "You stupid bitch. I have the device and your signed release. So what do I need you for now—except entertainment?"

Greed reached down and pulled her up by her hair, and then he slapped her powerfully across the face with the back of his hand. His ring cut Abby's cheek deeply, and the strong blow broke her nose and stunned her for a moment. He laid her on her back across his desk by jerking the fist still wrapped in her hair. Then he hiked up the tight skirt to her waist and fumbled with her bikini panties, trying to pull them off.

The feel of Greed touching her intimately woke up the warrior training Angela had given Abby. She slapped her heel against the side of his desk to trigger the release of the blade Stubby had hidden in the toe of her shoe, and then she kicked upward hard, stabbing Greed deeply in the groin. He bent over at the waist with a cry, clutching his crotch. Abby desperately groped around on the desk with her good hand and found a heavy leaded-glass paperweight. She smashed it down on his comb-over, and he fell to the floor unconscious.

Abby stood up and slowly pulled her skirt back down. She felt like she was going to throw up, and the room shifted around her like she'd had too much alcohol to drink. Blood streamed from the cut on her face and her broken nose; it soaked the front of her jacket and dripped down onto her shoes.

She took two deep, calming breaths and started to ramble. "Get it together, Abby, this is not the time to fall apart, girl. Greed might wake up any moment, so tie him up like Hawkeye showed you."

She stabilized her body by leaning back on the desk, and fumbling with her belt, she unraveled the parachute cord she had woven it out of and started to tie him up. It seemed to take forever because every move bumped her broken finger, and it hurt. She used the thumb and forefinger from the broken hand in a pinching action, her other hand, and her teeth to tie him up. The end result looked like a pig trussed by a drunken spider, but she thought it would hold him until Stubby arrived.

By the time she finished securing Greed, her teeth were chattering with cold, and she was shaking all over. The blood still dripped from her face, but she really didn't care; she knew there was danger, but she couldn't stand up to face it anyway. All she wanted to do was go to sleep, so she curled up on the floor as far away from Greed as she could get and waited for help, hoping that it would arrive before any guards did. As Abby's mind drifted, she recalled how she had teased Stubby about the obvious James Bond connection to the knife in her shoe; boy, now she was glad those were his favorite movies!

Forty - Six

As soon as Stubby heard the last supply cart roll away from the helicopter, he dropped out of the tail's hidden compartment. He didn't attach his collapsible artificial legs yet but swung himself along on his hands and leg stumps. He speculated that by moving without his legs, anyone watching video feed from the heliport wouldn't recognize his image as that of a human intruder; hopefully, they would dismiss him as one of the many cliff-climbing goats that populated the island.

He placed smoky lens filters over the ground level lights that illuminated the helicopter landing pad. That dimmed the bright lights enough to make a hidden spot for him to set up his equipment in the helicopter's shadow at the edge of the cliff.

After returning to the helicopter compartment, he put on his legs and pulled out a strong climbing rope, and then he activated the tiny, dim LED light on one end of the rope. He lowered the lit end slowly over the cliff's edge and waited. After a few minutes, he felt a tug on the rope and pulled up a duffel bag full of equipment tied to the end. Stubby then secured the unlit end of the rope to the helicopter's landing struts and lowered it back over the cliff again.

He unpacked the duffel bag. Step one was jamming the video security system with a previously recorded loop; during their mission, it would play back the previous day's recordings that Half-man had tapped into. Angela's plan worked on the theory that Greed was complacent enough to keep everyone on a repeating schedule, so the control room wouldn't notice that their system was playing the previous day's video for a while. And even when they did, they would probably think it was an equipment glitch at first; the week before Tony had switched recordings several times, so the guards would think there was just another system malfunction. Stubby waited five minutes in case anyone in the control room noticed the transition, but no one sounded the alarm, so he turned on the chip-communication program and sent a thought message: *All, system running, surveillance jammed.*

Finally, he ran the heat-sensor program—relocated from the drone into a handheld unit—to find the number and location of the fortress's current occupants based on their heat signatures. Then he patched it to Angela's tablet and to Tony's laptop so everyone would have real-time information available. Stubby took a moment to look at the readout and saw that Abby and Greed were alone in the office but that there were two guards nearby in the great room. Everyone else appeared to be moving about doing business as usual. Suddenly one person left the kitchen at a run and headed directly toward Greed's office.

Stubby took that as a signal to head to the office too, because it might have meant Abby needed his help before the thirty minutes were up. He cautiously crept down the stairs to the great room with his Zap in one hand and the heat sensor in his other. Once he had a clear view of the room, he realized both of the men his sensor had picked up were sleeping soundly; most likely they were the pilot and copilot, who had drank the water with Abby's knockout solution in it during the flight. Cuffing them still seemed like a good idea, and then he dragged their unconscious bodies out of sight behind the furniture.

Ange, Hook, two in cuffs. Great room.

He heard someone coming, so he hid behind the massive couch, too. It was an elderly male servant who headed away from the tower and down the hall toward the kitchen; Stubby realized he was likely the heat signature he had noticed running to Greed's office earlier. The little man appeared frightened and didn't even look around as he scurried through. Hopefully he hadn't noticed the two sleeping men when he had run by the first time, Stubby thought.

He continued on up the stairway leading to Greed's office with his Zap held in firing position. He slowly opened the office door, not sure what he would see on the other side, but planning to stun Greed immediately after yelling at Abby to get out of the way. Stubby expected that they would both be standing close to each other, involved in discussions about the device.

Instead, the horrible sight that met his eyes had him rushing to Abby, who was curled up on the floor. "Oh, baby, what hap-p-p-p-pened?" In distress, his stutter surfaced as he looked at her bloody, ruined face.

"He hurt me, Stubby, but I tied him up, so I'm OK now. Don't tell Tony. He'll be upset."

Stubby didn't think she was fine at all; she was cold, shaking, and he thought she was in shock, which he had heard could kill faster than her wounds would. She had two blackening eyes, swollen split lips, a crooked broken nose, and a four-inch-deep laceration on the side of her face that gaped open, showing the underlying facial muscle. Her neck and suit front—clear down to the hemline—were soaked in blood that was still slowly dripping from her face.

"He broke my finger!" Abby said through chattering teeth.

Stubby hadn't noticed that injury, because she held her hand cradled against her chest. The bastard—no wonder she was in shock! But he said as calmly as he could, "You did great, sweetie, but let me make sure he's tied up good and tight, and then I'll get you back to the helicopter for a nice nap and some pain medication."

"Did I kill him, Stubby?" Her voice was a whisper as she tried to talk past her swollen lips.

Her words struck his heart, because despite how Greed had hurt her, Abby was still afraid she had taken his life, and that revealed her basic goodness. He turned to Greed and saw he was breathing normally despite the large pool of blood around his crotch and his damaged head. Stubby Zapped him—a longer blast than was necessary—and added cuffs to Abby's cords for extra security.

"Nah, unfortunately, he's still alive, kid. But even if he were dead, it's called 'self-defense,' and no one would blame you anyway."

He took off Abby's shoes because he didn't think she could walk in them, and he used one to smash the prototype syringe into small pieces. He knew it wouldn't play well to the authorities if they suspected Abby had been there to trick Greed with the device. He retracted the knife blade back into her shoe and jammed the mechanism; they could come up with a good explanation for Greed's injuries later. Then he helped her to her feet and walked her back to the helicopter with his arm around her waist for support.

He found the medical kit in the duffel bag and gave her an injection of morphine for pain. Butterfly bandages and some antibiotic ointment were the best he could do for her gaping face wound. He taped her nose as straight as he could, splinted her broken finger by taping it to the one next to it, and hoped that would keep the broken one from flopping around too painfully. During the whole process, Abby looked at him with moist, sad eyes, and it was painful to see her like that. Not once did she complain or cry out because she knew it might attract guards to their location, and Stubby thought she was as brave as any solider he'd ever met. When the drug took effect and she started getting sleepy, he tucked her in the back of the helicopter with the pillow and blanket he'd used when he had hid in the tail compartment.

Then he untied the rope from the helicopter struts and stored it back in the hidden compartment because Hook and Angela had finished using it and were moving through the fortress. Then he checked that the programs were all running smoothly and disabled the helicopter's rotor blade—he didn't want someone trying to escape the island by flying off in the helicopter with Abby sleeping inside. He pocketed the critical part from the rotor, knowing that it disabled the blades and that it was a part impossible to replace with anything but the exact piece. Sometimes it was great to be a gadget guy, he thought. The last step was for him to go back to the office and crack Greed's safe.

But first he sent a thought message, deliberately neglecting to mention Abby's injuries so as to not to upset the team: *Hook, Ange, Abby is safe in copter. Greed cuffed and secure.*

Stubby checked the heat signatures before making the return trip to the office, and he saw a person slowly approaching Greed's door with his arm extended like he was holding a weapon. He was afraid that once the guard saw Greed tied up, he would sound the general alarm. So Stubby quickly ran down the stairs, across the great room, and up the tower stairway. Then he fired his Zap down the long hallway in its non–laser-guided mode. The wide burst of lightning-like electricity felled the surprised guard, scorched both hallway walls, and set a small tapestry on fire. He batted out the flames and camouflaged the visible damage by disabling the hall lights. Luckily, the electrical burst had also taken out the smoke alarm above the office door, or it would have sounded out over the small fire. He cuffed the stunned guard and dragged him into the office, locking the door behind him.

Forty - Seven

Hook and Angela backflipped over the side of the fishing boat into the dark tropical waters of the Caribbean Sea. They planned to swim to the cliffs that were directly below the helipad and bordered the fortress's main tower, well away from the closely guarded harbor entrance. Each of them towed a rubber neutrally buoyant bag full of equipment. Hook's bag was the biggest—containing mostly climbing gear—and he used his missing arm's propeller attachment to help him move it through the water; Angela's bag held Stubby's equipment. It took them about twenty minutes to swim from the boat to the island's breakers. They swam just below the surface with snorkels and swim fins rather than deep in the water like the scuba team.

The fishing boat had briefly paused to let them off, and then it had motored on to drop anchor closer to the harbor entrance but way back from Greed's warning buoys; the scuba team would enter the water from that anchored position. The boat would be unmanned from that point on.

Angela would spin the rescue story for the authorities by saying that Stubby had been night fishing and then had heroically responded to Dr. Newton's distress call because he had been the closest person who could help her. Then, she would say, he had paddled the small dingy lifeboat to the island to rescue her, together they had found the girls, and finally he had flown all three women to St. John using Greed's helicopter. There were huge holes in the story—most obvious was that Stubby would have had to subdue Greed and his security team single-handedly—and Angela knew the chief wouldn't buy it for a minute. But if they were careful not to leave any physical evidence behind and the rest of the team quickly resumed their flight crew identities, she doubted he would be able to assemble the pieces into the real story before they flew home. That would leave the glory for Ethel's amazing husband who could paddle like the wind, valiantly subdue numerous armed guards, and fly Greed's helicopter too. Angela was hoping the chief wouldn't look a gift horse in the mouth even though it stunk like an iceless fish market in the sun!

Both Angela and Hook worried about the force of the waves crashing against the cliff they needed to climb, because if they couldn't get out of the water immediately, the waves would toss them against the rocks, damaging the equipment and their bodies quickly. Almost nothing stood up to the power of an ocean meeting a rock with repetitive force. As a preventative measure, Hook had built a gun-like device that fired a sharpened steel rod with enough power to embed it deeply in the rock's face; the rod's free end had a strong rope tied to it. The plan was to fire the rod as they were carried by the waves toward the rocks and then to use Hook's arm-winch attachment to quickly reel themselves out of the ocean before they were battered against the cliffs. They would also tie the rubber equipment bags around themselves as a bumper against impact, lash themselves together, hold on for dear life, and hope it worked. There was no way to test the system before they actually used it, so that part of their plan had a scary, unknown quality. The drone's pictures had revealed a small shelf above the water line, and that platform was the resting spot they were aiming for. If the plan failed, they would be battered to death.

They stopped swimming and tied the bags and themselves into an awkward bundle when they started to feel the water pull them toward the island. They accelerated rapidly after that without swimming at all, and Hook fired the rod ten yards from the cliff's face. Angela closed her eyes, expecting her body to impact the rocks, but his winch system worked reasonably well, and a moment later they were pulled out of the water like a cork out of a bottle top. They were slightly scraped up and abraded from a few sharp rock points, but their neoprene wet suits had taken most of the real damage.

Resting on the shelf with their backs against the cliff, they agreed it wasn't an experience either of them ever wanted to repeat. They packed their swim fins and tattered wet gear into Hook's bag and took out black climbing gloves, shoes, and helmets. Under the wet suits they had on tight black nylon jumpsuits, and they used black paint on their faces; finally they added their vests, communication devices, and night-vision goggles. They didn't speak to each other, because the sound of the waves crashing below was too loud to talk over, but they had rehearsed the process so often it was automatic. Angela activated the tablet computer and slid it into the protected vest pocket.

Before they started to ascend, Angela left the bag of equipment for Stubby propped carefully on the shelf. She carried a tether attached to it on her belt so when Stubby sent the rope down from the helipad, she could fasten it to the tether, and he could pull the bag up from the shelf. Leaving the bag behind left her hands free to climb, and she could move better without its additional weight.

Hook led the duo up the cliff's face with the other bag on his back; he drilled into the rock with another of his arm's attachments and pounded in crampons as they moved upward. Those were an important safety device that would catch them if they slipped before they could fall too far. Most of the work of climbing involved forcing their fingers and toes into small cracks or onto tiny ledges and levering carefully upward. Hook had made several specialized fingers for his artificial arm that would fit into cracks too small for real fingers. Those steel fingers were strong enough to temporally support both their weights at the same time, and that advantage allowed them to climb where others couldn't. They froze as stationary black blobs on the cliff when the helicopter flew over delivering Abby to Greed.

Halfway up to the top, the cliff lost its steep slope and became completely vertical; the rock composition was much too dense to pound crampons into. That part was the harder, older core of the volcano cone. Even for experienced climbers like Hook and Angela, it was impossible to go straight up an almost smooth surface. So they tied themselves to crampons and rested their arms and legs while they waited for Stubby to throw down the rope from the helipad above. Angela had established basic time marks for each phase of the operation, so she counted off time in her head. The rope snaked down right on schedule. She tied the tether attached to the bag on the shelf to the rope, and she signaled for Stubby to pull it up. What she hadn't counted on was the heavy bag knocking her off the rocks as it came crashing by her on the trip up to the helicopter pad.

Fortunately the crampon she was tied to—and Hook's quick grab—limited her damage to a wide scrape on the side of her forehead, cheek, and chin. It stung a lot and would look like road rash for a while, but she thought it was pretty superficial as far as injuries went. Once Stubby sent the rope down to them the second time, the rest of the way was easy because Hook had tied on rope slings to sit in, and they just winched themselves up to the helicopter pad. When they arrived, the communication program was already running, Stubby had jammed the video security system, and the heat signatures were glowing red on their tablet computer. Stubby had communicated that he was on his way to Greed's office to pick up Abby, so they continued on with their plan to enter the fortress and to work their way down to the harbor.

The shape of Greed's fortress followed the island's topography. The great room had a long, wide hallway off the end opposite the main tower that led to several wings capped with smaller towers. The main hallway, which ended at stairs leading down to the harbor, was over twenty feet wide and about one hundred fifty feet long. It housed extensive collections of priceless art in huge glass cases that filled both sides along the whole length. Here and there paintings and sculptures on pedestals interrupted the flow of art cluttered behind glass. Many doors opened into the hallway, and the wings that intersected it led to the kitchen, the servants' quarters, and the guard housing. Angela knew some doors led to a media room, a library, the security command center, a game room, and numerous unoccupied guest suites, but others appeared to have no purpose on the blueprints, except maybe storage for more of Greed's expensive stuff. Guards patrolled the hallway regularly, and Angela believed it was probably booby-trapped in some way.

Parallel to the massive main hallway was a second smaller hidden passageway directly below it. That secret passage ran directly to Greed's quarters and had concealed entrances from various rooms, including the kitchen. Its purpose on paper was to allow servants to pass unnoticed, but the team suspected Greed used it for watching people and for moving his captives around. The secret hallway had elevator access to the harbor and the caves.

Angela and Hook's main job on the rescue was to disable as many people as they could, thereby helping the harbor team rescue Jasper and Emma with as little interference from the fortress's occupants as possible. But the first thing they needed to do was get to the command center. There, they would shut off the underwater percussion cannons and open the harbor's ocean gate to allow the scuba team to enter the caves. Angela knew the command center was the hallway's second door on the right, but it contained three heat signatures—likely guards that were armed.

From a strategic perspective, the hallway was a problem. Once they entered it, they would be exposed to anyone coming out of a door or connecting section. They couldn't shoot their Zaps with accuracy more than a quarter of the distance down its length, so they would be easy targets for anyone with a gun farther away than that. They might be able to duck into a room, but the door needed to be unlocked and the room unoccupied for it to be a safe refuge; all in all, it was a tricky proposition.

They checked the still sleeping pilot and copilot on their way through the great room. Then they waited until the hallway was visibly clear, checked for changing heat signs, and burst suddenly into the command center. One went in low and one high, just like they had practiced it, and in a matter of seconds, all three surprised guards were stunned and unconscious on the floor.

As Hook secured them in cable-tie cuffs, Angela thought to him, *Hook, look. The ocean gate is opened and the cannons are shut off already.*

He responded. *All, harbor is clear to enter, but watch out. Someone is going to leave by that route.*

He and Angela shared a look of concern, but Stubby had sounded the "all clear" that Abby was safe and Greed neutralized, so they decided to move forward with the plan. Hook took a minute to kiss Angela's scuffed face, and she kissed him back with feeling; but they suddenly became alert when the tablet computer showed a heat sign approaching the command center door. They froze in a crouched position, holding their breath, but the person passed by quickly, so Hook cracked the door and zapped the unsuspecting guard—who was the heat they had seen—in the back. They dragged him inside quickly and cuffed him with the rest.

They scanned for heat sources in the rest of the rooms that opened into the hallway, but they all were unoccupied; as added security, they turned the doorknobs as they passed by, but they were all locked. Finally, they arrived at the double doors in front of the guards' quarters, where they knew six warm bodies were seated around a table, probably having dinner.

Jasper, Tony, and Stubby had invented an ingenious door-securing device just for the guards' room. It was a thin, light-weight wire mesh that carried a big electrical charge. It was powered by a smart chip that sent the charge around any damage done to the mesh. That meant it remained active until it was shut down, no matter how much of the mesh was cut. It had a five-hour timer once activated, and after that it would shut down, destroying itself. Angela had decided that if they couldn't rescue Jasper within five hours, they would be out of luck, and the chief would probably arrive on the island by then anyway.

The mesh attached with supertacky glue strips and worked with any door material, but the guards' quarters had strong metal security doors, so they would conduct the punch of the electrical charge nicely. Angela and Hook covered the entire doorframe and knob with the mesh and turned it on. Once activated, anyone who touched the door—inside or out—would receive enough electricity to knock him off his feet, but not enough to damage him long term.

Angela had closely studied both the architect drawings and the composition profiles from Stubby's drone and had come to the disturbing conclusion that Greed had purposefully made only one exit from the guard quarters. She suspected that he had wanted to be able to confine any threat from a guards' mutiny. She believed Greed had built the area so he could electronically lock the security door from the outside and trap everyone inside like rats in a cage. Then he could do away with them, get a new staff, and start over if he needed to.

The reinforced walls, poor ventilation, and absence of any windows all spoke to Greed's paranoia and lack of value for human life. In a twisted way, it made sense to her; after all, he was outnumbered, he had a lot of valuable stuff around, and he hired people with questionable values and then gave them weapons. Angela figured he'd never consider the real reasons a rebellion might break out—namely the unpleasant working conditions and a mean, crazy boss. So Angela had made use of Greed's design by electrifying the door and essentially taking the men inside out of the fight for five hours. Hopefully, when the mesh self-destructed, the chief would be there with his posse.

She had just double-checked the mesh with a voltmeter when a man stepped out of a door across the hall with a gun in his hand. Angela cursed; she had checked that room for heat signatures before attaching the mesh to the guard's door. He was wearing a wet suit with a hood, gloves, and a face mask, and she knew immediately she had made a mistake by assuming all living people would have visible heat signatures. His wet suit was designed to keep his body heat inside to protect him from hypothermia, but it also must have canceled out any detectable infrared.

"Angela, watch out!" Hook yelled as he dove in front of her just as the man fired his gun.

Hook Zapped the diver unconscious as he shouted to her, but he fell to the ground when the man's bullet pierced his good arm, and it started to bleed profusely. Angela ran to him and saw that the bullet hadn't broken the arm bone but that it had blown a big exit wound in the muscle of his upper arm. She understood as his color paled that it wasn't pain or blood loss that scared him, but the thought of losing another arm. Unfortunately, the sound of his warning and the gunshot had activated the guards inside their quarters, and they tried to open the door. When they realized that they were trapped inside, they shot at the electrically charged door, and bullets pinged around the hall as a few passed through the metal.

Angela grabbed Hook under his shoulders and dragged him into the kitchen and out of the line of fire with her Zap clenched in her teeth. She crashed through the door like a wild woman and took a quick look around. She saw that the entire kitchen staff had also heard the shot in the hall, and they were standing in a line with their hands up. Angela motioned with her Zap toward the staff quarter's entrance, and they scrambled through it, knocking against each other. Then she heard the door's lock click into place. She shook her head because apparently Greed liked his household staff timid, obedient, and openly afraid.

However, there was one remaining person in the room. She was tiny, Asian, and middle aged. Angela looked into her dark eyes and saw sorrow laced with courage and determination; they showed a soul free of guile and full of goodness. Angela bet with herself that Greed had never looked into those eyes, or she wouldn't have survived on his staff. Undoubtedly, he had overlooked her due to her petite size, and that had been a stupid error on his part.

The small woman pleaded with her in broken English. "Please, missy, I help you."

Angela nodded, and the woman quickly tore a dish towel into strips and bound Hook's arm with a large piece pressing on the wound to stop the bleeding.

"Sir has my family. He hurts them. Please, missy, save us!" the woman explained as she worked.

That figures, the bastard gets his staff's cooperation by working over their families, Angela thought. She tried to explain. "We want to help you. Reed is no more after today, I promise. We won't hurt you, but stay out of the way. We will rescue the girls he hurts and the man and baby asleep."

The petite woman hugged Angela with tears in her eyes. "Bless you, missy, bless you!"

Angela turned to Hook, who was using a strip of towel to fashion a loose tourniquet. "How are you doing?" She noted with relief that his color had almost returned to a normal shade.

"Better cuff the guy in the hall, babe. I'm fine, but let's get on with the mission. The water team's almost here."

He checked the heat sensor readout. "Angela, someone's headed to the harbor down the secret passage. Let's go now!" He quickly demonstrated that he could open and close the hand on his wounded side, so she decided to scrap her plan to go back to the helicopter for the medical kit. Instead they would continue on, even though she knew he was in pain.

The woman showed them the kitchen's hidden door to the lower hallway, and she closed it after them. Angela looked around the passage and thought sarcastically, *Hook, no expense spared.*

The secret hallway was as plain as the upper hall was opulent; its rough rock walls were unadorned, and the floor was paved with simple slate tiles. It felt more like a tunnel hacked out of the island rock rather than a structure built with deliberation. Angela wrinkled her nose as they entered, because it smelled overwhelmingly of mildew, and the walls were damp with algae slime. A few small lamps lit the way, but many had burned out over time in the moist environment. Hook pulled Angela along quickly, but they both ran when they heard gunshots ahead.

Half-man sent a plea for help: *Ange, Hook, they know we're here, so time for reinforcements.*

Forty - Eight

Half-man tapped Tony on the shoulder and pointed to his own head. Tony knew what he meant by that gesture: get your head back on the job, and quit looking around like a tourist. All four men—Melt, Tony, Half-man, and Hawkeye—were being rapidly propelled deep beneath the ocean's surface by two underwater scooters. Greed's island security focused mostly around the harbor, so they were safe from observation, at least for a while, as they were still over a mile from its entrance.

Tony was enjoying the fast trip through the inky waters. He noticed many sea creatures were bioluminescent; fish in schools swam by with lines of bright-green dots on their sides, and various mollusks—and other things—intermittently lit up the sea floor. In his peripheral vision through the night-vision goggles under his swim mask, he saw several blacktip and hammerhead sharks cruise by, but the fast-moving scooters had kept them at a distance so far. He frequently looked down at Jasper and Emma in their glass box—which was safely secured to the front of his wetsuit with straps taken from Emma's baby backpack—but they looked asleep in their beds; Jasper was probably conserving energy for the task ahead.

They slowed the scooters to a stop as Hawkeye pointed out the edge of the rock barriers protecting the harbor's entrance.

Then they parked them on the sea floor and proceeded to swim forward cautiously, staying as deep as they could on the dredged harbor bottom; their visible skin was covered in black paint for camouflage, and the air they exhaled dispersed. They knew from the bugs that at least five guards remained in the harbor at all times. What was in the caves still remained a mystery, but everyone suspected they held additional threats.

Tony wondered to himself just how many guards a megalomaniac needed on an isolated island anyway. It seemed to him that five would have been plenty, but if he had counted right, Greed had at least fifteen or more in addition to his household staff. And complicating their arrival was the fact that they had all heard Hook's message that the ocean gate was already opened and someone was preparing to leave the harbor. That could have been as simple as a patrol boat going out for a routine check of the periphery or as risky as the big yacht leaving with Greed on board—and the massive boat would run them over on the way out of the small harbor.

Angela's master plan involved Hawkeye taking the lead once they entered the harbor, and then, using his marksman skills, eliminating the harbor guards before they knew they were under attack. Tony thought there was a big problem with that maneuver because Hawkeye would need to get close to the targets before shooting due to the Zap's distance limitation. He wondered how Hawk would manage that undetected. They stopped swimming for a minute and gathered around the waterproofed tablet computer Tony carried to look at the positions of the heat signatures sent from Stubby's equipment. Guards stood in groups, two by the submarine, three at the gangplank of the yacht, and four at the cave's entrance.

It was apparent that the guards knew the fortress had been invaded, because the movement of their signatures was agitated. Melt gestured to one of the guards by the yacht who looked like he was handing out things, and everyone understood it was probably weapons. Angela had made it clear that high-powered rifles could shoot people under water, so Tony stayed put. Hawkeye slowly swam up to the threesome by the yacht, Zapped the two closest guards, and quickly swam underneath the boat, using the curve of the hull as protection. The third man yelled and ran toward the group by the cave entrance, and Tony watched the bug's video as they all disappeared down the rock tunnel deeper into the caves.

When Hawkeye zapped the two guards, they fell into the harbor's water and sank beneath the surface, unconscious but alive and paralyzed by the electrical charge. Tony watched them sink to the harbor floor near him, not wanting to care that they were drowning. But he did. He didn't think he could live with himself if he stood by and watched two people die, no matter how evil they'd been. So he swam toward them, hooked their shirts in his hands, and towed them to the rocks that formed the harbor's entrance. He pulled them out of the water, turned them on their stomachs with their heads pointed down the rocks toward the water, and gave each several hard thumps on the back. After they both coughed out water, he cuffed their hands and feet, tied them together, and secured them to a strong piece of rebar sunk in concrete. Luckily for him, in the chaos caused by Hawk's Zapping the guards, no one had noticed him drag the men out of the water. He quickly swam back to assist Melt in removing the bugs the drone had planted.

Half-man had poked his head out of the water before Hawkeye had shot his Zap, and he'd recognized the woman verbally abusing a guard by the submarine. He heard her saying that she wanted them to get in the sub and power away from the island immediately. But the guard refused to follow her command despite the gun La Ruhr threatened him with, because, he insisted he would wait for his brother to arrive. Well, well, Half-man thought, it looks like witchy La Ruhr wants to get on her broom and fly away before things heat up. That made sense, because he had pegged her as someone who ditched when the going got tough. La Ruhr only looked out for number one, and to hell with anyone else. He quietly slipped out of the water and Zapped them both.

The witch was in midsentence and only had a moment to say "the insect" before she fell to the floor unconscious.

Half-man was satisfied with that brief response because it meant she'd recognized him, and she would have a lot of time in prison to think about underestimating James Dun. The irony was that if she hadn't been trying to force someone to do her will, then she might have noticed him sooner and then protected herself.

As Half-man reentered the water, a shot whizzed by him, grazing his ribs as it passed; the bullet didn't penetrate deeply enough to disable him, but he saw blood cloud the water and was glad they weren't swimming in the shark-filled ocean anymore. He removed his gloves and tucked them in his wet suit over the gash to apply pressure and to stop the bleeding before swimming to join the others.

Hawkeye managed to take out one more guard using the undirected electrical stream before Hook and Angela arrived. While the divers removed their scuba gear, she used a small medical kit that conveniently hung on the cave's wall to rewrap Hook's arm and to dress Half-man's injury. It was clear that Hook's wound needed surgical repair, but he growled at Hawkeye when he suggested that Hook take a backseat for the rest of the rescue to avoid damaging it further.

They concealed their discarded equipment by mixing it in with some diving things stored along the cave's wall, and they entered the tunnel as a slow-moving, cautious group. They knew there were at least three guards—maybe more—still at large, and that those men had the home-field advantage in a fight.

Forty - Nine

Madam La Ruhr pushed Abby into Reed's office, and as she closed the door, she said under her breath, "Nice fly for you, Sir Spider."

She walked away thinking that Dr. Newton might have had fine academic credentials, but she wasn't smart enough not to dress like a prostitute for a meeting with Reed; it was like waving a red flag in front of a bull, practically asking him to stomp and gore you. The doctor's appearance worked in La Ruhr's favor, though, because it would keep Reed fully occupied while she escaped in the submarine. La Ruhr walked calmly down the hallway, checking for dust with her finger as usual. She verbally dressed down the kitchen staff who were preparing dinner, and she personally signed the log in the command center before turning off the percussion cannons and opening the harbor gates. She explained to the guard captain that the Russian brothers would be servicing and testing the submarine in the next thirty minutes to prepare for another acquisition run the next day. She knew no one would dare question her authority in that situation, because they had all felt Reed's wrath when he needed new girls.

La Ruhr returned to her quarters and became a whirlwind of activity. She changed into jeans, a sweatshirt, and canvas shoes for travel, double-checked her emergency supplies, and changed all Reed's financial passcodes before locking her briefcase. La Ruhr had always considered her jobs temporary, so she kept personal things like clothing and shoes to a minimum and left them all behind when she changed identities. The basic rules she lived by were don't regret your choices, avoid looking back, and never second-guess decisions already made. Later she could use Reed's money to buy all new things anyway.

La Ruhr fully intended to pay the brothers and to give them the submarine after they let her off in a faraway port. She wouldn't double-cross anyone who helped her, because it came back like bad karma, and after all, she did have a few ethics. It never occurred to her that the submarine wasn't hers to give away, as she believed she deserved everything she could take from Reed.

The last thing she did before hurrying down the servants' hallway to the harbor was switch on the security system in the cave's tunnels. It was a booby-trap system with levels that progressed, so as intruders penetrated deeper into the caves, the penalties would increase until, as they approached the medical lab, a total roof collapse would bury all evidence of Reed's criminal activities there. La Ruhr didn't care if Reed was caught red-handed with his playmates, but she had planted evidence of her own death in the resulting cave-in, so she needed it to collapse soon after her getaway. She wanted La Ruhr dead and buried so with Reed's money she could live a new life as someone else. She didn't care who triggered the cave's collapse, but someone would try to get in or out eventually, not knowing that the security had been activated; if it was Reed himself, so much the better.

Her final act as La Ruhr was to notify Reed's banks to transfer the bulk of his money into a foreign account controlled by her. She knew some of his banks would balk without Reed's direct clearance, but others would follow through, knowing she was his business manager and believing her explanation of financial consolidation pending Reed's acquisition of a foreign-based megacompany. She almost hummed with pleasure as she contemplated her future as a wealthy woman—until she saw only one brother was at the submarine.

"Where in the hell is Rafael?" she hissed at him.

His brother shrugged. "I don't know! He just went for some supplies and didn't come back."

The brothers had spent the last two hours pretending to swim around checking the submarine's exterior, refueling it, and running the engine; but actually, they had been making solo trips into the fortress and stealing valuables. All the guest suites were loaded with expensive stuff and easily accessible using the hidden hallway, so together they had made multiple trips until most of the space in the submarine was full of art and antiques that could be easily sold. What his brother didn't know was that Rafael had been permanently delayed by Hook and Angela outside of the kitchen door.

"We're just going to have to leave him behind," La Ruhr insisted. "There isn't any time for fooling around. We need to go now!"

Unbeknownst to La Ruhr, the brothers had planned to leave her behind all along. They knew she had taken millions from Reed but was paying them only a small percentage of it, and that created hard feelings against her. They enjoyed her sexually—both individually and together—but had no illusions about the kind of person she was. They had laughed together about Madam Cold Fish and about how her aging passion was only ignited by money. On the small submarine her relentless orders would be impossible to tolerate, so they'd planned to get rid of her just before the trip started.

"I am not leaving without my brother. Not ever! We always stick together—we are brothers!" he insisted, curling his lips back over his teeth in a snarl.

La Ruhr grabbed his arm and attempted to drag him to the sub's open top hatch. He shook her off and shoved her backward. Then he made the mistake of grabbing at her briefcase as she lost her balance for a moment. She pulled a small gun from her pocket in response and pointed it at his chest, releasing the safety with her thumb.

"Get on that sub, or I will drive it myself, you stupid ass." She had planned for this possibility months ago by asking technical questions and having them give her a tour of the helm. It didn't seem that hard to drive to her; it went forward and up and down. If they could do it, she could do it! And if she didn't get the sub moving soon, Reed would smell a traitor, and she didn't want to end up like the girls; she would shoot herself before she allowed that kind of violation.

He said one word to her demand to get underway: "No!" But he put all the venom he had into it. His brother was everything to him, and he would die before leaving him alone on the island!

Into that dramatic stalemate Half-man suddenly appeared. They both looked at him for a brief startled moment before he Zapped them. La Ruhr fell down, unconscious but still clutching her briefcase, and that drew his attention to it. Half-man suspected it contained the keys to Reed's financial empire, so he tucked it under his wet suit, which was slung against his back.

But before he had stuck his head out of the water next to the dock, he had taken the precaution of disabling the submarine's main propeller; La Ruhr and her boyfriend wouldn't be going anywhere no matter how their argument had turned out. However, there was the missing brother they had talked about, so he alerted the rest of the team to that fact, not knowing the man was cuffed and cursing in the main hallway upstairs.

La Ruhr had called him an insect, and that made him laugh inside. What kind, he wondered—a pesky fly or a stinging bee?

But it didn't matter what she thought he was, because obviously she was a praying mantis. He cuffed them both, kicked her gun into the harbor, and then went back into the water just as the bullet grazed his ribs.

Fifty

The cave's mouth leading away from the harbor narrowed quickly into a spacious tunnel heading toward the island's center. The original cavern, which had been formed by millions of years of wave erosion, hadn't penetrated very deeply into the rock. Its internal space was like a rock cathedral with a tall ceiling and a floor covered by ocean water. Greed had completely changed its structure by dredging most of the floor deep enough for his yacht to moor there and then using the removed material for filling and elevating a portion above water level. He had also utilized dynamite to blast deeper into the island, forming tunnels and rooms of an unknown layout. He'd recycled the large rocks removed by stacking them to create a wave barrier out into the ocean securing and protecting the harbor entrance.

Angela had intuitively known the cave was the heart of Greed's operation the moment she'd seen it on the drawings; the fortress was for public show, but the caves revealed the real man who operated out of daylight, hidden deep under the earth. The caves presented a challenge to the team because the configuration of Greed's extensions wasn't known. Stubby couldn't read below the island's surface with his sensors, and they hadn't found engineering plans beyond the initial dredging and harbor expansion project.

The assembled team—minus Stubby and Abby—was about to enter the lighted tunnel at the back of the cavern when Angela heard a shout. "Hey, missy, no go there! He hurt you!" The petite kitchen lady was standing near the stairs, waving her arms at them.

Angela sighed loudly. "Hey, guys, hold up a minute while I see what she wants." She trotted back to the stairs. "What's up?"

The tiny woman was actually wringing her hands and hopping from foot to foot in agitation. "Missy, no go!" She made a slicing action across her throat with her index finger. "No go there!"

"All right, I get it. There's danger of death, but why?" Angela asked her.

In response, the lady made choking motions around her throat with her hands and coughed, bent over to the ground, pantomimed digging a hole and falling in, and finally spread her fingers and made slicing motions against her body.

Angela nodded. She had known from looking in the lady's eyes that she was more than she seemed and that she was aware of Greed's criminal activities "So he's set traps in the tunnel." She made go-away motions at the woman with her hands. "Thanks, but you go back now. We'll be ready for Greed's tricks, but we have to go in to get the people out. We'll be careful, so don't worry about us."

The lady gave her a brief hug and then turned and ran up the stairs. Angela hurried back to her team. "Greed has traps in the caves, and she was warning us. Seems like basic stuff—gas, holes, and sharp objects—and there may be other things she doesn't know about, so be alert."

"The traps must be run by a system separate from the rest of security. Because I didn't see anything like that activated or monitored from the control room, and I looked at every panel," Hook said.

"If there isn't a main switch in the control room, then maybe they're triggered on site just before the trap is sprung," Half-man mused. "He's so paranoid, and the space feels like it's his lion den, so I bet he has it under his control somehow. Maybe he monitors it from his bedroom."

"But if there's a central system, maybe when we find the first trap I could trace it back and try to reprogram it or to shut it down completely," Tony volunteered.

Angela thought for a minute. "No, that would take too long, Tony. But if we sent something ahead of us down the tunnel to spring the traps, we could just go around it safely after that." She looked around the cavern and spotted several sturdy flatbed carts that were used to move supplies around.

"Melt, go back and get those grappling hooks I saw on the dock by the stairs, and also get that coil of rope hanging on the wall."

The grappling hooks were mounted on long poles. Angela tied them to the cart handles so they could push the carts ahead of them down the tunnel. She hoped that if the cart triggered a trap, the poles would keep them back far enough that they would be safe.

"Logically, Greed isn't going to set a trap in a tunnel this wide. It'd take a lot of work and material to cover this whole space, and there're too many people coming and going who might accidently trigger it," Hook pointed out.

Angela nodded, agreeing with Hook's reasoning, but she still led the way, pushing a cart ahead of her. From the funnel-shaped back of the original cavern, a wide hallway almost the same size as the main one in the fortress stretched as far as they could see into the rock. It was dimly lit by security lights on the ceiling, and in contrast to the fortress's hallway, which was lined with cases full of valuable art, it had wide metal garage shelves full of supplies. Angela thought that Greed must have been prepping for doomsday, judging from the amount of stuff he had stored there. She saw hundreds of labeled plastic totes, tin cans, and boxes containing everything from applesauce to zucchini relish, all alphabetized in rows;

even personal hygiene supplies like toilet paper and mouth-wash were present.

The bottom rows were filled with jugs of drinking water secured by a series of locking cables. No thirsty person was getting water without Greed's permission. He was such a nice guy, Angela thought sarcastically. As they all ogled the sheer amount of things he had accumulated along the hallway, Angela realized he had hoarding behavior, which explained the expensive clutter Greed displayed everywhere in the for-tress above them.

"Keep alert. Remember that the remaining guards ran in here ahead of us," Hook reminded everyone. "Put on the head-lamp and gas mask from your vests now, and keep your Zap ready at all times. If Angela signals, we go to silent communi-cation using thoughts only, because sound waves transmit long distances through tunnels."

Angela assigned them positions: she and Hook led, one watching out and up and the other down for trip wires; Half-man and Hawkeye watched the right and left cave walls; Tony was in the middle of the group, carrying the glass box and com-puter; and Melt walked backward, watching the rear.

After they walked slowly in that configuration for about two minutes, the tunnel suddenly narrowed and split into three smaller dark branches. Two were big enough to still walk upright in, but the third required hunching over to move through it. Angela shone a bright light down each dark hole, but they twisted and turned so she couldn't see much beyond a few yards.

Angela snorted. "Here's where Greed made things interest-ing for us. It's like that kid's game—we're getting hotter and closer to what he wants concealed. I bet one of these tunnels leads to the girls, and one, to the lab and Jasper. Who knows where the other one goes, but they're all probably booby-trapped. I wonder if he knows how predictable he is. He thinks he's being clever, but it's just the opposite."

Tony looked down each hole cautiously. "It's creepy, dark, and scary, like a haunted house where something's going to jump out at you any minute."

Angela smiled. "Yeah, I think that's the atmosphere he was going for here. All he needs is a spooky voice telling us to turn back before it's too late. I for one love Halloween, and I can't wait to see what clichéd thing he has ahead for us."

She poked a cart down each tunnel as far as the poles would reach, but nothing happened. Then she attached a light to the end of one cart and roped the carts together to extend them as far as she could. The tunnels all looked dusty and unused. None of them appeared to be well traveled or more important than the others. She carefully looked for scratches on the walls, scuff marks, footprints, or anything that had been accidently dropped. To the casual observer, it would have appeared as if nothing had passed that way for years, but Angela knew better.

Finally she gave up and said, "OK, Tony, time to enlarge Jasper and see if he can track his body through one of these tunnels so we know which one to go down. This is obviously where Greed starts his keep-out policy, and I don't want to put anyone at risk unless I have to, so let's try this first."

Tony unstrapped the glass box from his chest and took it out of its clear waterproof bag. He saw Jasper was awake but had a grim look on his face. Tony knew Jasper was worried that he and Emma might not survive another size change. Tony understood it was his job to destroy the chip immediately if that happened, so he nodded to Jasper in acknowledgement of that promise. He opened the enlarging program on the computer. Jasper hugged and kissed Emma and then signaled for Tony to press enter.

Jasper's projection flickered to life, lying on the floor of the cave; he coughed, choked, and sat up, holding Emma. Everyone saw immediately that his image had more substance and definition than it had had before. His trunk was now only partly see-through rather than mostly transparent—but it still looked like static was constantly running through it—and the details of his extremities and face were better defined. Tony pumped his fist, grateful that the transition hadn't seemed as hard on Jasper, but his happiness was cut short when he looked at Emma, because she was definitely more ethereal and ghostlike than she'd been before.

At the cabin, Emma had had enough substance to wear clothes, sit in a swing, and to be held aloft, but her projection was visibly more fuzzy and indistinct. Abby's working theory about the difference in Jasper's and Emma's projections' densities was that since Emma had started with less mass than Jasper, her projection had been easier for the chip to do, and so she'd appeared more substantial than he had. Tony knew looking at them then that something else defined their appearances, because the projections had switched in clarity. He hoped Emma's new transparency wasn't a bad sign for her survival, because everyone on the team deeply loved her, but to Jasper she was as necessary as air.

Jasper stood up and held Emma close to his chest while murmuring to her softly and kissing her face; he had noticed her fuzziness too, and he was obviously scared like everyone else. But after a moment, he passed her to Angela gently and held out his hands toward the tunnel entrances. He turned his projection back and forth, trying to sense where his body was; then he tried moving down each tunnel as far as the carts had traveled, concentrating mentally on the space ahead. Tony fiddled with the program to boost the chip's feed, and then Jasper tried everything over again.

Finally he sadly said, "I just can't feel anything ahead, Angela. I'm sorry."

Angela was disappointed but not surprised. "Hey, it was worth a try, Jasper. Don't worry, we'll do it the old-fashioned way. OK, Melt and Half-man are one team, Hawkeye and Tony another, and Hook and I will take Jasper. Pick a tunnel, gentleman, push the cart ahead of you, and for God's sake, use the communication device frequently."

"Go slowly, stay alert, use your night-vision goggles and gas mask, and mark the turns carefully with chalk." Hook finished the lecture for her with a smile in her direction.

Fifty - One

The team decided which pair would investigate what tunnel by a quick game of rock-paper-scissors. Hawkeye and Tony got one of the tunnels large enough to stand up in. Tony pushed the cart ahead of him, looking at the floor, while Hawkeye scanned the walls and ceiling for trap triggers as they moved slowly through the confined, dark space. They wore their night-vision goggles, rather than their headlamps, to see in order to avoid alerting anyone to their presence. Hawkeye speculated that Greed had used a boring machine to make the tunnels, because there were repeating machine marks on the walls and the space was uniform in all dimensions, even though it twisted and turned frequently. The surrounding rock was hard, so blasting must have been necessary to break it down before the tunnel-boring machine could go through.

Most of the rock rubble was removed, but an inch-thick fine dust covered every horizontal surface. Tony was nervous, so he occupied his mind by wondering if Greed had brought in a dust-making machine for that purpose. It seemed impossible to get that much dust just from blasting and boring, and how else would powdery dust have gotten that deep underground? After all, there were snowmakers, foggers, and bubble machines, so why not a cave-dust blower? But knowing Greed, he had probably forced his staff to collect and spread the dust to a perfectly even thickness. Tony was glad he had on his gas mask, or he would have been coughing from the clouds of it they raised just by walking slowly through it.

They'd traveled about fifty yards down the tunnel when the floor under the cart suddenly collapsed and the cart disappeared from sight with a crash. Tony let go of the grappling pole just as it tipped upright and followed the cart into the hole. Both men froze in place while the dust cleared.

"Hell! A few more feet and I'd have been in there too!" Tony cried out, aware that he had made a mistake by letting his mind wander to dust machines instead of looking for booby traps.

Hawkeye put his hand on Tony's shoulder to steady him. "It's OK, it just means there's something important ahead. Let's hope the sound didn't alert anyone, but I don't think it did, because with all this dust, we would have seen footprints if someone else was down here."

He carefully moved forward to look into the hole. "Greed's serious with this trap. There's sharp spikes at the bottom, and he's greased the sides to prevent climbing out if you don't die right away."

He sent a thought message. *Ange, Hook, Half, Melt, just triggered a hole trap. We're OK, spikes in the bottom. Watch out.*

Hawkeye knelt down and carefully examined the trap's construction. There were two strong metal plates that slid into the cave's walls when the trap was set, leaving a piece of loosely attached canvas stretched over the hole to conceal it. Dirt and rocks were glued to the brown canvas, making it look like the floor of the tunnel was still intact, especially when it was covered with dust like everything else. When the trap was inactive, people could walk across the canvas supported by the metal plates under it. But the plates slid away when the trap was set, leaving the canvas to collapse when it was walked on. It was an ancient technique that used modern materials; it was simple but effective, especially when the hole was at least twelve feet deep and the floor was filled with sharpened rebar spears sticking up.

As Hawkeye continued to examine the trap, he saw that it hadn't been properly maintained and had been poorly constructed to begin with. The metal plates protruded from the tunnel walls about six inches on either side so weren't flush with the rock, and the canvas wasn't adequately camouflaged. He could see fabric cracks and ridges through the concealing dirt, even though it rested ten feet down in the pit on top of the spikes. He bet Greed had never gone down there to personally inspect it after its construction, or he would have noticed the flaws; probably no maintenance had been done on it after it had been built, either, and both were mistakes that worked in their favor. He sent his findings to the other teams to alert them so they could look for similar telling signs as they moved down their tunnels.

Tony asked, "How are we going to get across the hole?" He had stayed well back from the opening. "It must be ten feet wide at least."

The pole and cart combined might have been fashioned into a bridge, but the pole was still tied to the cart—now deep in the trap--and sticking up in the air out of reach. Even if they could have grabbed it, pulling the cart away from the spikes would have required them to lift it straight up, and the tunnel wasn't tall enough for that. Hawkeye started looking around for the mechanism that closed the plates back over the trap—so they could walk over the pit—but after a few minutes he decided it wasn't located near the trap.

Anticipating Hawkeye's decision, Tony said firmly, "We can't go back, Hawkeye. Jasper might be ahead."

"Then I see only one way to get across it, Tony. Run at it hard, grab the pole as you jump, and push off like a pole-vaulter to make it to the other side. You game for it?" Hawkeye asked.

"Sure, I did track and field stuff in high school. Sports are the best way to get girls, you know. So let's go, man. Bet I'll land farther on the other side than you do!" He paused for a minute. "But what are we going to do about any traps ahead without the cart to push in front of us?"

"How about if we throw something instead. You pitch high and I'll pitch low in case there's a light beam or a wire trigger. It's not as good as the cart, and it'll slow us down, but it's better than nothing."

"Maybe I could use what's left of the front pack, and you could throw the extra vest Angela packed for Jasper's body." Tony offered.

They both ran and jumped over the pit; then they continued down the tunnel, throwing and retrieving the pack and vest. Each man carefully examined the walls, roof, and floor of the tunnel before moving forward. Suddenly Hawkeye spotted a grid of nozzles quietly hissing out gas as they passed by.

"Tony, put on your mask now!" Hawkeye cried out loud. They both sprinted a good distance past the gas nozzles before slowing down. Then they caught their breath and returned to carefully checking the tunnel as they slowly moved forward again.

"There isn't going to be anything alive ahead. Greed wouldn't pump poisonous gas where it might accidently drift into the medical lab or kill the girls." Hawkeye reasoned. "There must have been fifty nozzles spraying gas. Greed wanted that trap to be fatal for anyone who survived the pit," he grimly said.

"I agree," Tony said while nodding. "So let's see what he's protecting ahead, because even if it isn't alive, it has real value to him." Tony bent to pick up the dusty front pack and threw it ahead again. "It can't be much farther."

"I noticed some of the nozzles were corroded closed, so nobody has ventured down here for a long time. So whatever it is, Greed doesn't need it often."

Slowly the tunnel opened up, and they came to a thick door made out of heavy black-iron bars. It completely sealed the entrance to a long, narrow cavern behind it. Hawkeye directed his headlight through the door's bars, and they were amazed at what they saw: row after row of all kinds of weapons, organized by class. There were simple blades, swords, and pikes, and more unusual hatchets, axes, and throwing spears. The were many various guns stored, some from modern times, and others, ancient. Greed had small missiles, anti-aircraft guns, various bombs, torpedoes, and even a couple of cannons. After looking around in amazement, they both backed slowly down the tunnel again.

"Holy crap—that's enough stuff to turn this whole island into gravel at the bottom of the ocean!" Tony said.

"Yeah, the only thing missing was a nuclear weapon, and maybe there's one that I missed. No wonder nobody goes down here!"

Tony shook his head. "Man, if Angela had known about this in advance she'd have thought the mission was too dangerous, and we'd still be home!"

Hawkeye agreed. "She could still abort the mission if she finds out that arsenal is wired to go off, but I think Greed wouldn't take the risk. Plus, we've come too far to give up now, and getting out will be dangerous too."

At that moment a thought message came through. *Hawk, Tony, they're shooting at us, come ASAP. Take the small tunnel.*

They swung back over the pit and headed back to the main tunnel in a run.

Fifty - Two

alf-man and Melt were hiding behind several large water barrels. Unfortunately, their skill at rock-paper-scissors had netted them the smallest tunnel, and they had hunched and crawled through about fifty winding, inky-black yards until it'd opened up into a space tall enough to stand up in. Once the tunnel had changed size, they'd realized that the area was occupied, because calypso music had echoed down its length. They proceeded cautiously, nervous that they would be easy targets if someone came toward them in the confined space.

In about one hundred more feet, the tunnel had abruptly widened into a large cavern, and after a brief thought discussion, Melt had decided to take a risk by peeking out of the tunnel for just a second. Half-man flattened himself against the wall while Melt glanced around the cave quickly; Melt had been noticed immediately by a guard who had raised the alarm by shouting to the others. Half-man thought how stupid the guards were to play loud music that advertised their position, especially if they were so nervous they posted someone to constantly watch the entrance. Because of that obvious mistake, he doubted any of the men inside had training in warfare.

Melt was an expert at memorizing details and had thought shared what he observed. On one side of the cavern there were three or four smaller caves closed with black-iron gates, and they probably housed the abducted girls. The other side had a crude setup for the guards, including a small kitchen counter with a microwave, a camp refrigerator, and a coffee pot; a composting toilet and several crude cots were next to the kitchen. The guards also had a worn recliner, an old radio, a CD player, and magazines.

When the guards had seen Melt, they'd started shooting their guns, and he and Half-man had ducked behind the water barrels, which had been their only available defensive position. The guards couldn't get a clear shot, but neither could they from their crouched positions behind the barrels. They couldn't back down the tunnel without exposing themselves further, so it was a standoff. Melt sent a thought message to Hawkeye and Tony for help, but while waiting for them to arrive, Half-man had an idea.

He was desperate to move things along quickly because he worried that if more guards came down the tunnel they would be boxed in, and concerned about the girls; they were so quiet, and he'd expected them to scream at the deafening sound of bullets firing in the confined space of the cave. Half-man thought maybe the cells were empty and the girls already dead; but why post guards if that was the case? All Melt had seen was a pile of dirty blankets on the floor of one dimly lit cell.

Half-man decided to act on his idea, so he took a deep breath, used the loud theater voice he could project to an entire coliseum, and said to the guards, "Shooting in a small rock cave is stupid. The bullets will ricochet and bounce back to hit you eventually. We are not interested in you. We are here to take the girls home. Reed will be in jail by the end of the day, and if you surrender now, I will put in a good word for you with the police chief."

Half-man repeated it again in Spanish and then waited for a reaction. He banked on the fact that at least some of the men had already run away from the harbor to hide there, so they hadn't wanted to fight then, and he hoped they wouldn't fight now.

He waited a few minutes with no response from them, so he sweetened the pot. "Reed is tied up in his office and has no power anymore. There is a large reward for return of the girls, and I will let you have it if you cooperate. Lie down with your hands behind your back, or I will shock you with electrical power." He repeated it in Spanish, reached the Zap around the corner, and sprayed an undirected blast of crackling blue-and-white electricity against the roof of the cavern.

After a moment, he slowly looked around the water barrel and saw three men facedown on the ground. Half-man wasn't a fool, so he stunned them anyway from a safe distance away. Melt kicked their guns away and cuffed their hands and feet, and then he searched them for the keys to the cells.

Tony and Hawkeye arrived, running down the tunnel after hearing the Zap discharges. "Looks like you managed fine without us." Hawkeye glanced around the shabby guard station with a look of disgust. "Where are the girls?"

Melt held up the keys. "Who wants to check?" He was afraid he would lose it if the girls were dead under the blankets, so he offered to let the other men look first. He was tough but not that tough, and his scars might have scared them anyway.

No one volunteered for the job, so Half-man reluctantly took the keys and slowly walked to the cells. He thought Greed had purposefully designed them to look like medieval dungeons; all that was missing was an iron maiden and a rack. He wanted to punch something—he was so mad! Wasn't it bad enough that Greed had taken them from their homes, had used them sexually, and had inflicted pain on them? But on top of that, he housed them like rats and terrorized them the rest of the time! He hoped Greed got every bit of that pain and suffering back, and more in prison. Quietly he unlocked the cell containing the blanket pile, and then, leaving the door wide open, he sat on the floor as far away from the blankets as he could get.

After a moment he said, "We're here to take you home. You're safe now. I promise."

Suddenly the blanket moved, and a naked girl dashed out of the cell door, grabbed a guard's gun from the floor, held it with a shaking hand, and pointed it at Tony, then at Melt, and then at Hawkeye. They all froze in place.

Half-man repeated himself in a calming voice. "We're here to take you home, and you're safe now. No one is going to take that gun from you. You keep it to defend yourself. Take another one for your friend and anything else you need to feel safe. It's going to be OK now."

The young woman trembled from weakness; her skin was a patchwork of wounds and dirt. But Half-man looked at the fire in her eye as she held the gun pointed at the men and breathed a sigh of relief. Everything physical would heal if her spirit was still intact. He slowly stood up, walked to the guard's cot, removed a blanket, and wrapped it around her shoulders gently. He was careful not to touch her skin or to make any sudden moves. She was rail thin with matted hair. He had a sudden urge to kick the guards repeatedly. How could a person be so lacking in basic human kindness that they turned away from those suffering innocents? He couldn't imagine it!

But he calmly said, "Is your friend all right?"

After recognizing the compassion in his eyes, she slowly dropped the gun to her side. "She's sick and has a broken finger and toe. Is Reed really going to pay for what he's done to us?"

"Yes, I promise. He might not pay with his life, but he won't ever do this to anyone again. I'm sure of that!"

Half-man walked back to the blanket on the cell floor and carefully pulled it back. The small occupant was unconscious, and he could smell the stink of infection in her wounds.

He called to Hawkeye. "Can we get them to Stubby in the helicopter? He's got the medical kit and can fly them to the hospital in St. John. This one needs help as soon as we can get her there."

Hawkeye brought him a fresh blanket to wrap the second girl in. "We can use the cot as a stretcher. Melt and I'll take them to the helicopter and come back to help with Jasper and Emma."

"Fine, let Angela know." Half-man turned back to the first girl. "Can you walk to the helicopter? Our friend Stubby can fly you home."

"I can walk, and I'll shoot Reed dead if I see him, " she responded grimly.

Half-man responded happily. "You go ahead and do that, honey, and then I'll kick his balls into his throat after you shoot him." He almost saw a smile through the dirt on her face.

He sent a thought message: *Stub, bringing injured girls to helicopter for medical care and transport.*

Hawkeye and Melt carried the unconscious girl on the cot back through the tunnel to the harbor, up the main stairs, down the long central hallway, through the great room, and out to the helicopter. During the whole trip the other girl constantly swiveled around, looking for danger and holding her gun cocked and ready. Melt was afraid she might accidently shoot herself, so he traded her gun for his Zap and let her stun any cuffed person who was waking up when they passed. He checked that the guards' quarters were still secured with the electric mesh and that the kitchen was empty of staff. They didn't have any trouble or see anyone not already cuffed on the trip, and that surprised him. It almost felt like the fortress was already empty.

Hawkeye settled both girls in the helicopter and let a sympathetic and recovering Abby administer first aid, because Stubby was still safecracking in Greed's office. He and Melt were shocked at Abby's damaged face, and they hugged her carefully. It didn't escape Hawkeye's notice that her facial injuries looked a lot like what Greed had done to the girls.

Hawkeye kissed her broken finger. "I'm sorry he hurt you, sweetie."

In response, Abby touched his face near his missing eye. "We all take our licks showing up for life and fighting for what's right. I'll be OK, but don't tell the rest of them about me yet. They don't need the distraction from helping Emma and Jasper."

Fifty - Three

As Jasper traveled underwater in the glass box, he could feel himself getting stronger as they moved closer to Reed Island. He had feared he wouldn't survive the stress of another size change, but the nearer he was to his body's location, the better he felt. Enlarging his projection still hadn't felt good—it was like being quickly deconstructed down to the molecular level and then reassembled—but it was survivable.

He wished Emma's projection was also stronger on the island. She hadn't changed in appearance after any of the previous size transitions, but this time she was obviously more transparent. As Jasper held her close to him, he had to be careful not to turn his hands perpendicular to her body because they would go right through her. It made him scared and angry; he didn't care much about his own future, but Emma had her whole life ahead of her, so she couldn't just fade away when rescue seemed at least possible.

Jasper knew they were moving down the tunnel toward the laboratory and his unconscious body. He couldn't feel it, but from the team's communication he knew where the other tunnels led, so they must have selected the one that headed there. Angela had stopped several times to shove the cart ahead through areas that looked like booby traps, but no traps had sprung. Hook pointed out that the small red light beam sensors in the rock walls were active, but they didn't trigger anything when they passed through them. Angela believed that meant they were expected in the lab, so the traps had been shut off—and that wasn't a good development.

Surprise always helped when the odds were stacked against you, Jasper thought, and it appeared they had lost that small advantage. Tony and Half-man had caught up to the group when they had stopped to discuss the first area that looked like an inactive booby trap; Melt and Hawkeye had rejoined the team from their trip to the helicopter with the girls shortly thereafter. Jasper mused cynically that everyone but Abby and Stubby would be present for the main event; he didn't expect a happy ending for the rescue after so much time had passed since Emma's abduction, especially because she continued to fade away.

Angela suddenly held up her hand, signaling to them to stop, because she saw a faint light leaking from around a closed door up ahead. She crept forward and tilted her head slightly so one eye could peek through the crack around the lock and look for a few seconds.

She returned to the group, and in a whisper she said, "I saw two guards with guns inside, a nurse, and three people working at computer stations. I didn't see Jasper or Emma, but there's a hospital bed behind a curtain, and I could hear a monitor beeping. I bet they know we're coming, because the guards have their weapons drawn, and they're pacing around the room."

"We can't blast in spraying electricity from the Zaps, because it might screw up the life-support machines," Hook cautioned. He gave Jasper a stern glance.

Jasper knew his face must have shown how he wanted to rip all the guards' heads off for what they had done to Emma, but he remembered that they all had promised Abby they would use as little violence as possible, so he swallowed his urges and decided to bide his time for retribution.

Tony spoke after a thoughtful pause. "I have an idea." All heads turned toward him. "Why don't we just send Jasper in alone? At some level they know what they're doing is wrong. And the last thing they'll expect is to have him show up and tell them in person."

"They're going to know I'm pissed, because I'm ready to trash the place and to personally beat them all up!" Jasper said with clenched teeth.

"So how about using that energy? He still looks like a ghost, and fear might prevent them from shooting or shutting off the machines long enough for us to take them down," Tony said in further support of his idea.

Angela thought about it and agreed. "Even if they attack him, it won't damage his projection, and hopefully it will distract them long enough for us move in."

Half-man volunteered to talk like Jacob Marley from *A Christmas Carol* and to speak from the computer as a disembodied voice. All Jasper had to do was move his lips and try to keep up, and if a disconnect occurred between Jasper's lip movements and Half-man's voice, it would only add to the ghostly feeling they wanted to create.

Hook removed the bottom of the supply cart—the one they had pushed ahead to trigger traps—to make a wheeled platform for Jasper to ride through the door on so he would look like he had quickly floated into the room. Half-man instructed him to hold his arms away from his body and to sway a little. No one who saw him would have mistaken him for a living human being, because even though he was just outside of the room where his body lay, he was still semitransparent with constant flickers of static.

Jasper wanted to get on with it. "Look, Angela, unless they hit the projection chip directly, I can't be hurt. Wrap some Kevlar around the chip, and I'll be OK, but come in pretty fast with Emma so we aren't separated for long."

They started the spook show by pounding loudly on the door, and then Hook crashed it open with a swift kick. Jasper glided in with his arms stretched out and swayed back and forth. He moved his head in jerky motions and stared with wild eyes directly at each of the people in the room one by one. The guards pointed their guns at him but seemed frozen with shock at his otherworldly appearance.

Half-man's voice was loud and booming and had computer-generated echoes and quavers. Jasper moved his lips silently and added toothy grimaces frequently.

"Where have you taken my body? My soul will haunt you until you burn in fire! You have violated the laws of man and God! Prostrate yourselves down and pray, sinners, for your lives!"

Jasper thought it was overkill, but Half-man's words had the desired effect, especially when a guard's bullet passed completely through his body and embedded itself in the wall behind him, showering rock chips into the room. Both guards then fled to a small elevator, tripping over things and pushing each other in their haste to get away. Angela rushed to the elevator behind them and zapped the control panel, trapping them between floors.

When Jasper had glided into the room, the three people at the computer stations had swiveled around in their chairs with their mouths open in surprise. But once the guards were gone, the nurse put her hands on her hips and simply said, "'Bout time you got here!"

Jasper stepped off the cart, walked toward the bed, and pulled back the curtain. He looked at the man lying there unconscious and didn't recognize him. The man was pale and thin to the point of emaciation, his eyes were sunken behind his lids, and his hair and beard had grown long. He looked emotion-lessly at the various wounds Greed had inflicted on his body and felt no connection to it. It was just a body without a mind; it was more of a damaged wax figure than a man, and it didn't feel like it had ever belonged to him.

He had a feeding tube sticking out from his abdomen and IV drips in each arm. A urinary catheter slowly collected urine in a bag, and a ventilator mechanically pumped air into his lungs through a tracheal tube. A beeping machine traced life-support data across a screen. The man on the bed was so far removed from who he was that he didn't even care that he was lying there naked, but Tony hurried over and tossed a blanket over his body.

Tony was angry that the nurse apparently hadn't thought Jasper was human enough to be humiliated by the exposure of his private parts to everyone. Jasper was unconscious and vulnerable, and he deserved someone to look out for his privacy! He shot the nurse an angry look, and she shrugged, embarrassed about it.

Jasper turned away from the man on the bed and walked to the pediatric incubator where Emma's body was lying unconscious. She also had tubes and monitors hooked up for life support, but her body was in better shape than his was, and it was a huge relief to him. Jasper was suddenly overwhelmed by emotion when he saw her there and alive; it was all too much for him, and he sank to the floor and choked back dry tears.

The nurse scurried over. "Now don't despair, honey. I've spent a lot of time and energy keeping you and the little one going as best I could. I'm Marybeth, and don't worry, we're going to get you and the baby home again." She started capping off the IV tubes and detaching EKG leads.

"Why did you help do this to them?" Angela asked angrily.

Marybeth replied calmly. "I didn't have a choice. Reed told me if I didn't help him, he would kidnap my granddaughters and play with them. I've seen what he does to girls, and I couldn't let that happen to them. I'm so sorry, but we did everything we could every day to stand in his way."

One of the computer guys said, "You're Jasper Higgs, and I'm glad to meet you at last! We knew you were coming back through the power feed changes, but we didn't know exactly when."

"You know how the chip works?" Jasper asked with concern.

"No, never did figure it out. We really didn't try too hard, because we didn't want Reed involved even a little bit. Kept putting him off with tech-speak and promises and then hoped you would figure it out from your end. Looks like you did, and I want to say your chip's pure genius!"

Angela broke in. "You guys can talk shop later. Let's get out of here now! Marybeth, can we transport the bodies safely?"

"Sure, I guess you're going to use the helicopter on the airstrip?" She continued to unhook machinery. "I see you brought a stretcher, and the incubator can be wheeled once I convert it to battery power."

"But how are we going to get to the airstrip with the equipment since Angela fried the elevator.? Go all the way back up and walk down to the hangar over the rocks?" Tony asked.

Marybeth smiled. "I've got a quicker route for you. Reed built us a small dormitory when he realized he had to keep Jasper alive in order to find the missing chip. He lied to the computer guys about the kind of job this was to begin with, and then he trapped us all here with armed guards twenty-four-seven, so we had to have some place to live. But I realized the back of the new room was close to the island's surface, so we spent time after lights-out digging a back door for an emergency escape route. It'll be a tight squeeze for you all, but after that it's just a short, easy walk to the airstrip."

One of the computer guys spoke up proudly. "You have Marybeth to thank for our not getting buried alive."

Angela looked at him with a question in her eyes. "What are you talking about?"

Marybeth explained. "When we dug the exit, I noticed a wire in the dirt, and when I traced it back I realized the whole area above the caves was probably drilled and loaded with explosives. My husband worked in demolition, so I recognized the wire right off. I think Reed's plan was to get rid of people and evidence by collapsing the caves with TNT. Then everything would be covered over with tons of rock and dirt, and he would walk away dusting off his hands."

The computer guy laughed. "Yeah, we spent a lot of time we were supposed to use to find the chip disconnecting booby traps instead! He had the traps sequenced, so the deeper an intruder got in the caves, the more stuff would be set off, until everything was destroyed."

Another computer guy continued. "We calculated that he had enough dynamite in the holes to destabilize the whole island, including his precious house. It was a really dumb idea because there was no guarantee that he wouldn't be home if someone penetrated deeply enough to cause it to blow."

Tony and Hawkeye exchanged a look, agreeing it was a really stupid idea; they both remembered the weapon arsenal, which would have probably exploded at the same time.

Marybeth smiled. "Just in case those guys missed a trick, I snipped a lot of wires and removed as many detonators as I could find while we dug out." She wheeled Emma's incubator into the center of the room. "I think we're ready to roll now."

Angela motioned to Melt and Hawkeye to lift Jasper's body onto the stretcher. She looked around. "Jasper, don't forget your computer and stuff." Tony turned back for it because he saw that Jasper was totally focused on Emma.

She questioned Hook and Half-man. "Do you guys need your wounds rebandaged, or are you good to go?" Both men indicated they would wait until later to deal with their injuries.

She turned to Marybeth and the computer guys. "We aren't going to have room for you on this trip, but I'll send the chief back as soon as I can. The guards are all tied up except the ones in their quarters, and those can't get out for another two hours. Reed is cuffed in his office, the household staff is locked in their rooms, and La Ruhr is tied up by the submarine. We'll leave you enough weapons to defend yourself, and the authorities should be here in less than an hour."

Tony was busy collecting hard drives and destroying data. "Sorry, guys, but Jasper and Emma can't risk a repeat of this situation. I'm sure you understand."

Marybeth led them through a door into an adjoining room filled with stacking bunks. She opened a small panel cleverly hidden behind the beds, pointed to a dark crawl space, and wished them luck. The team crawled through the claustrophobia-inducing dirt tunnel on their hands and knees. Melt dragged the stretcher with Jasper's body on it behind him, Hook pushed the incubator ahead of him with the top of his head, and Jasper carried Emma's projection carefully clutched in one arm. They finally exited into the dark tropical night, feeling as if days had passed since they'd dropped off the fishing boat instead of only a few short hours.

Fifty - Four

Stubby heard the sweet sound of the last tumbler falling into place. He looked at his watch. One hour and thirty minutes; not too bad for a lock he hadn't worked with before. He took a few deep breaths, loving the moment of anticipation just before opening a safe door and appreciating the beauty of the mechanism and his connection with it. He ran his hands over the smooth metal several times, and then he slowly opened the door.

Greed had installed a special high-intensity lighting system in the safe, and when the door opened it came on automatically—like a refrigerator door light—so the safe's contents sparkled to life in front of Stubby's eyes. It felt like he was entering Aladdin's cave as he stepped forward into the large rectangular space. Both sides were lined with waist-to-eye-level stacks of shallow, glass-fronted drawers holding mostly large loose gems and some fancy finished jewelry; they were the source of the glitter that had almost seemed alive to Stubby. They beckoned him forward, and he saw that most of the big stones were diamonds and that each one sat in an individual compartment lined with black velvet. He observed that every large stone was individually lit with an LED and that each compartment had an identifying number and gem description on a small silver plaque.

Stubby pulled out several drawers, and he discovered that behind the large gems were velvet bags filled to capacity with medium-sized clear and colored faceted stones. Stubby marveled at the number of priceless gems and wondered how many Greed had actually purchased. Nowhere did he see a gem the size most people wore for a ring; all were much bigger than that. Greed was short, Stubby thought, so it made sense to him that he wanted everything else big.

Below the rows of glass drawers, there were numerous cubbyholes containing large bins of paper currency that were kept in stacks held together by rubber bands. Most of it was US dollars, but other countries around the world were also represented. And above the sparkling gems were hundreds of framed bearer bonds and stock market certificates crowded together. They filled all available space to the safe's ceiling.

The back of the safe was occupied by a stack of gold bars; Stubby estimated the stack was eight feet tall and at least five feet deep. Each bar was stamped with its weight and purity. Looking around, Stubby felt a little of the mental rush Greed must have had every time he was in the safe, because seeing the wealth represented there was an overwhelming experience.

On a deeper level Stubby understood that the safe's contents represented what Greed was all about—that he could never have enough, was never satisfied, and craved more and more to fill all his empty spaces inside. Greed didn't know that all the treasure in the world couldn't make him feel whole any more than hurting women would give him the love and companionship he craved. He was a lost soul, and all his wealth wouldn't give him the peace and security that he really desired.

Even before he had opened the safe, Stubby had decided the approximate monetary value of the contents he would take with him. Stuff wasn't important to him and he lived a simple life, as did all the people on the team, but he felt some compensation was due for damages done. He believed that Greed owed the team not only for their lost time and the risks they had taken, but also for their pain and suffering, too. He knew that the gold's value would most easily convert to cash—its price per ounce was standardized daily all over the world—so he took one gold bar each for Angela, Tony, Half-man, Hawkeye, Hook, Melt, Dee, and himself. He took two gold bars for Abby, Jasper, Emma, and each of the rescued girls, because he felt they were owed more for the extra trauma Greed had inflicted on them. He calculated that seventeen gold bars—at twenty-seven pounds each—was about all the extra weight the helicopter could carry in addition to the girls. He stacked them on a small rolling cart Greed used for his office printer and dumped five drawers of gems—including the large ones and all the velvet bags behind them—into his safecracking tool kit. He thought they could sell the gems to fund the companies they had talked about, and their weight would be insignificant on the helicopter.

Stubby looked around the safe one last time and then walked out, locking the door behind him. He wasn't tempted to take more, because money was just another tool to him. He had seen that wealth and possessions didn't lead to happiness; having enough money was good, but having a lot of it was destructive. Look at all those famous Hollywood people, Stubby thought. So many lived out of control and full of pain despite piles of money—just like Greed.

Stubby had worn gloves to avoid leaving his fingerprints on anything, but he deliberately left Abby's blood, purse, shoes, smashed injection device, paperwork, and prints as they were. Angela's plan was for Abby to press theft charges against Greed—even though no one thought the miser would actually pay her huge price—which would give the chief an opening to search the island. Unfortunately, Greed had snapped, and Abby planned to take advantage of that by adding assault charges, so they needed as much evidence as possible because they would be up against Greed's many lawyers.

Greed was still trussed by the desk, but he was starting to groan and twitch, so Stubby Zapped him again on the way out. He still thought Greed was a very bad man, but the urge to beat him up for what he had done to Abby had softened into pity during the time he had spent in his office. Greed was one big empty space that no amount of hoarding would ever fill up.

Stubby exited the office and hurried down the hall and across the great room up to the helicopter pad. Both of the guards there were still snoring from the knockout drug in their water bottles, and he didn't see any other people. Abby had administered first aid to the rescued girls as best she could with a broken finger. One of them got off a wild shot at him, but Abby quickly assured her that he was really a white knight in disguise. Stubby blushed when he heard Abby's description of him, and the girl profusely apologized for her mistake. The smaller one seemed to be going in and out of consciousness, and Abby explained to Stubby that her wounds were infected and that she probably needed IV antibiotics at the hospital as quickly as possible. He loaded the gold bars into the helicopter's hidden compartment, gathered up his equipment and the climbing gear, replaced the part he had removed, and then prepared for flight.

They rose into the air, circled the airstrip until he got a visual on the rest of the team carrying Jasper's body to the second helicopter, and then headed for St. John. Once they were in the air, Stubby contacted Dee and told her to give the authorities the go-ahead; he knew Chief Lawrence had been standing by ready to search the island once they asked for his help.

Stubby knew the families of the girls would want to see them as soon as possible, but they also needed medical attention on St. John. So after consulting with Angela, he asked Dee to broadcast a general message alerting the families, the airport, and the hospital about their arrival. Angela hoped the resulting stir would allow the second helicopter to land quietly next to the plane the team had flown in on. They planned to quickly board the jet and to get away before the media descended, or the chief returned with some hard questions.

Stubby glanced at Abby cuddling the girls in the backseat of the helicopter; the smaller one was conscious and crying softly, but the other one clutched a Zap with a look of determination on her face. It broke his heart to see what Greed had done to all of them; he couldn't wait to reunite the young women with their families and to feel the joy of that sweet moment. Stubby knew it couldn't wash things clean again, but love filled the empty spaces of the heart better than anything else he knew of, and healing would occur once they were bathed in its warm light.

Fifty - Five

As the team approached the airstrip, motion-activated security and landing lights turned on, illuminating the darkness. When Jasper looked down at Emma in the light he realized her projection was fading away even further. His steps got slower and slower as he looked with horror at the baby slowly disappearing right before his eyes.

When he could see the ground through her face, he panicked. "Oh, God! Emma, Emma, baby Em! No...We have to go back right now!" Jasper practically howled in his grief. He turned to run back to the dirt tunnel's entrance to find Marybeth to help her, but Emma dissolved away to nothing in his arms after just a few steps back toward the fortress.

The men gathered around, and Hook put his hand on Jasper's shoulder. "I'm sorry, man. We all loved her, too. You did all you could to save her."

Jasper put his hands over his face in utter despair. "No, no, no!" It tore at his soul that they had come so far and had gone through so much only to lose his daughter steps from the helicopter. He felt like fading away too, because what was the point of all this without her?

At that moment Angela, who was standing by the incubator, shouted with joy. "She's waking up, Jasper! Come look at her! Emma's OK!"

He rushed over and looked into the incubator. Emma's blue eyes were open and blinking in the light. She looked at him, and he saw she was weak but alert; and in that moment of eye contact, he knew her mind was fully functional, and she was still the same Emma he loved. He closed his eyes in relief and gratitude, and then he opened the top of the incubator and disconnected the tube directing oxygen to her nostrils; she was a healthy pink color and breathing regularly, and the tube would tangle if she moved.

"Hey, sweetie. Let's take this off. You don't need it anymore." He kissed her face and she gave him a weak half smile. Jasper was sure she remembered him. Emma's projection had weakened the closer she had gone to her body until they had slowly united again. Why that wasn't happening with him too, he wasn't sure; maybe it was because his body was in such rough shape or because he carried the chip. Perhaps uniting again wasn't going to be possible for him, but it didn't matter as long as Emma was whole.

"Hook, do you think we can leave the incubator behind now that she's awake? We could use the extra space in the helicopter," Angela said.

Hook knew Jasper's projection couldn't support Emma's body weight, so he motioned to Half-man to pick her up out of the incubator. "She looks pretty good. I think if we just leave the IV drip port and other stuff as it is, she'll be fine without it."

When Half-man gently picked her up, Jasper noticed Emma didn't have control of her limbs; they flopped limply like they had when she had been a projection. But her eyes were bright and lively, so he hoped she would regain strength in time. Half-man helped Jasper cuddle her for a moment by supporting her weight as her father kissed her face and hugged her tenderly. Jasper felt like sun was streaming out of every pore; he wanted to sing and dance because maybe everything would work out after all.

"So how come she returned to her body and you haven't, Jasper?" Angela asked.

"I have no idea. I don't know why she projected with me to begin with, and I don't know why she's back either. I suspect it's because she never fully projected like I did, so her image couldn't be sustained when physically close to her body. I'm just happy she's OK—that's all. I don't care what happens to me."

They looked up when they heard helicopter sounds, and they saw Stubby circling overhead. Angela waved at him. "Let's go, people! We can't be too far behind him."

Angela held Emma in her lap in the copilot seat as Hook did the preflight checks. Jasper's body was stretched over the laps of the four men wedged in the back, and his projection occupied the jump seat. The men tried to ignore how light Jasper's body was—it felt like a corpse was lying on their laps—for it was both sad and creepy at the same time. They tried to distract themselves by focusing on the joy of Emma's return to her body, and they took turns naming all the good things she had ahead of her to experience in life.

As they rose into the air, Hook sarcastically said, "I hope everyone enjoyed their tropical island adventure tonight."

Hook landed at the St. John airport just yards from the idling private jet that had brought them and partially concealed the helicopter behind it. Stubby had landed the other helicopter three hundred feet away on the tarmac closer to the small terminal building.

Dee was dressed in an official-looking nurse's uniform and was standing with Dwight in his wheelchair near the first helicopter. But what the hat and blanket actually concealed were the hastily unloaded gold bars and rescue equipment that she had removed from the hidden compartment. As a distraction from the transfer, Stubby and Abby had gathered the crowd around them—on the opposite side of the helicopter—and had delivered a short statement about what had happened on Reed Island.

As soon as Dee saw Hook's helicopter approaching the airport, she bustled around using important-sounding scientific terms and took Stubby and Abby from the group, saying that Abby needed a medical exam. She was upset about Abby's injuries and used that to add authenticity to her abrupt interruption of the crowd's questions. She pushed the wheelchair and guided Abby and Stubby toward the jet, and Stubby clutched his tool kit closely the whole time.

Their exit happened just as medics unloaded the girls from the helicopter and onto the ambulance amid their crying families; the crowd's attention quickly shifted to them, and they shouted questions about their captivity and took pictures.

When Abby saw Emma was awake, she gathered her out of Angela's arms and danced around in happiness while kissing her and crying at the same time. Suddenly she noticed that Jasper, Tony, Angela, and the rest of the team were staring at her with looks of horror. They saw her bruised eyes—one of which was almost swollen shut—her misshapen broken nose, the deep laceration on her cheek, her splinted finger, and the blood that had soaked the front of her white suit almost down to the hemline.

She sighed. "OK, Greed beat me up—so what? I fought back, and he lost—end of story. I'm on pain relief and I'll heal. So don't get all upset and full of 'should haves,' 'could haves,' and 'would haves.' Besides, we got Emma and Jasper back, so we won!"

Jasper had a big lump in his throat, and he kissed her battered face. "Thank you, Abby. Thank you, everyone!" His voice broke with emotion on the last word, and he looked away.

Tony gave Abby his most serious look. "We have to tell Mom now. No way can we hide it from her when you look like this!"

"Yeah, I figured as much, and she's bound to see the media coverage anyway. She's going to be mad, but there isn't anyone else I trust to fix me up, so we do what we have to do."

Abby turned, saw Jasper's wasted body, and looked away in horror. The monitors were beeping, and air was pumping into his lungs, so she knew he was alive, but he didn't look it. Thankfully most of him was covered in a blanket, because just seeing his sunken face and wasted arms scared her. It also puzzled her that he paid no attention to his body at all, purposefully ignoring it. She thought he acted like he and his body would never be reunited, but she would soon set him straight about that! Getting Emma back wasn't the end of the story for them and their future.

The team worked together to finish loading the waiting jet as the pilot did the final checks. Dee had already checked them out of the hotel and had had their suitcases delivered to the airport and loaded in the plane. She had also arranged for the fishing boat to be returned to dock and the underwater scooters retrieved. She greased everyone with generous tips and convoluted explanations. Abby knew Dee's amazing beauty alone turned people into adoring puppies who were willing to do anything she wanted without questions. To everyone's amazement, they were soon in the air, flying back to Seattle with their mission accomplished. The whole trip then seemed unreal.

When they had been in the air an hour Tony couldn't put it off any longer, so he dialed his mother's number. He couldn't get a word in past "hello" and held the phone away from his ear as she yelled at him in Italian. She was really upset because she had seen the news, and they hadn't told her they were taking a trip, let alone a dangerous one to a faraway place. Tony felt that even though they were adults, to her they were kids who had gone to the mall without permission. He shuddered to think what was going to happen after she knew Abby had been hurt on their illicit trip.

Finally he had had enough and yelled, "I love you, Mom, but be quiet for a minute, and I'll explain everything." Unfortunately, once she was listening, he didn't know where to begin; it was all so complicated.

Angela snatched the phone out of his hand. "Aunt Sophia, we have been rescuing Jasper Higgs and his baby daughter, Emma. You remember the crush Abby had on the computer game guy, don't you? Well, he's the same guy, and Abby needs your help because she got beat up a little, and Jasper's in a coma. We're flying into Sea-Tac Airport. Can you meet us there and help us, please?"

Angela paused, but everyone could still hear Sophia's loud voice from the phone. Abby and Tony shrunk down in their seats. "Yes, I was involved and didn't tell you, Aunt Sophia, but can you yell at me later, please? We need your help now, and we're sorry we upset you. Maybe we could have handled it differently, but it doesn't mean we don't love you."

After a little more discussion, Angela hung up. "OK, everyone, there will be hell to pay, but she'll meet us with the trauma wagon at the airport." She sat down with a sigh next to Hook and leaned against his shoulder for comfort. Aunt Sophia had always been a force to be reckoned with, especially when the Italian came through.

"Going up against her is scarier than going to Reed Island," she said to Hook with feeling.

Fifty - Six

When the plane was halfway home to Seattle, Chief Lawrence called. Abby put him on the large video screen at the front of the jet, but she blocked his view of the plane's interior. She thought there was no point in buying trouble, but it proved to be unnecessary as the chief had identified the players already.

"Hello, Dr. Newton, the versatile Stubby, Ethel, Dwight, Dee Light, Jim Osborn, and the rest of your fantastic team. Thank you for what you did, but don't give me any details, because I want to remain as puzzled as everyone else when I'm questioned. But I thought you all would like to know what happened on Reed Island after you left."

Abby asked, "Is Reed in jail now?"

"Not exactly. I think even before you arrived a plan was set in motion. Because as far as I know, no one has been invited to the island in years, and many of his staff took advantage of your visit to escape what was essentially slavery. When I arrived, the whole place had been stripped, and only the heavy furniture remained. Everything else was gone, but you could see where it had been displayed or stored."

"But when I left there, the place was packed with art, valuable collections, and antiques. He was a hoarder! Where did all that go in such a short time?" Abby exclaimed.

"I figure they were loading stuff on Reed's yacht the whole time you were there, probably using the hidden hallway. It must have been like an ant colony! The yacht was gone when we got there, so they must have sailed immediately after the second helicopter left, because we were only fifty minutes behind you."

"I'm confused, Chief. Who left in the yacht? Don't tell me Reed got away!" Abby twisted her hands in distress.

"No, he was right where you left him tied up in his office. The only people still on the island when we got there were ten guards, Reed, and La Ruhr. Everyone else sailed on the yacht with Reed's loot, I think."

"The guards we cuffed were the ones left? What about the men we locked in the guard quarters?"

"The ten they left behind—including the brothers—were the bad ones. I know because they made lists of their crimes and hung them around their necks. Some of it was simple stuff, but some was horrible to read. I guess when you live on a small island, everyone knows the rotten apples, and Reed fostered an attitude of violence and power over others. But I guess what they did traveled back around and bit them in the end."

From her seat behind Abby, Angela smiled and spoke up. "Oh yeah, and I bet the little kitchen lady was the organizer. No wonder the rescue went smoother than I'd expected."

Abby looked at her in astonishment. "Smoother than you'd expected? Two people shot, and I got my face rearranged. That doesn't sound smooth to me."

Angela snorted. "Consider the situation, Abby. There were many armed guards, extensive security, booby traps, and we had no way off the island except by Greed's helicopters. The rescue should have been much harder for us to do, but people were working behind the scenes to help us, so bless them."

The chief continued. "La Ruhr and Reed were stripped naked, and their crimes were written on their skin. They were completely covered with what they did to hurt people—even their eyelids and lips were written on. They cut La Ruhr's hair down to the scalp, but someone buried a knife in Reed's heart. The knife said 'for my sister' on it."

After a moment of silence, Abby said, "He's dead, then."

"Very. I think he was dead before the helicopters flew off. Like I said, it all looked preplanned. They had years to think about how they wanted to end it. Those people on the island suffered, so I'm not in a hurry to find the yacht. It broke my heart to read some of what was written on Reed's skin. La Ruhr was vindictive, mean, and self-serving, but Reed was evil. I have La Ruhr in custody, but she acts like she has brain damage or something. I don't think she's faking it, but she'll get a psych evaluation."

"You're a good man, Chief. Did they open the safe in the office?" Stubby asked.

"No, that was closed, but whatever's in there will probably go as damages to the many people he wronged. I know as soon as this hits the news tonight, people will be lining up for restitution. It's going to take years to sort it all out!"

"What about Reed Island?" Abby asked.

"If he didn't have a will filed, and I checked and didn't see one, it'll belong to the people. The mayor is already rumbling about making it into a tourist attraction."

Hook shook his head and sighed. "I guess since California makes money from Alcatraz tours, why not."

"They left all that giant ugly furniture behind, and it fits the spooky vibe some people like. Maybe Reed will haunt it if they bury him there," Abby mused.

Jasper was angry about using the island to make money. "There should be a memorial to the people who suffered and the girls Reed killed there."

The chief heard him and nodded in agreement. "Reed exploited people, and we won't do that, I assure you." He paused and thought for a moment. "Oh, I wanted to tell you that there's a reward for finding the kidnapped girls and that belongs to you. So where do you want me to send it?"

Hook answered. "Put it in the pot for the memorial. Everyone fine with that?" He looked around as people nodded.

"Well, I want to thank you again for cracking the nut I've been trying to open for years. It makes me sick to think of what he was doing, and I couldn't stop it. Sometimes the law is a hindrance instead of a help."

Abby spoke up. "His crimes finally caught up with him, Chief. There's justice in that. But I guess you won't need us to return for a trial, and I'm happy about that."

"No, just send me a statement to have in my files, and please add a picture of your battered face as evidence of the assault. But maybe you'll come back and enjoy a vacation some day on our beautiful beaches. We owe you that and so much more, too."

Abby knew she spoke for everyone on the team. "Chief, it was our pleasure to take that slime bag down. You don't owe us anything."

Fifty - Seven

Dr. Sophia Newton was waiting on the tarmac with her arms folded, a scowl on her face, and one shoe tapping. Standing behind her was her nurse-assistant, Tommy, who was leaning on the trauma wagon. He had been planning to remain neutral, but he had a slight smile on his face in anticipation of interesting drama, because very few people crossed Sophia without paying a penalty, and that included her children.

The trauma wagon had been built from the same model of truck that Tony had used for his mobile computer business. He and his mother had had a fun six months outdoing each other during their trucks' customization processes. Sophia's truck was a cross between a mobile clinic and an ambulance; it contained a complete laboratory, a suite for minor surgery, a basic pharmacy, and a digital X-ray machine. She drove it around the country, helping out victims of disaster when she could, and her staff used it to give free medical services to poverty-stricken and homeless people two days a week.

As the jet taxied to a stop on the airstrip, the whole team inside lined up, watching Sophia with trepidation from the airplane's windows. Everyone who had crossed a parent recognized the look on her face, because it clearly said, 'You are in big trouble and will be grounded for life!'

Angela finally spoke. "I love her to death, but I'm really scared of her, too."

Abby gathered her courage and straightened her shoulders. "OK, I'll go out first, and the rest of you come out when it looks safe."

She walked down the stairs and stood in front of her mother, looking her straight in the eyes. A small bead of sweat trickled down her back, and she fought the impulse to run away. Abby had changed from her blood-encrusted suit into a dark dress with a matching beaded sweater. The outfit swap had been a strategic move to diffuse the impact of her injuries, but she hadn't applied any concealing makeup, knowing her mother would appreciate the honesty of her showing her face without downplaying what had happened.

Her mother slowly took in the extent of Abby's facial injuries and her splinted finger. Then her stern look suddenly dissolved into one of anguish, and she softly said, "My God, Abigail. I just want to know why! Why did you go away to help a stranger without telling me?" Tears ran down her face. "It was obviously dangerous, and I wouldn't have let you go!"

Abby enfolded her mother in her arms. She could count on one hand the number of times she had seen her cry openly. Abby knew she frequently worked with terminal children and their families; yet she always remained a pillar of strength, no matter what the outcome was. To see her cry over her injuries was awful to behold, and her gut clenched in a combination of guilt mixed with love.

"We're sorry, Mom, but that's exactly why we didn't tell you we were going. You'd have stopped us, and I couldn't have lived with that."

"You and Tony could have been killed! I might have lost both of my babies, and I didn't even get to say good-bye!"

"Look, Mom, you taught us to do what's right and to stand up for ourselves even if we're afraid. You were there, Mom, because you were in our hearts every step of the way." Abby hugged her tight, kissed her cheek, and blotted at her mother's tears with a tissue from her pocket.

Finally her mother sighed. "All right, you're here now and safe, but don't think we're done discussing this, young lady. Where's your brother? Is he hurt, too?"

Abby motioned for the rest of the group to deplane. The first off was Tony, and he hugged his mother with a guilty look on his face.

"I love you, Mom, and I'm sorry we made you worry. Believe me, we don't want to go through anything like that ever again!"

Next Hook came forward, holding hands with Angela. Sophia took one look at his bloody, dirty, bandaged arm and motioned him to the truck. She shot Angela a stern look. "I know you're hip- deep in this, my girl, and you're the one who should have known better. We'll talk later—you can be sure of that."

Half-man came up next and held Emma out for Sophia's inspection and for his protection, too. She took one look at the baby's dangling, lifeless limbs and immediately turned on doctor mode.

"Get this baby on board, Tommy, and check her vital signs."

Finally she turned to Jasper's projection, which was standing by his body on the stretcher that Melt and Hawkeye carried. His body was still hooked up to life-support machines and an IV drip. She immediately recognized Jasper Higgs from his picture by Abby's girlhood bed, but she didn't express a flicker of surprise at his projection's unusual appearance. She had seen lots of strange things in the twenty-five years since medical school, and as far as she was concerned, he was just one more patient who needed her care.

Sophia growled at his projection. "Whoever has been taking care of you in your comatose state hasn't been doing a very good job of it. But I assure you, that's going to change right now."

She looked over the tattered, dirty, and exhausted group. "Everyone get in the truck." Then she barked commands through the open door. "Tommy, take us to the celebrity ward at the hospital. It'll be private, and it has its own entrance. See who's on orthopedic rotation tonight for Abigail's finger, and we'll need a good cosmetic surgeon for her, too, so if Ted isn't available call, Pete. See if Dr. Hanson will fly in from Spokane tomorrow. He's absolutely the best doctor for long-term coma patients."

She settled down next to Emma in the truck with a stethoscope in her hand. "Oh, and call ahead to the hospital so we can have breakfasts waiting while I deal with the gunshot wounds."

From the truck's window, Abby noticed Stubby and Dee sneaking away from the plane toward a waiting taxi—probably to transport the gold to a safe location. She covered for them by loudly saying, "Mom, we need diapers and formula for Emma, too."

At the hospital the next day, every television carried the news of Sir Reed's death and the heroic rescue of the kidnapped girls. The chief had kept Jasper and Emma out of the story, but Abby's part had been played up instead, and her lab was besieged by the media. She gave her staff ten days of paid vacation and closed shop, hoping things would settle down after that. Halfman kindly created a disguise for her so she could move around without flashbulbs and microphones shoved in her face. The fact that her broken nose was taped in a splint and her cheek sported over fifty black, spidery stitches worked to conceal her identity, too.

Once Hook and Half-man's gunshot wounds were doing well, Sophia sent everyone but Abby, Jasper, and Emma back to Ocean Shores for recovery. She gave both men antibiotics, pain relief medication, and strict instructions for wound care. Both warriors said, 'Yes, ma'am' and agreed to follow what she recommmended to the letter. Sophia had a specialist evaluate and treat Hook's injury. To his relief, his arm would have no permanent damage.

Sophia observed quickly that her daughter loved Jasper and Emma deeply, and that he returned her feelings. She realized she had to accept that her little Newt had grown up, which was a bittersweet feeling for any mother. It had always been hard for her to let go of control, but she finally admitted to herself that her children did have the right to make decisions without consulting her first. They were grown-ups, even though it felt like just the day before she had been changing their diapers. She decided to be proud of what had happened instead of angry, even though it had scared her so much.

She knew Abigail had been attracted to Jasper for years, so maybe he was her intended life partner. Sophia had always dismissed her early crush on him as puppy love, but perhaps it had turned out to be a fairy tale of enduring love. She supposed it was time to step back from running her daughter's life; after all, she was finally getting a beautiful grandchild to spoil, so she kissed Emma's cheek with a smile on her face and a measure of acceptance in her heart. She knew letting go would take practice and persistence, like so many things in life that are hard but important to do.

The next day Sophia sat down with Abby and Jasper's projection to discuss the recovery plan for his body and for Emma. She said she saw no reason for Emma to stay in the hospital, because Abby could do the necessary physical therapy, and the cabin was a diverse environment that would help Emma normalize more rapidly than staying with her father in a confined room. Already Emma was waving her arms and legs a little and squirming her body around slightly, but she still had a lot of development to catch up on. Both girls could visit Jasper frequently and video chat with him as his body rested and recovered in the hospital. But Sophia thought that since Emma wasn't tethered to Jasper by the chip anymore, she should be a little more independent of him. Jasper's body would rest while Emma's was stimulated.

Jasper passionately hated the idea of separation from Emma. He said he didn't care if he was ever reunited with his body, and that the thing on the bed was keeping him there against his will!

He paced and grumbled and pitched a tantrum Abby believed was worthy of a sleep-deprived toddler. But Sophia repeated what the coma specialist had said.

"Recovery depends on the body and mind working together again, and to do that, I believe, your body and its projection must stay physically close, promoting the necessary harmony to merge." She pointed out that Jasper's body was still much too fragile to leave the hospital, so there he would stay until she released him.

Abby knew her mother was right and that closeness had already worked to unite Emma with her projection. But she didn't use logic. Instead, she walked up to Jasper's projection and gave him a passionate kiss filled with all the longing for him she had.

"So, Jasper, do you ever want to actually feel that? Do you want to have a physical relationship with me sometime? Do you want to toss Emma into the air and to teach her how to catch a ball? Well, do you?" she said.

He stared at her, angry and upset. "Of course I do!"

"Then please stay here and recover enough for Tony to try to put you back into your body by ending the program. I'll take good care of Emma—you know that. Mom says it will only take two weeks until your body is well enough to try it. Do this for us as a family, Jasper."

Jasper suddenly felt like a jerk. "I'm sorry, Abby. I'm just so sick of this situation. I don't know if I can go back. I'm afraid ending the program will fail, and my projection will stop, but my body will still be a vegetable. Then you and Emma won't have anything left of me. I don't think I remember how to be human anymore. I've changed. I'm just a mind now, and better a brain without a body than a body without a brain. Let me go home with you and just live as a projection."

Abby stroked his cheek. "Jasper, remember what it was like when this all started? Keep that faith, and trust the process just a little longer. You washed up in the globe at the right place, and at the right time. How amazing was that? We've come so far, and it's going to be a happy ending for us. I believe that, and you need to, too."

Even though Jasper finally agreed to follow Sophia's plan, it didn't stop a big hole from tearing in his heart as he watched Abby and Emma walk away and close the hospital door behind them, leaving him to sit alone and stare at the corpse on the bed that used to be someone he recognized.

Fifty - Eight

Abby took her time with Emma seriously; she researched child development, created spreadsheets, and made daily goals for them to achieve. She smothered Emma with all the love and affection she could, but she also approached her recovery scientifically, and that gave her a framework by which to measure progress and to highlight problem areas. Abby consulted with child-development experts by e-mail, made video records to review during naptime, and took copious notes for her mother and Jasper to review. And she documented all progress in a daily log with sequential video clips.

Abby decided that learning boiled down to play, but it had to be directed play with a purpose. Everything she did with Emma encouraged her to improve her skills; Abby didn't just hand her a toy—she made her reach for it to strengthen her arms and grasp. Every spoonful of food was a reward after Emma shaped a sound with her mouth. And Abby constantly talked to her; she told her what they were doing and the names of things around them, and she repeated sounds and words over and over again. They had fun, but they both worked hard, too.

One day Abby discovered that Emma hadn't been unconscious as a projection as they had assumed. She knew games Abby had made up and played with her before they had traveled to Reed Island, and she could pick out the books she wanted Abby to read to her, because she knew the stories they contained already. Best of all, after comparing standardized charts to what Emma could do, Abby realized that she wasn't behind in her developmental milestones at all; her brain must have played catch-up while her body had rested unconscious on the island.

Abby knew that Emma had had a profound speech delay before her abduction, but when she returned from the island she was able to make a variety of sounds, including "shhh," "bah," "uh-o," "mammm," "woo," "bee," "da," "dee," and "wow." She didn't tell Jasper about Emma's verbal progress, because she wanted to surprise him when he came home. She coached Emma to say "Dada" over and over again, imagining the look on her father's face when his daughter called him daddy for the first time.

Abby loved Emma and treasured their time together. She saw the intelligence in Emma's eyes, and the innocence, too. She kissed her frequently, cuddled her close, and she told her she loved her multiple times a day. The relationship seemed so pure to her, with nothing complicating the exchange of love between them, and both of them flourished as they invested time and attention in each other.

However, the rest of the team exchanged concerned looks over Abby's obsession with Emma. It was all she talked about, and it was all she cared about; if anyone came to the cabin to visit, she brushed them off, saying she was on a schedule with Emma that had to be followed. Angela noticed a brittleness in Abby's demeanor, a superficial gloss in her expression, and a deadness to her eyes. That concerned her much more than the multicolor bruises slowly fading from Abby's face. She recognized the dangerous mental quicksand Abby was sinking into and called Dee for help.

Dee came to visit, bearing toys for Emma that had shapes, textures, and sounds to enthrall her. They all played on the floor awhile, and then Dee asked, "How are you doing now that we're home?"

Abby looked away, refusing to make eye contact. "Just fine. My face is healing, and I love being alone with Emma like this. I think my nose is going to end up straighter than it was before Greed broke it, so I can't complain."

Dee touched the stitches on Abby's cheek gently. "I'm not buying that, girl. So how are you doing really?"

"Fine, like I said. Take it or leave it, Dee. I'm not prying into your experience on St. John, so why don't you respect me and leave it alone?"

Dee was shocked at her rudeness because it was way out of character for Abby, and that told her she was on the right track. "Feel it, heal it, and let it go. That's the path to recovery. You aren't doing that. You're burying it inside instead, and that isn't healthy, sweetie."

Abby got more defensive and snapped back at her. "The dress worked, Dee. Is that what you want to hear from me?"

Dee watched moisture form in Abby's angry eyes. "Hey, I'm your friend, remember? I love you, and you're safe with me, so let it out."

Abby struggled with the lump in her throat and finally said, "I could have been one of those poor girls. That's what Greed wanted. Me dirty, cold, starved, tortured, and then killed and discarded like his trash."

Dee remained silent for a moment and then said, "And what else, honey?"

"He broke my finger like a pencil, Dee. I heard the snap of it and then the crunch of my nose breaking. He had a ring with a knife in it that cut my face wide open. The blood ruined my white suit, so I threw it away. Three hundred dollars down the drain."

Dee gathered her up in her arms. "And what else?"

There was a long pause while Abby struggled with her emotions. "Then he pulled me by my hair across his desk, and he was ripping my panties off and touching me. I heard...I heard... oh God, Dee. I heard him pull his zipper down." She sobbed. "Another minute and he would have...he would have...," she said.

Dee stroked her hair gently. "OK, let's give it a name so you can deal with the fear: it's called rape. He tried to rape you, but he didn't, because you stopped him. You stopped him cold with a knife to the groin. Good going, girl! And if he hadn't been standing there unzipping his damn pants, then he wouldn't have been open to a direct hit, so it served him right. Then you bashed him in the head for good measure. He underestimated you, Abby—big time."

"But he could have, he wanted to, and he was going to do it!"

"Yeah. So what? There's a lot of 'could haves' and 'what ifs' in the whole situation. He could have discovered the device was a trick, but he didn't. He could have shot you immediately, but he didn't. You can't be thinking about what might have happened, because it didn't. Think about what you did do instead: you knocked him out and tied him up. That's exactly what your plan was, and you were amazing under incredible pressure!"

"No one has hurt me on purpose before, and I could see in his eyes when he pulled me across his desk how much he liked doing it. He was excited by my blood and wounds. He was a horrible, twisted man!" Abby blotted her nose and eyes with a tissue Dee handed her.

"That's all the more reason to take him out of business, honey. You did very well. You didn't let him get away with hurting you. And Stubby said you didn't complain about the pain or act scared at all."

"Hard to be a baby when I saw what the girls had endured. They're heroes to me."

"You weren't a baby, and you're my hero, Abby." Dee pulled back and looked her in the face. "But I will admit in retrospect that maybe we could have toned down the outfit's impact a little."

They hugged again, and then they sat down with tea and cookies. Abby felt like Dee had lifted a big weight off her shoulders. She realized that she had been on guard ever since her experience in Greed's office. At night she woke up with her heart pounding at every little sound, she kept the cabin's doors and windows locked at all times—even though the weather was warm—she kept her cell phone and a Zap nearby, and she had avoided walking the beach alone with Emma. Worst of all, she knew she was making rituals around checking security multiple times a day because it made her feel safer inside her head. A little obsessive-compulsive behavior was normal for her, but she knew she had been close to developing a problem that would need therapy and maybe medication.

Looking at her behavior clearly, Abby realized she probably had some post-traumatic stress symptoms. She resolved to ask Angela to design some therapy to deal with it, because no way was she going to let a creep like Greed take away her peace and sense of security. She knew recognizing what was happening to her was the first step home and out of his office for good. She decided she would start by adding baby yoga to her day with Emma; she could also meditate for centering and inner peace when the baby napped. No more rumination on what had happened with Greed, and no more constant vigilance. So when Dee left to go back to Seattle, instead of locking the cabin's door, Abby left the screen open so she could enjoy the fresh air, which was a small step in the right direction.

Fifty - Nine

Jasper's projection paced around the hospital room where his body lay, and he muttered under his breath about things Sophia couldn't understand. She finally had to force him to sit down with her for a doctor-to-patient talk. In her opinion, Jasper's projection—which she understood came from his mind—needed to simmer down so his brain could rest, and if he'd been a normal patient, she would have prescribed a mild sedative to help him adjust. But she stopped herself, because was it even possible to medicate a projection? She could inject his body, and it might alter his brain's projected activity, but it might not be safe because there were a lot of unknown variables at play. It was a dilemma not faced before in medicine, she thought, so it was time for an old-fashioned nonpharmaceutical solution.

After watching him pace back and forth, not even acknowledging her presence for five minutes, she sighed and said, "Sit down, Jasper. What's the problem?"

"No problem. I just want to get this over with." He spoke to her, but he didn't sit down and instead continued to move. She thought it was like the stereotypical patterns of caged animals who repeat the same movements over and over obsessively.

"It's never going to be over, Jasper, no matter how much you want it to be. What happened to you was real, so it's part of your history now. The only thing you can do is use the experience for growth and move on with your life from here."

Her calm reasoning made him angry. "You don't know what you're talking about! You can't possibly understand what it's like to be me right now! And there isn't a solution, because I can't modify the chip or the program without creating errors."

Sophia sighed again. He was young, intense, and so full of strong emotion and passion. One of the gifts of aging is perspective on life—knowing nothing lasts forever, good or bad. It all passes into history eventually. "Tell me then, and make me understand, Jasper, so I can try to help you."

"I can't wait in this in-between state anymore! It was fine when he wasn't here." He pointed to the bed and his body. "But now that he's close, he tries to draw me back in, and I want to be away from here."

"You can feel your body wanting its brain activity back?" She was astonished by his revelation.

"Something like that, but the chip is in the way because it's fighting my body, trying to keep my projection intact." He grimaced. "You know how they say you can't be in two places at one time? But that's how I feel. It's like my brain is tearing into two pieces every minute, and I can't stand it!"

Sophia called up his medical data on her tablet. "Let's see. In one week you have gained ten pounds, but you need forty more. I could try pulling your tracheal tube and seeing how your body does. Then if your lung function is acceptable, you can talk to Tony about whatever you need, and we can schedule the merging after a final clean brain scan. That would be in about two days."

Jasper sat on the bed suddenly. "You think I can handle it that soon?"

"Look, Jasper, you aren't handling it very well now, so it's up to you, but I'm worried that the feeling your brain's tearing apart isn't good for it. If we pull the tube and you stop breathing, then we can replace it and wait a little longer. Your body must breathe on its own, and that isn't negotiable with me or with my daughter."

Pulling the tube was a tense moment. Sophia had Tommy standing by with an Ambu bag and oxygen just in case Jasper didn't breathe and they needed to reinsert it and put him back on the respirator. There was a long minute after she removed it when nothing happened, but then his chest shuddered, and he took one shallow breath and then another before finally settling into a good rhythm.

Jasper watched his chest rise and fall on its own with mixed feelings. The person on the bed was looking more like he'd remembered him every day, except for the new scars left by Greed. Abby had given him a shave and a haircut, and the nurse sponge bathed him frequently. But he still felt disconnected from his body and ambivalent about uniting with it again.

His projection wanted to float away and to let the poor man he once had been rest in peace. Only the frequent visits from Abby and Emma kept him from doing just that, but it was so very tempting to open the hospital door and to disappear into the night forever. He would have taken the chip with him, because once the chip was destroyed, his projection would end, and maybe his mind would too. At least as a projection he could think and feel like himself.

He was unaware that Sophia had added clinical depression to his medical chart when she saw that he didn't care if his body breathed or not. That had concerned her.

Tony visited Jasper the next day. "I've figured it every which way, Jazz, but I can't find a new solution. You're right—we have to destroy the chip to stop your projection. Emma just went back naturally, but if that was going to happen to you, I think it would have by now."

"I know, TNT. Melting the chip either works, and I'm back in my body, or I'm gone forever. But either way, it would be a better existence than the limbo I have now."

"Yeah, Jazz, but killing the chip is so final. It's a big risk, and it might not work, and then what happens to you? Will your body be a vegetable, or will we need a medium to communicate with you, or what?"

"I don't know, and that's why it should be only you and me melting the chip."

Tony thought for a minute. "No way, Jazz! Abby put it on the line for you, and I'm not doing that to her after all she did to get you back. You just can't fade into the sunset without any responsibility for what's left behind, dude. What happens when the chip melts affects the whole team, and they deserve to be a part of it, too."

Two days later they all gathered around a metal bowl filled with wood chips to start a fire. Sophia opened the hospital room's windows to prevent the smoke alarm from sounding, and Tony lit a candle and placed it in the bowl. Abby brought champagne and tried for a celebratory mood, but it fell flat due to the team's general feeling of apprehension. Jasper made a short but heartfelt thank-you speech and kissed Emma. Then he tipped the candle, starting a small blaze, and, before anyone realized what he was doing, he tossed his chip into the flames. There was a gasp in the room as his static-filled image faded in and out, and then he was gone.

Everyone turned to the bed, but his body continued to breathe calmly as if nothing had happened.

Sophia took his vital signs and said, "It's up to Jasper at this point. There's always uncertainty about when a coma patient will wake up." She didn't add what she was thinking to herself, which was "if they ever wake up at all."

Abby tried to stay strong. She made a rotating schedule so someone Jasper knew was with him all the time. They read to him, talked to him, and tried to stimulate him physically for ten hours a day. And after seven long days, Jasper groaned, opened his eyes, and told Abby to quit singing the Barney song to Emma again, please.

It was great to still have his mind intact, and he loved Emma and Abby, but after a day of drifting in and out of consciousness, Jasper thought it was the pits to be back in his body. He hated it! The lights were too bright and sounds too loud; his mouth tasted awful, and the EKG leads itched like crazy. It was weird to hear his own breathing and to feel his heart beating all the time. The weight of his limbs was heavy, and it took so much effort just to sit up in bed. It felt like he was imprisoned in a heavy, awkward costume made out of flesh. It didn't feel natural at all!

In his body, he had to eat by chewing and swallowing each bite, and then he had to go to the bathroom to dump what was unused; shaving, trimming his nails, brushing his teeth and hair, and sleeping all seemed like a waste of time to him. Not only that, but he also had odors, hair, saliva, mucus, and earwax. It was gross to be alive like that. It took effort to move around, and he was full of aches and pains. He missed being a simple projection because it had been so much easier to just live in his head.

Sophia refused to let Abby see him struggling to cope with his body, and after three days of listening to his whining, she got him to stand up and walk to the shower with her help. There, sitting on a bench under the beat of hot water, his attitude started to change. It felt good to be really clean again, and he could smell the coffee and maple syrup from his waiting breakfast. The sun shone brightly through the window in his room, and he could hear birds singing. In that moment his spirits lifted a little, and he was finally grateful to be alive.

Later he checked his e-mail and wrote in his gaming blog for the first time in months. He was still very weak; his joints hurt and his muscles trembled after only walking around his room twice. He overheard Sophia ordering a hospital bed to be delivered to the cabin for long-term convalescence, and that made him mad enough to ask Tony for some resistance bands so he could start exercising, which was exactly why Sophia had let him eavesdrop on her conversation to begin with.

When his outlook improved he realized that everyone had worked hard to get him back, and he was acting like an ungrateful swine in return. Not once had Hook, Half-man, or Abby complained about the injuries they had received during his rescue. He was human again, whether he liked it or not, so he'd better start counting his blessings. He started by being consciously grateful for everything—even going to the bathroom and breathing. He tried to stay in the moment and to appreciate it fully. Then one night he cried alone in his hospital bed, overwhelmed with joy for the chance to see Emma grow up and to have Abby in his future.

The next morning Sophia signed his hospital release papers. Jasper wasn't very strong physically yet, but she could see the man he once had been in his eyes, and, more importantly, the stronger, wiser man he was becoming.

Sixty

Abby was excited because Jasper was coming home to the cabin and she hadn't seen him for more than a week. She'd made a pot of nourishing soup that was on her mother's list of things he could eat and some brownies that were definitely not. She had cleaned the cabin, removing anything that might have reminded him of their ordeal—including the empty globe and sound equipment—because she knew he was struggling to adjust to his changed life. Then she checked on the sleeping Emma and waited outside nervously for his arrival.

After the car pulled up, she watched Jasper slowly extract himself by levering out with his hands and carefully placing his feet down. She knew better than to rush out and help him, as her mother had given her strict advice to assist only when he asked for it; she had said he wasn't a baby like Emma, and treating him like an invalid would only make him angry and delay his recovery. Abby thought that advice was easy for Sophia to dispense but harder to do in reality when you loved the person who was struggling. She would have to be on constant guard against her natural nurturing tendencies.

"There you go, old man." Tony grabbed Jasper's elbow to steady him on the uneven surface as he stumbled. Slowly he moved down the walkway and sat beside Abby on the cabin's front porch.

"Old man? Hey, TNT, you come back from mostly dead and see how you feel! Give me about six months, and I'll make you eat those words. I promise." They both laughed as Tony headed for his truck.

Abby put her arm around his waist, and Jasper took her hand and, facing her, spoke seriously. "I've wanted to do this before, but I wasn't sure how it was all going to end up. I didn't think it was fair to ask you until I knew Emma and I would survive. But I promised myself it would be the first thing I said to you if I came back here." He took a deep breath to calm himself. "You mean everything to me, Abby, and Emma and I both need you forever." He took a ring out of his pocket. "I love you so much, so will you marry me, please, and make a family out of one lonely man and a baby? I promise I'll cherish you and never betray your trust as long as I live, and even past that if I can do it."

Abby had tears in her eyes and had to speak past the lump in her throat. "The answer is yes, a thousand times, Jasper! You were my first love as a girl, and that has only grown deeper in the time I've spent with you. Even when you were mostly dead, I loved you, Jasper, and Emma couldn't be more my daughter than she already is."

He placed the ring on her finger and kissed her gently on the lips. "The ring was my grandmother's. I want it to be a symbol of our love like it was for her in her life. The center stone is an alexandrite, and it changes color from blue to purple depending on the light. I think that quality is like me when I met you—part projection and part man."

She looked at the ring shining on her finger. The gold band was formed in a vine-and-flower pattern, and the center stone was tear-drop shaped and accented by two small sparkling diamonds.

"It's beautiful, Jasper, and I love it! But is that all the engagement kiss I get? We're fiancés now, and I can't wait to ramp it up, because we both have real bodies now." She had a gleam in her eye.

In response, Jasper pulled a prescription out of his pocket and showed it to her. On it her mother had written, "Do not elevate your blood pressure for the next two weeks, or your migraines will intensify. So behave yourselves, both of you."

Abby shook her head. "Oh, no! I was hoping to make up for lost time a little!"

Jasper pulled her on his lap and nuzzled her neck until she giggled. "Just sitting next to you is getting my blood pressure up, and we've only shared one little kiss. I don't know how I'm going to make it two weeks. It seems like I've already waited my whole life for you. My imagination needs a lecture from the doctor, because it's going nuts right now."

"That's good, because I feel the same way about you. I know. How about if we plan the wedding for two weeks from today? That'll keep us busy, and we'll have a honeymoon to look forward to."

"I didn't think a wedding could be done in two weeks unless it was at a Vegas Elvis chapel, and I don't want that. But I guess if you could rescue me, you can do almost anything. In the meantime, I'm going to need a lot of cold showers to follow your mom's prescription."

"Dee can make it happen—she's a wizard. And we'll keep it simple." Emma suddenly announced that she had woken up from her nap, and they went inside to rescue her from the crib.

At her crib's side, Emma looked up at Jasper with a happy face and distinctly said, "Dada."

He scooped her up in his arms and held her close. "Wow, you said daddy! My sweet baby girl, I've missed you so much." Emma patted his face with both her small hands and gave him a dazzling smile, and Abby laughed at the identical expressions of joy on their faces as they gazed at each other.

Then he and Abby exchanged a look that said this happy moment alone was worth fighting for. Jasper lightly touched the scar forming on Abby's cheek, thanking her without words for what she had gone through on the island.

Abby put Emma on the floor and went into the kitchen to dish up the soup. Emma showed off for her dad by scooting on her bottom over to the drawer that contained plastic storage bowls and spoons for her to play with.

"It won't be long until she learns to walk and gets into more trouble. We need to babyproof the yard so she can come out and play with us," Abby commented over the noise of plastic banging on the floor.

Jasper looked around the small cabin. "It's weird. I've never actually been here, but I know where everything is and how the couch feels to sleep on. In some ways I felt more normal as a projection than I do now back in my body. Sometimes it feel like everything was a dream that I just woke up from, or I think I'm still in the globe, floating in the ocean with no hope of rescue. I'm having a hard time establishing what's real. My life before the chip seems unreal to me now, and what happened to me as a projection feels unreal, too. And my body's so different that it's like I'm living in somebody else's skin. I just don't feel like me at all, and that's hard to deal with."

Abby kissed him with compassion in her eyes. "That's all the more reason to wait a few weeks before jumping into Jasper the Husband, which will be another big change."

She added a set of measuring spoons to Emma's pile. "I've been thinking about life a lot lately, and experiences always change people, especially big traumatic ones like we just went through. I believe what we call reality is actually an illusion people create to make life feel safe, predictable, and permanent. Life is actually temporary and short, but we try to ignore that fact and to create a sense of continuity and feelings of security so we can function. Then something comes along that forces us to see clearly how fragile our existence is, so it disillusions us, and then it takes time to build back the illusion—and our reality—to feel normal again."

He rubbed at his temples with both hands. "I want it to go away like it never happened so I can be myself again."

She could tell he had a headache and needed to rest. "If it hadn't happened, Jasper, than we wouldn't have met, and that would be awful. Also, Angela would still be tortured by her bad memories, Greed would be doing business as usual, the kidnapped girls wouldn't be returned home again, and people on the island would still be trapped and exploited. Lots of good came out of it, and I hope remembering that balances out how bad you're feeling right now." She glanced at the clock, dispensed some migraine medicine her mother had sent ahead, and handed it to him with a glass of water.

"I'm restless all the time. I can't concentrate or think straight. My body isn't automatic any more. I have to send specific thoughts through my brain, like 'don't step off that edge' to make sure I don't. It's like driving a bus instead of riding along, enjoying the scenery. In the past my foot wouldn't have stepped off the edge by itself, and my brain could think about other things."

She put Emma in her high chair. "I think those automatic, well-traveled neuronal pathways just need some reminding, and they'll be active in your subconscious again. Why don't you try doing the things you enjoyed before Greed? Even if you have to fake it until you make it, it'll give you some structure to build on and something to calm and focus your mind with."

He joked with her while she spooned baby cereal into Emma's mouth like an expert. "Well, I could design a new game where you have to neutralize guards on a tropical island to rescue prisoners and get the gold."

Abby laughed and gently scraped the cereal spillage from Emma's lips. "That might be a little too much for your brain right now, but you could keep it in mind for later. Just don't expect me to want to play it."

After Emma was fed, they called Sophia, who was delighted about their engagement, and announced the quick wedding timeframe to the team. They spent the rest of the afternoon e-mailing people about the date and time, and the list turned out bigger than they'd anticipated it would be. Abby couldn't leave out her staff at the lab, and they decided to invite the rescued girls and their families; Jasper also contacted his estranged family at Abby's urging. Once they had a firm number of attendees, Abby called Dee and held the phone away from her ear as her friend screamed in delight and then demanded total control of the festivities.

They strolled down to the beach to watch the sunset and to meet with the team to decide how to set up their nonprofit organization. Stubby had distributed the gold bars, but the gems were locked in a local bank's safety deposit box. The master plan was to sell some of the stones several times a year and to deposit the money into an account that would be given out as needed to do good work in the world. Every disbursement would require approval and signatures from multiple team members. But the definition of "good work" was flexible and open to change over time. They hoped to quietly help as many people as they could worldwide and to include earth-friendly projects, too.

Hook had established a trust account for the rescued girls using their gold bars. Some of the money would be available now for therapy, but most wouldn't be released until they were twenty-one. No one wanted them to be victims again because of their money, so Hook had carefully protected them legally, even from their own families.

After the meeting they played with Emma, gave her a bath, and put the sweet-smelling sleepy girl to bed. Abby said, "Tony told me he would sleep in his truck if you want to use his room tonight, Jasper."

"No, I'll use the couch again. I think it's a good idea to have Tony sleep here as a chaperone. Your mom probably has some sort of extrasensory doctor power, and I wouldn't put it past her to show up unexpectedly just to make sure we're following her prescription."

They held hands on the couch before bed, and Abby lifted Jasper's hand close to her face. She looked at his fingers one by one, tracing the veins, touching the fine hairs, and rubbing his nails back and forth with her thumb. She kissed the front and backs of each finger and tasted them with the tip of her tongue.

He cleared his suddenly clogged throat. "What are you doing?"

"I'm memorizing your hand. I held it as a projection, and I longed to know what it was like for real. I've wanted to touch you and to just take you in for so long, Jasper. Would you mind if I unbuttoned your shirt and touched your chest?"

Jasper gulped audibly. "Oh yeah, you know I'd like that, but my blood pressure would go through the roof, along with my brain! I can already feel the sizzle."

She sighed and reluctantly said, "Well, OK, then, let's put that thought on hold for now. I don't want to give you a nasty headache just so I can have my way with you."

He laughed. "You can bet that in two weeks, I'm never sleeping on the couch again!"

Sixty - One

Dee planned the wedding ceremony on the beach because it was the only space where everyone would fit comfortably. She found the perfect dress for Abby—pale coral with multiple layers of chiffon, each one a slightly different shade than the others. The color complemented Abby's red hair and fair skin without washing her out like white would have. It was sleeveless with a sweetheart neckline and an empire waist, and it was accented with a satin belt that tied in the back and was covered with faceted clear crystal beads. The dress floated like a cloud colored by sunrise when Abby moved, and the long belt trailing down her back sparkled in the light. Abby loved it immediately, as Dee had known she would.

Dee rented chairs for the ceremony and tables for the casual dinner afterward. She decorated the coral-colored tablecloths with shells and glass Japanese fishing floats in bright colors; there were enough floats for each guest to take one home as a party favor. Abby laughed when she saw her bringing in boxes of them. Jasper understood that to Dee floats were a symbol of the unique way their love had begun, and she wanted to celebrate it, but the memory of living in a globe wasn't a pleasant one for him, so he just tried to be a good sport about it. She added bouquets of mixed flowers bunched with sea grass and tied them with ribbons that matched the floats' colors.

Dee left cooking and serving the dinner to Hook, Half-man, Stubby, Melt, and Hawkeye. They decided on a luau-style roast pig served with platters of fresh fruit, three types of homemade yeast rolls, a variety of salads, and mixed grilled vegetables. Condiments from the simple to the complex would be provided so guests could make pork sandwiches or top the salads. Instead of a wedding cake they would make a tower of several types of colorful cupcakes and add an ice cream bar with toppings galore. They also decided to serve s'mores around a bonfire on the beach for kids and adults too.

Dee planned dancing to live music, games, conversation, and champagne toasts well into the night when the beach would be lit by thousands of tiny white lights and several bonfires. It would be a total celebration not only of love, marriage, and the creation of a new family, but also of a successful rescue against the odds and the ultimate triumph of good over evil. Abby couldn't imagine a better wedding and reception party, even if she had had a year to plan it. It was her dream wedding to the perfect man for her, and she floated along, filled with happiness as it all came together.

The night before the wedding, they sat around the camp-fire and discussed their future plans. Hook and Angela wanted to expand their rain-forest PTSD treatment center by building cabins instead of using the current hodgepodge of tents. They wanted everyone's suggestions for a central building in their compound, and soon the plans included several meeting rooms, a kitchen, a laundry, and multiple bathrooms with showers. They all agreed that the design should be rustic and simple to blend with the surrounding forest; Half-man suggested adding a tree house for meditation, too.

To Angela's shock, a vote was taken, and the project passed as the first thing to be funded by their nonprofit company. They discussed expanding the scope to treat other people with

PTSD—not just soldiers— and Angela and Hook were happy to add more cabins to their original plan. Abby suspected the camp would have a long waiting list no matter how many cabins they built.

"I know the ancient forest does most of the healing, but what do you think about including a chip in the therapy program to erase traumatic memories, too? I know it helped me a lot," Angela said to Jasper.

"Bad experiences are part of life, Angela. Everyone has them sooner or later," Abby responded. "And they can teach us something valuable in the end. Real life isn't all sweetness and light, and it takes time to find the silver lining. There can be gifts in processing trauma, like wisdom and inner strength."

Jasper disagreed. "Normally I'd prevent the use of my technology outside of this circle, but I saw Angela's pain, and she wasn't getting any good out of that no matter how long she processed it, Abby. Sometimes it is more than a person can bear to think about."

"But isn't it playing God to decide what to erase from someone's mind for his or her own good?" asked Half-man.

Angela reasoned in favor of the chip. "No, because we aren't deciding—they are. They know what memories are torturing them and what they can't shut down no matter how hard they try. Those selected experiences we could offer to tone down—not to erase them, but to push them into the background of their memories like mine were."

"So the decision to use a chip has to be on a case-by-case basis," Abby said. "And someone like my mother needs to screen potential candidates, because I disagree, Angela, and the people themselves may not be the best ones to decide. It should be determined by a team of trained experts."

Jasper made the time-out sign between the cousins. "There's a lot of traumatic experiences in the world that happen to innocent people—like the girls—through no fault of their own. And why should they pay for that for the rest of their lives? Tony and I could work on a chip to filter selected memories for pre-screened people who ask for it. Then a place like Angela's forest would help with the rest of their recovery."

"It would prevent suicides and homicides, because pain drives a lot of destructive behavior in people," Angela reasoned.

"Medical referrals only to start with. Otherwise we'll get people like wives with cheating husbands, because they'll want to avoid the pain rather than kick out their spouses and do the work of recovery," Abby shot back.

"Or maybe she'll just shoot the cheating bastard instead!" Angela countered, and then she reconsidered and compromised with Abby's viewpoint. "All right, everyone write down your ideas and feelings about using the chip for this, and I'll run them by Aunt Sophia tomorrow after the wedding."

The meeting broke up then, and Stubby demonstrated his prototype boomerang ball to everyone's delight. With a ball that returned to the thrower, you could play catch with yourself or practice tennis or baseball without a backboard or catcher involved. The team invented a group game where they rotated and caught each other's returning balls or else they lost points, and it was more fun than Frisbee. Abby knew Stubby had other wonderful toy ideas that he just needed to develop. Tony and Jasper were eager to form a toy company with Stubby to assist him in perfecting his ideas and to help him get his products marketed. Jasper offered to advertise Stubby's toys on his gaming networks and blogs.

Abby didn't wonder what Half-man would do after the wedding. He and Dee had become instant friends. Dee wanted his theater skills in her club's drag show, and Half-man was clearly intrigued with the fun of that idea.

To her surprise, her mother phoned to discuss Melt, although she referred to him as Mel. Sophia said she thought the military hadn't done a very good job correcting his burn scars, and she knew a surgeon who could normalize his appearance, which would include adding a prosthetic ear. Abby was upset with her mother's attitude and idea; Sophia had always talked about accepting people as they were, and she wanted to improve Melt's looks—that didn't make sense. Abby just tensely explained that her mother would have to talk to Melt about further surgery, and not to her.

Sophia explained that she wanted to give Melt a chance to mostly erase his scars if he wanted to, and she planned to offer him a job in the trauma wagon no matter what he decided about his scars. She said knowing what Melt had overcome was an inspiration to everyone he came in contact with. But Abby knew he was a shy man, and she didn't think he would like being on display as a heroic icon, so again she told her mother it was Melt's decision.

Sophia's offers didn't make sense until Abby remembered a wistful look her mother had sent Melt across Jasper's hospital room and his quick smile and wink in return; suddenly it all fell into place. Well, well, her mom and Melt—wasn't that interesting? It would be fun to see how it played out, because it must have been a case of opposites attracting; her mom was definitely an extravert, and Melt, an introvert, not to mention that he was at least eight years younger than Sophia. But Abby thought none of that really mattered, because her mom had been alone for many years, and Melt was a sweetie. She wished them both much-deserved happiness.

Finally she tracked down Hawkeye, who was sitting by himself on the driftwood bench where she had originally found the globe. To play the part of an airline worker on the jet to Reed Island, he had shaved his beard and cut his hair, and now regularly wore his prosthetic glass eye rather than the patch. That had transformed him from a rough pirate to a handsome man, but he often wore a look of sadness on his face, and Abby knew he still didn't have any sense of self-worth. She'd been working on a possible idea for his future, and it had come to fruition, so she took a letter out of her pocket and handed it to him.

"What's this?" Hawkeye asked her.

"Read it, Hawkeye. I recommended you to the Olympic Shooting Team as a potential coach, and they decided they want you to train the US team for the summer games in two years."

He was astonished. "Why would you do that, Abby?"

"Because you're the best coach ever, and they want gold for the United States. You're still a famous marksman, you know."

He read the letter through twice and turned it over and over in his hands as if the words weren't real. Abby waited patiently and was finally rewarded with a glimmer of hope in his eyes.

"They really want me?" He sounded like he couldn't believe it.

"Of course they do, because they're not stupid. You're the best teacher I've ever had, and I've had a lot. You're a natural coach, so go and have fun. We're sure to win a gold medal this time."

Later, Abby saw him showing the letter around to everyone with pride rather than sadness on his face. No one but Hawkeye himself had ever questioned that he had a lot left to contribute to the world.

Sixty - Two

On the way home from the island Abby had removed her hair extensions—Greed's savagery had loosened most of them anyway. At the moment, her original short cap of red hair curled softly around her face where it had grown out since she'd found the globe. For the wedding ceremony, she wore a crown of flowers intertwined with crystals and ribbons that trailed down her back. She went barefoot in the sand, as did most of the wedding party.

As a wedding present, Sophia gave them the deed to the Ocean Shores cabin and half the property it was built on, acres of valuable beachfront property. The other half of the acreage she deeded to Tony to build a house on if he wished.

It was a lovely, generous gift, and Abby couldn't think of anything she would have wanted more. Jasper was already muttering that he could work from anywhere and that he wanted to expand the cabin into a real home. He wanted to add a guesthouse for visitors and sell his place in Seattle because Abby's apartment would be big enough when they needed to be in the city for her work.

Angela was Abby's maid of honor, and Dee, her only bridesmaid. Tony was Jasper's best man, and Stubby, his groomsman. Everyone looked great in pale gray suits and

dresses accented with coral-colored flowers and bouton-
nieres. Hook, Half-man, Hawkeye, and Melt wore their dress
uniforms and looked wonderful. Emma was carried by Sophia
and was a flower girl, and she was a sweet confection in a
pale-pink ruffled dress, a diaper cover, and socks; she even
had tiny sparkly pink buckle shoes. The new grandmother
and granddaughter both had fun scattering colorful flower
petals in the sand.

Abby didn't care that Emma almost stole the show as she
was passed around to guests and thoroughly loved on during
the ceremony; she was such a sweet baby, so who could resist
her? Abby often thought about the weeks she had carried her
around like a limp doll and had played game after game, hoping that Emma would someday respond. What a joy it was for
everyone to have her and Jasper back safe and sound!

The ceremony was simple and short. Abby and Jasper had
written their own vows, and there wasn't a dry eye after they
declared their love and spoke pledges about their future life
together. Jasper told Abby that she was the angel he had thought
she was when he'd first seen her, and she said loving him had
sculpted her soul from a young age. Soft classical music played
as the waves that had brought them together washed up on the
beach in the background.

Abby and Jasper discussed taking a honeymoon but decided
they wanted to stay home as a family instead. There were jokes
about the adventurous tropical island getaway the couple had
had before the wedding, but that had been in no way a honeymoon. Angela and Hook volunteered to stay and tend Emma at
the cabin so they could at least spend their wedding night at a
local hotel. Angela had set up champagne; white candles; and
a lovely repast of cheese, crackers, fruit, chocolate, and small
cakes, and it was all waiting for them in their room. Best of all,
Jasper had a new prescription in his pocket written by Sophia
that simply said "enjoy" on it.

Epilogue

They laughed, they loved, and they deliberately spread goodness and light into the world; and Abby hoped that somewhere, Greed was grinding his teeth, knowing that.

www.ingramcontent.com/pod-product-compliance
Lightning Source LLC
Chambersburg PA
CBHW060140260626
47160CB00001B/58